JOURNEY

OF THE

ZODIARKS

Magic Unleashed

JOURNEY
OF THE
ZODIARKS
MAGIC UNLEASHSED

BOOK 1 IN THE JOURNEY OF THE ZODIARKS SERIES

TK Fretresé

ISBN: 978-1-950479-00-9 (paperback)
ISBN: 978-1-950479-01-6 (eBook)
Second American Edition: March 2019
Printed in the United States of America

Cover Art Illustration: © Tremess / Adobe Stock
Stock.adobe.com
Extended License Acquired
Cover Design by TK Fretresé
Book Design by TK Fretresé
All interior illustrations / sketches by TK Fretresé

Darkness Reigns, Cover Art Illustration: © Luis Louro / Adobe Stock
Stock.adobe.com

This book is dedicated to my Zodiarks, my children.

You have my unconditional love and devotion.

My deepest gratitude to my husband (my best friend) for always

being an encouraging companion.

TABLE OF CONTENTS

Magic
Unleashed

CHAPTER ONE
Shrouds of Darkness

"**M**assster, what do you wish of usss, for we are many, and can do many powerful thingsss?" asked a small goblin with a hissing lisp, pacing around the room in circles with its head hunched down beneath its black hooded robe, staying concealed within the shadows dancing along the walls from flickering candlelight within the high stone tower.

"Tell ussss your thoughtsss. We wish to ssserve you, oh, great massster. What evils shall we commit in your most powerful evil name?" hissed the creature, with a raspy voice no louder than whispers. Slowly, the goblin took careful steps to approach the master's side, bowing its head down lowly in submission to the DARK ONE.

A single window pane crusted in filth at the height of the tower rattled from the frightful storm outside—for a moment, it was the only noise in the room amongst the two powerful figures.

Beneath the black sky, forceful winds were assaulting the great mountain, which concealed the castle; relentless lightning bolts plunged down from the storm clouds and struck its rocky surface. As the winds whipped through the trees and howled outside, bits of dust lifted free from the caked-on grime covering the window, and dust drifted down from the rafters onto the cold stone floor.

Several thin candles held in brass holders were scattered on narrow ledges around the dim room. Randomly, they slipped off the ledges and splattered hot wax onto the floor as large bolts struck the side of the mountain, nearest the tower. Having heavier heft to them, thick pillar candles held on firmly to their spots as the storm raged on, and the fires upon their wicks wildly danced along the walls. The heat of their flames became mixed with the stagnant air rising up through the vent in the floor—a disgusting mixture of sweat, decay, and mold from the dungeons below in the belly of the monstrous castle.

In the center of the room stood a tall figure shrouded in shadow, and it wore a long, hooded, black cloak which concealed every inch of the tall frame—hiding the wearer's face. Not even the candlelight's luminescence was able to penetrate the evil shrouding the DARK ONE's features as the figure stood next to a large ornate pedestal made of marble. At the pedestal's precipice, it held an oversized basin constructed of pure gold that was

2

adorned along its rim with gems of different hues, and melted silver filled the inside of the basin… appearing as a shimmering liquid amidst the palpable darkness in the tower.

Legion watched as the DARK ONE leaned over its edge and peered deeply into the center of the basin. Slowly, the silver liquid began to swirl, and it gradually picked up speed.

Legion crouched down on the floor and cowardly held its head in its hands, fearful of the intensity of its master's rage as the DARK ONE stared into the swirling mass.

Something foul had crossed the master's gaze!

"Massster, what angersss you so? We have captured many caravans of travelers as you demanded. Are you not pleased with ussss?" the goblin asked, tilting its head left to right, listening to the goblin voices inside itself argue with each other in his mind. "Massster, we are *Legion* and can do whatever you ssseek. Demand of usss anything, great DARK ONE, and it shall be done in your name." Slowly, Legion stood with its head bowed lowly in respect to its master. The small goblin was much too afraid to make direct eye contact with the DARK ONE, for fear of what harm might be afflicted upon the creature—a goblin possessed by many.

Legion closed its eyes and began tilting both its dirty, large, pointy ears—covered with bristly hairs and entwined with ear wax—down toward the vent in the tower's floor. "We listen.

3

Sssweet criesss come up from the dungeon. Do their screams not pleassse you? Is it not soothing to Master's earsss?" the goblin asked, not expecting an answer, whilst creeping about the room in the shadows… taking pleasure in the sorrowful wailings of captives coming up through the vent. Legion lifted its long, pointed nose into the air and breathed in a deep whiff; the smell of human sweat and blood permeated the air and filled his nostrils.

Still, the figure shrouded in black peered deeply into the swirling silver mass without speaking a word. With intense concentration, the DARK ONE stared into the gem encrusted basin.

Legion's tongue flicked out of its mouth at the air and its rows of sharp teeth became wet with drool as the goblin's stomach growled for food. "DARK ONE, it hasss been long since Legion hasss had meat. We hunger! Dead flesh, raw and sweet, or cooked till juicy tender! We hunger… for meat!"

Still, the DARK ONE ignored the words of the goblin and continued to stare into the bowl, until finally breaking the heavy silence. "There is a threat in the town, Bernard. A seed that must not be allowed to grow! It must be cut at its roots before it strengthens and finds others of its likeness! It must be sought out and destroyed." The DARK ONE's deep voice filled the stone tower and caused the goblin to tremble. "Send spies by air into this town. Find the one that would grow like the mighty oak to be strong enough to rise against *ME*!"

"Yesssss Massster! Your *will* is oursss! It shall be done," the small goblin obediently replied.

"First, tonight everyone will feast! Order the Generals to choose seven prisoners to take from the dungeons to the kitchen cooks and have them prepared. They will need to add extra wood to the stockpiles for the ovens. Next, the Generals are to gather every soldier and laborer into the dining hall, and have everyone eat their fill of flesh until their stomachs stretch and can hold no more. The prisoners… *I* hear their relentless cries for mercy and their dreadful pleas to be released from their torments. *I* will grant them the freedom they so desperately seek. Have the Generals provide a slow death to those remaining in the dungeons after the feast," the DARK ONE calmly instructed without the smallest tinge of emotion—feeling no remorse at ordering the deaths of mothers, fathers, and their children who were crammed in the dungeons. "Have them empty all the cells. Make certain none are left alive. My dungeons will be refilled… in time. After that matter has been taken care of, send the winged-spies to Bernard, and end this threat to my reign."

"Yesss Master! All will be done as you have told. We shall send spiesss by air, frightening to the sight. Wings large and mighty with sharp beaks that bite!" the goblin agreed, and with a burst of swirling black smoke, Legion vanished from the stone tower.

CHAPTER TWO

Bernard

As twilight approached and the sun's light faded, the usual wintery chill was felt throughout the town, Bernard. Thick clouds rolled in across the sky and blanketed everything above the quaint, charming area, thereby decreasing the comforting glow of the twin moons and blocking out the light of the stars. Tall, ornate polls adorned the sidewalks, and from them hung large cast-iron lanterns with glass panes on all sides, bursting magically with bright flames upon the onset of every evening's twilight. At night, the beautifully lit cobblestone streets sparkled from the lights of the grand lanterns throughout the close-nit town filled with average citizens who were oblivious to the perils in the world—caring only about the troubles within their town.

Shopkeepers all over—except for those at a couple taverns, which stayed open till much later—were performing their nightly rituals of cleaning and closing their stores. Through glass window panes, people could be seen waving their hands at brooms to sweep the floors, wiggling their fingers at books to have them place themselves neatly back onto shelves, and at pots and dirty dishes to have them take a soak in hot soapy water, while sponges lifted from the washtubs to scrub them clean. Some could be seen swinging both their hands back and forth as if conducting a symphony... mops washing the floors, pencils and crayons putting themselves up into containers, and sponges wiping tables and windows clean!

At the horse stables, several white carriages—lined inside with plush velvet and adorned on the outside with silver and gold-leaf designs, bells, and other over-the-top stylings—were being cleaned and readied for the next day of business by the staff. Meanwhile, the horses were being fed their nightly supper and placed into the barn stalls for a good night's rest by one of the regular volunteers, a young woman barely out of her teenage years named, *Amora*.

"Amora, are you done with those horses yet? It's time to go!" Mr. Higgins called from outside the barn. The short, plump man stood just outside the open barn doors, pacing back and forth excitedly! He was dressed in his casual work attire consisting of a faded brown coat, dirty brown boots, a stained grey shirt, and brown pants, which he wore when helping out with barn work, such as slapping a fresh coat of paint on something that no longer reflected the crisp clean image of his business, cleaning out the stalls, or carrying fresh bales of hay and water into the barn. However, on most days he was one of the drivers for the luxurious carriages and he dressed much fancier for that—a clean, pressed, white shirt, black slacks with a matching pair of shiny loafers, and a heavy coat and hat.

"Come on!" Mr. Higgins pleaded as he stepped up onto a stool and peered over the stall doors to see if Amora was actually finishing up with her last horse or petting it like she did with just about every animal she came across. "That horse is fine. Look, he's all tucked in and ready for a good night rest," he anxiously remarked while rubbing his short fat fingers through his sparse, greasy, brown hair that shown a bald spot at the top of his head. "I don't want to be late for the party ya know, and it will be starting any minute! Now give it a rest! Our work is done for the day," he fussed, still leaning over the stall doors to watch as she fed a carrot to the horse and ignored him completely. "I got a date for this one, and I don't want to keep the lady waiting!" he said, growing more frustrated and getting ready to turn on his heels to leave her in the barn without him.

"I'm almost done. I just need one more minute," she yelled out the stall doors as she finished feeding the horse and picked up a brush off the rickety wooden stool next to her—giving the animal a few more gentle brush strokes.

"Why don't you ever use your magic when doing these chores? The horses would get fed and brushed much faster ya know!" Mr. Higgins replied with a huff of sarcasm and stepped down off the stool. He knew how head-strong Amora could be when she was fixated on something, so all he could do was throw his hands up in the air and pace-around while he waited.

"Magic is not for everything. Sometimes it feels good to get my hands dirty... to do it myself. Take the horses for example. They are not objects to have my fingers wiggled at! They are beautiful, strong animals with personalities, and they deserve the hands-on approach. I enjoy taking my time doing things for them without magic," she answered, smiling and then changing the subject. "Anyway, who are you going to the party with this time?" she asked, rolling her eyes and thinking about his last date. "Is it Rosemary, again?"

"No, no! Not her! She's got too much of a temper for me," he laughed, remembering the last party he had attended with Rosemary (he shuddered at the thought of it).

Amora finished with the last horse and laughed as she exited the stable, "Yes! I remember it all! Last year at that party she thought you were attracted to Miss Petrol because of the way you were looking at her during the fire-dance as she pranced around the bonfire, dancing to the music in her rather... well, let's just say 'short' attire!"

Amora walked over to the messy wooden table on the other side of the barn, and placed the brush on top of it and slid the stool she had used underneath. "Let me think... oh yeah! Then, Rosemary grabbed one of the cakes sitting on the dessert table. I believe it was strawberry! Next, without saying a word to anyone, she went looking for you! She found you talking with a group of guys huddled together gabbing about their dates, and she hit you in the face with the entire cake in front of everyone! Cake was splattered everywhere! Even a couple of the guys next to you were wearing a slice or two themselves from the blast!" she explained, barely able to control her laughter as the memories played inside her mind.

"It wasn't that funny!" Mr. Higgins pouted with a grin that spoke otherwise. "It took me nearly an hour to get all that icing off my face and out of my ears," he said, trying his hardest to keep from laughing, but before he knew it, the laughter burst from his mouth and joined in with Amora's! "That woman always had a suspicious nature, if you ask me. That's just plain and simple." Quickly, he thought about several other dates with Rosemary where her suspicion seemed to join them like a third wheel.

"So, who's it going to be this year Mr. Higgins?"

11

"Well, I don't quite know how to say this—" he paused with a long sigh. "I'm going with… Miss Petrol."

A look of shock leapt across Amora's face as she let out a gasp of surprise. "Oh! So, you *were* attracted to her that night during the fire-dance! Mr. Higgins, you are a scoundrel! You know, I think Rosemary really did like you! She talked about you every chance she got to about half the folks in town, and it broke her heart to watch you gawking at Miss Petrol that night!"

Mr. Higgins stared down at the ground to avoid the judgmental look Amora was giving him. His cheeks became red with embarrassment as he continued, "I know. I know. I just couldn't help myself. Miss Petrol is so pretty, and she always smells like those sweet cranberry muffins that she makes at her bakery." Mr. Higgins closed his eyes and took in a deep breath, "I can almost smell those muffins baking in the oven right now, and when she doesn't smell like muffins, well, she usually smells like warm chocolate chip cookies. Amora, you know me!" he pleaded for her sympathy. "How am I supposed to resist a pretty woman that always smells like my favorite sweets from a bakery?" he asked rhetorically.

Mr. Higgins looked up, and Amora shot him a knowing glance that she understood what he must have been thinking. She fully knew about his weakness for sweets—from all the times she had caught him taking extra breaks at work to sneak in a cookie, a

12

cupcake, or some form of chocolate pastry. So, she could imagine his weakness for wanting to date a woman that always smelled like muffins and cookies. Not to mention that she was always baking them and letting him be the taste tester anytime they crossed paths.

At the thought of all the possible cakes, pies, muffins and cookies that Miss Petrol had probably been baking all day with her assistant, Mr. Higgins decided it was time to leave and maybe make a quick stop by her bakery. "Well—" he let out a yawn with a stretch, "I'm going to head on home. I need to get cleaned up and changed for the party." He stepped outside the main barn doors and took in a deep breath of the cool crisp late evening air. "It's a nice night out. I think I'll walk over to her bakery, and say hello, before I head home. I should be able to catch her before she finishes cleaning for the night, and I'll see if she needs help with anything."

"Is she the owner of that fancy new bakery that recently opened near the town square?" Amora asked as she removed her black coat from the hook on the wall it was hanging from and put it on. Quickly, she glanced around the barn to make sure everything was done, and things were back in their proper places before turning off the lights and leaving for the night. Quietly, she closed the main doors and latched them shut, then joined up with Mr. Higgins, whom was waiting outside for her.

"Yep! That's the one! That shop makes the best of everything, if you like sweets!" Mr. Higgins reached into his coat pocket and took out a chunk of shortbread wrapped in brown parchment paper with his name scribbled on it.

"I've been saving this piece of shortbread since lunch. I was gonna have it during the walk home, but since I'm heading over to the bakery first, you're welcome to it," he said, holding his hand out with the wrapped morsel in it.

Amora looked at the tightly wrapped brown package in his hand and crooked her eyebrows in a frown at the thought of eating anything that had been stored next to his body inside his coat. The thought of how warm the shortbread was due to his body heat was certainly disgusting enough to solicit dry-heaving and a full-blown gag, but she didn't want to insult him with her true feelings.

"No thanks. You go ahead and enjoy it. I'll just grab something to eat a little later," she said, faking a smile meant to look genuine.

"Okay. Suit yourself," he replied, then greedily opened up the parchment package and began stuffing the shortbread into his mouth.

"Did you remember to add the extra hay to the stalls?" he inquired with full cheeks in mid-chew.

"You ask me that every night, and the answer continues to be... yes! Tonight, *you* should be more worried about what

14

Rosemary is going to do when she sees you with Miss Petrol as your date!" Amora added, giving him a stern but curious look.

A cold shiver ran up his spine at the thought of seeing Rosemary again. "Guess I'll have to steer clear of the dessert table at this party, too!" he jokingly said. "I'll just deal with whatever comes. Who knows... maybe she'll be with somebody new, and I'll be a distant memory to her. One can only hope!"

"Are *you* going with anyone special tonight?" he asked.

Amora dusted off some dirt from her black pants, and then tossed her long black hair over her shoulders and began putting it up into a loose ponytail. "No. You know I'm not dating anyone."

"What about that young man...ya know, the one that works over at the shop around the corner?"

"You mean the bookstore?"

"Yeah! The bookstore! What about him?" he asked curiously, tilting up an eyebrow at her. He had always wondered if there was something between those two.

"No. We're just friends, but I think he might be going to the party tonight."

"You better go catch him before he leaves and ask him to go with you! It wouldn't be proper for a young woman as pretty as you to go alone to the town's biggest social event! Especially, if you don't have to! People might start saying that something must be wrong with you in the head," he said, snickering at the thought.

15

"Get out and have some fun. I won't take no for an answer!" Mr. Higgins paused for a second and thought up a clever way of motivating her. "Why, if I see you at the party alone tonight, then I might even have to dance with *you* and tell everyone we came *together*!" Mr. Higgins gave Amora a wink to cement the unpleasant thought deeply into her mind as a friendly warning.

Amora shuddered at the thought of Mr. Higgins' threat and was quickly convinced to either go to the town's event with someone, or not to attend it at all. "Alright. You've made your point. I'll ask him if he wants to go to the party with me, but don't make too much out of it if we show up together. I don't want to make him feel uncomfortable. We'll just be there as friends," and she gave him a look straight in the eyes, trying to gauge if he was actually listening to her or not. "Mr. Higgins. I mean it. Please, don't go around pointing out to anyone that I'm there with him… that's if he even *does* agree to attend with me. He and I are just friends, and he'll never forgive me if rumors start floating around. You know how people in this small town can talk and spread gossip!"

Mr. Higgins flashed her a mischievous smile that revealed little about his intentions, "I hear ya. Well, I better get going. See ya tonight, and remember this party is at the Central Park Plaza and it starts at seven o'clock. I believe there's going to be another huge bonfire setup like the one from last year, too. Should be fun!"

Mr. Higgins scrunched up the empty brown wrapper that now only held a few crumbs of shortbread and placed it into another pocket and began walking away down the cobblestone path. "See ya later," he said, waving goodbye.

"Bye," Amora replied kindly with a quick wave of her hand, then headed down a different path towards the bookstore around the corner.

CHAPTER THREE

Bookstore

*T*he streets were quiet as Amora headed towards the bookstore with only a person scattered here and there—the evening air quickly growing chillier as night continued to settle in. Her fingers were becoming numb from the bitter cold as she clumsily grasped at buttons on her black coat, sliding several of them through the holes to close it enough to contain some warmth against her skin.

Within minutes, she spotted a familiar faded wooden sign hanging beneath a long wrought-iron bar over the front entrance of the store, which was a large, heavy, walnut door battered with age. Everything in the street was still and quiet except for the creaking sound the sign made as it swayed on its hinges back-and-forth from a passing breeze. The sign read: <u>Bernard Bookstore, Old & New</u>.

Several glass windows dotted along the front of the store gave the impression that the building was closed for the evening—there were no visible signs of light shining from the inside—but Amora knew her friend better than that. It was more likely that he was still somewhere inside the store—perhaps in a back room—since he regularly enjoyed browsing through the books and reading during the evening hours after the store had closed.

Amora stepped up the stone steps and knocked on the door.

One Knock. Two Knocks. Three knocks.

No one answered.

She pressed an ear to the cold wood, listening for any sounds… nothing.

"Magnar, are you in there?" she whispered through the door. No response.

She felt her heart begin to beat faster with worry as she thought to herself, *where is he? He's got to be inside somewhere.* Quickly, she stepped down the stairs, rushed over to the nearest window, and cupped her hands against the glass, straining her eyes as she tried to make out images on the other side.

Within the darkness, she could see a faint glow—a small flicker of light—against what she thought was probably the back of the store; although, she had never been to that area before, and had never heard her friend mention anything about the books back there. She squinted her eyes more to focus on the soft light, and for a second, she thought she saw a tall silhouette walking away from the dim glow towards the front of the store. Immediately, the tension in her body began to melt away and was replaced by cheerfulness as she recognized the silhouette and ran back up the front steps to be greeted!

"Magnar!" she exclaimed with a happy and relieved smile. "I thought something had happened to you... I knocked several times and called for you, but you didn't come to the door, so I was starting to get worried. I'm glad you're okay." Quietly, so that he wouldn't notice, she took in a deep gulp of air to calm herself from her panicked worry.

"Amora—" he said, confused about her being there, but happy to see her. "What are you doing here? I thought you would be heading home by now to get changed for the party everyone seems to be going to." He glanced slightly over his shoulder back towards the flickering light in the back, and she could clearly tell he was preoccupied with whatever it was that he had been doing.

"Come in," he said, holding the heavy walnut door open, gesturing for her to step inside out of the cold. "Sorry I didn't answer the door right away. I was reading something in the back."

"No problem," she smiled, following him through the store towards the back.

The building was quite large and had both a bottom and top level with a spiraling staircase. They walked past aisles of towering bookshelves and past randomly placed small antique tables that held unlit lanterns and random items. The wooden floor planks creaked underneath their weight as they walked towards the flickering light in the distance, which seemed to be oddly growing dimmer the closer they got.

"I haven't really given much thought about the party this year. Are you going to it?" she casually asked.

"I thought about it, but I always feel awkward at those things. I've never really been good at dancing or socializing. I never know *what* to say to those people!" he threw his hands up in the air with a big huff of frustration at the thought! "They always want to know… am I dating anyone? Do I like my job at the bookstore? What are my plans for the future? The questions seem to never end, and I don't feel like dealing with that stuff tonight," he complained, nearing the lantern that had been emitting the soft glow of light at the back of the store—sitting atop an antique wooden side table painted green, which had cracked over the years. Upon approach, the flame of the lantern snuffed-out into a puff of smoke, and again, the room was engulfed in darkness.

Although not being able to see a thing, Amora could hear Magnar fumbling around on the table as he reached out for the lantern.

"I'm going to try to relight it," he said.

"Okay."

Magnar began focusing his mind on igniting a flame on the lantern's wick—he wanted to show off the magic he had been practicing to Amora. He held one of his hands out towards the wick and firmly spoke, "*Incendo Ignis,*" but only a few orange sparks appeared within the glass-covering of the lantern, and flickered down onto the wick, quickly fizzling out into a dull puff of grey smoke.

"Well, that wasn't supposed to happen," he said, forcing out an unconvincing laugh, meant to hide his embarrassment.

"It's alright. Magic takes practice."

"Alright," Magnar replied, unconvinced that it took as much practice for her, as it did him. "Let's see *you* do it then."

"Alright, I will." Quickly, she held up a hand in front of the lantern, spoke the words, "*Incendo Ignis,*" and snapped her fingers! Immediately, a bright burst of orange, yellow, and red sparks appeared inside the glass in a glorious sparkly display similar to the fireworks that could be seen dazzling the night sky at grand celebrations thrown by the town! Whimsically, the beautiful sparks swirled down and ignited into a bright burning flame that was dancing on top of the wick!

"Well, it seems to come easily enough for you," he replied, frustrated that he hadn't been able to do it himself. "So, why did you stop by tonight? I mean, I'm glad you're here, but why?"

Amora's cheeks became red as she thought to herself about what Mr. Higgin's had said earlier that evening—about her coming to the party and asking Magnar to be her date! Decidedly, she knew she could *not* let him know that she wanted to go the party—and most of all, with him! That this was the *real reason* she had stopped by tonight!

"No reason!" she exclaimed, louder than she had anticipated, and immediately she was given a reprimand of a *shh* by Magnar.

"Can't a friend just stop by to talk with another friend on a boring night?" she continued, much softer. "I just wanted to stop by. That's all," she said as convincing as she could.

As the words left her mouth, she bit her lower lip and knew it was a gamble if he would believe her not. Quickly, she followed it up with an exaggerated facial expression that she tried hard to make convincing... a scrunched-up half-smile mixed with a grimace that implied, *I have other things to do if you don't want my company.*

Luckily, Magnar's attention was already fixated on something else, and he had barely mustered up a glance in her direction while muttering, "that's fine." Intensely, he was searching dusty bookshelves for something—his eyes intense and barely blinking. He held the lantern up near his face while leaning over closer to the shelves and began running his lengthy fingers along the spines of the old books with faded lettering—carefully reading each title.

Amora stood silently and watched him in the lantern's light; his almond-shaped hazel eyes burned with intensity as he searched through the books and his thick, shiny, dark hair looked glorious in the perfect haircut, ending just above the neck near his ruggedly defined jawline.

She smiled as she thought of how well she knew him. He was always well-mannered and polite to elders, and he preferred to wear what he thought of as sensible clothing—consisting of the usual dark pants, long sleeved shirts, and practical worn-out shoes—which Amora thought could use replacing.

"What are you looking for?" she whispered as she walked over to stand next to him and leaned in closer to get a better look.

All the books had hard covers, which appeared timeworn and tattered, and each silver and gold lettering title was so time-faded that they were barely readable. Cobwebs stretched across the top two shelves of every bookcase with spiders happily going about their business, and not a single strand of the webs appeared to have ever been broken or disturbed by anyone. The wood of the bookshelves was aged and cracked in different areas, and thick layers of dust with no visible signs of tampering layered the shelves. In fact, Amora began to wonder how they were going to remove even a single book without leaving traces of their presence in the dust if he actually *did* find what he was looking for, but she knew that Magnar was going to see whatever this was, through, and would probably just get frustrated with her if she were to suggest they not move any of the books for that reason. So, quickly she decided it would be better to just keep quiet and let him find whatever he was looking for.

"If you'd like, I could help you search for what you're looking for? I'm going to light a couple more lanterns, first."

Suddenly, Magnar turned his head toward her, "No! No more lanterns!" he snapped.

Shocked and upset by his angry outburst, Amora whispered, "okay," and turned her face away from his. "I was just trying to help!" she snapped back.

"I'm sorry—" his tone much gentler this time after realizing the error in his outburst to her. "I didn't mean to snap at you. It's just that Mr. Galdipp, the owner, told me this section is restricted to everyone... including me. He would be beyond upset if he walked by the store and saw lights through the windows, and then came inside to find me and you reading in this section."

Amora looked puzzled as she tried to make sense of why the owner wouldn't want anyone in a certain section of his store. "Why does Mr. Galdipp even have a restricted section? I thought the whole purpose of having a bookstore was to sell books—any books—to customers. Having a section restricted for *everyone* doesn't make sense."

"I agree," he said, pausing for a brief moment as he returned his attention back to the books on the shelves. "I know he has to be hiding something... BIG... and it weighs heavily on his mind. I've seen customers venture back here to browse through these books, but before they can get even *one* off a shelf, he charges back here and becomes extremely upset! He starts shouting, and within minutes, the customers either leave the store expressing some choice words as they exit, or they apologize for no reason and return to another area of the store to look through other books... across the room over there," he said, gesturing with a tilt of his head towards a general section on cooking, cleaning, and casting basic spells. "Afterwards, Mr. Galdipp mopes around the store and hangs his head down like he's actually sad about what happened. As if he didn't want to act that way towards them, but for some reason, he felt he had to."

"Wow! That's odd! He's usually one of the nicest people in town. I would never have thought he would be like that to anyone!" Amora replied, shaking her head in stunned disbelief.

"Exactly. He's a really nice guy, and if there's information back here that will help me find a way to help him, then that's worth the risk!"

Amora quickly nodded in agreement.

"So, for the past couple of nights, I've been sneaking back here to look through some of the books after he's left for the night and I've closed the store."

"Okay, but won't he eventually figure out you haven't been leaving right away after closing?" she asked.

"I've got that covered. I told him that I've been trying to brush up on my magic skills. You know—" he paused and smiled, "to be able to do just a few of the things that already come so naturally to you."

"Magnar—" Amora remarked with a shy smile and a faint hint of blush warming her cheeks.

"Anyway, he believes that I've been staying late to study the magic books and practice awhile before I head home every night."

"Smart. That's actually a good cover story. Believable," she said, smiling back at him.

"You're not gonna believe this, but I came across a book the other night, and… felt drawn to it for no explainable reason. At first, it didn't stand out to me; the book looked plain and I was going to ignore it and move on, but I couldn't! I had to open it! So, I did, but I only had enough time to read through a couple pages, because Mr. Galdipp surprised me and returned to the store that night. I had to close it in a rush and put it back, fast!" he explained with his words sounding hurried, as if a part of his memory had just kicked in and he was reliving the experience in his mind.

Amora hung onto his every word as he continued explaining, "Did he catch you?"

"No, luckily not! I was able to put the book back and run into another aisle. Quickly, I grabbed one of the magic books off a shelf—just seconds before he came around the corner—and I immediately began firing off spells to light the wick of a lantern sitting on a small table near me! Mr. Galdipp didn't suspect anything. He even told me I was doing a good job and to keep at it. He rationalized most of the lights being off as my way of practicing so that I could use magic to eventually learn how to turn them all back on!"

Magnar took a moment to soak in his victory and laughed at the absurdity of how he had managed to escape being caught!

"Anyway, as long as he believed it, right?"

Enthusiastically, Amora nodded her head up and down, "Right!"

"That's why I forgot where I put it and why it's taking me so long to find it again." He took in a big frustrated sigh as he held the lantern up near his face again and began searching through the titles on another dusty shelf. "I've got to find it and show it to you! I've never heard of, nor read anything like this book before!" The adrenaline and excitement were building in his veins at the thought of sharing his findings with her, and his hazel eyes became filled with determination to do so!

"Maybe I can help. What does the book look like?"

"The cover is tattered-brown-leather with faded gold letterings on the front and along the spine. I could barely read the title, but I think it said—" he paused, trying hard to remember, "Yes! Now, I remember! It said: The Zodiarks."

"The *Zodiarks*?" Amora's mouth twisted into a perplexed expression. "I've never heard of that!"

"I know. Me either."

"I wonder what that means. Who were they?"

"I don't know. I didn't have the chance to read too far into it, but I can't wait to read more!"

"None of this makes sense. Why won't Mr. Galdipp let anyone into this section? Why does he even have a restricted section? Why are all of the books back here so old, and why is no one allowed to read them? What's in them! Who were the *Zodiarks*? For that matter, what *is* a *Zodiark*?" Frustrated and annoyed with all the secrecy, Amora breathed a deep sigh and looked around at all the bookshelves in the restricted area covered in cobwebs and dust.

"Believe me, I agree! I have all the same questions that you have. So—" he paused and looked at her—his expression was a mix of we are in this together and I can't do it alone. "Help me out… start searching through the lower shelves closer to the floor. Maybe he suspected for some reason that I was messing around with that book, and instead of confronting me and being wrong, he decided to move it to one of the lower shelves."

"Sure," she agreed without hesitation.

"I'll hold the lantern between us, so you'll have enough light to see. That way, we won't have to light another lantern and call more attention to ourselves in here."

"Okay, that's fine," and she quickly squatted down next to him and began searching the lower shelves for the book he had described.

Several… long… quiet… minutes ticked by on the wall clock. The only sound penetrating the cumbersome silence of the store. Tick… tock… tick… tock… tick… tock. Until, finally…the silence was broken.

"I found it!" Magnar shouted excitedly.

CHAPTER FOUR
The Secret Book

"Shh," Amora whispered as she snapped her head around to look in between the bookshelves toward the storefront windows to see if anyone was walking by and had heard Magnar's outburst! The glow of lanterns hanging from a few wooden polls across the street in front of the store provided her with enough light to see that everything looked deserted outside. "I thought you said we needed to be quiet!" she whispered harshly to him.

"Sorry," he whispered back, sitting the lantern down onto the floor so that he could use both hands to gently begin pulling the thick book off the shelf, trying carefully not to leave any obvious disturbances in the dust near it. "Okay... just about there," he said as he slowly pulled the book free. "I've got it!"

Quickly, Amora turned to see Magnar holding the book he'd been desperate to find! "Good, and I don't think anyone was outside to hear your shout either. So, we're good for now. Everyone's probably at the party anyway," she said with a sigh of relief. "We should be able to take our time tonight reading it."

Carefully, he held the heavy book in his hands to prevent damaging the dry brittle leather the pages were bound to. "Grab the lantern," he instructed. "There's a table and some chairs in the back. We can read the book there."

Amora nodded and grabbed the lantern. Quietly, she followed him to the back of the store where there was a plain wooden table and four chairs surrounding it. She placed the lantern in the middle and sat down next to him and watched as he gently brushed the dust off the front cover and read the faded title out loud: _The Zodiarks._ The spine of the book creaked as he opened it and began flipping through the pages to find where he had left off reading the previous time.

While Magnar flipped through the pages, Amora looked at each of the intricately drawn illustrations depicted on them and was in awe! Nothing looked familiar to her, but each was amazing!

In the drawings, the sun shone brightly in each of them with a blue sky filled with puffy humongous white clouds. Some illustrated large birds soaring over and through them! Several drawings had gorgeous brilliant-hued flowers that almost overcrowded the trees and shrubs in lush green forests. Others

32

depicted large waterfalls flowing over high cliffs into big plumes of frothy-white water, and some showed beaches with crystal turquoise water, white powdery sand, and all types of colorful fish swimming amongst beautiful corals!

None of the illustrations showed images of the world she had come to know!

She had always known her world to be cold and harsh. Summer was always chilly, and everyone had to dress in layers, while winter was even more bitterly cold with heavy snowfall at times. Neither spring nor fall were any better. Both of those seasons were characteristically known by their cool, monsoon rainfalls that battered the roofs of buildings and created treacherous mud, which horses and carriages had to be pushed and pulled through!

There were no bright colors to be seen anywhere, only dull shades of cream and a variety of grays. When the ground was dry, the soil proved to be uncooperative and often times infertile. When it was drenched in rain water, the mud resembled a thick brownish-red sludge. Even the trees were different from the drawings—dull, lifeless, and struggling to maintain any leaves.

Neither Amora nor Magnar had ever seen the bright rays of the sun the drawings indicated had once existed, nor had they ever seen a blue sky. As Amora continued looking at the drawings, she began to feel as if her world had undergone a change, somehow.

Something had caused everything she had come to know, but what, and why?

A sadness filled her heart as Magnar continued flipping through the pages and stopped to view another drawing; this time the illustration was of a meadow filled with bright colorful flowers. She had never seen a real flower before or even a drawing of one, and her heart felt heavy that such beauty was being withheld from the world, and for what reason, she didn't know. To her, the reason did not matter, because nothing could justify the denial of these beautiful things from herself, or anyone else in the world.

A moment later, he began flipping through the pages again, and her eyes became fixated on an image in a drawing that he hadn't paid much attention to, but rather, passed by carelessly.

"Stop," Amora requested. "Go back a couple pages."

Magnar said nothing but did as she asked.

"There!" She stopped him again in order to carefully study the image on the page. Amora was in awe at the creature depicted! She had never seen, nor heard of anything like it before! It was enormous, compared to the other animals in the previous drawings, and it had two huge wings stretched-out, with an enormous wingspan! Its neck was long with large bony spikes dotted along the back of it, and the body of the creature seemed to be covered in the same boney material that covered its neck. There

34

were several sharp spikes—much larger than the others—that went down the length of its back, all the way to the tip of its oversized tail! Amora realized the boney material must have been some sort of protective armor.

"Have you seen anything like *that* before?" she asked, pointing at the creature in the drawing. "What is that thing?"

Magnar grinned while thinking, *I knew it! You're glad I dragged you into this*, and Amora instinctively knew his thoughts, and replied to him with a nod and a smirk that meant, *Yes, you're right. I'm glad I'm here… now get on with answering me!*

"Yes. I read about it on one of the pages in this book. It's called a dragon!"

"A what!" she exclaimed in disbelief.

"A *dragon*!" he confirmed.

"Wow!" she gasped and leaned in closer to the book, staring at the page as if expecting the image to change or come to life!

"If you feel anything like I did the first time I opened this book, then you have a million or so questions. For one, how could any of the animals and plants in these images have really existed, and yet, be kept from everyone's knowledge?"

Amora nodded her head, yes, and continued looking at the dragon on the page—ignoring the silliness of her thought about wishing the creature could somehow jump out of the book and show itself!

"What *is* this book?" She was brimming with curiosity from every question imaginable now, but fear quickly gripped her heart as the words left her mouth, and slowly, she looked up at him as if scared to hear his answer—his next words might do her in; the world she thought she knew was crumbling down fast around her and this would seal her fate.

Magnar paused, feeling her thoughts float from her mind into his. "It's a history book. Looks like it dates back really far!"

As the words left his mouth, an eerie silence filled the room.

The wall-clock stopped ticking.

The breeze outside stopped blowing.

The sign hanging over the front entrance ceased its creaking.

Everything stood still. Eventually, Magnar broke the silence with whispers to Amora, who was still sitting quietly by his side, flipping pages of the illustrated book and browsing through the drawings.

"I figured out where I left off reading, and we don't have any more time to spend looking at these drawings. Let's begin."

Quietly, Amora looked up into his eyes, nodded her agreement, and together they began reading the forbidden book.

****

Years faded into millennia, and the world was as bright and vibrant as ever, thriving under the watchful eyes of the *Zodiarks*—an elite group of people mysteriously established and tasked with the responsibility of protecting nature and all its beauty. Most inhabitants of the planet, *Gekala*, were pleased with the Zodiarks and their deeds, but found it reassuring to have others appointed to watch over them as a safeguard that their unmatched magical power was not unknowingly being misused. So, a petition asking for a council tasked with keeping watchful eyes on the Zodiarks was created, and it passed through cities and towns everywhere. Millions of signatures were collected and so the measure was passed; a respectable council of wise Elders were to be appointed to watch over the Zodiarks!

Life flourished and citizens were happy living out their daily lives. The Council of Elders did as requested by the people, and provided moral support to the Zodiarks and guidance in their deeds. Loved by millions, the Zodiarks were thought of as royalty! They were given housing in a huge castle in the grandest of all cities, *Zareck*! Huge towers, standing at each side of the castle and scattered throughout the city, rose high into the sky—their peaks above the clouds!

Over a hundred buildings housed families, dining halls, taverns, and all types of stores. Everyone felt safe behind the city's high, massive, stone walls, broken only by their impressive entrances with large, stone archways holding gated-doors made of thick woods embellished with artful, metal designs and secured by thick iron hinges. Behind the walls, the citizens of the bustling city proudly displayed bright banners strewn up high between lampposts, each with gold lettering that read: *Zareck! Home of the Zodiarks!* At every twilight, the street lanterns hanging from the lampposts and those mounted to the stone walls came alive, bursting on the wicks with huge flames—magically lighting the city!

The citizens were loyal to their Zodiark leaders. Children freely played in the streets, pretending to be Zodiarks, dressing like them in modest robes with sashes they had gotten from their mothers, and would cast simple magic while using their limitless imaginations! They often dreamed of growing up and being chosen as the next Zodiark to join the secretive and elite group!

All over the world, towns and villages became filled with rumors about the secretive magic performed by the Zodiarks up in the towers—behind closed and locked doors. Eavesdropping servants, spying through cracks in the stones and listening through vents, often sold the few bits and pieces of information they had gathered to unsavory individuals lurking in taverns as visitors to the city—their homes often far away.

During the night at any tavern, loud laughter and boisterous stories could be heard about the Zodiarks! People claimed they saw them performing rituals up in one of the towers around a large marble pedestal that held a gold basin adorned on its rim with beautiful gems of different hues, and it was filled by using a pitcher containing a silver liquid! Servants claimed to witness gems being placed into the basin: some were red as flames; others were turquoise like the sea; bright green like newly sprouted plants; cloudy white like the frothy sea-foam of waves tumbling onto sandy shores; or were radiant yellow as bright as the sun!

Servants told stories about the silver liquid in the basin changing into water and flowing over the sides down onto the floor by the gallons! Some spread stories about flames rising so high that they touched the ceiling during spells, which left black char marks that servants had to paint over the next day! Others told tales of white smoke swirling up and filling every inch of the room as thick as fog, or of large spiny sea crabs crawling forth from the basin by the dozens and swarming the room until one of the Zodiarks gathered each of them up into a net made of silver thread, and secretively carried them away somewhere!

Thousands of stories were made-up to fill pastimes and to provide entertainment to many people across the world, but the truth of what went on behind locked doors during Zodiark rituals was not even known to the council of Elders who were appointed to watch over them. The only assurance the Elders had that the Zodiarks were not performing any types of harmful magic was due to an initiation ritual the Elders (from long ago) had created with the consent and help from the first Zodiark. The ritual centered on a spoken promise each newly elected Zodiark had to say in front of their kinship while holding a golden chalice encrusted with gems that contained powerful magic, which was placed on it by the other Zodiarks.

After speaking the promise aloud, the new member held the chalice in one hand while extending the other to be cut by a ritualistic blade held by another Zodiark. The wounded hand was then held over the chalice and the blood dripped into the red wine inside. Next, each member drank from the chalice, and the bond created between them sealed the terms of the spell—that if any Zodiark, who had recited the promise and drank from the chalice, did any harmful magic... the price would be their imminent death!

The Promise:

"Do what ye will with harm to none,
To the Zodiark Circle, you are forever joined—we are as one,
Let that be thy conscience and thy guide,

41

Many purposes wielding magic together simultaneously with
Zodiark pride,
A link added to the chain, another drop into the sea
Joining you to the Zodiark family,
Powerful magic is indeed a part of thee,
Unique and strong, it is a great responsibility!
View it not with a light heart or mind,
Intention to kill shall destroy thy own life-vine,
Do what you wish with full knowledge and understanding,
Positive deeds in the world shall flourish, but darkness within
thyself will be a poison without ending."

After years of harmony and peace, the sky gradually began darkening. Storm clouds steadily rolled in and stretched their full lengths, until blanketing the sky. Deep rumblings echoed through the air as dreary clouds transformed from bright, puffy whites into dismal, dark shades of gray, casting away the sun's glory of golden rays and its warmth. Loud claps of lightning and booms of thunder became the weather's music, silencing the beautiful songs of birds and other wildlife as they dashed away to hide! White flashes of light streaked across the sky over the city, Zareck, and began jumping from cloud-to-cloud—multiplying till the bolts seemed to stretch across the entire world! The seas of *Gekala* became restless! Waters began churning within their depths and rogue waves—more than seventy feet high—raced across the seas searching for ships to devour! The world itself had plunged into mourning! The most powerful Zodiark had reached the end of his old age... and died!

Stunned at nature's reaction, which was unlike anything seen before, the Elders immediately gathered traveling supplies and took to their carriages in search of a new Zodiark—someone strong enough to replace the fallen member.

Immediately, people all over the world began sinking into depression from the constant grey skies and cold rainstorms that kept popping up day-and-night. Complaints filled the talk in taverns as people griped about the rains flooding their fields, drowning their crops, and making life miserable and muddy!

Others acted as if they could care less about the unfavorable changes taking place in the world. Their focus was aimed at the open *Zodiark* position! Straightaway, people began submitting themselves for the lucrative role—by any means possible. Gifts ranging from: cakes several layers high and loaded with frosting; pastries and pies; silks; gift baskets filled with assortments of chocolates; exotic fruits; unwanted pets of every type; and boxes filled with linens in varying colors began piling up at each Elder's home! Their doorways became littered with piles of it, and each item had a message tag attached, which stated to some degree: "*Look no further! I'm the perfect choice! The new Zodiark!*

Anytime, day-or-night... I can visit and provide a demonstration of my skills!"

However, the Elders were annoyed by the pointless bribes piling up at their homes—blocking their doorways! Servants struggled to push past the towering piles to gain entry inside the Elders' homes. Workers tasked with ridding the Elders of the unwanted pets, were often attacked as they struggled to cage or leash them! A few sustained injuries while trying to coerce the barrage of uninvited visitors to leave. One servant had a huge tiered cake topple off its stand and fall onto his head, covering him from head to toe in thick icing! While another had several heavy boxes fall from the top of a pile, and was knocked out cold on the Elder's front porch!

Thousands of hopeful travelers made the long journey to the city Zareck, and soon filled every available inn! Each person was hoping to get either a glimpse of one the Zodiarks or was hoping to meet with an Elder. The bustling city quickly became overcrowded, and with all the hype and commotion stirring about, the taverns quickly became the liveliest places to find good ale, wine, and gossip!

One spirited night in a packed tavern near the center of the city, patrons filled long tables with endless food and ales, and sang songs glorifying the Zodiarks! Froth spilled from their mugs as they clinked them together, drank, and cheered each other on, and the barkeeps could barely keep up with the orders coming in. As one of the hired-hands was picking up dirty dishes and wiping spilled ale off the tables with a dirty rag, he overheard two men from the town, *Bernard.* They were talking about someone who lived along the outskirts of their town.

Quickly, he noticed everyone sitting at the table with the men were listening intently, and not uttering so much as one word. Quietly, so as to go unnoticed, he moved over to the table the men were sitting at and began slowly picking up the dirty plates and bowls among them, keeping an ear close in order to eavesdrop on their private conversation—hoping it would make for juicy gossip later!

The men spoke about a person who was very private and a loner—someone that emanated a dark energy and was always seen wearing a black hooded robe with their face hidden.

The voices of the men were low, as if they were almost afraid to tell more. One of them took a nervous glance over his shoulder towards the other patrons in the tavern who were sitting at tables behind them and to the sides. He almost took notice of the man listening-in, but was falsely reassured, as the humble-looking waiter gathered several more dirty forks and spoons from the table, and placed them inside one of the discarded mugs; then, he began wiping sauce off the far end of the table with his rag.

45

The conversation continued, and the men spoke of a two-story house on the outskirts of their town (the home of a private and evil individual). It was covered with rotten, wood planks, which were infested with vermin. A few, filthy, grime covered windows were at the front of the house, and through them, no one passing by ever saw any light. The other side of the windows only showed sets of pale curtains, slightly parted, and darkness. The windows' shutters had lost most of their paint years ago and hung crooked on rusty hinges. Roaches ran across filthy ledges and gutters, and huge spider webs stretched across the dirty front porch. Wrought-iron railings stood on each side of the front steps—unsecured to their cement structure—rickety and leaning towards the ground. Monstrous crickets with black stripes across beige, humped backs and long oversized legs, jumped freely up and down the walkway-path leading up to the front entrance. The front door stood as a sizable barricade between the outside world and the one dwelling inside the rotting home, and it appeared to be the only structure fully intact and not submitting to the surrounding decay. It was worn and had chipped paint with a couple spots of splintered wood, but the structure appeared unbreakable and the door was always shut!

An old stone chimney stood at the apex of the house, and both men agreed that occasionally, on their way out of town, they would see black smoke billowing out. However, the smoke didn't carry the pleasant scent of food cooking over an open fire, or pastries baking in a wood oven. No! Then, both men placed their hands over their nose to demonstrate how strong and foul the odor in the air would be, and described the stench as bitter herbs charred over flames.

Lastly, they spoke of an old, wooden fence that enclosed the property, and had only one gate in which to enter or leave through. Over the years, vines had crept onto the fencing and weaved their way in between the crevices. They had grown thick and had clusters of poisonous, but rather juicy-looking berries that were tempting to eat. So, the townspeople had to make sure all the children knew not to take any of them! The vines were protected by long, razor-sharp thorns that were a formidable warning of the cuts trespassers—who dared to cross—would inevitably endure. The entire property pulsed with the dark energy of the one living inside!

Suddenly, one of the men stopped in the middle of his story and stood up, looking over at the clock hanging on the wall. Hurriedly, he tapped his traveling buddy on the shoulder, and he, too, saw the time and began rushing!

"Sorry everyone, but we'll have to tell you the rest some other time," the man standing up informed. "We've got to get going!"

Everyone at the table immediately began complaining about the sudden stop in the men's tale!

"Oh, come on!" one of the men groaned.

"Don't leave now!" another pleaded. "Let me buy you gentlemen another round of ale, and you can finish telling us your story."

"Yeah! It was just getting good!"

"Surely, you can stay a few more minutes!" another insisted. "What's so important anyway that you have to leave right this second?"

"We've got an appointment to meet with one of the Elders," the other traveler expressed excitedly. "We can't be even one minute late!"

"Well, guess none of us can argue with that," one of the men at the table responded, throwing his hands up, knowing the conversation was definitely over no matter how the others tried to convince them otherwise. No one was going to give up a chance to meet with an Elder!

"If we're late, then we've missed our appointment and that's... that! However, before we go, I *will* tell you two more things."

The men at the table nodded and became quiet as they listened.

"I for one, have never actually met the person living in that house, but I've lived a long time, and I've seen things, and heard enough stories from others to make me think I know a thing or two. Firstly, whoever that is living in that old, creepy place, could very well be strong enough to replace that fallen Zodiark. Secondly, no one in Bernard wants that to happen! I would be willing to bet that every single person in our town has got all their fingers and toes crossed, hoping someone... anyone... gets chosen as the new *Zodiark*, instead of the person living there!"

"I'll chug to that!" the other man unexpectedly shouted, breaking the silence of the others at the table. Quickly, the rest of the men joined in, grabbing their mugs, chugging the remainder of their ale!

"Hey! You there!" he shouted at the young man cleaning up at the end of their table. He had fully realized by now that he had been eavesdropping, considering he was still working on the same pile of dirty dishes that he had begun with.

The young man looked around, quite unsure that he was the one being spoken to.

"Yes, you!" the man insisted, appearing to read his mind. "Get another round of ale for our new friends here! I'll pay for it on my way out!"

Quickly, he nodded and collected the pile of dirty dishes into a stack and dashed off to bring them fresh mugs of ale filled to the brim with white froth! As the drinks arrived, the men cheered while they were being passed around the table, and the travelers from *Bernard* paid their tab and left.

CHAPTER FIVE

A Grand Celebration

*T*he following day as sweet-smelling morning dew settled on the ground, bells began ringing and horns began sounding throughout the city! The last of the traveling Elders had returned during the wee hours of the night; after which, the council gathered in secret to discuss all they had seen and heard. The decision had been made!

Immediately, people previously tasked with spreading the exciting news that a new Zodiark had been chosen, were woken in the early morning hours by private messengers! Hurriedly, they jumped out of bed, threw on their clothes and shoes, and took off running up and down the streets in all directions throughout Zareck! Each person shouted at the top of their lungs, "The new Zodiark has been chosen! The new Zodiark has been chosen! A grand parade will be held here, in the city Zareck, in three days to honor the new Zodiark! All are invited! Tell everyone you know!"

Sleepy citizens and visitors peeked out their windows, wiping the sleep from their eyes as the announcers continued shouting the message! Quickly, everyone shook off their groggy haze and realized what they were saying! People came rushing out of their homes and the inns, pouring into the city streets, cheering joyfully and talking amongst each other about the exciting report!

Straightaway, many rushed back into their residencies and sent magical mail to friends and family, announcing the news! Orbs popped up in homes all over the world, containing the face of the sender within it, joyfully declaring a message about the new Zodiark and the upcoming parade! Some popped up over beds of sleeping relatives, shocking them wide awake and causing a few to fall out onto the floor! While others were surprised in lavatories, or at kitchen breakfast tables during the morning meal, causing some to spit out their food at the orb's sudden appearance! The news spread far and fast over every land, and millions of people were splendidly excited!

Everyone immediately began making preparations to travel with family and friends to Zareck! Quickly, they rushed to buy supplies for the trip; stores were emptied of their baked goods, clothing, candles, incenses, and other miscellaneous supplies. Beautiful horse-drawn carriages trimmed with silver, gold, and precious colorful stones were booked for rental, which left many to find other means of transport for the long journey!

Some casts magical charms on carriages in order to expand cabin size, allowing for lots of extra people to be loaded into the space! People whispered incantations, waving their fingers at storage bins and casting charms, causing bag-after-bag to be loaded beyond practical capacity! Some chose to travel by air, riding on majestic, white swans; while others traveled on large bullfrogs with their throats puffed out in pride, making huge jumps towards the city. A few, who considered themselves more elite than the others, were seen riding side-straddle on graceful unicorns, prancing their way towards Zareck!

The weather returned to normal upon the induction of the new Zodiark; the clouds cleared, the rain ceased, the seas calmed, the skies were again blue and dotted with puffy white clouds, and the sun shone brightly with its golden rays warming the tropical air. The harmony of nature had been restored! Everything was perfect, and people were arriving by the dozens at the gates of Zareck to watch the impeding parade!

Travelers, young and old, received a warm welcome by the citizens of the city! Bands playing drums and blowing horns delighted the visitors on every main street, welcoming people of all ages to dance and join in the cheer! Bright banners hanging over the entrances said, *Welcome to Zareck*, and blew in the breezes. Colorful streamers hung from poles, and flags with the word, *Zodiarks*, were nailed to doorposts and window ledges from second and third stories of buildings!

Shop keepers set up lavish open-air markets with booths filled with exotic fruits, vegetables, breads, and pastries of all varieties to delight the senses and taste buds of the tourists! Stores stocked their racks with beautiful clothing for those needing pants, shirts, formal attire, dresses, hats, shoes, or bags! Many had magical charms placed on them to change color with the sun and moons, or for purses to allow extra things to be piled inside! Several vendors filled their stations with expensive bottles of wine and barrels of ale, ready to sell and pour to thirsty adult visitors who were wishing to enjoy themselves a little bit more.

Other vendors were selling juice, natural spring water by the bottle, and extra-super-duper fizzy-delight sodas in candy flavors! Immediately, the children entering the city with their parents spotted the bottles of fizzy sodas and took off running to stand in the long lines to purchase one! All the excited children were jumping up and down and shouting for the soda! The sounds of bottle tops popping open filled the air as soda bubbles and fizz began spewing out the tops and down the sides of the long-necked bottles! All of the children immediately began guzzling down the soda, paying no regard to the sticky mixture sliding onto their hands and spilling to the ground!

Into the wee hours of the night, the celebration raged on until the crowds gradually dissipated—most people returning to their lodgings, sleepily dragging their feet, plopping into bed, while others found chairs scattered along the streets and slumped into them, quickly falling into drunken slumbers. A few fell asleep before being sober enough to leave the taverns—their heads laying on wet, messy, bar tables, snoring in pools of their own drool with their fingers still clung to the empty mugs beside them.

Gradually, the warm humid air of the night shifted into to the cool, crisp of morning as the sun began to rise, coloring the sky light shades of pinks, purples, and sea-blues amidst strands of white clouds. Groggily, people woke up and opened their windows to let the fresh air in and feel the warm rays of the rising sun cascade through the windows. The smell of sausage, eggs, bacon, grits, pancakes, waffles and biscuits began drifting through the air as people started cooking breakfast in sizzling hot skillets and ovens all over the city, while others took showers and got dressed for the exciting day ahead!

Without delay, bells began ringing throughout the city, tolling back and forth, sending out their beautiful sounds! The much-anticipated parade was about to begin! Frantic and excited energy pulsed through the air as people ran to look out their windows to see how many were rushing into the streets along the parade route to get a good viewing spot! Hurriedly, children and teenagers raced each other down stairs, outdoors, and through the streets with great excitement to join the growing crowd! Everyone was clamoring for the perfect spot to see the Zodiarks!

At the first sounds of the bells, some hastily ended their showers... jumping out while still covered in soap suds, tripping over rugs as they scrambled to reach for their towels, or being blinded by shampoo soap dripping down their foreheads into their eyes—screaming as they rushed to turn the faucets back on to resume rinsing suds from their hair! Others hurriedly threw on their clothes, some with shirts inside-out, mismatched socks, or dresses stuck awkwardly into stockings. A few people choked down their breakfast in huge mouthfuls, scrapping forks and spoons against plates as they shoveled the food down!

In the streets, people were being ushered to the sides by designated parade staff in order to make the way clear for the parade's marching bands and dancers! At the farthest end of the city, near the center, stood an impressive stone castle, which was home to the Zodiarks, and it was lined on both sides with huge towers reaching high into the clouds.

On the wide stone steps leading up to the castle's doors, stood a group of bare-chested men adorned with tribal tattoos along their arms and markings on each person's face. Each man was wearing arm-bands and anklets made of green leaves weaved together, and their green shorts matched. Several of them had a large drum strapped to their chest and were holding padded sticks in their hands. The other men stood silently next to them, holding bigger padded sticks without drums. Beyond the steps, there was a circular white platform waiting for them with three additional drums on it, much larger than the ones strapped to the men!

Quickly, a man of only several feet tall came waddling up the steps to stand in front of the tribal men. He gave them a brief nod, then stepped onto a small platform with a microphone stand on it, which had already been adjusted to fit his height. His face was lightly covered with a mix of brown and white feathers, and his large, round, yellow eyes peered out over the cheering crowd as he seemed to briefly study the onlookers for any signs of trouble. As he looked them over, he adjusted the tight belt underneath his round, plump belly, and craned his neck upwards for a better view, causing his oversized, pointy, yellow, beak to look even more curvy to those nearby.

He was nicely dressed for the occasion, wearing dark slacks, a pale, olive-green, button-down shirt, and a dark vest over it, which all looked very good despite a few brown feathers poking through some gaps between the buttons of his shirt. A gold chain clipped onto his lapel, hid its other end in his vest pocket, until he pulled out an expensive gold pocket watch to check the time, then replaced it to its spot.

"Hello everyone!" he said confidently into the microphone as he waved a feather-covered hand at the cheering crowd! "Welcome to the inauguration ceremony of our *newest Zodiark*! I am Sir Beaksmith, one of the Elders, and I'm proud to announce that after months of searching the world high and low, all the Elders have agreed... we have found the perfect person to carry on the works of our fallen Zodiark. This person has proven to not only have the magical strength sought after in a Zodiark, but also has superb moral character, and is the youngest to ever have been chosen! Let us show our newest Zodiark our greatest and warmest welcome!"

Again, the crowd erupted into loud cheering and applause!

"Today, let us honor and celebrate *all* the Zodiarks!" and with both hands up in the air, Sir Beaksmith shouted into the microphone, "Let the celebrations begin!"

Quickly, Sir Beaksmith scurried off the platform as two people hurried to remove the microphone from the path of the tribal men on the steps. Slowly at first, the men carrying the drums began to beat their drumsticks against their drums in a synchronized rhythm, while descending the steps towards the other awaiting platform holding the humongous three drums. In perfect step with each other, the men beat their drums and stepped up onto the platform, allowing the others to take their positions at the larger drums. Together, they joined in a slow, steady, synchronized beat, gradually increasing to a magnificent crescendo—raising the platform to hover above the ground, then moving it down along the parade route!

Immediately, the marching bands and dancers wearing vibrant and dazzling costumes joined in the parade! Trumpets, horns, clarinets, flutes, and saxophones rang out their musical notes in amazing tunes! Baton twirlers repeatedly threw their ribbon covered sticks high into the air as they marched onwards in front of the cheering crowds lining the streets! People were high-fiving each other, dancing, jumping up-and-down, and waving to those in the parade! Others, who were standing on balconies overlooking the parade route, were throwing down huge handfuls of colorful confetti as the people marched by during the splendid celebration!

Suddenly, the castle doors at the top of the steps began to swing open, revealing the seven Zodiarks standing together on the other side. Their appearances were regal in their formal attire of long royal blue robes, pristine whites showing beneath golden sashes tied at the waist, and gold and silver necklaces hanging around each one's neck with matching golden slippers for shoes. A special thread of silver unicorn hair had been intricately woven into the stitching of their robes, causing them to shimmer when touched by the warm rays of the sun.

A gold crown with seven points sat on the top of each Zodiark's head. Each point contained a rare precious stone—chosen as a symbol to represent one of the many cherished elements in the world. *Sapphires* collected from within the deep seas represented water. Light *topazes* found in the places where strong winds constantly blew represented air. Flawless *diamond soul-stones* found within the soil of volcanos represented the people's unbreakable spirit. *Emeralds* found deep within lush jungles vibrant with life represented vegetation. *Crimson garnet inferno-stones* found within caves near steam vents represented fire. *Rose quartz* found within distant fields of flowers growing at the pinnacles of rock-covered mountains represented love. Lastly, the black *onyx* stones found deep within the darkest ice caves represented death.

On a platform made of marble they stood—most of them with old wrinkled faces and grey beards, except for the newest member. A teenage boy with green eyes, fair skin, and with no hair even yet upon his face was standing (front and center) among them, waving a hand over the platform while whispering something no one else could hear. Immediately, the platform began moving, levitating off the ground, and descending slowly down the steps following the performers! The crowd cheered joyously while the Zodiarks waved as they passed by!

Straightaway, following them were the Elders, which were each being seated on carrying-chairs with plush cushions covered with purple velvet linens and stuffed with soft feathers. The poles attached to the chairs were covered in polished gold with leaf decorations artistically cut along the entirety of them. Spectators gasped at the gold's brilliance shining in the light—at the impressiveness of the chairs—as their servants carried them through the parade behind the Zodiarks!

As the parade continued on, children along the streets were entertained by adults who had been hopeful at being chosen as the new Zodiark. The children huddled around them as fun magic tricks were performed; their favorite spell being one in which a man held his hands out together, causing a dense cloud to form and lift up high into the air above them. Then, he would instruct one of the children to point a finger at the cloud, causing a bright spark to shoot forth from that finger and explode the cloud into a big shower of candy raining down over the excited children! Others were twisting balloons in their hands in the shapes of all types of different miniature dragons and other creatures and were making them come to life by flying them through the air, circling them around the children, and swooping the creatures down low over their heads, causing them to duck and laugh!

Up high on his chair in the procession, Sir Beaksmith waved at a group of giggling girls who were enjoying a small mound of candy produced by a street magician's cloud trick along the side of the street. The magician caused a storm cloud to swell, until it burst! Greedily, the young children were stuffing their mouths with chewy gummy candies, yellow lemon sour balls, green lime firecracker-poppers, sweet winding rainbow lollipops, and nugget-bars covered with creamy milk chocolate.

"Look! He's waving to us!" one of the boys said, ramming his skinny arm into the ribs of another to get his attention.

Quickly, a girl who was scarfing down a melting chocolate bar, shot her eyes up to Sir Beaksmith! "Wow! That's an Elder!" she gasped, hurrying to wipe the chocolate off her face with a sleeve of her shirt. "Mind your manners! That's an Elder who's waving to us!" she sternly instructed the other kids, as she knew her own mother would have done if she had seen them—luckily, she was too busy watching the parade and dancing to the music!

Immediately, the other children stood up, wide-eyed and smiling from ear-to-ear at the Elder and began waving wildly at him with sticky messy candy in their hands!

Delighted at the sight of their happy faces, Sir Beaksmith smiled, but then something in the corner of his eyes caught his attention. Instantly, he motioned with a feathery hand at his servants to stop marching, and he keenly focused his sharp eyes up ahead at something silver and shiny underneath the platform carrying the drummers. Brightly, he saw the silver object flash again! Without delay, Sir Beaksmith hurriedly motioned his servants to let him down off his carrying-chair just as a loud noise sounded through the air....

CHAPTER SIX
Dark Horizon

*B*oom! Without warning, a huge explosion from inside the platform holding the drummers sent men and debris flying through the air! **Boom! Boom! Boom!** Sounded three more explosions along the parade route! Suddenly, an ear-piercing noise began sounding throughout the streets, forcing everyone down onto their knees and clasping hands over their ears! Mind searing pain filled each person's head as they kneeled down in the crowds. Blood began oozing from their ears, dripping down the sides of their faces! Men, women and children tore at their ears while grimacing and wailing in pain!

Suddenly, millions of sharp metal shards began raining down from the sky—mercilessly, each razor-edged blade moved with purpose! The sky became darker and darker as the shards rained from the sky, blocking the light of the sun—slicing the skin of its victims. Screams filled the streets! People everywhere were trying to get up in a frenzied hurry to run underneath the nearest shelters, but the shards were quick in striking their targets, sending people tumbling over bodies—tripping over the dead! Shards struck eyes and people tried to free the metal from their face—pulling the metal out with their eye firmly attached to it with veins stretching and clinging to the socket. Others tried to free the shards from their legs, shoulders, hands, and abdomens—screaming as they tore it through muscle on the way out.

Among the chaos, a thick, black fog began to creep through the streets, until it surrounded the city! Darker the sky grew, till becoming charcoal as night—all light from the sun had perished underneath the thick blanket. Those alive were frantically calling to the Zodiarks! "Please! Help us!" they shouted, to no avail!

Before the Zodiarks could do anything to help, the fog moved towards them and intensified into a denser black mass that fiercely swirled and caged them! Instantaneously, the cage developed into a roaring black tornado… trapping the Zodiarks inside! Separated from the Elders and those crying out for help in the streets, the Zodiarks frantically searched for a way out and began trying different spells to take down the cage! Horrified expressions filled their faces as they looked at each other… realizing that nothing was working.

Swiftly, two of them stretched their hands up towards the sky and began shouting new spells!

The roar of the whirling massive tornado was deafening, and its winds tore at the buildings near it—ripping roof tiles off, and freeing doors from their hinges, sending them soaring up into the sky!

Immediately, the other five Zodiarks joined in, flinging one spell after another—each one failing against the mega-tornado encapsulating them!

As the others soon paused their attempts—unsure of what else to do—the youngest Zodiark began trying additional new spells! Fast and hard, he flung one after another at the tornado, which seemed to be alive and pulsing with shadow-energy. The tornado seemed to be growing larger—engorging itself on the energy produced by the peoples' fear and pain, like an evil beast, becoming more enraged while continuing to trap them.

"Dispergo! Dismoveo! Dissupo! Dispello!" the young Zodiark shouted, but the winds only slowed for a brief moment, and then intensified as the top of the storm climbed even higher into the black clouds above!

Over the deafening noise, the Zodiarks cringed at the sounds of their people screaming and shouting in horror!

"What's that!" yelled a little girl, standing next to her mother while gripping her hand so tightly that the woman's face winced in pain!

"Look! There in the clouds!" hollered a man, hiding within a damaged clothing store; the tornado had torn tiles off the roof and shattered all the windows along the storefront. Broken glass clung to the window frames, and clothing was strewn all over the floor alongside pieces of glass. Cautiously, the man held the door slightly open as he peaked outside to watch a terrifying creature descend out of the clouds!

"What is that thing?" a panicked woman shouted.

"Where? I don't see it!" a little boy yelled, as he peaked from behind a large stone column that was holding up a damaged archway and tavern sign.

"There! Above the tornado! In those dark clouds!" an elderly man replied, pointing at the sky.

Without warning, the enormous monstrous figure in the sky plunged downwards from the dark clouds—its large horns atop its head pointed toward the ground during its descent! Screams filled the streets as the black, silver-eyed dragon flew only inches above everyone's head… the power of its wings in-flight forced the people to fall onto the ground!

As the dragon flew, stones lost their strongholds within the buildings and came crashing down onto the streets! Several of them hit the dragon as they fell, buts its thick, scarred, black scales acted as a protective armor, causing the beast to feel nothing! Quickly, the dragon ascended back into the sky with its huge, leathery, black wings stretched wide and it dashed its long spike-covered tail at one of the Zodiarks' towers, causing a section of the roof to cave-in on several servants who worked for the Elders––who were hiding inside!

As the dragon reached the pentacle of the dark clouds, it closed its wings and descended again, rapidly, towards the people frantically running through the streets! Swiftly, the dragon dove down… rolling its body in the air as it picked up speed! A second before hitting the ground, the dragon up-righted itself and stretched out its huge wings above the people. The sharp claws at the tips of its wings scratched at the sides of the buildings, leaving deep gashes along the stones!

Purposefully, the dragon ravaged the city and tormented those within it! Pass-after-pass, it made back up into the sky and again down through the city—growling and feeling its hunger grow! Without mercy, the dragon began grabbing straggling runners with its feet! Women and children were clutched so tightly within the dragon's violent grip, that their bones began to crack, and blood spewed from their mouths as they struggled to breath.

As the dragon again reached the clouds, it paused and flapped its black wings to hover. Slowly, the dragon lifted its feet towards its massive jaws, which were filled with rows of razor-sharp serrated-edged teeth. Its silver eyes—intense with malevolence and vengeance—looked at those crying within its grip. Without hesitation, the dragon ripped the people in half, freeing their torsos from their dangling limbs, and greedily ate their flesh!

Still, its stomach was unsatisfied, and its evil heart felt nothing as it cruelly threw the remains of the blood-soaked limbs down onto those running and watching in horror! Again, the dragon swooped down, making a few more attempts to collect its desired pounds of flesh... soaking the dragon's mouth with the blood of the innocent.

As the tornado continued to trap the Zodiarks and render them powerless, the dragon repeatedly made its descents, until unexpectedly choosing to land inside the city just beyond the entrance of the front gates. As the creature landed and slowed its wings, dust flew up from the dry ground and clouded the air.

Onlookers hiding within dilapidated buildings watched the behemoth fold its wings down by its sides and sit straight-up in a poised and prideful stature. Seemingly, the beast was brimming with pride at all the destruction and fear it had wrought... as it waited for someone.

****

Within the black sky, flashes of white lightening began dancing from cloud-to-cloud; at first two in the distance, but quickly multiplying into a crescendo filled with dozens of blindingly bright bolts within the coming storm! Without warning, searing hot streaks began jumping down from the charcoal clouds, striking the buildings throughout the city! Crisp crackling sounds filled the air as thunder shook the structures violently. Suddenly, a tremendous bolt of bluish-white lightning shot down from the sky and struck the locked gates at the front entrance—decimating the steel bar holding the doors closed and ripping them at their iron hinges!

Suddenly, a huge burst of wind blew open the doors! There, in the midst of the broken gates stood a tall figure clothed in black metal armor. The figure stood, like a statue taking the moment in, and pulsated with evil energy, which felt thick and palpable—similar to static electricity—in the air.

Abruptly, the clouds released their bounty, producing a torrential downpour of rain, which slid down the shiny black helm covering the person's head, and the drops cascaded down along the smooth metal armor along the figure's arms, chest, and legs… down onto the steel boots that resembled claws. Slowly, the figure stepped forward, moving towards the dragon. The mud on the soaked ground splashed underneath the weight of the boots as the figure walked into the city with purpose and steady steps—walking toward the massive whirling tornado.

As the figure neared the dragon, the beast shot its silver-eyed stare towards frightened people sneaking glances through broken windows. Viciously, the dragon snarled, then crouched down on its legs and lowered its head all the way onto the ground, submissively, as it recognized its master and cowered itself in the presence of… *the DARK ONE.*

Protectively, the beast shot its head toward soft sounds coming from behind a column that had crumbled half its length to the ground. "Who is that?" the dragon heard a young boy whisper to his mother.

As the two of them watched in horror, the mother looked down at her scared son, but stayed silent and simply shook her head that she didn't know, whilst giving him a firm look that he should not utter another word. She greatly feared provoking the wrath of the dragon further, due to her son's whispers, and preferred not to gain the attention of the one the dragon was yielding to!

Boldly, the DARK ONE approached the monster tornado! Huge winds, filled with dirt and debris, swarmed the Zodiarks imprisoned inside! Slowly, the figure raised both gloved hands to the storm and began shouting over the noise. The DARK ONE'S voice was carried on the winds and was louder than the storm… filling the entire city!

"Zareck!" the intimidating figure laughed. "The ruined city of the Zodiarks! Tell me, did everyone enjoy the parade you so foolishly threw?" the DARK ONE sarcastically asked.

Everywhere, the people cowered: within dilapidated buildings; behind broken columns and shattered windows; and peeked through crevices; sneaking glances from behind doors hanging sideways on bent hinges as the DARK ONE continued, "Tell me! Where... are... the... Zodiarks?" (over pronouncing each word). "Where were they while the dragon destroyed your city and ate your young... your old... the women... and the children?" the DARK ONE asked, turning around in a circle with hands held out, in jest, as if waiting to receive an answer that would never come. "The *Elders* say the Zodiarks are the most powerful in our world, *Gekala*! Isn't that the reason you fools... celebrate them! Why they are treated as royalty!" the DARK ONE angrily shouted, then returned to face the revolving prison whirling upwards, touching the sky! "*I alone...* am the *most powerful*!"

Standing there, in the midst of the rain, the figure raised both hands towards the sky and shouted to the storm:

> *"Dark souls, those foul, and bitter with rage,*
> *Rotting flesh long since buried in the grave,*
> *Warring within the storm... obey ME!*
> *Hear the one that commands you!*
> *Freedom for but a little while,*
> *Through gateways... returned from the tomb!*

Immediately, evil souls began appearing as fleshless bodies (by the thousands) within the massive storm swarming around the Zodiarks! Grimacing pain-filled faces—having empty eye-sockets filled with shadow—stretched their mouths wide open! They began to wail and moan as they broke away from the storm and went rampaging throughout the city! At the same time, portals appeared within the sky and down in the ground everywhere within Zareck! Souls with evil intentions began to climb out of them, but hands belonging to others reached for them and eagerly dragged them back inside!

Souls with ghastly faces and horns at the top of their heads flew out from the tornado and rammed themselves into the buildings as they saw the portals opening nearby—long transparent arms reached out to grab them, dragging them back to the realm of spirits they had fled from! Stones weighing hundreds of pounds were knocked free from the buildings as the sinister spirits rammed into homes, inns, shops, and taverns—trying to escape the reach of the hands! People ran out of their hiding places back into the streets, because the spirits had found them and tormented them with scratches and deep bloody gashes, which appeared randomly on their skin from spiteful souls who were envious of the flesh they no longer had!

Abruptly, a huge burst of energy from within the twister sent the remaining souls scattering throughout the city as the Zodiarks broke themselves free—ceasing the tornado's winds! Immediately, each of them created spells and furiously hurled them at the evil figure standing in front them without the slightest sign of fear or intimidation!

"*Praeligo Potestates Eius!*" shouted a Zodiark as he threw a spell from his hand to bind the attacker's powers!

"*Immobiles Motus Eius!*" shouted another to suspend the attacker's movements!

"*Silentium Lingua Eius! Non Verba de Labiis Suis!*" to mute the tongue and stop the words!

"*Incrementum Gravitatem! Conquinisco Usque ad Mihi! Manibus de Terram!*" to force the attacker down onto both knees with gloved hands placed flat upon the ground!

"*Draco-Musca Effictum Ignis, Caveam Bestia Flamma Apud Annulos Ignis!*" shouted the newly elected Zodiark! Instantly, a reddish-orange flame shot forth from his stretched-out hand and became transmogrified into a large, four-winged, fiery dragonfly! Quickly, the dragonfly soared up to the clouds, then dove down to the kneeling DARK ONE and started making loops around the attacker, lassoing the evil inside its flaming rings!

"*Tremefacio Terram!*" shouted another, while the dragonfly trapped the DARK ONE within the scorching flames! Suddenly, the ground underneath the city grew agitated and began to shake. Everywhere, the buildings started swaying as the sodding and stones underneath them shifted from their places! Long cracks split apart the stones in the streets and huge sections of dirt fell into the amounting deep places, revealing themselves underneath the city! Within seconds, the ground beneath the dragon separated itself and the behemoth took to the sky—circling high above within the black clouds!

Every Zodiark stood together, as a team, boldly in front of the DARK ONE! There, each stood without fear, nor hesitation as the battle ensued between *them* and the enraged *evil* inside the flaming lasso-cage!

With a hand stretched-out, the young Zodiark bravely shouted the words:

"Terraemotus!

Erupit Terram!

Luto Cataracta Circumventuros

Malum et Ascendo Versus Caelum!"

Slowly, an arrow of white light was emitted from his hand, and it dove deep into the soil ahead of them! Rapidly, the ground beneath the DARK ONE began to shift, crack, and tear itself open as the ground throughout the city quaked—ripping apart! Vents beneath the ground hissed loudly as the Zodiark's spell forced

74

them open, and superheated steam began billowing up through Zareck's streets—changing the air into a sticky hot heat.

"*Dirumpe et Terramque Spargens et Ascendum!*" the young Zodiark shouted as he flung another spell at the evil black-armored figure. Instantly, a wide area of ground began to break and separate around the attacker! Suddenly, without warning, everything in the city fell silent. The steam in the deep vents ceased billowing out, and the few remaining souls still flying through the streets were dragged into the last portal seconds before it closed and vanished from sight.

Everywhere, people stopped running. Some had perplexed expressions on their dirt streaked faces as they look around for an explanation… wondering to themselves, *was everything finally over?*

Aimlessly, people began walking around. Men, women, and children exited from their hiding places and walked out of buildings. They were tired, hungry, and bleeding and were holding dirty torn pieces of cloth on wounds as they stumbled out of doorways and walked up the broken street toward the Zodiarks and the DARK ONE—still kneeling inside the dragonfly's fire-rings.

As they walked, several people looked up as they heard the faint sounds of the dragon's wings flapping as it flew overhead through the clouds; the beast was struggling with thoughts of intervening on its master's behalf.

As everyone gathered into the crowd, a few yards away from the figure in black, abruptly the silence broke! In the deep cracks created by the last spell, huge columns of gas mixed with dirt and debris, burst from the ground on all sides of the DARK ONE and soared into the sky!

Loudly, the dragon screeched as it balked at the Zodiark's spell that trapped its master, but obediently, it did not intervene! Enraged, the behemoth's silver eyes glared down at everyone gathered on the street of the main parade route near its master. Swiftly, it dove down and made a low swoop over their heads— knocking several onlookers to the ground—but then quickly resumed its flight back to the sky!

Everyone started to scream and run, but quickly stopped at the sound of the Zodiark's voice.

"Fear it not! The dragon is only a puppet of the evil trapped within the cage!" the oldest of the Zodiarks sternly spoke as the other six stood at his sides. "We have its master. The source of its hatred and violence! We can communicate with the beast and send it away."

"No! Kill the dragon!" an onlooker shouted!

"Yes! Get rid of the beast!"

"It killed my father… and I watched as it ate him! Destroy it!" shouted a young blonde girl in the crowd.

"I want it dead, too!" shouted a woman holding a baby in her arms; both of them were wearing torn clothing stained with a mixture of blood and dirt. Tearful streaks showed clean lines on the woman's otherwise filthy face underneath her exhausted green eyes.

"Pierce its heart with one of your spells!" yelled a boy, somewhere in the middle of his teen years. "It has no right to live after what it's done!"

"Yes! Kill it!" the crowd shouted together.

"I want its head on display at the city's front gates!" yelled an elderly woman with curly white hair. Her arms were covered in bloody scratches and a dark bruise was on the side of her face from being knocked down during one of the dragon's low-passes over them. She clutched her back in pain and frowned at the Zodiarks for considering sparing the dragon's life!

"Kill the dragon! Kill the dragon! Kill the dragon! Kill the dragon!" the crowd of wounded people shouted in unison with their fists pumping threateningly at the dragon in the sky!

"Silence!" one of the Zodiarks shouted, but instead, the crowd grew louder! "We are bound not to do harm! It's part of an oath we took, and we are sworn to uphold it. We cannot break it… not even now."

Immediately, the crowd erupted with indignation at their beloved Zodiarks! "What! Not even when the people you serve are murdered!" a man shouted at them.

"What good are you then to us!" yelled another.

"No harm, huh! Well, does that mean you're going to also let that person you caged live too?" asked a woman in the middle of the dismayed crowd.

"Yeah? What are the Zodiarks going to do with *the DARK ONE*?" an injured boy yelled. Immediately, noisy chatter filled the crowd as everyone conversed with each other as to what they thought their leaders should do.

All of a sudden, before any of the Zodiarks could answer, the high walls of dirt and debris surrounding the DARK ONE came crashing down! As the columns plummeted, dirt was scattered over the people on the street before the thought to run for cover entered their minds! Thick dust saturated the air, making it difficult to breathe… causing the people to choke, gasp, and cough in the mess. People squinted their eyes to find each other and see what was going on through the haze.

Gasps sounded throughout the crowd as eyes saw the evil in black armor gripping the fiery lassos! Suddenly paralyzed with fear and feeling helpless to do anything, everyone watched an energy field, made of intense concentrated negative emotions, emanate from the DARK ONE, encompassing the attacker within a dark orb that glowed red. Quickly, the orb began to pulse and increase in size with each beat of the DARK ONE's evil heart—a heart filled with hatred and envy!

Without strain, the DARK ONE ripped apart the lassos and became free from the gravity spell—that had forced the powerful evil to kneel on the ground—up-righting to stand in front of the Zodiarks. Standing in the midst of the orb, strong and unharmed, the DARK ONE glared unflinchingly at the Zodiarks. The orb—unbeknownst to them—was draining energy from the dragonfly and the Zodiarks, siphoning their light essences and transferring them into that of shadow. Quickly, the lassos shriveled on the ground and the fire engulfing them became extinguished with an insignificant puff of smoke, then vanished!

"Was that the best you could do!" the DARK ONE sarcastically said to the Zodiarks—each of them facing the DARK ONE and poised to attack with more spells at the ready! "I *allowed* you to throw any spell you wanted and *that* was your best!"

An evil laugh came from the one in black armor.

"I did nothing! I all but laid down and gave myself to your whims, and still you show nothing!" (the hatred grew with every word). "All of you are weak!" the DARK ONE screamed at them! "*You... are... nothing... to... me!*" (the words hatefully and purposefully pronounced). "These Zodiarks are no more fit to rule a world... than a rat is fit to be a king!" the DARK ONE announced to the listening crowd without removing the glare off the Zodiarks.

"Then, who should rule? *You... DARK ONE!* Did you seriously think the Elders should have chosen, *you,* as the next Zodiark! That you would do a better job taking care of this world than me! That *you* would be able to manage things in it to keep it beautiful and strong!" the newly elected Zodiark replied.

"I am stronger than any of you! I *will* rule this world! Everyone will bow to me—no silly spells required," the DARK ONE sarcastically answered, referencing the gravity spell that had been used to force the evil-doer to kneel on the ground, which had been skillfully broken. "I care nothing for the beauty you speak of. It reeks of Zodiarks! I will remake this world to be as I am. In everything... there will only be MY image!"

"Never!" the young Zodiark shouted, but before any of them could say a single spell, the DARK ONE's dragon swooped down from the black clouds and scorched the buildings lining both sides of that street with blue flames from its mouth!

Immediately, chaos ensued as the people took off screaming and running in all directions, and the DARK ONE's eyes approvingly met his beast's! Loudly, the black dragon called to its master, and then flew off to make a full flight over the city. Then, the DARK ONE returned the wicked glare back to the Zodiarks who had become distracted.

With hands raised to the sky the DARK ONE spoke:

"Malum Abundivit!
Nigrum Nubes de Caelum!
Tenebrosus Materia!
Rubrum Orbis!
Da Mihi Vestra Potestatem Indu Magna Supplementum!"

As the last word departed, an evil red glow appeared in the DARK ONE's eyes beneath the black helmet and the orb of energy began to pulsate faster.

"Duo Sphaerae Cum Ignis.
Crescer Indu Manus Meas.
Levo et Miscere Indu Unum!"

With hands held out, smaller spheres containing a reddish-orange liquid appeared in each of the DARK ONE's hands. Slowly, the viscous substances inside them swirled as the orbs lifted and floated into the air, till joining together into one massive sphere.

"Ignire," the DARK ONE whispered to the sphere, and with a flash of red light, the sphere became lit on fire and flew towards the Zodiarks!

Just then, Sir Beaksmith came running out of a nearby building where he had been hiding and watching the events unfold! "*Obex!*" he shouted. Instantly, an invisible barrier of energy sprung up around himself! "*Celeritate,*" he commanded, and with lightning speed, Sir Beaksmith rushed towards the Zodiarks! Panicked and with no time to think, he grabbed the youngest of them—the newly elected—and instantly the barrier stretched to encompass them both as they dashed away a mere second before the sphere burst over the others and ignited them with scorching flames!

In horror, as Sir Beaksmith pulled him away, the young Zodiark looked over his shoulder—his eyes widening at the sight! The faces of his comrades were screaming in agony as: flames incinerated their robes and other clothing; hair burned in flashes of bright flames; searing heat crisped and charred flesh; and bodies collapsed onto the ground... writhing in pain as death approached them.

"Wait! We can't just leave them!" the young Zodiark pleaded with Sir Beaksmith. "I can say a spell. I think. I don't know... but I can't just leave them... to die!" His mind was spinning, dizzy with thoughts as he searched for something—anything—that he could say or do to help. Salty tears burst from his eyes and poured down his cheeks!

"I'm sorry. There is nothing we can do," Sir Beaksmith replied. "He *will* kill you, too, if we stay any longer. You're strong, but not enough to defeat him. All the Elders knew he was strong enough to be chosen as the next Zodiark. Even stronger than you. Maybe the strongest anyone had ever seen! Several Elders interviewed him, back when we were searching for the next to be chosen, but his heart... it was so dark... filled with evil and shadow. None of us could bring ourselves to choose him! We thought he might try to disrupt the parade somehow, but none of us thought he would go this far! I'm so sorry! All I can do now is to protect you. We must leave before he realizes you're missing." Tightly, Sir Beaksmith gripped a feathery hand around the lad and pulled him away.

"Okay," the young Zodiark replied, choking back tears and wiping them from his eyes, "but one day the DARK ONE will pay for this!"

Sir Beaksmith nodded and with a whisper, spoke the word, "*Vanisco,*" and with a small flash of light, they vanished.

Triumphantly, the DARK ONE continued watching the flames consume the Zodiarks, without noticing the departure of one.

"Let this day mark a new beginning. The reign of darkness has come! Never shall another word in this world be spoken about the Zodiarks!" the DARK ONE commanded, knowing that the people who were hiding, watching, and listening would spread the news of all that had happened. "The Zodiarks are dead! Never again shall they be revered! Let shadow end the light." For a moment, the DARK ONE stood, staring down at the heap of charred flesh on the ground still smoldering, then vanished into thin air from sight.

Loudly, the dragon in the sky roared a warning to those below, then flew off at its master's departure, as a thick, sluggish, white fog began to crawl over the city's high walls into Zareck. Slowly, cold air poured into the city and frosted the broken shards clinging to the window panes. The chill of the DARK ONE's reign had begun....

CHAPTER SEVEN
It Can't Be

Quietly, Amora shut the book on the table and stared down at its cover. "I can't believe it," she whispered. Her throat felt dry and scratchy as she tried to force what little moisture remained in her mouth down into the pit of her stomach, which was nauseated due to the shock and disbelief she was feeling after reading everything in the forbidden book with Magnar. Tears pooled in the corners of her eyes, and her rosy cheeks paled as the illustrations depicted in the book—of the dead bodies and charred Zodiarks—played over-and-over again in her mind.

Without a word, she stood up from the table, scooted her chair back to its original position, and turned herself away from Magnar.

"Are you okay?" he asked, still sitting at the table, but turning to face her.

Unable to answer, she placed her hands over her face, and soft sobs became all that was audible inside the bookstore.

Quietly, he stood up and walked over to her. "I'm sorry. I shouldn't have shown that book to you. I didn't mean to upset you like this," he whispered, and gently swept aside strands of her black hair from the sides her face. "Please, don't cry."

"No. I'm glad you showed me," she insisted, removing her hands from her face and wiping away the tears sliding down her cheeks. "I can't believe something like this has been kept a secret for so long. That no one has ever spoken about or heard of Zodiarks or Elders."

Not knowing what to say, Magnar nodded his head and glanced up at the wall clock to read the time. It was well after midnight, and he was beginning to worry that if neither of them showed up to the town's party, then people would begin to gossip about anything they suspected the two of them had been up to.

"We should get out of here and head over to the town's social for a while—" he paused briefly. "So, people won't come up with their own conclusions about why neither of us were there."

"You're probably right. I know Mr. Higgins will be full of questions tomorrow at work if I don't at least make an appearance there tonight, but I need to head home first and change for the party. I can't go smelling like hay and horses!" she laughingly replied, but Manger wasn't listening, and he felt a million miles away somewhere deep in his thoughts. A blank, expressionless look set across his face, and his hazel eyes were staring at nothing in particular in front of him.

"Magnar!" she said forcefully with a snap of her fingers a few inches from his face to bring his attention back from wherever it had disappeared to. "Are you okay?"

Startled, he quickly moved his head back in reaction to her hand. "Sorry. My mind just wondered off for a minute."

"What were you thinking about?" she asked.

"The man in the book…the Elder it kept referring to," he began, but then stopped as he drifted quietly back into his thoughts.

"Do you mean Sir Beaksmith?"

"Yes. I can't stop going over the drawings of him in my mind," he replied, but then paused again to think something over––wrestling in his mind with some notion he was desperately trying to make sense of.

"Magnar, what is it? What are you thinking?"

"Amora, this is going to sound strange… impossible even, but if what we just read in that book is true—"

"Yes, go on," she insisted. "After what we just read, nothing seems impossible anymore. What is it that you want to say?"

Magnar took in a deep gulp of the cold bookstore air and then quickly blurted out his far-fetched idea. "I think Sir Beaksmith is the owner of this bookstore, Mr. Galdipp!"

"What!" she exclaimed. "How could it be him? The things in that book happened forever ago. Everyone would be dead by now," she stated, trying to make sense of what he was suggesting.

"I know it doesn't make sense, but the man in those drawings looks very similar to Mr. Galdipp—the same large, round, yellow eyes, short stature and round middle, and pointy nose. The difference is only the grey feathers Mr. Galdipp has, but that's from his old age."

Calmly, she placed a hand on his shoulder, "Sir Beaksmith would have to be at least a couple hundred years old to be who you're thinking of. How could he have lived for that long?"

"Yeah, you're right. I know that's impossible," he said, moving his hands up to his head to rub his fingers against his temples in a circular motion to relieve the headache setting in. "Unless—"

"Unless what?" Amora asked, half-heartedly interested in the answer.

"Maybe he performed some sort of spell or ritual that gave him a longer life."

"Magnar, I think you're grasping at straws, but either way, we need to get going," she dismissively replied.

Hesitantly, he looked over at her to see the impatient look on her face just as she glanced up at the wall clock. It was now a few minutes past one in the morning. Thick frost had taken hold of the windows lining the bookstore and created whimsical patterns made of ice crystals, and the temperature inside the store had transitioned from cold to freezing, numbing the toes inside their shoes.

"I'll put the book back on the shelf. Then, I'll walk you home if you want. I can wait for you outside while you get ready for the party, and then we'll walk to it together. You shouldn't be alone on the streets this late at night," he suggested.

In agreement, she nodded her head and turned to look at the flickering flame inside the lantern sitting on the table next to the book. "I doubt there's anyone passing by the store at this late hour… I'll meet you outside the front door at the steps. Remember to blow out the wick after you've put away the book," she instructed before walking away towards the front of the store.

The floor creaked underneath Magnar's weight as he walked over to the table and carefully picked up the old tattered book in one hand and the lantern in the other and headed over to the shelves where the book had been displaced. Gently, he slid the book back into its spot on the dusty shelf, then walked over to the table the lantern had been removed from. He held the lantern up to his face and stared at the flame as he took a moment to contemplate all that he had learned that night. Finally, with a quick breath, he blew out the flame and replaced the lantern to its position on the table, grabbed his black coat off a nearby hook, and hurried out the bookstore to meet up with Amora, whom was shivering in the cold, despite her coat being buttoned up to its neckline.

"I put everything back exactly how we found them. No one will know what we were up to," he said, locking the door and joining her at the bottom of the steps.

Amora dug her frozen, reddening hands deep into her coat pockets to warm them as she replied, "Thanks."

The night air outside felt colder than it had inside the bookstore, and their breath fogged with each inhalation as they walked side-by-side down the cobblestone streets—turning left, right, this and that way, towards her home... going in the same direction of the party. A thick blanket of grey clouds, which smelled of impending rain, filled the sky and it was already beginning to mist. The trees along the streets were gently swaying back and forth as the wind picked up, and dry crinkled leaves rustled on the ground as the breezes scattered them in the grass and along the roads.

The rain soon began to change from mist into a heavy drizzle, and the wind whipped the cold droplets into Amora's face, stinging her cheeks and eyes. Without complaining, she held her head down while she walked and did her best to shield her face with her hands. Out of her coat pockets, they quickly grew redder and began itching due to the frigid weather; so, her pace quickened to reach home and get inside out of the cold for a while before heading to the party.

Soon, the nearer they came to her home, the more a familiar smoky scent penetrated the cold night air. "Do you smell that?" Amora asked after taking in a big whiff of it.

Magnar took in a breath, deep into his nostrils, and closed his eyes at the wonderful smell. "Ahh, that's firewood burning. We must be near the party and they've lit the bonfire!"

"Look in between those houses over there." Amora pointed to a space between two moderate-sized homes, and hues of bright oranges and reds flickered through the leaves of the bushes from something happening in the distance. "Can you see what I'm pointing to?"

Magnar leaned closer to her and bent down to get a better view to see what her eyes were looking at. "Wow! Is that the bonfire?"

"Yep, sure is!" she exclaimed. "We're almost to my house. It's down this street. When we get there, you can come inside and warm up while I get changed for the party. We can head back up the road, this way, but we'll cut between those two houses over there as a shortcut to reach the town social quicker."

"Sounds like a plan!" but suddenly something caught Magnar's attention moving around high in the trees behind one of the houses. "Wait a second. Did you hear that?" he asked, leaning over and whispering into her ear.

"What? I didn't hear anything," she whispered back, glancing around to see if anything was nearby.

Magnar paused and listened. "There! There it is again! Sounds like tree branches cracking!" With curiosity and a bit of caution, he looked up at the trees and searched in the direction the sounds had come from, but could not see what was causing the noises.

Silently, they both stood still and watched the trees. Increasingly, a sickening nauseous feeling began to sink into the pit of Amora's stomach, and she knew something about this was not right. It felt odd, like something in the trees did not belong and it was… watching them. Even more than that, she felt like whatever it was… it was actually there to watch *her*.

CHAPTER EIGHT
A Spy in Bernard

S uddenly, there were sounds of branches cracking as a large figure jumped across several branches near the top of the trees, knocking a large tree limb down to the ground! Splintered wood scattered as the huge branch hit the ground with a *thud* and broke into large chunks.

"Up there! I see it! It's right there!" Magnar exclaimed, pointing at the top of the trees! "It looks like some sort of bird," he said, staring at the perched creature. "Wow! Amora, I remember seeing it near the bookstore, too! It was sitting on the roof of the building directly across from the bookstore. I only glanced at it then, and didn't think too much about it, but I'm sure it was the same bird."

Amora tilted her neck to look higher up into the cluster of trees to see a heavy, black, feathered fowl sitting on top of a large branch—partially hidden by leaves. Motionlessly, the bird stared down; the intensity of its pupil-less white eyes glared down at both of them—barely blinking its thin eyelids as it tracked their movements. Amora realized the feeling inside the pit of her stomach had been confirmed! Something about this was definitely wrong!

As to not draw attention to her movements, she reached a hand out, painstakingly slow, toward Magnar and tightly took hold of his hand.

"Ouch! What are you doing?" he reacted at the squeeze of her hand, giving her an annoyed look.

"Listen. Don't make any fast moves, but I think that's a *Vulturk Death Gazer*."

"A what?" he whispered, looking back up into the trees. "A Vulturk Death Gazer... I've never heard of that. What is it?" he quietly asked, trying not to draw more attention towards them from the creature.

"It's some sort of grisly looking vulture-like bird. They're extremely ugly and have vicious tempers to match. At least, that's what I read about them, and it looks exactly like the drawings I saw in a book."

"What book?" he asked, keeping his eyes fixated on the vulturk watching them.

"It was a fairly new book with a stiff spine, crisp pages, and a green cover. It was lying on top of a stack of books on one of the small tables at the bookstore. There was nothing too special about it, and I don't remember what the name of it was, but I found it one night while I was waiting for you to get off work. I only had time to read several pages, but I thumbed through most of the pictures. Mostly, they were of grisly looking vulturks that had black feathers covering their wings and bodies, and they had long, thin, greyish necks. Thin skin covered their featherless faces, and some had black beaks with a tint of light brown along the curvature, while others had dark brown beaks with a yellowish tint. Also, I remember each one had three long toes on their feet with sharp claws on the end. Probably to help them tear into rotting flesh, since they're known for eating the dead."

"Yep. That sounds like a similar description to our visitor up there. Do you remember anything else about them?" he asked.

Amora took in a deep breath of the cold night air, which fogged as she blew it out, and gathered into her hands the hair which had fallen loose from her ponytail during their walk. She loosened the remaining portion, to fall with the rest of it, and tossed all of her hair over her shoulders behind her, then resumed explaining the information she had found in the book.

She explained that a page in the book told about people who believed the vulturks acted as spies that were sent from an unknown region to gather intelligence for sinister purposes. However, no one had been able to track the birds long enough to

95

prove that theory, or to find out who could be using them in such a manipulative way. Next, she explained how the pupil-less white eyes of the birds made others question if they were hollow inside––meaning they were soulless creatures that did not care about right or wrong, but rather, were driven by their whims and were highly aggressive (which also meant avoiding quick or jerky movements near them).

"So basically, we should hurry up and get out of here, but walk away, slowly. That's what I'm hearing," Magnar said, beginning to slowly step away, backwards, in the direction toward her house.

"Yep! That's right," she replied. Slowly, Amora turned around with Magnar, and carefully they took slow steady steps away from the glaring vulturk.

At first, Amora felt her body tense up as she tried to concentrate on the speed of her paces, but the farther away she got from the vulturk, the more she felt her body begin to relax. Within minutes, they both quickened their paces back to normal and felt relief flood through them as her house came into view.

"SCREECH!"

"Screech, Screech, Screech!" the vulturk called out as it stretched its long wings and swooped down from the tree.

"Watch out!" Magnar shouted. Quickly, he grabbed Amora and pushed his body weight against hers to knock them both onto the ground a second before the bird glided over where they had stood!

"Screeeeeeech!" the vicious vulturk yelled as it passed over them and flew off into the distance.

"We need to get out of here and warn the others about this thing. No telling how long it's been in town, or why it's here," Magnar said as he helped her up and dusted leaves off the back of her coat.

"Right," she nodded. "Let's cut through that shortcut to get there as fast as we can! No walking… we're running all the way! Agreed?"

"Let's go," he agreed. With a hurried pace, he followed her through the shortcut toward the direction of the rising bon fire smoke. The chilly air stung his lungs as he huffed deep breaths in-and-out through his open mouth; with each pound of his feet against the ground, he kept up with her speed as she sprinted across one street and down the next! Within seconds, the back of his dry mouth began feeling prickly and rough. Thoughts of drinking warm apple cider or hot cocoa with marshmallows began filling his mind.

Of course, he thought to himself that he would not indulge, until after they had warned everyone about the weird bird hanging around town, but then thoughts of warm, chewy, chocolate-chip-nut cookies began pushing aside his top priority. Forcibly, he tried to push away the savory images of herb biscuits with butter, pot roasts and leftover boiled potatoes with carrots scattered along the bottoms of the platters—swimming in pools of gravy—or the almost empty bowls containing all sorts of different types of breads, which some old lady had kindly covered with a cloth napkin to prevent from becoming too hard in the night air, and his mouth watered at the delicious thoughts.

As he ran, his stomach growled loudly at the thought of snatching up one of those crusty pieces and dipping it in leftover gravy! No matter how hard he tried to focus on the creepy bird, the growling in his stomach returned his hungry thoughts to foods which might not have been completely finished off at the snack tables!

"We're here!" Amora yelled to him, barely glancing over her shoulder as she ran through a large open archway towards the gathered group of partygoers.

Lively upbeat music was playing by a popular band on a raised makeshift stage, while couples were energetically dancing in front of them. Men were twirling around ladies, and their beautiful dresses and skirts were flouncing up at the turns. Several gentlemen stood along the sides of the dance floor preferring to talk with each other, and a mixture of nicely dressed individuals were sitting at picnic tables sharing stories, jokes, and gossip with neighbors and friends. Everywhere, cheerful sounds and laughter filled the air as people sipped on wine, ate baked goods—from Ms. Petrol's bakery, which she had kindly donated to the event—and stood in the lines forming in front of the oak ale-kegs in order to refill their mugs at the tap.

A couple young children were laying in their mother's laps, fast asleep, next to plates of half eaten strawberry cake—undisturbed by the music, nor the voices of their mother's, who were enthralled in the conversations taking place. In the midst of the celebratory chaos, Amora noticed there was a gap in the line of kegs, in which one must have gone missing. Presumably, there were probably a few mischievous teenagers, lurking about somewhere, that had sneakily stolen the keg to drink some ale with friends behind a neighbor's house in order to be undetected by their partying parents.

"Amora! Glad you could make it," said an approaching plump man. It was Mr. Higgins! Amora was surprise at how nicely he was dressed in his best pair of black slacks and a clean crisp white shirt! Usually, she only saw him wearing clothes with dirt and grass stains at the horse stables, which included a bit of a pungent smell; she was not used to him looking so... clean!

Cheerfully, he strolled up to her and was holding a fat slice of strawberry cake on a paper napkin in one hand and a pint of frosty ale in the other. At first glance, Amora guessed it was probably his third or fourth of each.

"I was beginning to think you wouldn't make it, but why haven't you changed your clothes for the party?" Before she could answer, he looked around and continued, "Hmm, well... never mind that now. It's almost over and a few people have already gone home, but here, I brought you a slice of strawberry cake. It was as popular tonight as it was during the last party," he jokingly laughed and gestured at a smear of the icing on his shirt. "Here you go," he said, kindly handing the slice of frosted cake with thick pink icing into her hands.

"Thank you, but I really don't have time right now. I need to––"

"Nonsense!" he interrupted, dusting crumbs off his hands. "There's nothing you need to do, except enjoy yourself."

"But––" she insisted.

"No buts! Now, mind your manners and introduce me to your friend here." Mr. Higgins quickly turned his attention to the young gentleman standing next her, who was giving the snack tables a good look. "Hungry?" he asked, giving him a bit of a sideways glance with a raised brow.

"Mr. Higgins, this is my friend Magnar," she began to explain, but then again was interrupted by the eager man, who she could tell was sizing them up as a potential couple in his plotting mind.

"Yes! This is the young man you told me about. I know very well who are," he eagerly replied. "You work at the local bookstore. Right?"

"What?" Magnar's attention was removed from wondering what was left to eat on the snack tables over to the conversation he abruptly now found himself in. "Oh, yes. The bookstore. Yes, that's where I work." he answered briefly, still not paying much attention to the conversation.

"Well, nice of you to come. I see you eyeing those tables over there. Let's get you a plate of food. I think there may be some roast left in one of the pots, and we've barely touched any of the fruit pies," he said with a friendly slap on his back. "Come on. Any friend of Amora's is a friend of mine, and here, you can have my pint of ale. I just poured a fresh mug. Plus, Ms. Petrol thinks I've had enough anyway," he laughed and pointed towards a tall woman wearing a short, red, flouncy dress who was standing near the bonfire and giving him a stern look of warning.

Like a child reprimanded by a parent, Mr. Higgins flashed her an annoyed glance, then, with a sulk, he handed over his pint of ale to Magnar.

"Can you believe she thinks I drink too much?" he asked rhetorically, stumbling as the words left his mouth. Quickly, both Magnar and Amora reached out and caught him by an arm, causing half the ale in the mug to spill on the ground.

"Sorry about that. We can top you off at the kegs. Now let me go! I don't want anyone making a fuss over me." Being a prideful man, Mr. Higgins pulled his arms away and straightened his legs up under himself. He could not bare to supply Ms. Petrol with just-cause to imply she was right, nor that it was okay to prevent him from drinking as he pleased.

"Let's get you some food, and I'll grab a cup of warm apple cider. That should make Ms. Petrol happy. Oh, and Amora, the band will be taking a short break in a few minutes, but then another song meant for dancing will be gearing up, and these legs have life left in them yet! You'll either dance with me, or with this young man." Mr. Higgins flashed her a sly grin, and she knew very well what it meant and what he was trying to do. "You know, I'll come looking for you if I don't see you and him already on the dance floor, but first, if you want to change out of those work clothes, then head over to Ms. Petrol's house. It's right over there... down that street," he said, pointing towards a row of absurdly tall, but thin houses, grouped in a perfect line on Candlestick Street. "Her house is the seventh on the left, and I'm sure she'd be fine with lending you any dress in her closet."

Just as Mr. Higgins got the last word out of his mouth, Ms. Petrol walked up, and Amora found it hard to believe that a woman as beautiful as her... was dating a man like Mr. Higgins. She thought he was nice-and-all, but still, why? As she approached, her curly ringlets of chestnut hair bounced against her shoulders and rested on the soft fabric of her burgundy knitted shall wrapped around her. Her skin was the color of fresh snow and appeared as if it had never known a ray from the sun that seldom shined through the blanket of grey clouds—which Amora had become accustomed to.

Coming up to stand next to Amora, she stood slightly taller in her heels, and Amora looked admiringly at the makeup on her face. It was not too overdone. The hues Ms. Petrol had chosen were soft natural beiges with a hint of rosy pink against her cheeks and a touch of strawberry on her lips. Amora had not spent much time learning the ways of applying makeup, but she did notice how the colors complimented her green eyes.

"You must be Amora! Mr. Higgins has told me so much about you. All nice things of course! He speaks very highly of you. Like you're the daughter he never had," she happily complimented her with a polite lady-like shake of her hand.

"Hello," Amora shyly greeted, wondering if she had noticed her observing her makeup.

"Yes! This is the one I have a hard time tearing away from those horses every night, and this guy right here is her gentleman friend, Magnar. He works at that bookstore. You know, the one Mr. Galdipp owns not too far from the stables," Mr. Higgins cut in, and gave Magnar an awkward pat on the back, which implied they knew each other better than they actually did.

"Nice to meet you." Magnar greeted her with a brief wave of his hand.

"Yes, the pleasure is all mine dear," Ms. Petrol politely stated, and then turned her attention to the unkempt Amora standing next to her. Quickly, Ms. Petrol gave her a full-body glance over, and suddenly her expression turned sour. One would have thought she had just eaten a bitter stink bug after looking at the frumpy clothes and coat Amora was wearing, along with the messy hair and her lack of face coloring.

"Amora. Dear, you're not dressed for the party. Why don't you and your friend head over to my house and take a look through my closet. You're welcome to choose anything you'd like," she nicely offered, but her eyes implied that, *no*, would not be taken for an answer.

"That's what I told her," Mr. Higgins piped-in. "See! She's as sweet as she is pretty!"

Immediately, Ms. Petrol's cheeks turned rosier than the hue of her blush as Mr. Higgins wrapped his arms around her curvy waist and drew her in close for a kiss!

"Mr. Higgins! Stop it!" she giggled with a huge smile betraying her laughter with the truth—that she was highly enjoying his public display of affection! "Not in front of them."

Gently, she pushed his hands away and noticed the kiss had left his mouth with a tint of her strawberry lip color. Flirtatiously, she wiped it away with one of her fingers and shot him a playful wink that they would continue that later.

"Sorry about that," she apologized. Her cheeks still pink with embarrassment at her momentary loss of composure. "Anyway dear, I think most of my clothes should fit you. A couple things might be a little big on your frame, but others will do just fine. A nice belt around the waist could also help if you need it. Just choose whatever you'd like, but we really should be getting back to the party. By the look of things, the band will be starting their next song set soon," she motioned at the singer standing next to one of the tables finishing off his ale, and the instrumentalists collecting their empty plates and heading towards the trash bins to discard them.

"I see. Well, it was good meeting you… and I see why Mr. Higgins is so taken with you," Amora replied.

"Thank you dear. Have a good night," and with a polite smile and nod of her head, Ms. Petrol took hold of Mr. Higgins held out hand, and headed off with him towards the crackling bon fire.

"I guess we better get going, too, so you can change at Ms. Petrol's place, or you'll never hear the end of it from that Mr. Higgins," Magnar said, looking around at the remaining partiers scattered about, who were enjoying themselves with drinks, plates of food, and laughing at each other's jokes and stories being told in their friendly conversations. Carefully, he looked up at the trees surrounding the area of the town social. No bird. Relieved, he took in a big breath of the cold air into his lungs and let it out with a long sigh of relief. "I don't see that D*eath Gazer* anywhere. Guess we must have scared it off back there."

Amora's eyes shot up at the trees, too, in search for any signs of the vulturk. Nothing. "Good. Let's just get out of here. I'll get changed, so Mr. Higgins won't have anything to tease me about later, and we'll head back over here as fast as we can. Then, I'll make sure to spread the word about the bird we saw. If we can just tell a couple people tonight at this party, then enough gossip should spread around town by late tomorrow to warn just about everyone."

"Right. Let's go," Magnar agreed as he put down the half empty mug of ale Mr. Higgins had given him onto a nearby snack table and headed out with Amora.

CHAPTER NINE
Death Gazers

*A*s the two walked down the dimly lit street away from the party, the music resumed as the band members rejoined on stage, and it began sounding farther away. The scent of wood burning from the tall bonfire was still pleasantly lingering and drifting through the night air as Amora and Magnar approached Candlestick Street.

"Her house should be right over there," Magnar said, pointing to a tall, but relatively narrow house that was the seventh on the left, and tightly squeezed in between the sixth and eighth.

"Shh," Amora whispered. Her eyes had become fixated on one of the roofs.

"Ouch!" Magnar complained, grimacing from the pain shooting up through his forearm as she gripped a hand onto him and dug in her fingernails to gain his attention and halt his footsteps with hers!

"Why'd you do that! You know… that really hurt," he griped, unclenching her hand from his arm and rubbing the offended area. "What are you staring at anyway?"

"Look… at… the… roofs," she whispered through clenched teeth, not blinking, nor taking her eyes off the roof closest to them. Her chest was heavy with fear, and she felt as if she had to force her lungs to accept each inhalation of forced breath inside.

"What… the roofs," Magnar replied. "Why would I care about the roofs?" but just as the words left his lips and his eyes looked up, fear gripped him, too!

"CAW! CAW!"

"CAW! CAW! CAW!"

"CAW! CAW! CAW! CAW!"

The roofs of every house on both sides of Candlestick Street were lined with huge, black, grisly Vulturk Death Gazers! Each vulturk perfectly sat next to the other (in a line of twelve or thirteen) at the highest points on each house. Coldly, every set of empty white eyes glared down at the two of them as they stood motionlessly on the street.

"SCREECH! SCREECH! SCREECH! SCREECH!" one of the hideous vulturks sounded and hissed at them.

"Look at the one hissing at us. I think that's the same vulturk from earlier," Amora whispered, trying to move her lips as little as possible to prevent provoking the birds into a frenzied rage. "It's looking right at us... like it remembers us."

"Yeah, and it brought friends, and they don't look happy to see us either," Magnar whispered. His gut began filling up with acid, produced by his fear of impending doom, which was quickly building up inside himself. Slowly, the bitter acid began rising from his stomach into his throat and it burned as it slid upwards. Instantly, the corners of his mouth turned into a frown at the sour taste coating his tongue, and uncontrollably, he began choking and coughing out the stuff!

"CAW! CAW! CAW! CAW! SCREECH! SCREECH! SCREECH! CAW! SCREECH! CAW! SCREECH!" hundreds of vulturk voices sounded together in alarm! Immediately, they began launching themselves off the rooftops into the sky to join together in a circular formation, creating a huge black swarm over Candlestick Street!

"Run!" Amora shouted! "Get to Ms. Petrol's! Now!"

Beneath the frenzied black swarm, both of them took off running towards Ms. Petrol's house! Their feet were pounding fast and hard against the street as they ducked and dodged swooping vulturks—one after another, they dove down from the swarm to attack them!

"Faster! Run!" she screamed to Magnar, who was behind her and struggling to keep up with her pace as hordes of vulturks dove down and tried clawing at him before flying back up to rejoin the swarm! Successfully, he dodged each attack—ducking, dodging, running to the right, then swiftly changing direction to the left—until unexpectedly, the largest vulturk dove down and took hold of him from behind!

The Vulturk Death Gazer was three times the size of the others and had gripped the back of Magnar's coat with its large talons!

"SCREECH! SCREECH! SCREECH!" the bird squawked and hissed.

"Get off me!" Magnar yelled as he fell to the ground on his stomach—his face hitting hard against the street. "Get off me you blasted bird!" he yelled again, struggling to free himself from his coat! The grisly vulturk clawed viciously at the fabric, shredding it apart with its nails and beak!

Suddenly, an intense rush of pain filled Magnar! With a long powerful slash of its beak, the vulturk had torn a long section of fabric off his coat and flesh had become entwined with it! Instantly, blood began seeping out of the exposed wound. "Amora! Help me!" he screamed to her in blood-curdling shouts! "Amora!"

At the sound of her friend's screams, Amora instantly turned around and saw him pinned to the ground on his stomach beneath the vulturk they had seen earlier high in a tree, and she quickly realized it must be the leader of the others! "Magnar!" she yelled.

"Hold on! I'm coming!" Horrified at the sight of the huge vulturk on his back, she no longer cared for her own safety, and her fear began dissipating away. Straightaway, Amora took off running towards him as six more vulturks suddenly dove down in her direction from the black swarm! However, in that moment, her fear had completely gone and she felt something strange building up inside herself—in her core.

Immediately, she stopped running and faced the swooping vulturks head-on. Boldly, she stared at them as they approached... meeting the empty, cold look in their white eyes with a coldness of her own.

"CAW! CAW! CAW! CAW!" they squawked as they neared.

"Amora! Watch out!" Magna shouted, still struggling to fight off the bird perched on his back and hissing wildly!

"Hang on Magnar!" she yelled.

I've got this, she told herself as all six of the vulturks approached her. Their long black wings were stretched wide as they soared closer and closer; each of them lifted up their claws, preparing their assault on her flesh! Just then, a mere second before they could take hold of her, Amora flung out both of her hands—one palm facing towards Magnar and the other towards the six vulturks!

"*Ignis!*" she shouted. Instantly, searing hot flames leaped out of her hands in streams at the vulturks!

111

"CAW! CAW! CAW! CAW!" the birds screamed in agony as their black feathers ignited into brilliant flames! Straightaway, the six vulturks crashed to the ground and writhed in misery, and Magnar pushed the ablaze vulturk off his back onto the street!

"SCREECH! SCREECH! SCREECH! SCREECH!" the vulturk hollered as it convulsed next to him, slapping its wings against the street in reaction to the extraordinary hurt bursting through every part of itself as the flames consumed it!

"Come on Magnar!" Amora yelled, motioning with both hands for him to get off the ground and join her in running to Ms. Petrol's house. "Run! Before the others come!" she warned, pointing up towards the hundreds of birds still circling overhead in the black swarm. Their white eyes were peering down at them as they circled above (watching the vulturks burn in the smoking fires on the street below and waiting for a cue from their leader to continue their assaults).

"SCREECH!" their leader bellowed its last command with its dying breath from the ground; then, it stirred no more! The flames consuming the creature ceased as it died, but the smoke lingering from its charred flesh continued rising up into the sky and mixed with the winds created by the wings in the black swarm. Collectively, the anger of all the vulturks seemed to intensify— palpable in their glaring white eyes—as they inhaled the smoking remnants of their leader!

"Magnar! Run! They're coming! RUN!" Amora shouted as loud as her voice could strain out the words! Her light brown eyes appeared larger at the sight of the entire swarm shifting their direction in unison! Hundreds of grisly vulturks stretched their wings wide and began diving towards them—the sounds of their wings and squawking became a deafening noise!

Fighting back the rush of pain in his back, Magnar pushed himself off the ground and took off running with her! His heart was beating fast in his chest as he forced himself not to give into the throbbing pain coursing through his back.

Don't pass out, he thought to himself. *Her house is right there. It's right there! We'll make it... just a little bit more... just a little bit further,* he repeated over and over in his mind, until finally opening the unlocked door to Ms. Petrol's home... slamming it shut just as one of the vulturks slammed its body against the door's frame on the other side!

CHAPTER TEN
Rest for the Weary

*B*reathing heavily in and out—trying to catch her breath—Amora huffed, "We made it! I'll turn on the lights," and with a flick of her hand accompanied by the word, "*Lumen*," the living room lights flickered on. Quickly spotting the sofa, she walked over to it and collapsed her exhausted body onto the soft cushions.

"Thanks," he replied, plopping onto a comfortable chair next to her. "Thanks for saving my butt back there. That bird would have killed me if you hadn't ended it first," he said, letting out a huge sigh of relief and wincing in pain at the same time as he accidentally rubbed his back too much up against the chair. "How'd you do that anyway? I don't know any magic like that."

"I don't know," she sighed, leaning her head back on an armrest of the plush sofa. "I can't explain it… it just came to me."

"Well, thanks." Magnar leaned his head back, too, and closed his eyes.

For several minutes, the two of them sat silently and listened to the angry vulturks swarming outside Ms. Petrol's house—their angry cawing and wings beating against its exterior. Amora was exhausted from the long day and her muscles were fatigued from the running. Empathetically, she looked over at her friend, who was sitting with his eyes closed, almost falling asleep in between winces of pain stabbing him with every breath as his chest heaved and moved the muscles in his back.

Despite her tiredness, Amora forced herself not to fall asleep. She had to clean and dress his wounds before a nasty infection took hold, and it was likely that Ms. Petrol had something at the house that would be useful. "Magnar, you still awake over there?"

"Ugh," he grumbled, barely opening his eyes.

"I'm going to take a look around. We need to clean up your back before infection sets in," she told him.

"Ok," was all he mustered, still leaning his head on the chair.

"Maybe there's a medical kit or something in the bathroom. I'll be right back." Amora forced her aching body off the sofa and headed into the bathroom. "*Lumen*," she said, turning on the bathroom lights. She opened up a small linen closet next to the shower and took out a couple clean towels, and found a box filled with: a glass bottle of antiseptic liquid; a tube of antibiotic cream;

115

some white dressing bandages; adhesive tape; and a pair of scissors.

This should do, she thought to herself. *I just need a couple more things.* She took the box to the living room and placed it on the table by the sofa, then headed into the kitchen.

"*Lumen*," she repeated to turn on the kitchen lights. Quietly, she searched for a clean, small, kitchen towel and then filled the washbasin up with water. "*Glacio*," she said, waving a hand over the water in the basin. Instantly, the water became frozen!

I just need something to break this up with, she thought. Amora looked around for something hard and sharp. She opened the cupboard drawers and cabinets, but found only spoons, forks, plates, cups, and cooking pots, but nothing to break apart the ice. *Wait. There!* She spotted a small kitchen knife lying next to a basket of apples on the counter. *That'll work*, she thought. Immediately, she picked up the knife and began banging away at the block of ice, jarring Magnar awake!

"What are you doing in there?" he asked (in a rather complaining tone).

"Sorry. Just one more minute." Quickly, she finished breaking apart the ice and placed chunks of it into the kitchen towel and wrapped them up. "Okay, I think I have everything we need to clean your back and dress the wounds, but it might hurt a little, though."

116

"Fine. Do whatever you have to," he consented.

"First, I need you to lay down on the floor," she instructed.

"Okay." He stood up from the chair and laid down on the floor—flat on his stomach.

Amora placed the towel filled with ice down next to him, then grabbed one of the towels—she had placed along with the supplies—off the table and balled it up into a makeshift pillow. Gently, she placed it underneath his head. "Is that better?" she asked.

"Yeah. Thanks," he replied, shifting it slightly to make himself more comfortable. "I'm probably gonna regret asking this, but how bad is it?" he asked, referencing the slash wounds the vulturk had made across his back.

Amora grabbed the box and the other towel off the table and sat down next to him on the floor. Her stomach soured at the sight of the bloody mess mixed with ripped fabric, but there was no time to waste! She had to get it cleaned and bandaged soon or infection would set in… despite knowing that peeling his coat and shirt off his torn skin was probably going to hurt like crazy! "Let's just say that you'll live, but it's got to get cleaned up first," she answered.

"Oh, it's bad. I can hear it in your voice. I *know* it's bad!" he shuddered. "I'm going to die, aren't I? Come on. Tell me. I can take the truth of it!" he insisted, cringing at the anticipation of the pain to come.

117

"No. You're not going to die," she reassured him. "Really! You'll be fine. We've just got to get this taken care of, but yes, it might hurt a little," she said, watching him grip the towel beneath his head with both hands and stuff his face into it. She cringed at knowing that in order to help him… first, she had to cause him more pain. "I'm going to start now." She took in a deep breath to calm her nerves and swallowed the lump of dread forming in her throat. "First, I'm going to remove your coat and then your shirt. Straighten your arms for me," she instructed him.

Reluctant to feel the pain he knew was coming, Magnar did as he was instructed.

As gently as she could, Amora slowly removed the shredded coat off his back as silent tears began streaming down his face. Next, she helped him roll onto his side and unbuttoned his shirt. After returning him back onto his stomach, she then carefully peeled the bloodied fabric off his back, but this time he could no longer contain the pain inside. Screams leapt out of his throat!

"Stop! Stop! Please! It hurts!" he yelled, but she knew it had to be done. So, with one huge yank, she pulled the cloth free form the tangled mess of torn skin!

"OUCH!" he screamed, arching his back with the pain!

"You did it! It's over! That was the worst of it," she comforted him, sitting the bloody shirt onto the floor next to the coat. Her own tears were now streaming down her cheeks at seeing him collapse onto the floor in pain. "I'm sorry, but that was the only way to get the shirt off of you. I had to pull it."

"Just finish it," he replied, returning his sobbing face to his makeshift pillow.

Without another word, she reached into the box and took out a medium sized glass bottle filled with antiseptic liquid and began drizzling it all over his wounds. Magnar arched his torso at the sting of it and buried his mouth into the towel-pillow to better muffle his groans. Next, she poured a bit of it onto a section of the towel in her hands and lightly dabbed it around the torn skin. Gently, she wiped all the smeared blood off his back until his skin was clean. Then, she took out the tube of antibiotic cream from the box and began rubbing it along the sides of his larger wounds and over all the small scratches.

For Magnar, the cream felt soothing due to the numbing agent in it, which alleviated the stinging.

After that, she dressed them in the white bandages, which she cut to fit the size of every wound, and then properly secured them in place with the adhesive bandaging tape. Finally, she took the ice wrapped up in the kitchen towel and placed it on top of the white bandage secured over his largest wound, so that the coolness of the ice would help minimize any potential swelling. Quietly, she sat next to him for several minutes, holding the ice in place on his back and listening to the sounds of the vulturks outside the house grow fainter. Soon, she could barely hear the black swarm at all.

"We should get moving. Mr. Higgins will probably be walking Ms. Petrol home soon, and I need to get this mess cleaned up before they get here," she said, removing the damp kitchen towel off his back, which had become wet from the melting ice. Her stiff muscles ached as she got herself up off the floor and extended out a hand to help him do the same.

Not in the mood to say much of anything, he took hold of her hand and got up—wincing again in pain.

"There's a coat hanging on the rack by the door. It looks like a man's coat, so it's probably Mr. Higgins'. I don't think he'd mind letting you use it… considering everything that's happened tonight," she said, looking at him and waiting for some sort of response, but none came. Quietly, she walked over to the coat rack and removed the black coat off the hook. "Here, let me help you put it on."

With no words, Magnar stood and allowed her to help him slip his arms into the black coat. The arms were a bit oversized and the coat fit loosely over his frame, but he was relieved that at least it wouldn't fit snug over his bandages, which meant less pain.

After helping him put on the coat, Amora cleaned up the mess in the living room. She replaced all the items where they belonged back into the box and dumped the ice from the towel into the kitchen basin. She put the box away back into the small linen closet where she had found it and placed the used towels into a pile on the bathroom floor, but just as she was about to turn off the bathroom light... a distant sound caught her attention!

CHAPTER ELEVEN
No Safe Place

*A*mora stood very still and listened. There it was again! *What is that?* she thought. *It sounds like... somebody is blowing a horn.* Frozen in place, she stood and waited to see if the sound would happen again. Not a single audible noise anywhere. The house was perfectly silent, and she could tell that Magnar was in the living room trying to hear it, too.

The seconds felt drawn out. Time was stretching itself and an uneasy feeling was beginning to alarm every sense in her body. Things felt... strange. Suddenly, there it was again! A deep sound that seemed far away in the distance, but it was growing louder each time she heard it.

"Magnar, did you hear that?" she asked, leaving the bathroom and whispering, *"Nullus Lumen,"* to both the bathroom and living room lights to turn them off.

"Yes. I heard it, too," he whispered.

"What do you think it is?" she asked, fumbling around in the dark and knocking into the furniture, until she found Magnar standing next to the front door and joined him.

Again, the deep noise played through the air. This time, joined by beats with a deep base sound. "Boom, Boom, Boom, Boom…" the beats joined in.

"It sounds like someone's blowing a large horn, but those beats… they sound like drums," Amora whispered.

The drums were beating in rhythm and all together the sounds grew louder and louder. "Whatever it is, it sounds like it's getting closer. Go look out the window," Magnar instructed her. "Maybe you can see who's doing it."

"Okay. I'll try," Amora replied, and walked over to one of the living room windows.

Carefully, as to not draw attention to the house, she slowly slid back the curtains and peeked outside through the windowpane. The street was dimly lit by a lantern hanging on a pole outside, and the swarm of vulturks had gone. Absolutely nothing was stirring outside, which caused her sense of unease to intensify. Things did not feel right. Surely, there should be lights on in at least one of the other houses from people returning home late from the party, but there was nothing. Every light was off.

"See anything?" he asked.

"No. Nothing, but isn't that weird? Shouldn't there be lights on somewhere from people getting home late from the party?"

"Maybe they're all doing what we're doing. They could have heard the same noises we did, and turned off their lights, too," Magnar reasoned.

"Wait. I see something. There's someone across the street looking through a window on her top floor." Amora watched the woman—hiding behind what was likely bedroom curtains—and waved a hand at her to get her attention. Quickly, the woman shook her head, *stop it*, and yanked her curtains closed!

"That was weird," Amora whispered to herself.

"What did you say? I couldn't hear you," Magnar asked.

"Oh, sorry. I was talking to myself, but I waved at the woman who was peeking through her curtains and she shook her head, *no*, at me. Then she yanked them shut," Amora explained, confused about the woman's odd behavior. "Magnar, I have a terrible feeling that something is very wrong."

"Yeah. I'm starting to feel it, too. Keep looking and see if you can see anything else," he replied.

Amora drew the curtains closer around her face to conceal herself and continued looking out the window. Her eyes squinted in the darkness, but in the distance, she began to see orange-ish lights popping up near each other. "I see something."

"What is it?" he asked.

124

"It looks like orange-ish and reddish lights glowing and flickering not too far away from where the party was. Wait! There's more of them now. They're popping up everywhere out there," Amora informed him. Carefully, she studied the glows and flickers of the lights, and her mind began calculating the possibilities of what they could be. Suddenly, her eyes opened wider as horror took hold inside her! "Magnar! I know what they are! They're fires! People are setting everything in Bernard on fire! We've got to go! Now!"

"What!" he exclaimed, thinking she couldn't be right! "Fires! That doesn't make any sense," he argued, but the surge of adrenaline in his body forced his mind to the truth—yes, she was right!

Suddenly, screams filled Candlestick street as people came running away from the party towards the houses! Amora's eyes met with an injured woman who was limping up the street and shouting at the top of her lungs, "Goblins! There are goblins in Bernard! Run! They're killing and setting fires! Everyone, get out of here! Now!"

"My gut tells me this attack has something to do with that forbidden book we read and the vulturk that followed us from the bookstore, to here. Maybe those birds *really are* used as spies somehow, but that means whoever was spying on us knows we found out about the Zodiarks. If everything in that book was true, then that means the DARK ONE must have found out that we know the truth. Everyone thinks the DARK ONE has always been the ruler of this world. No one has ever questioned anything. I'm guessing the DARK ONE wants it to stay that way," he paused and continued connecting together the thoughts processing in his mind. "The DARK ONE went to great lengths for the Zodiarks to fade from memory and history. Even what's taught in schools— in history books—are all lies and makes no mention of the Zodiarks, and those lies have fueled the knowledge the DARK ONE wanted... until I found that old book and showed it to you."

For a moment, he thought to himself about how he had stumbled upon the tattered book on the dusty bookshelf in the forbidden section at the store, and how he had been so determined to show it to Amora and read it with her.

"This is all my fault," he whispered. "If I had just obeyed the rules and stayed out of that forbidden area... if I hadn't found that book... if I hadn't shown it to you, then maybe none of this would be happening right now."

Without a word, Amora stood motionlessly by the window and stared outside—watching random people duck into the houses of individuals who were trying to help. Several good intentioned townsfolk were holding their front doors open and waving for people to run inside. It was obvious that each person was thinking that everyone would be safer in their homes, but Amora had a dreadful feeling sinking deeper into the pit of her stomach. A feeling that implied those efforts were in vain. Somehow, she knew the people in those homes were not safe and the goblins were going to find them. Surely, the goblins would not stop until they had searched every crevice in Bernard to find Magnar and herself... if what he said had any truth to it. The houses on Candlestick Street would soon be burning along with the rest of the town!

"Amora. We need to go before the goblins reach this street," he told her, reaching for her hand. He could already feel beneath his feet the beginnings of vibrations from the war drums as the goblins drew closer, and it would only be a few short minutes before their ghastly faces would be in sight.

Barely hearing his words, her eyes became glassy as she watched the horrific scene of people fleeing for their lives outside the window. *Goblins are real. Are they really after Magnar and me? Could they be in Bernard for any other reason? No, probably not. They're here because they're after us... because we read that book... because we know the truth,* she thought to herself. She had only read about goblins in books or heard rumors about them from traveling drunkards who had temporarily set up tents on less traveled streets in Bernard. Those people would beg for scraps in between uttering nonsense of broken phrases about things they had seen during their wayward travels. However, no one ever took them seriously. She had always thought goblins were nothing more than wild myths.

"Goblins… are… real," she muttered.

"Yes! Now, come on! We've got to get out of here!" he reiterated, gripping her hand tightly and leading her to the front door. Slowly, he turned the handle as lightly as he could to minimize the sound and cracked the door open a few inches. Through the small space, he searched for signs of goblin activity, but he could only hear the sounds of the drums growing louder by the second. Candlestick street had become deserted, except for a little girl and her mother ducking into a house across the street and shutting the door behind them.

"I don't think the goblins have reached this street," he whispered, opening the door wider and slipping outside with Amora on his heels.

Immediately, she noticed the orange glow of lights penetrating the black sky in the distance and understood that was where the goblins had first begun their assaults on the town. With electrified nerves surging through her body at the sight of the glow, she took in a deep breath of cold night air and closed the door behind her. The air was smoky and thick with the smells of charred buildings, smoldering timbers reducing to ash, and death. Disgusted by the goblins' atrocities, Amora grimaced at everything the smoke in the air symbolized and at how it burned her lungs at each inhalation.

"Let's hurry," Magnar said, looking around for goblins. "This time, I think I might be the one to know a shortcut. Look," he said pointing. "Let's head up to the top of this street and then cross over to the other side. There's a path in between a couple houses. It's narrow, but we can squeeze through and it'll lead us to the outskirts of town... to an area of thick trees and overgrown bushes. If we can get there undetected, then I can lead us deeper into the woods, until we reach a place where they grow thickest." Hesitantly, he looked into Amora's eyes, which were looking back at him with cautious curiosity.

"Wait. What do you mean... where the trees grow thickest?" she asked, looking rather dismayed about his idea as it took root in her mind. "No! You don't mean... you couldn't possibly mean– –"

"Yes," he interrupted. "Amora, it's the only way we'll be able to get the goblins off our trail. They won't follow us in there."

"But—"

"I know, and I'm scared too, but if we plan on living, then we'll have to go through Kembrull Forest," he said, firmly committed to his plan.

"Fine! If that's what we have to do, then so be it, but what about our parents? We can't just leave them here! To die by the hands of… goblins!" she declared. "You know as well as I do that if the goblins are here in Bernard to kill us for reading that book, then they'll go after them too! What if they think we read the book and told them about the Zodiarks?" she pleaded, her eyes welling up with tears as she spoke. "Magnar, please. Before we leave, let's go back and see if there's anything we can do to help them, and if there isn't, then we'll go immediately to Kembrull Forest, and I won't say another word about it."

Contemplating her compelling suggestion, Magnar looked in Amora's eyes and wiped away the silent tears sliding down her cheeks. His head was spinning with all the different scenarios that could happen if they returned to the center of town in search of their parents, but instead, got themselves captured by the goblins. In every scenario playing in his mind, they were either captured, tortured, or worse… killed and eaten by those blood thirsty things! However, he did not feel too keen on the idea of running away and not helping them either, and he knew she was right to want to return for them. Now was the time to take hold of his fears and summon up the courage to do what needed to be done.

"Okay. We'll go back," he finally answered, whilst swallowing down the lump of dread that had traveled its way up into his throat from his stomach.

"Really!" she exclaimed, throwing her arms around him. "Thank you and don't worry! They won't even see us, and I

promise that if there's nothing we can do, then we'll get out here…
fast!"

"Ouch! Please… no hugs," he replied, wincing in pain from her enthusiastic embrace of gratitude for agreeing to help her save their parents.

"Oops, sorry about that, but you'll see we're doing the right thing! Let's go!" Without waiting another second, she took off running down the street as fast as she could back towards the location of the party… towards the center of town!

CHAPTER TWELVE
The Goblin Camp

"Shh! Get down!" she ordered, abruptly grabbing Magnar on the arm and pulling him into a crouching position next to her behind some overgrown shrubs. "Look, over there," she whispered, across the street in the dim light of a lantern attached to the side of one of the homes was a small shadow against the side of a house. Slowly, the hunched-over form crept from the rear of the home towards the front porch where the lantern was hanging, and Amora desperately wanted to see the creature for herself. In her mind, she willed it closer to the light, *Come on. Come on, just a little bit more.*

"You there! Get over here!" a raspy voice snapped! "Didn't I tell you to search the other street?"

Amora strained her eyes in the dark of night to see the new figure marching towards the shadow.

"Yes, but I thought—" replied the smaller of the two.

Finally, the shadow stepped into the lantern's light and gaveway to a short goblin of about four feet high with rough dark skin and patches of wiry black hair covering his body. The goblin was dressed in dirty pieces of cloth that had been stitched together—which Amora guessed were from discarded ripped clothes the creature had picked out of garbage heaps somewhere—and it did not have any shoes on its grungy feet. As for the rest of him, as it spoke, Amora noticed several teeth were missing from its mouth, and those that it had were badly discolored (various shades of browns and yellows) from stains—probably from eating its meat raw. An unsightly hump had taken root in the goblin's spine—forcing it to walk hunched over—and its black eyes were cast down cowardly as it waited for the other goblin to approach, who was nearly within the light.

"You thought nothing!" a raspy voice hissed at the other, abruptly swinging a hand out and striking the smaller goblin!

Amora gasped in shock at the violent action and shot Magnar a glance of surprise at what they were watching, but he placed a finger to his lips and shushed her. His intense eyes were filled with a warning… not to make any sounds that could alert them to their hiding place in the bushes.

"The General told me to send a scout to Candlestick Street to search for them! This street has already been cleared stupid," scolded a rather ugly looking female goblin of about five feet tall with short blackish-grey hair and a nasty attitude.

Her face was full and round with a double chin, and her yellow eyes were filled with madness as she squinted at the goblin. As she spoke, Magnar and Amora could see that her wide mouth was crammed with rows of sharp misaligned teeth, and again, she raised her plump hand to strike him once more across the face. Her clothes were even filthier than his, but were more intact with less rips and need for stitching. However, being much heavier in size than him, her stomach-rolls of extra girth spilled out from beneath her shirt and over the top of the pants that were fitting a bit too tightly around her waist, but she made no effort to conceal any portion of herself. She was proud of her size and knew that being a larger goblin increased her rank over others.

"Sorry," the small goblin apologized, cowering his face even more with his hands placed at the sides of his face to block any other incoming blows. "I'll go at once!"

"Hah, and risk letting a General find out that a scout under my supervision disobeyed me! Never!" she declared, gripping the goblin by the throat with one hand and squeezing it as she lifted him off the ground. "Do you know what the *Generals* would do if they found out about this? Both our heads would be severed with a dull axe, and they would place our bloody skulls on pikes for display. Then, our headless corpses would be fed to the load-pullers before they chained them up to those carts... the ones carrying the cages full of Bernard's people. Our bloody meat would supply the pullers with more than enough energy for the long haul back to the dungeons."

"I... can't... breath," the goblin interrupted, gasping for air and struggling to loosen her grip from his throat.

"No! We won't allow them to find out about this," she proclaimed. "You're coming back with me and you won't say a word to anyone about this. They will think Candlestick Street was searched, but you didn't find the girl, nor the boy that vulturk saw. Understand?"

"Yes. Anything you say," the goblin strained his voice to answer with her hand still tightly gripping his throat. "Not... a... word... to... anyone."

"Good, but if you disobey me again, I'll rip your limbs off myself before the Generals have a chance to send out the order, and I'll feed your raw bloody meat to the others. Now come on!" She released her grip from his throat and dropped him to the ground.

Quietly, the injured goblin rubbed his neck as he followed her back to the goblins' temporary camp in Bernard, and within seconds they were out of view.

Amora flashed a look at Magnar that he knew all too well. She wanted to follow the goblins to the camp!

135

"Oh no! No... we're not going," he stated sternly.

"It's our best chance at finding them."

"Amora... no! You know that's a horrible, terrible, very, very bad idea!" he firmly insisted!

"We have to! I'd bet you anything they've taken our parents there!"

"So, what if they are there? It's still a goblin camp and we both know what that means... lots of goblins! Plus, you heard as well as I did what she said about those *Generals*. What do you think they'll do if they find *us*?" he asked rhetorically. "I'm sorry, but neither you, nor I are going to that camp and that's the last word on it," he demanded, turning his face away from her and waiting for her to break the silence between them with more bickering on the subject.

With his arms crossed, he waited several seconds, but there was nothing. *That's not like her,* he thought to himself, and turned around to confront her for what he expected to be another round of arguing, but she was gone!

"Amora! Amora, where are you?" he frustratingly asked, trying to keep his voice low enough that nearby goblins would not hear him.

"Come on!" he heard a voice say from across the street. A female's figure—several houses farther down—was darting behind trees and bushes as she ran towards the camp!

****

"Shackle the rest of the scum and throw them in the cages with the others," commanded a large dark-skinned orc with bloodshot yellow eyes and a mouth full of sharpened pointy teeth, "Get the load-pullers ready. We leave at dawn's first light."

"Yesss, General. I get it done for you. I do it at once!" a tiny goblin of merely three feet tall eagerly replied, and scurried off to find others to help him complete the tasks the General had ordered of him.

Quickly, while the General's back was turned, Amora and Magnar ran past him unnoticed into the goblin camp and ducked behind several trash receptacles crammed together next to one of the buildings. "Shh, get down and stay quiet," Amora whispered, as she squeezed her head in between two bins and squinted her eyes to get a better look at the General—who was too preoccupied with barking orders at the others to even notice anyone was watching him from across the cobblestone street.

"You there!" he snapped, pointing to another minuscule goblin walking past him and carrying pairs of iron shackles in his hands.

Immediately, the goblin stopped in his tracks and felt his legs begin to wobble underneath him as he looked around, hoping the

General towering over him was speaking to someone else—anyone but him. "Me?" he asked softly with his head bowed down and his eyes staring at the rusty shackles in his hands.

"There's no one else here," the General sarcastically retorted with a cruel sneer.

"Right, General. No one here but me," the goblin lowly replied.

"Stop talking!" he yelled down at him. The entitled General reveled in the intimidated and fearful expressions of the lower class. So, he lifted his snout into the air and peered down his nose at the puny goblin and balled his fists, while flexing the rows of muscles down the lengths of his tattooed arms and chest—demonstrating his larger size and higher rank. "Your kind should not be allowed to even speak to us, *Generals*! You are the filth that sticks to the bottom of my feet and wedges between my teeth. I should have your loose tongue cut from your mouth for speaking to me. No! I have a better idea. I should rip it from your mouth myself and feed it to the load-pullers."

"Sorry, General. No more talking. I talk no more," he pleaded, and flung himself down onto the ground with his hands covering his head protectively for fear of being struck by the hefty orc.

"Hahaha!" the General laughed. "Get up, filth. You amuse me, so I'll allow you to live… for now. I want you to find the woman and her scout that searched Candlestick Street and bring them here to me. They haven't reported in yet, and delays will not be tolerated."

Amora quietly watched as the seven-foot-tall General continued giving instructions while belittling the goblin; she cringed at the sight of a long piece of thick drool that slid out of his mouth and dripped down one of his long tusks protruding from his bottom lip. Fixated on the disgusting saliva, she watched it drop onto a rather large scab covering a new scar on the General's bare chest, then finally, it dropped onto the ground just as the small goblin hurried away to find the woman and her scout.

Amora looked at the tattooed markings on the General's face while he talked to the goblins passing by regarding issues within the camp. The markings resembled tribal tattoos etched in flesh (meant for identifying the clan he or she belonged to). She knew he was proud of the markings by the way he held his head up confidently and spoke to those with similar tattoos—even to those within lower ranks.

"We need to get going," Magnar said, interrupting Amora's stare at the General—in awe of his massive size compared to that of the goblins. "Remember... *our parents*," he whispered, giving her arm a firm tug to pull her towards him—it was time to go.

"One more minute. If we stay and watch, then maybe we'll learn something that could help us," she insisted, still staring. Carefully, she watched the General walk up an elevated patch of land, overlooking the goblin camp, as the first few rays of morning's light began cutting through the thick blanket of storm clouds overhead. Like an animal sniffing for rain, the General raised his face to the looming storm and took in a deep whiff of air—heavy with the scent of water—and closed his eyes as a chilly mist began to dampen his skin.

For a moment, he stood motionless in the mist. Then, he reopened his bloodshot eyes and watched the on-goings of the other goblins across the vast camp within the heart of Bernard. In one section there were rows of tents—most constructed from shoddy fabrics that had been stitched by the lowest classes of goblins—being held upright with large, sturdy, wooden planks that had been placed in their centers to construct temporary housing units. Inside the tents, were modest piles of sticks and leaves that had been lit on fire to keep the off-duty goblins warm as they slept on thin blankets.

Several goblins were walking through the camp carrying handfuls of furry animals with bashed-in skulls and broken necks. Selfishly, they held them close to ward off attacks from those who might be interested in stealing their meager meals! Quickly, they rushed towards their tents to cook up their rodents and tree-dwellers, but only one of them made it safely back to fill the cooking pot! Immediately, he sat down on the hard ground inside his tent and sunk his razor teeth into the furry flesh—tearing fur and ripping off chunks of the oily fatty meat from the bone, spitting it into the sizzling pot, which hung from a thin hook above the fire.

Meanwhile, another goblin endured the mischievous wrath of two others... both of equal rank. Slowly, they snuck up behind him and removed freshly sharpened knives from their pockets. Without warning, they plunged their blades into the sides of his ribcage multiple times and hurled vicious insults! Immediately, the wounded goblin screamed in pain as he collapsed onto the ground—loosening his grip around a recently slain rodent that rolled off his fingers onto the ground. Quickly, one of the attackers grabbed the prize and took off running with the other goblin fast on his heels—both bursting with maniacal laughter at their unfair win.

In another area of the camp, goblins were hauling buckets filled with rotten meat over to filthy pens where the restless load-pullers were being caged. At the sight of the meat, the animals pawed excitedly at the ground with their wide feet and shook their mighty heads back and forth in excited anticipation of the hard-to-come-by meals!

"Alright, alright. Calm down ya stupid beasts," said a rather nasty goblin known for his cruelty.

One of the load-pullers, in the pen in front of the goblin, watched excitedly as he dragged the heavy bucket towards him.

Loudly, a chain *rattled* and *clanked* as the animal yanked and pulled his neck against the collar that was fastened too tightly around his throat—connected to a chain that restricted the range of his movements.

"I said I'm coming!" he yelled in anger at the beast. "Why do I have to feed you stupid things? Worse than ground-runners you are! Stupid brains. Yes, all load-pullers have stupid brains! Smaller than us goblins… is what you have. Small as a pea. I smash it in my fingers. Starve… you should, but do they care?" the goblin asked, looking around to see if any Generals were close enough to overhear him before ranting on. "No! They not care! I not eat yesterday, but *Generals* not care… other goblins not care."

Again, the load-puller clawed at the ground and shook his massive head, loosening slobber from his bone-crushing jaws as he hungrily drooled for the rotten meat to be tossed from the bucket.

"Food should be mine! So rotten and delicious, but they catch me if I take it. They catch me and feed *me* to load-pullers, if I do. No, they think goblin should starve. *Feed the pullers*. Feed the *pullers* they all say. Goblin should feed *Generals* to the pullers, then goblin in charge."

The goblin halted dragging the bucket—several feet away from the puller's reach—and removed one of the stinky bits from the mess of food. The stench permeated the air, and the load-puller lifted up onto his two hind legs, waiting for the goblin to toss it so he could snatch it in his mouth.

Half-heartedly the goblin tossed the fleshy bit a couple feet towards the puller, and it landed with a *plop* on the ground between himself and the beast.

"Generals think you better than servant goblins. Go get meat then," the goblin cackled as he watched the load-puller yank his weight against his chain while trying to stretch his front legs out to grab the meat, but it was too far away. Over-and-over, the puller strained his body with all the force of his muscles towards it, but the collar and chain held firm. The powerful beast roared with frustration at the goblin, but the goblin continued standing there, watching and mocking the puller, and again tossed another chunk of food out of the puller's reach.

"See it, I do. Why can't they? Big animal... dumb animal. Strong you are, that is why you pull heavy carts, but you not smart... like goblin," he laughed, not seeing another goblin walk up behind him, who was also carrying a bucket filled with rotting meat.

"Hey you!" he said, startling him.

"Yes! What is it? You see I'm busy!" the goblin replied, trying to hide his worry that the other goblin had seen him taunting the beast, and would report him to one of the Generals. "Well, hurry up! What is it you want?"

"Nothing from you. I do you a favor. Watch that one," he said pointing to the load-puller in front of them. "He's not like others. He remembers things. A tricky one."

"I don't need hear you! No help I need! Go! Go way-way!" the goblin yelled at him and shooed him away with his hands from himself, his bucket, and his load-puller!

"I just telling you…"

"No! No say more words! I bite you! I bite hard! Rip your heart out with teeth! I feed *you* to load-puller. Yes. Yes! Make problem go away," he continued, ignoring the other goblin, and again took another chunk of rotten meat out of his bucket and threw it beyond the load-puller's reach.

The load-puller narrowed its eyes at the small goblin and turned its body away from him and the meat.

"What! Turn back on me!" the goblin gasped as he watched the load-puller walk away and sit on the ground with its back still turned.

"I tell you… *no trust him*," the other goblin again warned, dragging his own bucket to feed a different load-puller.

"Shut it! No words to me. Okay. No words! No need help!" the small goblin hissed, flashing a warning-look in his direction, then refocused his attention back to the angry puller who was now refusing his food. "You dumb, dumb. You forget to eat," he said, kicking a side of his half-empty bucket. "Oh, I see this. I know what *you* do. You too good to eat food from goblin. You better than goblin," he said, pacing around the bucket and scratching his dry itchy scalp as he thought about what to do next. "You not better than goblin. Eat food!" he shouted, gripping the edge of the bucket, dragging it a few feet closer. "Here, I say eat!" the goblin demanded, reaching all the way down to the bottom of the bucket to grab a large chunk of gooey stinking meat, which he hurled over his shoulder without turning around—oblivious to the position of the load-puller... who had gotten up!

"Watch out!" the other goblin shouted.

The clever load-puller had faked his disinterest in the meat long enough to sneak up behind the goblin as he was pulling the next chunk of rotten flesh out of the bucket. Swiftly, the load-puller grabbed the unsuspecting goblin in his massive jaws and chomped down on him!

"Nooo! I kidding," the goblin gurgled as he took a shallow breath and was swallowed into the puller's gut.

"Well... guess I go tell General," the other goblin reasoned, viewing the bloody mess of scraps that had spilled from the bucket onto the ground. Quietly, the goblin grabbed the empty bucket and scurried off to tell one of the Generals about the incident.

CHAPTER THIRTEEN
Scorched Memories

Gradually, the mist transitioned into pummeling sheets of heavy rain that battered the streets of Bernard and the goblin camp, but still the General stood on the hill, holding his gaze firm. Soon, his attention turned towards the middle ranking goblins who were hauling chains and piling them with iron shackles on top of wooden boxes—materials they had used to imprison their captives with before carting them off.

"Faster! Pull, you filthy dogs!" ordered a different General, who was circling around the goblins pulling the chains through the thick sludge. The ground had become knee-deep with mud and they struggled to keep a firm hold on the slippery chains as they hauled and pulled on them—one goblin lined behind another.

"Get up, you filth!" yelled the General as he took a black leather whip—looped at his side—and cast it at one of the goblins who had lost his grip on the chains and had fallen on his face into the mud! The lash of the whip sliced into his dark meat and sent chilling screams into the air from the goblin's lopsided mouth!

"I said… GET UP!" the General again shouted while the goblin was struggling to rise, and he sent forth another cracking lash of his whip at the flesh on the goblin's back! Upon feeling the pain of the whip, he lost the position of his hands in the mud and again slipped back into the wet goop.

"GET UP, YOU FILTH!" the General screamed over the noise of the rain and sent several more lashes of his whip at the goblin as he tried to stand. This time, the leather struck the back of the goblin's legs and crippled him, which sent him, yet again, plunging back down into the sludge!

Finally, his legs straightened up underneath him, and the goblin wiped the rain and mud from his hands and face, then retook hold of the muddied chains. "It not happen again General," he cowardly replied with eyes casts downward—afraid to look at the General's face, who was leaning over in front of him. The General's long tusks, protruding out of his mouth, were almost touching the goblin's cheeks as he stared at him and challenged the goblin's resolve to accept his punishment without resistance.

"It better not," the General coldly replied, and returned his attention back to supervising the other goblins pulling the remaining chain lengths.

"You there!" the General shouted through the rain to two goblins passing by with iron wrists and anklets in their hands. "Go shackle the rest of the Bernard scum and load them into the cages."

"Yes General. At once," they replied and hurried off.

Amora watched to see which direction they headed, but quickly they disappeared between two buildings, causing her to lose track. "Look," she pointed, seconds before they vanished from view. "Let's follow them."

"No. We need to get out of here before someone sees us," Magnar sternly replied, preferring to be the voice of reason.

"Come on! Our best chance at finding our parents is walking away, and you know as well as I do, that wherever they're holding the captives is exactly where those two are going. Following them is the only way we'll find out if they're still alive or not."

For a brief moment, he looked at her and thought about it. As much as he did not want to admit it, or to follow the goblins deeper into the camp, he knew she was right. They had not seen a single person, but they had to be somewhere in the camp, and those goblins would lead them straight to the spot!

"Fine, but stay quiet and keep low," he agreed reluctantly.

"Okay, but let's hurry!" she whispered excitedly.

Silently, they left the safety of their hiding place behind the trash receptacles and snuck past bushes and along the sides of

148

buildings, until slipping down the same alley the goblins had disappeared into.

"Over there," Magnar whispered and pointed down at two rows of goblin-sized footsteps in the mud that led further down the alley and then turned sharply to the right. "Goblin tracks. I bet that's the way they went."

"Then that's the way we're going," she ordered.

With hurried steps, the two followed the tracks right, left, straight, then another right down alley after alley, until reaching the edge of where the mud met the smooth stone of the cobblestone street. They had completely disappeared.

"What now?" Magnar asked, looking down at the stones for any residual muddy signs to indicate where the goblins had hurried off to.

"I don't know, but if we keep going that way," Amora pointed at the street in the direction the tracks had faded towards, "there's another path that leads to one of the grassy knoll areas. That could be where they're keeping everyone," but as the words left her mouth, she looked up to see Magnar's forlorn face staring at something. Her eyes quickly followed his to a disfigured building with charred timbers—some of which were still smoldering despite the rain.

The structure had once been a toy store that had held many precious memories from her childhood when her parents would take her to play with the new thing-a-ma-jigs and carry out—in a specially wrapped package—one new toy of her choosing. However, now the place stood in ruins. It had lost its charm—the cool crisp colors and inviting atmosphere were gone. The roof had been reduced to ashes and the walnut wooden beams had become blackened and rain soaked. Items that had once adorned beautiful oak shelves were now broken—smashed into pieces by the goblins who had run through the building with lit torches to ignite the goblin-fires. The large cover over the entrance's awning, which a friend of the family had painted of a child holding a ballerina music box, was almost unrecognizable—ripped and badly burned. The sign over the front door—which she had looked up at at least a million times as a youngling—was now hanging crookedly on broken hinges and swaying with a creaking noise in the breeze, and a thick layer of char hid its once artful letters.

"Look at what they've done," she said in a low voice as she walked around to the front of the store and looked to her left, right, up and down the street at other charred buildings lining that side of the cobblestone road. Slowly, she turned around to look behind her and that side, too, was also littered with blackened structures with caved-in roofs, busted doors, and shattered windows. One of them still had greyish-white smoke smoldering up from deep inside where embers had been burning long through the night—reluctant to be doused by the rain.

Her heart sank as she took in all the destruction the goblins had wrought in their search for her and Magnar. Buildings that had once bustled with life and made the citizens of Bernard proud of their charms had all been reduced to pitiful eye-sores. She knew some of the town's people had even lived in small homes above their stores, but now both had been transformed into nothing more than heaping mounds of scorched blistered woods left soaking in the rain to rot and fester with mold.

Briefly, she closed her eyes and searched her mind for memories of being a young girl in Bernard. A slight smile lifted the corners of her mouth as she remembered skipping up and down the cobblestone streets on her way to one store or another. She had enjoyed visiting with friendly store owners and townsfolk who would cheerfully greet her, and sometimes when her parents were not looking, a few of the owners would give her candy from the assortments kept by the registers. One of the bakeshop owners, which specialized in cakes and fruit pies, would sneak her a piece of freshly baked cake neatly placed on a clean white plate—meant for paying patrons to sample before making a purchase of one of their many tiered offerings. In her memory, she could almost smell the sweet scents of chocolate, strawberry, and lemon cake layers being pulled out of the ovens, but as she took in a deep breath, all she could smell was burnt wood and rain. At the foul smell of the odors, she re-opened her eyes and the smile receded from her lips.

The town she had grown up in with Magnar had been destroyed by goblin-fire, and the only thing left to do was rescue their parents (if they could), escape, and bring the one responsible for sending the goblins in the first place to justice!

"You think things here will ever be the same again?" Magnar asked, standing next to her and looking around at the destruction, too. "Do you think they'll ever be able to rebuild all this?"

"I don't know, but I hope so."

"Yeah, me too," he replied. For several minutes they stood there in silence while getting drenched in the rain as they stared at the places that had meant something to them. Soon, a numb feeling removed the shock and sadness, and then resolve settled in. They needed to move on and finish the task that had brought them to this place.

"Come on. Let's get moving," Magnar said, breaking the silence. "Soon enough the goblins will be coming back and probably this way, and if all this was done because they were trying to find us, then we should make sure those foul things never get what they were after!"

"Right! Let's find our parents and get out of here!" she fervently declared, and immediately the two ran towards the next muddy path leading to the grassy knoll area where they suspected the goblins had gone and were holding their parents captive!

CHAPTER FOURTEEN

Cages

"**S**hut up! Filthy people scum!" shouted one of the goblins circling around the cages stuffed with captives. Cruelly, she struck a short metal rod against the iron bars, clanking metal against metal. "Shut your mouths! Too many voices! I shut you up! I shut you all up if I drag scum out of cages and hit many times with my rod. I'll do, if you not quiet!" she threatened, striking the sides of the cages several more times.

"Hurry! Get down," Amora whispered, running behind several wide trees with thick trunks across from a small group of goblins who were placing shackles on the wrists and ankles of those being prepped for transport. From behind the trees, she and Magnar watched them clasp on the rusty iron cuffs and shove people up a rickety latter—only a couple feet high—into iron-bar cages sitting atop large wooden carts already hitched to load-pullers.

"Over there," Magnar gestured towards tall, thick, overgrown weeds. "We can get a better look at who's in the carts from there."

Amora took a quick look at the tall weeds and grass. Then, she nodded her head in agreement. Carefully, they crouched low to the ground and snuck into the weeds, until they were only a few feet away from the nearest empty cage.

With keen eyes, they searched each prisoner's face for their parents - looking from one crammed cage to another. Faces of women, children, and men were tired and dirty with streaks of mud mixed with tears upon rain-soaked skin. Their hair was drenched and matted with dirt, bits of leaves, and grass. Amora felt sorrow for the terrified young children who were clinging tightly to their mothers. She knew they were frightfully worried about what horrors the goblins had in store for them once they reached whatever place they were headed—praying against all hope that place wouldn't be dungeons.

Many of the captives had lost their shoes at some point during the chaos of being snatched from their homes—probably asleep in their beds—during the middle of the night and dragged by goblins across cobblestone streets, dirt paths, and knolls to this holding area scattered with cages. Amora looked at the empty cage near them, and knew it was meant to hold her and Magnar as well, but she wasn't about to let that happen! Quickly, she resumed her search for the faces of their parents, but instead, she found the face of a child looking back at her from inside a cage. It was a little girl sitting on the lap of her mother and she was holding a large rip in her shirt closed with one hand, while wiping away the rain from her eyes with the other. Amora noticed the young girl wasn't wearing any shoes and her feet were streaked with brown mud and something red. Immediately, she realized the red was probably blood seeping from deep cuts received while being forced to walk barefoot in the dark, and then stumbling on something sharp such as rocks or broken tree branches along the way, but goblins cared nothing for the comforts of people, much less young ones.

"There!" Magnar blurted out. "I see them! Over there in that cage, but the load-pullers are already starting to haul them away!"

Instantly, Amora's eyes darted towards the direction of where he was looking, and she spotted the sad faces of their parents! Everyone was sitting with their backs slouched against the railings of the cage and their heads were bent low as they sobbed in despair. Two of the load-pullers had already left towards the pathway leading out of Bernard, and the third was yanking his weight against the cart to gain momentum in order to follow the others. All of a sudden, she felt her stomach fill with desperation and fear!

Frantically, she looked around for a way to stall the load-puller from leaving, but she couldn't find anything nearby that would be able to distract it without gaining the attention of the goblins surrounding the remaining carts! She was unsure about what to do next as her eyes desperately searched for something to throw, or for something shiny that might catch the eyes of the beast and slow its pace behind the others long enough for them to free their parents. Promptly, a heavier feeling sank deep into her heart as she realized that even if they did find a way to gain the puller's attention, they still wouldn't have a way to get over to the cage or unlock the latch without alerting the goblins to their presences.

"I see them, but how are we going to free everyone without getting caught?" she asked, while craning her neck above the tops of the weeds in order to get a better look at several rather oddly shaped, rusty, sharp items scattered on two rotting crates the goblins had flipped over to use as tables. "There's some tools on those dilapidated wood crates, right over there. One of them looks like it may be a curved blade of some sort and it has a pointy tip."

"So, what? We can't get to it without being caught."

"We have to try something," she replied in a huff and plopped back down into the cover of the tall weeds. "If I could just find a way to grab that knife, then all we'd have to do is catch up with the load-puller. I bet we could find a way to toss it up into the cage, and then when the goblins aren't looking, someone could pick the lock from the inside. If that much works, they could all make a run for it!"

"Yeah, but there's no way we're going to get anywhere near that crate without being seen! Look! Do you see that ugly old goblin standing next to the empty cage they lifted onto the last cart?" he asked, pointing at a fat goblin covered with wiry sprigs of grey hair on his leathery skin, wearing shredded clothing, and a rather nasty looking expression on his face. His bulging yellow eyes were constantly darting left, right, and looking behind himself in dire paranoia.

"Yes. I see him, but what about it?"

"He's looked in our direction three times and stared hard into these tall weeds, but hasn't spotted us yet. Each time I see him looking, I slowly crouch down even lower, almost lying flat on my stomach, and have been pulling you on the arm to do the same without worrying you as to why I'm tugging so hard. I don't know how much more I can keep spotting his looks in time, or how long our luck is going to hold out, especially if you stand up to reach for anything on that crate!" he reasoned with her, hoping that since he was the one with a sound head on his shoulders, she would give in to listening to him this time, and not make any more impulsive moves against his better judgment.

"I agree! That's why I'm not going to stand up and reach for it," she replied with her head tilted to the side at him.

"What—" he asked, with his eyes squinting and a puzzled expression that meant he was weary of what plan she was concocting in that mind of hers (which he knew he was probably not going to like).

"I'm grabbing that knife!" she declared with a stern look, but then quickly allowed her face to again soften. "I'm going to use a levitation spell to do it. That way, I won't be standing or causing any undue attention in our direction. It's a win-win!" she informed him (in a manner of being pleased with what she thought was a *genius idea*).

"A levitation spell?" he hesitantly asked. "Amora, we don't know any advanced levitation spells decent enough to even come close to being able to do what you're thinking."

"That's where you're wrong, because I do know one!"

"No. You don't."

"Yes! I do!" she insisted rather forcibly.

"No! You don't! I've seen you perform the spell you're thinking of, but something always goes wrong! Please, just think about it! We only know simple magic like scrubbing floors with mops dancing across the hardwoods, sending sudsy sponges to wipe windows clean, causing books to jump off cluttered tables and arrange themselves on bookshelves, or making messy stacks of paper and coloring sticks—children have been using— suddenly pick themselves up into neat stacks, or causing them to march in organized rows and place themselves into storage bins! Neither of us know anything remotely advanced enough… *to risk our lives.* There are probably a hundred goblins in town searching for us! At best, they're keeping that last cage empty for us, but it's likely they would prefer to separate our heads from our shoulders and take those to one of their demented Generals instead!" he argued, trying to make his point clear and strong enough to deter any haphazard or impulsive actions she might try to carry out on her own that could get them caught.

All of a sudden, they found themselves in a stand-off with each other, and the tension between them felt intense as they stared at each other. Amora bit down hard on her bottom lip to prevent saying anything cruel—upset that he didn't yet trust her instincts.

Neither of them wanted to relent to the other, but Magnar decided to at least change his tactic and try gently reasoning with her instead. Either way, a decision had to be made quickly before the load-puller carrying their parents' cage got too far away to consider a rescue in the first place!

"I need you to listen to me on this," he said, softer this time. "You'd be risking both our lives if you try that levitation spell. I really think it's time to accept there's nothing we can do to help

159

them, here. I'm sorry, because I know how much you don't want to hear this, but we need to leave for Kembrull Forest… while we can."

Amora released the grip of her teeth off her bottom lip and broke her stare away from his hazel eyes. Silently, she sat in the mud by his side in the cover of the tall weeds, and briefly looked down at the sludge surrounding them, while the rain continued pouring from the grey clouds overhead. Her clothes were soaked, and the coat no longer provided her with any warmth in its drenched state. She felt her body beginning to shiver and all she wanted was for things to return back to the way they were—before goblins, before goblin-fire, and before reading the book… when ignorance was still bliss. However, she wasn't about to give into her fear or sorrow! She had listened to his words, and yes, there was some validity to what he had said. Even still, she knew she'd never be able to forgive herself if she left for Kembrull without at least trying something more! She was doing the spell with or without his consent, and then she was going after that load-puller!

Her eyes were ablaze with determination as she looked up at Magnar, but before he could utter a word of protest, she turned her attention to the rusty knife on the crate and spoke the spell. "*Levate et Veni ad Mihi!*" she whispered, and with her hand stretched out she twisted her fingers towards it in a lifting manner. Slowly, the knife began to twitch upon the rotted top of the wood crate, but it didn't levitate up into the air as she had hoped. However, determination was coursing through her blood, and instead of giving up, she hardened her focus and again spoke the spell. "*Levate et Veni ad Mihi!*" Again, the knife twitched, and this time lifted about an inch or two up into the air, but then dropped back down onto the crate with a *thud*, which caught the attention of the old goblin! Instantly, his bulging eyes darted towards the crate and he hurried his hefty girth over to it! Carefully, the grey-haired goblin bent over the crate and looked the items over.

"Look at what you've done! He's going to find us now... thanks to you!" Magnar lashed at her.

Her heart began pounding fast in her chest after hearing his angry words and wondering if he was right as she watched the goblin study the items. *Is he right?* she thought to herself, but suddenly a rush of relief washed over her, and a grin parted her lips!

"What are *you* grinning about? You've killed us. Do you realize that? Any moment, that goblin is going to find us and alert the others! They'll grab us and drag us, kicking and screaming, to one of those demented Generals! We're going to be beaten and tortured for information about that book. Then, once they're satisfied and we've told them everything we know, they'll take that blade you wanted so badly and spill our guts with it! Yeah, right here in the mud, they'll cut our bellies open and let us watch our innards fall out and splash into the sludge. Then, they'll toss our lifeless bodies into that empty cage to haul us back to their master! So, wipe that grin off you face!" he angrily blurted in a panic!

"Are you finished yet?" Amora whispered, still grinning at him, but Magnar refused to utter a word in reply. "They're not going to find us, because that one has already dismissed that the sound he heard even came from that crate."

"What?" Magnar asked, looking back at the goblin who had lost interest in determining the origin of the sound—watching it waddle away back to the empty cage.

"See. It's fine. No harm done," Amora reassured him, watching the goblin resume his post next to the empty cage.

For several minutes, they sat silently in the wet weeds, staring at the goblin and waiting for the remainder of his attention to find other distractions. Again, his bulging eyes resumed darting back and forth in paranoia towards other areas of the expansive knoll. Further away, one load-puller still remained and was being prepped by goblins for departure, and there was one last wooden cart being readied to carry the empty cage—the one the old goblin was guarding.

"This is taking way too long," Amora whispered. "Our parents will be long gone if we wait here any longer," but just as the words left her lips, she heard a weird call in the air! "What is that?"

Amora perked up and tilted one of her ears up higher to hear it better, and again someone made the throaty sound.

"I don't know, but whatever it is, it's gotten the attention of our goblin. Look! He's leaving," Magnar replied, surprised and relieved that they hadn't yet been discovered.

"One of the goblins must be calling to him for something. Look, he's heading past those tents towards the area where they're keeping the last load-puller."

"Well, now's your chance," he suggested. "Do the spell again while he's distracted and maybe we can finally get out of here. I'm freezing! I can barely feel my legs! Plus, I wouldn't mind getting out of this mud and finding a nice warm place to rest awhile."

Amora looked at him and raised her eyebrows in surprise at his sudden change in attitude! Now he was actually encouraging her to do the spell! Quickly, she acted on his change of feelings and focused her full efforts on moving the rusted knife off the crate. Again, she stretched out her hand and twisted her fingers in an upward manner, simulating the lift of the knife up into the air, as she spoke the spell, *"Levate et Veni ad Mihi."* This time the knife lifted effortlessly several inches off the crate and smoothly floated in the air towards her and sat down gently in the palm of her hand.

"Finally! Can we get out of here?" he asked, not waiting for a reply as he began standing up.

With a raised eyebrow, she looked at him… noticing the grouchy tone in his voice. However, she could tell he was relieved and also somewhat impressed that her spell had actually worked despite being scared, frustrated, and chilled to the bone.

"Sure, let's get out of here!" she readily agreed.

CHAPTER FIFTEEN

The Biggest in Bernard

S neakily, they crouched—keeping their bodies as low as possible—to remain out of sight within the tall weeds. Amora brushed aside the wet blades of grass as she followed Magnar out of the overgrown knoll, but her hands had grown so cold from sitting in the rain that she could barely feel the textures of the thin grass blades against her numb fingers as she pushed her way through them to where the field touched the edge of a cobblestone road. Carefully, she stepped out of the weeds onto the road, which was wet and slick with mud. Her sludge covered shoes provided no additional traction against the stones as she continued to follow closely behind him across the street over to a row of buildings that had blackened timbers—like those they'd encountered earlier before entering into the knoll. These had broken windows with sharp slivers of glass hazardously still clinging on their panes, and ceiling timbers that had given way during the goblin-fires, which had crashed to the ground and taken with them most of the roof. Many of the buildings had heavy smoke damage—even if the fires hadn't burned them down—and looked as if they had been wrecked enough that they could collapse at any moment.

Eventually, the rain lightened into a mist, which was accompanied with a haze of thick fog mixed with the scent of the smoke lingering in the air. The fog settled low over the ground—limiting visibility to no more than a few yards ahead. Quietly, the two walked up the streets and made left and right turns down others as they walked towards the area they believed might allow them to catch up with the load-pullers. Everything had become quiet. There were no more sounds of goblins doing tasks, or Generals barking orders, nor goblins fighting in their tents. No longer could they even hear their own footsteps against the cobblestone streets. The only thing to break the silence was the slow drips of water down timbers into the puddles beneath them, and the occasional cracking of rotten wood.

"Where is everyone?" Amora whispered. She clasped her hands together and blew her warm breath into them a few times, trying to warm her frozen digits as they walked.

"I don't know," he replied, trying hard to see ahead of them through the dense fog. "You'd think we would've passed someone... anyone by now."

"Do you think we're too late? That maybe all the goblins have left, and the pullers went in a different direction after we last saw them," she continued, her teeth chattering from the cold as she spoke.

"Maybe, but I was sure they were coming this way and that we'd run into them. Those pullers are large and heavy—"

"Stupid and slow," she interrupted, trying to make him smile at her attempt at humor, but the pain of the cold took the fun out of it. Her bottom lip had begun quivering uncontrollably now as her body temperature slowly decreased from wearing freezing sopping-wet clothes.

"Yeah, and that too," he replied smiling at her, but then quickly noticed her skin had turned pale and her lips appeared different in color, like cyanosis was setting in. "Are you alright? Your lips are turning blue."

"I'm fine. We just need to find our parents and get out of here. At this point... that's all that matters," she stated stubbornly.

"No! That's not it at all. *You* matter," he said softly, walking and looking down at the cobblestones for fear of seeing her reaction to his heartfelt words. For a brief moment, neither of them spoke as they walked on in awkward silence, but then he continued on, "If it makes you feel any better, I stopped being able to feel my feet a couple hours ago," and just as she looked at him with concern, he made a goofy face at her to ease the tension between them.

"Stop it," she said, smiling at him. A small chuckle, that she was trying to hold back, escaped her shaking lips while she was trying to manage a proper scold, "That's nothing to joke about," but before she could continue her lecture, she spotted a tall figure in the fog approaching. Suddenly, her heart was in her throat and silence gripped her lips!

Immediately, Magnar saw it, too! "Shh, in there!" he told her, and without hesitation he grabbed her by the hand and quietly ran with her into one of the destroyed buildings nearby. Quickly, they darted behind a partially burnt wall missing its top half, but still intact enough at the base for them to conceal themselves. From inside their chests, their hearts were pounding audibly in their ears—growing louder by the second into a deafening crescendo! Fearfully, they both hid behind the wall and peered around its edges to watch the figure in the fog—each standing as motionless as a statue.

168

Larger the figure grew with each step as it came closer, until the fog soon parted enough to reveal the monstrosity within. A General! The largest either of them had ever seen! This one was taller than those at the goblin camp! His body was thick and rippled with muscles, and his face was boxy in shape. His bloodshot eyes were intense with evil and his wide mouth housed a tusk on each side of his bottom lip. They were like spears for goring flesh! The muscles in his legs stretched the faded puke-green fabric of his pants to their limits, and his feet were grotesquely wide—to carry his large size—and were filthy with mud and blades of wet grass. His toenails were thick, yellow, and curved from lack of care. As he came closer, the General closed his eyes and tilted his face to the sky. Next, he took in a long, deep breath of the cold air into his hairy nostrils. He seemed to roll the scent around in his mouth a few seconds, before letting it out and opening his eyes.

Suddenly, several smaller goblins came into view as they hurried to stand at his side!

"What is it?" one of the goblins asked, standing no more than waist high at the General's hip. The goblin could barely stand still as it anxiously awaited his answer!

"Yes, tell us!" another hissed, constantly switching its weight from one foot to the other!

"Shut up! All you!" another angrily hissed at the others. "He smell it. The air tell him!"

Violently, the pack of goblins turned and hissed back at him! "You not tell us! You no rank high!"

Instantly, one of them pulled a small blade from his torn pants pocket and held it threateningly at the goblin. "I gut you! Flay you like fish! We eat!"

"Yes! Do it! Do it!" the others began shouting! "Kill him! Kill him!"

"Take words from his lips!" another chimed in.

"Quiet!" the General's deep scratchy voice shouted as he slapped one of the goblins across the face with one hand, causing it to lift off the ground and fling backwards high into the air, until hitting hard against the cobblestones with a thud!

"I smell them. They are here," the General stated, without giving the least bit of acknowledgment to the goblin struggling to stand up, rubbing his bruised leathery skin.

"You smell their meat!" one of the antsy ones eagerly commented.

"Yes, yes! Scouts not find like General do!" said another.

"Their scent is strong. Find them. Bring them to me. I'll toss them in the cage myself," the General ordered—unmoved by the emotions of the others. Slowly, he turned his face to look at the charred buildings lining both sides of the cobblestone road.

170

"They're close. Search every building till you find them! Go!" he commanded them.

Immediately, the air filled with throaty, maniacal, high-pitched, staccato sounds of goblins excited to begin the hunt! Instantly, they dispersed and took off running in all directions towards the blackened structures destroyed earlier by the goblin-fires they had set!

Swiftly, Amora and Magnar whipped their heads away from the edges of the wall and slouched their backs against it as they mentally processed what they'd just seen! "What do we do now?" Amora whispered, struggling to get the words out as panic tightly gripped her throat, making it a challenge to speak. Her heart was racing faster now, and she desperately tried to think of a magic spell or anything that could help them out of this predicament, but her mind was blank! She couldn't think—there was too much fear taking hold of her!

"I don't know, but we can't stay here," he replied, sitting next to her against the wall and looking frantically around what was left of the room for anything that might be of some use. "You still got that knife?"

Amora felt around in her wet coat pockets until her frozen fingers touched the rusted metal. "Yeah. It's right here," she said, pulling out the curved blade and showing it to him.

"Good. Hold onto it, because we may need it sooner than we thought," he strongly suggested.

Without hesitation, she quickly nodded in agreement and clutched the blade tighter in her hand. "Maybe we can sneak out that window," she said, gesturing at the open pane on the far wall—likely opened by someone who had used it to escape the goblin raids. However, there was one problem with using the window that she could see... broken glass!

"Okay, let's go before they get over here," he said, leaning his weight against the wall as he stood up, and held his hand out to help her off the floor, too.

"Wait. What about the glass?" she asked, pointing at dozens of broken shards scattered on the floor beneath the window near a rock that had been thrown through it at some point. "There's no way we can walk over it without the goblins hearing us," but before he could answer her, they heard a low squeaking sound coming from a damaged door being swung open on broken hinges somewhere in the back of the building!

"They're coming!" he exclaimed in a panic, and without thinking, he rushed towards the open window!

"Magnar, wait! The glass!" she warned, but it was too late. He was already hurrying across the shards, stepping as quickly as he could over them and they were crunching beneath the weight of his feet!

172

"Stop! They're gonna hear us!" she warned again, but he was not slowing down and was almost at the window!

"Amora, hurry! It doesn't matter anymore! They're already inside! Now come on!" he insisted, and just as he reached the window, one of his feet landed on a large shard of broken glass and it crunched loudly beneath the bottom of his shoe!

Suddenly, another door at the back of the room swung open hard and hit the wall behind it from the force! Immediately, the sounds of loud maniacal grunts mixed with hideous laughter was on the other side of the burnt store shelves that had toppled over during the fire—now leaning against each other in the middle of the room just beyond the other side of the wall they had hidden behind moments earlier!

"They're here! Come on, Amora!" he beckoned, waving his hands at her frantically for her to hurry up and get over to the window! Quickly, Magnar reached the window, brushed off the last remnants of glass and climbed out onto the other side!

"Come on!" he called to her from the other side of the window with his hands stretched out to help her cross! Hearing the grunting and laughing getting closer, Amora no longer cared about the goblins hearing her feet against the glass, and she took off running towards the window! She could see him on the other side waiting to help her (just a few more feet away), but suddenly a sharp pain filled her ankle and sent her plummeting to the glass covered floor—knocking the knife out her hand!

"We've done it! We've caught the ugly she-scum!" one of the goblins hissed to the others, while one of them gnawed its teeth into her ankle and gripped her legs with its scaly hands!

Amora struggled to loosen the goblin's hands from her legs as it bit down harder into her ankle, sending pain coursing through her!

"Get off her!" "Magnar screamed from outside the window. "Amora! Your knife!"

Fighting against the pain, Amora spotted the knife a foot from her among the glass, and she pulled herself along the floor towards it! Blood ran down her foot as the goblin's razor-sharp teeth tore into her flesh and his claws scratched at her legs! Frantically, she reached for the knife—brushing away glass as she strained her arm to reach it!

"Take her leg! Rip it from socket! She no need two," another goblin shouted, as it entered into the room to join the others.

"Get off me!" she yelled, reaching desperately for the small, round, wooden handle of the knife… almost grabbing it with her stretched out fingers, but the goblin chomped down harder on her ankle, and sent a new wave of pain surging through her leg! Loudly, she screamed in pain and her hands flung down to grip her leg in response! Again, she tried to pull the goblin's hands away from clawing her leg, but still she could not free herself from the grip of the vile creature!

"The knife! Grab the knife!" Magnar shouted.

The pain began causing a dizzying haze to fill her head as Magnar yelled, and she felt herself struggling to focus on his voice, but then she felt something else—an unexplainable strength surging from deep within in her core! All of a sudden, she felt stronger and more determined not to give into her pain! With one powerful lunge of her body towards the knife, she shoved the remaining shards out of her way, and grasped the handle of the knife! "Got it!" she yelled to Magnar, and sliced at the goblins hands with the sharp curved blade!

"Ouch!" the goblin screamed, letting go of her leg and ankle as it fell backwards onto the floor. "She-scum cut me!" the creature whined, staring at the gashes across the backs of both its hands, and listening to the mocking maniacal laughter erupting from the others watching him on the floor—fueling the goblin's anger! "I not take you to General now. I eats you instead!" the goblin hissed. Swiftly, the vile thing growled and pushed itself up off the floor and charged at her with its rows of razor-edged teeth threateningly bared!

With all the force she could muster, Amora plunged the rusty blade forward into the goblin's belly just as he landed on top of her!

Ghastly screams leapt from the goblin's throat as he looked down at the knife—her hands still gripping the handle!

"Finish him!" Magnar shouted from the window.

Amora's intense eyes rose from looking down at the knife, up to meet the eyes of the goblin. Her fingers tightened around the handle and she pushed her weight against it, pushing the blade in deeper! Then, with one forceful shove, she slit the goblin's belly open, spilling its entrails on top of her!

"She-scum! She killed him! Look, she killed him dead!" several goblins began shouting, filling the room once again with maniacal laughter and grunting!

Amora pushed the dead goblin and his entrails off of her onto the floor, and hurried towards the window as the others drew in closer, encircling the corpse!

"Let's eat him," one of the grunting goblins suggested to the others, and quickly, they began ravaging the bloody mess of torn leathery flesh right there in front of her!

For several seconds, Amora watched in shock at the cannibalistic behavior of them devouring their own kind!

"Don't watch! Get out of there! The General had to have heard that!" Magnar shouted, reminding her of the very real danger they were still in if she did not get through to the other side of the window right away! Quickly, she propped herself up onto the frame and lifted one leg through, and then the other with his help.

None of the goblins even looked up to see her escaping while they continued focusing on the feast of raw goblin flesh.

"I know a shortcut from here into Kembrull Forest," he said, taking hold of her hand. "Follow me!"

"Where's the girl?" they heard the General's voice yelling at the goblins back inside the room as they took off running. "You... let... her... escape!"

"Look General, what the she-scum done," one of the small goblins pointed to the bloody mess of intestines and organs scattered on the floor.

"Yes," another hissed. "She done it. She-scum strong."

"Yes, yes. She... have a goblin blade," another hissed, circling round the corpse and wiping bloody strings of flesh off his mouth with the back of his hairy hand.

"I'll gut every one of you myself and place your bodyless heads on spikes if you don't get out that window and find them... NOW!" the furious General bellowed, his voice echoing off the structures down the street!

"Yes General!"

"At once!"

"Right away!"

"We find them!"

"We bring them screaming!"

177

"Get out there! Find them! Find THEM!" the General yelled again and again!

With hurried steps, Amora and Magnar ran as fast as their feet could move down one street, then another, turning left and right as they listened to the maniacal grunts and laughter from the goblin pack hunting them!

"They're getting closer! How are we going to lose them?" Amora asked, holding his hand and running as fast as she could, trying to keep up with his pace!

"Just keep running!" he ordered, pulling her with him off the cobblestone street and into a large wooded area filled with trees and bushes! He knew the goblins were on their heels by how much louder their sounds had become, and he looked over his shoulder to verify where they were! Everywhere, he saw bushes rustling as hordes of the vile creatures ran along the ground, and leaves falling as dozens of others climbed up the trees and jumped from branch-to-branch!

"Come on! Faster!" he shouted over the noise of the goblin horde and quickened his pace!

"There's more of them aren't there? It sounds like every goblin in the whole town is after us!" she said. Her heart was pounding into a crescendo of rapid beats in her chest, and her feet were hitting the ground hard with every step—matching his swift pace!

"We'll be safe once we're inside Kembrull Forest!" he tried to reassure her. "We just need to get there before they do!"

"How do you know that? You don't know anything about goblins!" she replied, thinking that he did not have a clue about what he was talking about!

"I heard a man in the bookstore one night talking to someone about goblins."

"That's what you're going by! We're risking our lives heading into Kembrull Forest because you overheard someone talking!" Amora yelled.

"It was a man that had visited the store several times before… a traveler. He said goblins hate Kembrull Forest and he had escaped them once by entering into the outskirts of it! I know it's a long shot, but it's the only chance we've got!

"How will we know we're in Kembrull Forest?" she asked.

"He said the woods of Kembrull Forest are thicker than others! I guess look for that," Magnar answered.

For an hour, they ran hard and fast through the forest, while pushing their cold hungry bodies to the limits as they kept pace ahead of the frenzied goblins! Neither of them looked back for fear of stumbling as the yards changed into miles. As they ran, the air grew colder and the last remnants of the fog lifted through the trees, which looked thicker and older than the ones they had passed, thus far. Closer together the trees grew, and their deep

179

roots curled in and out of the rich soil. The leaves of their thick canopies overhead soon began blanketing out the light of the dismal day as they entered further and further into the dark forest. Soon, even the maniacal sounds of the goblins began to fade, until turning into nothing more than faint grunting in the far distance. Then, there was nothing. In the dark forest, only perfect stillness and quiet marked the place where the wind did not blow, and where goblins dared not venture.

"Magnar, stop," Amora said, slowing her steps and pulling against his hand for him to slow to a complete halt.

"Why? What is it?" he asked, huffing to catch his breath. "Why are we stopping?"

"Magnar, weren't we supposed to stop at the outskirts of Kembrull Forest?" she asked, glancing around at the eerie looking trees surrounding them in the dark woods.

"Yeah, why?"

"Because," she paused and hesitated to say it, "we're already *inside Kembrull Forest*, and the goblins stopped following us a while ago."

Magnar looked around and realized she was right. They were way further inside Kembrull Forest than they should be....

180

CHAPTER SIXTEEN
Kembruss Forest

*I*n silence, Amora and Magnar walked into the dark forest. Not a sound disturbed its eery quiet, except for their footsteps on the dry crinkled leaves hued yellow-gold, burgundy, and amber, which had fallen from the autumn canopy high above. Slowly, the time passed as they journeyed deeper and deeper inside the forest—rays of light lessening with every step. As the light faded, the temperature began to drop, causing their breath to fog in the air and their bodies to shiver. The trees were changing, too. Their lengths were taller and trunks wider—from centuries of aging—and most were covered in an odd-looking thick bark. Clumps of pale-green lichens grew along their sides and long strands of it dangled low to the ground from their branches—brushing against them as they walked.

"Let's rest here awhile," Magnar said, resting his back against one of the trees and clutching Mr. Higgin's wet coat tighter around himself.

"Sounds good to me," she agreed. Exhausted, Amora plopped down on a large twisted root—partially exposed out of the ground—and slid her frozen hands inside her coat pockets. Startled by the feel of wet rust against her fingers, she plucked the bloodied goblin blade out of one of the pockets and held it in the flat palm of her hand. She was stunned that she still had it, and realized that without thinking, she must have placed the blade back inside her pocket after killing the creature, but she could not remember if she had done it before or after she had rushed out the window—everything had become a blur.

"You've still got that thing, huh?" Magnar asked, watching her hold the blade in her hand with a blank expression on her face while staring at it.

"Yeah. I do," she said, not looking away from it. She had never killed anything before and the feeling she had at best was… a strange emotion. She didn't feel the remorse she thought she would. Instead, she felt numb. Where was the guilt she was sure she would be plagued with once things had settled down and she'd had a chance to comprehend what she had done? The guilt wasn't there… not even a little.

"You can put that thing down you know," Magnar said, interrupting her thoughts. "I don't think we're gonna see anymore goblins for a while… at least not in Kembrull Forest."

"Yeah. I know," she replied, and with a deep sigh, she let the blade drop from her hand onto a pile of leaves. All of a sudden, overwhelming emotions consumed her as everything she was feeling merged into one powerful emotion: the hunger; cold; exhaustion; shock at killing a goblin; losing their parents and watching everyone be hauled off in cages caused an unfamiliar pain to surge through her fatigued muscles. Her mind was spinning and all she wanted to do was burst into tears, but then as quickly as it began, all her thoughts ceased and again she was numb.

"I found some wood we can use to build a fire," Magnar said, searching in the dim light to gather broken branches off the ground. "Can you grab those over there behind you?" he asked, gesturing at some dry wood lying only a foot away from her near a large tree root that had grown awkwardly above the ground.

Without a word, she reached for the small broken branches—perfect for kindling—and placed them on top of the small pile Magnar had stacked near her with the others he had found.

"Grab those two small stones by the tree for me too, and I'll see if I can get this fire started," he instructed.

Again, saying nothing, Amora did as he asked and brought the stones over to the pile of wood. After a few minutes of more searching in the dim light, he added some dry leaves and more wood to the pile, and then sat down in front of it with his legs criss-crossed. Patiently, he struck the rocks together several times slightly above the dry leaves, while Amora quietly waited, sitting across from him on the other side of the pile. A few minutes later, sparks flew from the stones onto the leaves and ignited a fire!

"Quick! Help me blow some air on it," he urged, swiftly leaning over to gently blow into the small flame to make it become bigger.

For a moment, the small flame flickered as if it were going to extinguish, but with Amora's help the flame grew and spread across the other leaves. Once satisfied the fire had properly caught onto the wood, Magnar added a couple more sturdy branches to the campfire and encircled it with additional rocks he had found. Next, he spotted a large dead root lying on the ground already half-broken and he dragged it closer to the fire.

"Take off your coat and shoes," he said, slipping his arms out of Mr. Higgins' soggy coat and tossing it over the broken root—along with slipping out of his shoes to place them next to the fire, too. "We can dry everything out while we get some sleep."

"Okay," was all that she could muster up to say in her numb state. Quietly, she peeled off her wet coat and placed it over the root, and then removed her shoes and sat them next to the fire to dry.

"We'll rest a few hours and then try to find some berries or nuts to eat. There's got to be something edible growing in these woods," he said, curling up on the ground and trying to get into a decent position for sleep. "Are you going to be okay?" he asked, worried that she wasn't saying much and still seemed deeply bothered by everything that had happened, and rightfully so.

"I don't know! I feel... nothing!" she blurted. "I don't feel anything about anything right now," she confessed while trying to find a place to sleep on the ground close to the fire—somewhere she would be comfortable enough to drift off for a few hours.

"Feeling numb seems like a good emotion to have after everything that's happened. You're probably just tired. We both are," he said, yawning and closing his eyes with his head laying against the crook of his arm.

"But—" she hesitated.

"You're lucky. I wish all I felt right now was numb," he interrupted.

"You seem fine to me."

"Then I'm a better pretender than I thought. My mind is spinning with the memories of everything that's happened and with... the guilt," he revealed, and paused as his words sank into the silence of the woods. "If I'd obeyed the rules and just stayed

185

out of the restricted section of the bookstore… if I hadn't read that book… if I hadn't showed it to you," he continued on with every word seeming to sound more choked in his throat than the last. He struggled to fight against the sorrow welling up inside himself in order to explain that she was not the only one having difficulty processing all that had happened. "What I'm trying to say is none of this would have happened if it wasn't for me. I'm… I'm sorry Amora," Quietly, he sobbed and wiped away the water pooling in his eyes with his free hand, missing those that had splashed down onto the arm he was using as a makeshift pillow underneath his head.

"I won't let you do this. No. You can't take the blame for everything that's happened!" she snapped, leaning up on her elbow next to the fire to look over at him. What happened was not your fault!"

"Amora, if I'd left that book alone, then the goblins would have stayed wherever they came from. They wouldn't have come to Bernard in the first place. Our town wouldn't have been destroyed, and the black swarm of Vulturks wouldn't have attacked us. I know you're trying to be kind, but face it… everything that happened was because of me," he maintained, giving further in to his self-pity and guilt.

"I understand that you feel responsible, but I think that you were destined to find the truth. Someone eventually had to, and it was your instincts that did it. Somehow, you knew something wasn't right, and you went digging around to prove it. None of this is your fault. You didn't attack us, and you're not the one who sent those goblins into Bernard, and you didn't order our town to be burnt to the ground or its people captured and carted off to who knows where. No! All of that was done by someone else, and I bet we both know who that was," she stated steadfastly, and watched his head lift up off the crook of his arm for his eyes to meet with hers across the other side of the fire. "I know the same thought has crossed your mind at least once."

"You think the DARK ONE we read about in the book is somehow still alive and did those things?"

"Yes. That's exactly what I think. That's who sent the Vulturk to follow us at the bookstore, the Vulturk swarm, and the goblins."

Magnar laid back down and rested his head back against the crook of his arm and proceeded to close his eyes with a big yawn. "Even if you're right… what can we do about it?"

"I don't know. Maybe nothing," she said, copying him and resting her head also in the crook of her arm. The warmth of the fire felt good against her skin and the crackling sounds of the wood slowed the racing thoughts in her mind. She could feel her eyelids growing heavier with every passing second as she struggled to stay awake in order to finish their conversation, but sleep was coming for her like a thief in the night seeking to whisk her away into an abyss filled with dreams to escape her own sorrow. Frankly, she welcomed the opportunity to leave her problems behind, even if it was only for a few hours. "We can try to figure out where they took our parents. Maybe there's a way to rescue them," she said, yawning and giving in to what felt like a ton of weights forcing her eyelids closed.

"Yeah, but there's something I forgot to tell you."

"What?" she asked, letting out another big yawn and listening to the crackles of the flames against the wood, and enjoying the heat against her face while she waited for him to answer. "Magnar... what did you forget to tell me?" she asked again, struggling to reopen her eyes to see him across from her on the other side of the campfire. Red and orange sparks flew up into the air as the flames embraced the wood and she watched several float up, until disappearing altogether. "Magnar, are you still awake?" she asked softly.

"Maze... white werewolves..." he mumbled, his voice trailing off as he fell asleep into the deep abyss of dreams waiting for him.

"What did you say?" she sleepily asked, her own eyes too heavy now to remain open. Again, another long yawn escaped her lips and she took in a deep, comforting breath of the crisp cold air mixed with the scent of the burning campfire wood. "I didn't hear you," her slurred voice trailed off as she, too, surrendered to the sweet abyss of dreams far away from her problems.

CHAPTER SEVENTEEN

Howlers

*U*nnoticeably, the hours rolled by one after another beneath the autumn canopy as the flickering flames of the campfire dwindled to the soft glow of reddish-orange embers. Occasionally, specks of orange drifted up into the air while the wood whistled and popped, sending fragrant swirls of smoke up from the logs and hot ash. While the two slept, the last rays of daylight faded and soon the forest had reclaimed its perfect darkness—as the last flame ceased with a final puff of smoke. Only the residual warmth in the embers kept the cold at bay while they sank deeper into the abyss of dreams as they laid curled up on the ground with their head lying comfortably on the crook of an arm.

Blissfully, each one's subconscious mind plunged them into happier times filled with laughter among friends, and joyous gatherings at parties where foods were plentiful and spread across from one end of the table to the other with drinks flowing freely. Soft smiles stretched the corners of Amora's and Magnar's mouth as they dreamed of children playing alongside those tables while parents danced to boisterous music, ate, drank, and made witty toasts with mugs held high up with the other guests. Deeper into the dream abyss they sank—each dream seeming more real than the last.

Abruptly, long, high pitched howls, "Ooooooooooooo," pierced the air and jolted Magnar awake! Straightaway, he sat up with his eyes wide open and looked around in every direction— his eyes darting left and right—to see what was making the howls. However, no matter how hard he strained his eyes in the darkness he couldn't see anything more than vague shapes of trees.

"Ooooooooooooo!"

There it was again! More howls rang out from somewhere within the forest, but it sounded as if more voices had joined in! At once, Magnar sprang to his feet! His heart was beginning to pound in his chest—a feeling he was coming to know all too well– –and quickly he began to search around in the dark for Amora. He needed to wake her, but could not risk calling out her name for fear of drawing unwanted attention from whatever creatures were making the howls. If what he suspected them to be was true, then alerting them to their presence in Kembrull Forest was definitely something he would rather not risk doing, but the howls were growing louder and closer... fast!

Quietly, he scrambled around in the darkness with hands held out to feel for where Amora was sleeping on the ground. Upon feeling the side of her arm, he tripped over a partially exposed tree root (he swore it hadn't been there before) but quickly regained his balance and stooped down next to Amora to shake her awake and cover her mouth with his hand.

Again, the howls rang through the air, "Oooooooooooo."

"Amora. Shh, don't make a sound. We're not alone," he whispered, giving her a gentle shake to wake her from her sweet slumber.

Frustrated, she jerked her arm away from his hand and wanted nothing more than to return to her dreams—pleasantly miles away from reality. "What is it?" she grumbled, yawning and refusing to open her tired eyes.

However, before he could answer, another long howl rang out, "Oooooooooooo!"

Instantly with eyes wide open, Amora sat up straight and looked in the direction of the frightening howl, but her eyes saw nothing but the encompassing darkness. Immediately, another set of howls picked up where the last had left off, but this time in a different direction! At once, she felt her heart beating faster and the pace of her breath quickening at the surge of adrenaline in her veins. She could taste the fear in her mouth—a metallic bitter taste that coated her tongue as panic took hold of her.

"What are those sounds?" she whispered, no longer feeling tired, but instead wide awake with a renewed sense of urgency.

"Those?" he asked, listening to another wave of howls. "That's the reason I woke you," he stated, up righting himself off the ground and helping her to do the same—both taking a moment to listen to another set of them.

"Ooooooooo... Ooooooooo... Oooooooooo!"

Neither were able to determine from what direction they were coming from. Some of the howls seemed close, but others were softer and seemed to be coming from somewhere deeper within the forest.

Again, Magnar tried to see through the darkness, but all he could make out were more trees and the lichens hanging down from them like nets that might ensnare those who weren't careful.

"Do you know what's making those howls?" Amora asked, reaching down to the root she'd laid her coat over and sat her shoes next to. Hurriedly, she gathered them up and put on the shoes and dry garment—buttoning it up. Then, she slid her hands along the dry rough root to find where Magnar had placed his items and kindly handed them over for him to put them on.

193

"Thanks," he said, taking his shoes and the oversized black coat from her hands. "White werewolves," he whispered, as he slipped on his shoes.

"What did you say? I couldn't hear you."

"White werewolves," he repeated, this time louder. "White werewolves are making the howls. At least, I think that's whose making them. I read about them in one of the books back at the bookstore. Someone had left it lying on a table, and I was going around the store that evening collecting the books people had decided not to buy. I was placing them back onto the shelves when an image on the front cover of one caught my eyes. It was a simple drawing of an animal I had never seen before. Being curious, I sat down and read a few of the pages and they were about white werewolves that live in Kembrull Forest."

"And you're telling me this, NOW!" Amora snapped, upset that he had not warned her before venturing into the forest.

"We weren't supposed to go past the outskirts. The werewolves have never been seen in that part," he reasoned.

"Well, we're obviously *way* past the outskirts now!" she snapped again, trying to keep her voice low enough to refrain from alerting the werewolves to their location.

"I know, but we can't turn back. I'm sorry, but I thought I was doing the right thing."

"Why can't we?" she asked, taking in a calming breath to soothe her frayed nerves.

"Well, for one thing, I have no idea where we are, or how to find my way back to Bernard if I wanted to. Secondly, some of the goblins may have stayed behind in Bernard in case we returned," he explained.

For a moment, neither spoke as they listened to more howls coming from all directions within the forest—some louder and closer than others.

"Okay, what now?" Amora asked, after taking the time to breath and take hold of her nerves—at least enough to think rationally about the new situation she now reluctantly found herself in.

"Now, we get through Kembrull Forest."

"I can barely see my hand in front of my face. How are we supposed to find our way out?"

"Keep putting one foot in front of the other. We must've slept long into the night, so it'll be daylight soon, but until then, step carefully and stay close. We don't want to become separated," he instructed, looking around to determine the best direction to head towards. "Let's go this way," he said, pointing to the far side in front of them.

"How do you know that's the right way?"

"I don't, but we came from that direction over there," he answered, pointing behind them. "So, we should keep moving this way across the forest, till we reach the other side. Maybe we can find a town once we're outta here."

"Okay, but why not the other two ways?"

"Well, the loudest howls seem to be coming from those. That probably means the white werewolves are traveling those two paths. Even if one of them *is* the right way... it's too dangerous," he reasoned in his matter-of-fact tone. "The only good option is this way," he said, again pointing straight ahead beyond the nets of dangling lichens and a number of spooky looking trees with oddly contorted branches.

Instantly, Amora felt her gut sour at the sight of the creepy trees lining the way he had chosen, but she knew he was right. At this point, the only way to get through Kembrull Forest was to go deeper into it in order to reach the other side of the outskirts. However, it would lead them through ominous tree-arches that seemed to be the beginning of a waking-nightmare that would not bode well for anyone.

"Magnar, I don't like the look of those. I don't feel good about this the least little bit," she stated, dreading the path ahead.

"I know, but it's the only way," he said, taking the first step towards the darkest path.

CHAPTER EIGHTEEN
The Trees

Forward, Amora carefully walked with Magnar beneath the natural archway—periodically tilting her head to look up at the branches as she passed underneath them. Immediately, her pulse quickened and every molecule inside herself screamed that she should turn back, but she could not. Step-by-step, she closely followed behind him deeper into the forest. With each step (slow, careful, and precise) they moved through the darkness, stepping over broken branches and rotten roots that jutted up from the ground. The dangling lichens clung to their coats with their tendrils, causing them to forcibly pull off the strands. Gradually, the air became colder, the wind was still, and the howls had lessened to only a few sporadic ones. Perhaps the white werewolves had become distracted by something and were no longer tracking them. Maybe the trek through Kembrull Forest was not going to be as bad as she had

197

thought. Maybe, everything was somehow going to be okay... maybe.

"What else did you learn in that book about the white werewolves?" she asked, hoping he might reveal some minor detail that would ease her mind.

"I read it a long time ago, but I think it said something about them having a ghostly appearance, and they're quick!" he said, trying to remember the details from the few pages he had read.

"Oh, great! That means they'll be practically impossible to outrun if they start chasing us!" she shrugged, stepping over several more large chunks of broken branches littered on the forest floor. "Anything else I should know?"

"Only that no one who's ever entered into Kembrull Forest beyond the outskirts has ever been seen again, but that doesn't mean that's what's going to happen to us!"

"Well, that's encouraging," she huffed, feeling a scratchy sensation at the back of her throat as she spoke. Come to think of it, she could not remember the last time she'd had anything to drink, and her stomach had been hungrily growling for the past hour. Frankly, she wondered how Magnar had not noticed the loud sounds yet, but she guessed he was probably just as hungry, too, and he had not heard hers due to the loudness of his own.

"Wait, I remember one more thing," he said, thinking back to something vague he had read.

198

"What?"

"It was the last thing I read before putting the book away. Something about the forest and a maze."

"A maze… what do you mean?" she asked, as another growl rumbled through her empty stomach, causing her to place a hand over the empty organ.

"I can't remember any more than that," he stated, pushing aside a low hanging section of lichens that were dangling from a branch. Kindly, he held them to the side for Amora to pass through too before letting them go. "It was time to close that night and I didn't think much of the book at the time. So, I put it away and finished up some other things. Then, I locked up the store and went home… never looked for it again."

Again, Amora's stomach growled, but at least she was beginning to get a better look at the trees and shrubs with daylight approaching—the first few rays were starting to push through the canopy. "It's almost morning," she said, gesturing upwards at the rays poking through the leafy roof.

"Good. Maybe we'll finally find a way outta here," he replied, looking around and studying the natural structures they were passing by. "We've been walking for hours and I still can't figure out if we're going in the right direction, or if we're any closer to the outskirts."

"Yeah," she sighed, barely paying attention to his words as she searched the ground for fallen nuts. "Do you think this forest has anything we can eat? Maybe some berries or tree nuts…"

"I don't know, but I wouldn't trust anything even if you did find something. Who knows what's poisonous, here."

"Yeah, you're probably right," she agreed, cringing at yet another hunger pang.

"The sooner we find our way outta here, the sooner we can find a town and get some food," he said, urging her to keep moving, despite having the same hungry feeling inside the pit of his own stomach.

Quietly, the two continued walking onwards past wiry shrubs covered with thorns and thin trees that reached high into the canopy. However, the further they walked, the more the trees began to seem… different. First, Amora noticed the change in their branches. They were no longer thin, but were now fatter, and most had pointy tips on their ends that resembled spears—nothing like natural wood.

Next, she noticed the bark was beginning to look different, too, within the soft light. The bark appeared thicker, tougher, and older with specks of grey, and there was some sort of reddish substance that stained sections of the trees. Interestingly, not a single leaf grew where the stains were. As she passed underneath the huge heavy tree branches stained with the muddied reddish

color, she apprehensively darted her eyes back and forth...
searching for danger.

"*That's odd*," she thought to herself, looking up at their
contorted shapes.

KEMBRULL FOREST... the Dark Woods

Quietly, she continued walking behind Magnar, who did not seem to be paying much attention to the eerie scenery surrounding them. Instead, he was completely focused on something else. She guessed he was probably trying to keep track of the natural landmarks they had passed in order to keep track of where they were, and to figure a way out of Kembrull Forest. Of course, he did not have time to observe the changes in the trees as intently as she did, but a nagging feeling was tugging at her that it was important she make him aware of it. There was something *very strange* about these trees and she couldn't quite figure out what it was.

Several times she had heard what sounded like bark cracking along the trees they had recently passed, and once she thought she had seen the movement of a branch! Yes! Amora felt there was something definitely weird going on in this part of the forest. The trees felt alive with a *dark presence.* They had an *evil* energy to them....

There it was again... the cracking noise! Quickly, her eyes darted in the direction it came from—somewhere in the distance, maybe to the right. *Over there! Was that a tree twisting itself towards them? No! It couldn't be!* she told herself, hoping her eyes were playing tricks on her. Unfortunately, a foreboding feeling was sinking into the empty pit of her stomach as she squinted her eyes in the pale morning light. Suddenly, an awful thought crossed her mind, *the trees were watching them!*

"Magnar wait. I need to get a closer look at something," she said, walking away from him towards a fat tree with blackish-grey bark and low hanging branches stained with the reddish substance.

"Why? What are you looking for?" he asked, halting his steps and watching her walk towards the tree—which was similar to dozens of others surrounding them.

Cautiously, she neared it and studied the details in the wood. Pieces of bark had been chipped off a branch, as if something or someone had torn them away in a struggle… and there were *claw marks!*

"Magnar! Come here and have a look at this," she said.

"At what? It's a tree," he replied, uninterested and thinking this was a waste of time, but obliging her anyway. "Okay, I'm here. What do you want me to see?" he asked, standing beside her in front of the tree.

"There's something odd about this tree," she whispered, not taking her eyes off it. "Look… there," she instructed, pointing to one of the long white lines scratched across the wood. "What does that look like?"

"Amora, we don't have time for this. We need to go," he replied, looking away from it.

"I'm serious! I need you to look," she sternly insisted. "Tell me what these lines look like to you."

Reluctantly, Magnar sighed and turned to face the tree to study the lines she was pointing to. Quickly, he glanced at them, but just as he was about to turn away again and spit out a slick answer to appease her, he spotted another set of the lines on a higher branch. Carefully, he backed away from the tree, keeping his eyes glued to the lines, until he was far enough away to look the entire tree over. It was covered in the white claw-mark lines and reddish stains!

Immediately, Amora knew something was horribly wrong! "Magnar, what's the matter? Why do you have that look on your face?" she asked, stepping away from the tree towards him.

"There," he pointed.

Amora turned around and followed his eyes with hers to see the tree was covered with claw-marks, causing her to gasp at the sight of them.

"It's not just the marks I'm looking at. Look at the long one, right there, in the middle of the tree. Do you see it?" he asked.

"The claw-mark... yes, I see it."

"No. Not that. Look harder and trace the line with your eyes. Do you see what's *inside it*?" he asked, his voice cracking at the thought.

Carefully, Amora's eyes traced the claw-mark and soon she had found it, too... the object that had spooked Magnar with understandable fear!

"Is that—" she paused, unable to finish her question.

"It's a white werewolf's nail," he affirmed, his voice trailing off and his face becoming pale.

Quietly, they stood and stared up at the nail stuck in the tree. Their minds raced at the endless possibilities of how it got there and about what the reddish substance covering many of the trees might be.

CHAPTER NINETEEN

The Goo

*T*heories filled Amora's head about what the reddish substance could be, and without thinking, she reached a hand up to a low hanging branch and touched it.

"Stop! Don't touch that!" Magnar urged, swiftly pulling her hand away from it. "You don't know what that stuff is!"

"It feels thick and wet," she stated, rubbing the viscous goo between her fingers. "It's oily." With curiosity, she gave her fingers a sniff. The goo badly stunk, causing her to turn away in repulsion! "Whatever this stuff is, it smells horrible… like something died." Instantly, as the words left her lips, she realized maybe that was exactly what had happened! "Wait a second… this stuff can't be," she paused, looking at Magnar's face for confirmation that he was thinking the same thing.

As if reading her thoughts, he nodded in agreement. "I think so, too," he confirmed—his eyes large with worry. "It's blood. Some of that reddish stuff... *is blood.*

"But how?" she asked, not expecting an answer she knew he was unable to give. Suddenly, her fingers began to burn, and the goo changed to a darker hue. "Ouch!" she yelled, gripping her fingers tightly with her other hand.

"What's wrong?" he asked, wanting to help without any idea of how.

"It burns!" she cried, grimacing in pain and frantically rubbing her fingers against the fabric of her coat—trying to remove the goo. "I think it's eating my skin!"

"What? It can't be!" Quickly, Magnar took hold of her hand and examined the raw, reddening skin that had been exposed to the substance. She was right! The thin top layer of each digit was dissolving! Magnar's stomach soured and vomit climbed up into his throat at the sight of the exposed tissue, but he looked away and swallowed it back down.

"How bad is it?" she asked, staring down at the dirt and leaves on the forest floor to keep from looking at her hand.

Bravely, he looked again at the swollen red fingers, and decided it was better not to worry her. There was nothing either of them could do at the moment to make the injury better, and their main focus needed to be on getting out of Kembrull Forest as soon as possible. Then, he would find her some help... someone to heal her fingers.

"Magnar, how bad is it?" she repeated.

"It's not as bad as you think... probably just feels worse than it is," he lied, hoping to ease her concern. "Once we get out of this forest, we'll find a town and search for someone that can help. There's bound to be somebody who'll have the medicine we need to properly treat it."

"Okay," she replied, removing her hand from his, but still keeping her eyes from looking at it. "Let's get out of here. I don't want to end up like whoever died on this tree." "Right," he agreed, looking around at all the other fat trees with dark stains splattered on their limbs and trunks.

"Wait a second," she whispered, her brow furrowing as she pondered over a question that had popped into her head. "If some of the stains are blood, then where are the bodies or the bones? Shouldn't there be some carnage left-over from whatever happened?"

"I've been thinking about that, too. Maybe part of that reddish stuff is some sort of flesh-eating enzyme the trees excrete from their bark, and it attacks whatever it comes into contact with. Over time, the enzyme helps the tree to eat its victim by dissolving their flesh and bones into a digestible liquid the tree's roots can absorb," he suggested, with a rather disgusted expression on his face at the idea of *man-eating trees*.

"You think these trees are actually capable of eating people?" she asked, looking up at the tree in front her with tingling fear sensitizing her skin.

"I know… a scary thought right," he replied. A cold chill ran down the length of his spine and his body shuddered. "Come on, we better get moving. We've still gotta find a way out of Kembrull Forest before the next sun set, or else we're gonna have a long night."

"After you," she said, motioning for him to resume leading the way.

With a nod, he walked back toward the area they had detoured from, "I think it was this way."

CHAPTER TWENTY
The Life Within

*A*s they journeyed deep into the heart of Kembrull Forest, all either could see were hundreds of sinister looking trees looming ahead, but bravely they continued their journey. Dry brittle leaves rustled and crunched beneath their shoes as they stepped carefully over rocks and roots, ducked beneath low branches, and pushed aside nets of lichens. Nervously, they looked up as they passed beneath huge branches that had become entwined in a sort of gripping embrace—dripping the reddish goo into puddles beneath them on the forest floor.

The light from the noon sun penetrated the canopy enough to illuminate the area better for them to see where they were going... slightly warming the forest from the morning's bitter cold. Strategically, Magnar tried to keep mental notes of the natural landmarks they had passed to prevent from walking in circles, but twice he thought he had seen the same funny looking tree.

"Magnar," Amora said, interrupting the silence between them.

"Yes?" he asked, stepping over another root haphazardly poking out of the ground. He noticed each root seemed perfectly positioned in various ways to cause either of them to trip, and the forest appeared to be filled with more of them now, than earlier.

"I was wondering about something," she continued.

"What?"

"I was thinking about the claw-marks we saw."

"Yeah, what about them?"

"Do you really think those trees could eat a white werewolf or…. a person," she choked out, looking down at the ground and stepping carefully over several more roots. "Can a tree really do that?"

"I don't know, but I'd say that's probably the most unlikely, but yet reasonable answer. To tell you the truth, nothing in this place would surprise me." Unexpectedly, Magnar let out a tiny chuckle, "Guess we know the reason no one ever lived to tell any stories about Kembrull Forest."

"I knew you were going to say that," she laughed, mustering what little strength she could.

Abruptly, a loud cracking sound spun Amora's head to look behind her—a rather nasty looking fat tree covered in ashen-grey bark and stains had lost a branch. Frozen in place, Amora stood staring at it… expecting to see the tree move. However, nothing was happening, but Magnar was quickly getting farther away. Filled with anxiety at the thought of being alone near the creepy plant, Amora quickly ran to catch up!

"You okay?" he asked, barely noticing that she had not been there the entire time.

"I'm fine," she replied, taking in a gulp of air with a quick glance over her shoulder back at the tree—swearing its position had somehow already slightly changed. "That's weird," she mumbled.

"Did you say something?" Magnar asked, focusing most of his attention on mentally taking notes of the odd landmarks and getting them out of the woods.

"How do you think the trees... g–get their victims?" she stuttered, continuing their conversation in an effort to take her mind off her sore feet, empty stomach, and the fear of being grabbed and eaten alive by the plants.

"I was wondering the same thing," he replied. "It must have something to do with those cracking sounds we keep hearing... and the ends of their branches... look at that one over there," he said, pointing to a long crooked branch. "Its tip looks like a spear. They probably move when someone's not looking and gore them with *those* things... like a meat-kabob on a stick."

"I feel like they're watching us... waiting for us to trip or something, so they can kabob us."

"I've been feeling the same way, too, and those cracking sounds—" he paused, looking up at another group of trees towering overhead with interlocking branches—another natural archway for them to pass underneath.

"Go on," she urged.

"Well, it's just that—" again he paused.

"What is it? Go on... tell me," she insisted.

"You're not going to like what I'm thinking," he cautioned.

"I know, but there's very little that you could say in a place like this that I'd actually like. Just spit it out and get it over with. What is it that you're thinking?"

"Well, I think the trees have been trying to... catch us. They're hunting... *and we're the prey.*"

Upon his frightening words, Amora gasped... her eyes darted back and forth at all the sudden cracks of bark throughout the forest.

Magnar took in a big gulp of the crisp air and blew it out in a long sigh—briefly fogging it in front of his face. "The sounds we've been hearing... I know what's causing them."

"Go on... what?" she asked, biting her lower lip anxiously... worried that what he would say next was going to send her over the edge of tolerable insanity.

"They're coming from the trees… from them shifting their branches towards us after we've walked past them… and sometimes before," he said, nervously looking around.

"No!" she exclaimed, suddenly noticing the increasing number of branches pointing towards them. *Trees can't do that… right?* she asked herself. "A few minutes ago, I thought I saw one of them move! I knew it! I heard a loud cracking noise and caught it moving out the corners of my eyes! It stopped the moment I turned around."

"I have more bad news," Magnar whispered, hesitating to look at her.

"I know I'm not going to like this," she huffed. A sudden rush of blood surged through the nooks and crannies inside her head and banged against the nerve endings, causing a painful headache to set in as she waited for him to continue. She already knew exactly what he was going to say, because it was the very thing she had been fearing since they had come into the dreadful forest—something that ended with the words… *we're lost.*

"The landmarks… I've been keeping track of them, but they're changing," he stated. "Groups of mushrooms, scattered patterns of rocks, and nets of lichens were my marks to remember."

"Go on…" she encouraged.

"Well, we've started doubling-back and passing them a few times. At first, I thought maybe I had just remembered them wrong, but it kept happening, and now I'm sure we're lost."

There... the words she had been hoping not to hear had been said. They stung like pointy thorns, and suddenly her headache was worse! Heavy thoughts raced through her mind as the words, *we're lost*, sunk deeper into her consciousness. She asked herself a myriad of questions:

Did we escape the goblins just to be turned into plant food?
Are the ghostly white werewolves going to find us huddled
somewhere by a tree in the middle of the night and mercilessly
attack us?
Had the goblins been smarter than us, because at least they knew
better than to run into Kembrull Forest?
Would we have been better off captured in one of those cages
being hauled to the dungeons by the load-pullers?
Are either of us ever going to see our parents again?

"Did you hear me? I said we're lost," he repeated, wondering why she had not said anything. "You okay?"

Amora forced her eyes to look at him—despite the headache that made her head feel as if it weighed several more pounds than

216

it did. However, as she opened her mouth to form a reply, howls in the distance stole her attention!

"Wait. Did you hear that?" she whispered, gripping his arm in a frightened clutch and peering over her shoulder to look behind herself towards the direction the sounds had come from. Again, the howls rang out... this time followed by more cracking of tree bark.

"I heard them too," he whispered, desperately searching in the dim light for signs of white werewolf movement.

Here... there... no... over there! Howls pierced the forest from multiple directions!

"Where are they coming from?" Amora asked.

"I don't know, but listen... did you here that?" he asked, turning to the right.

"Here what?" she replied, turning to follow his eyes to see what he was intently staring at.

"Over there. I heard something... it sounded close. Look at that grey tree between those tall thin ones," he whispered, pointing to a short swollen tree covered in the reddish stains a few yards away. "I think the noise came from there."

"Look! Its branches are pointing directly at us!" Amora said, noticing the other trees around it had their branches pointing in normal directions—up, down, left, and right.

"It's hunting us!"

217

All of a sudden, a huge gust of wind *whooshed* past Amora and Magnar just as the entire forest erupted with the sounds of cracking bark! The tops of the trees swayed as the wind passed through them, and several large branches collided with others— sending splinters of wood tumbling to the ground. Debris of leaves and soil swooshed high into the air and into Amora's and Magnar's faces as they tried to shield themselves with their hands, waiting for the strong gust to pass.

"Let's get outta here!" Amora shouted over the roar of the wind. "Do you know which way?"

"No!" he yelled back.

"Well, staying here isn't an option! It looks like there are several pathways up ahead, but I don't have a clue where we are. Magnar, it's up to you to choose one of them. Pick one!" she ordered, fearing if they didn't leave at that very moment, a tree branch from above might come crashing down on them.

Frantic, Magnar looked in every direction and computed all the possible routes as quickly as he could. *This way? That way? Over there? We should go that way! Wait. No! Maybe that way,* he contemplated.

"This way!" he said, faking confidence in his decision while eyeing a narrow dirt path he hadn't noticed before. Without hesitation he said, "Follow me," and quickly took off running toward the dirt path that *zigged* and *zagged* between trees, lichens, and shrubbery.

"Come on! Faster!" he urged, running as fast as his feet could carry him!

"I'm trying to!" Amora fussed, trying to catch up behind him. With barely enough time look ahead of herself, she jumped over large roots poking up from the ground and ducked beneath branches—losing her balance only once after an unnoticed branch swung out at her, causing her to briefly stumble as she dodged it.

Swiftly, they ran along the path, following its twists and turns as the forest came alive! Huge branches crashed against each other as they cracked themselves loose in an effort to spear them… each one only a second too late!

"We've got to find a way outta here!" Amora yelled, her heart pounding and lungs burning with each breath of the sharp cold air.

"Look! Over there! Do you see it?" he shouted.

"See what?"

"Up there! It looks like a big wall or something… made of bushes… and tall! If we can find a way inside it, we'll be safe from the trees!" Magnar's eyes traced the length of the green wall in the distance. It appeared to reach high into the canopy above, and as far left-to-right as he could see. "Come on! Look for a way inside!"

219

"Magnar, wait! I don't think this is a good idea!" Amora warned, but Magnar wasn't listening.

"Come on! I think I see a hole we can squeeze through… there!" Magnar shouted, pointing up ahead to a small empty space within the wall, but it was past a cluster of deadly-looking plump trees covered with grey bark and the reddish stains… with their branches already pointed towards them.

Hard and fast Magnar ran with his heart pounding rapidly in his chest, and the muscles in his legs were burning with fatigue, but still he rushed towards the green wall standing in the midst of the forest. He was determined Kembrull Forest was not going to claim their lives!

"Amora! You keeping up? Are you with me?" he asked, glancing over his shoulder to make sure she had not fallen too far behind him since his legs were longer than hers, which benefitted him with a longer stride.

However, before she could answer him, her eyes widened with horror! "Magnar, watch out!" she shouted.

Immediately, he slid as he tried to come to a halt after turning back around and realizing that he had already reached the cluster of engorged trees.

CHAPTER TWENTY-ONE
Doubt

*I*nstantly, the tree cracked loose its long, creepy, spear-tipped branches. Then, it swung them at Magnar just as he was sprinting past them! Amora watched with horror as the largest branch slammed hard against his chest and sent him flying high into the air! For a moment, he appeared suspended above the forest floor before gravity plummeted him back down with a painful and loud *thud*!

"Magnar!" A blood-curdling scream leapt from Amora's throat as she ducked beneath the tree's branches to rush to his side! Quickly, she slid onto her knees in the dirt next to him—her voice filled with panic and fear as she checked over his body for injuries.

"Magnar, are you okay? Magnar... please, answer me. Are you okay? Sit up slowly... is anything broken?" Right away, Amora helped him sit upright as he shook away the hazy daze inside his brain from hitting his head against a rock. Slowly, he comprehended what had happened and took in a few shallow breaths—wincing as the air re-inflated the lungs inside his bruised chest. A sharp pain stabbed at his tender ribs as he did so, causing him to erupt with several dry coughs and spat dirt mixed with saliva onto the ground.

"Don't speak if it hurts too much," she cautioned, softly brushing away the loose dirt and bits of leaves from his hair and clothes.

"I—I—I didn't see it," he stammered, choking on the last remnants of dirt inside his mouth—grimacing at the awful taste. He figured if a person mixed dead insects, decayed plants, and animal droppings together, then that would be close to the disgusting mixture on his tongue!

"Come on, I'll help you up," she said, looking back at the tree—feeling relieved they had managed to get by the first one in the cluster. After standing up, Amora reached down and helped hoist her friend onto his feet and shake off the remaining debris.

"Thanks," he said, placing a hand over his throbbing chest where the branch had knocked into him.

"You would've done the same for me. Now, we have to find a way past the rest of them," she said, pointing towards the others within the cluster up ahead… in front of the green wall.

"Maybe, we can try to go around them," he suggested, trying to take a step forward, but stumbling as the pain in his ankle shot up through his leg. "Ouch!" he hollered, abruptly lifting the foot off the ground and falling onto his rear.

Quickly, Amora knelt back down next to him and asked, "What wrong?" as he tightly gripped his ankle.

"It's my ankle... I must've twisted it."

"I can't look at it here. We need to get you up and moving... place your arms over my shoulder and I'll help you. Lean as much of your weight on me as you can, but you'll have to find a way to push your mind past the pain, until we can find a safe place to rest."

"No. I'm too heavy... I'll be fine. Just give me a moment," he shrugged, rubbing his sore ankle and looking at the trees ahead. "I need you to make sure we stick together when we run past those things," he stated, frustrated with himself that he had gotten hurt and was going to slow them down at the worst possible time.

"Stop it! Stop being so stubborn and take my hand for goodness sake!" she firmly insisted, knowing that his pride had been wounded and he was sulking like a child. Right now, the only thing that mattered was finding a way out of the forest before the white werewolves returned at twilight.

Reluctantly, Magnar realized there was no use in denying she had the better idea between the two of them. So, without another word, he stretched out his hand and took hold of hers with a defeated sigh.

"Good. We agree on something," she said, relieved that the conversation wasn't going to turn into a pointless debate. Tightly she gripped his hand with both of hers and leaned back to use her body weight to pull him off his backside up onto his feet.

"Ouch!" he complained, accidentally placing too much of his weight onto the injured foot—hobbling as he lifted it off the ground and placed more weight onto her shoulders as he draped an arm across them.

"Whoa, take it easy. I've got you," she reassured him, supporting his weight.

"No. I knew I should've done this myself. I'm gonna slow you down. Without me, at least you've got a chance! All you need to do is make it past those trees to the inside of that wall. Then high-tail it out of Kembrull Forest! I'm sorry I brought you here... to this place. I thought it was the right thing to do... but I was wrong. Amora, you've got to make it out of this forest. Leave me here if you have to." Slowly, Magnar tried to place the entirety of his body weight onto his injured foot, but within seconds the pain re-flooded the injured tissues and forced him to lift it back off the ground again—gripping Amora's shoulders even tighter.

"Enough! We're both going to live past tonight... if that's okay with you! Now, let me help you and no more arguing about it! If you end up staying... then so am I," she demanded, piercing his eyes with a stern look that meant business.

"O—okay," he stammered, relenting to her decision.

Firmly, she took hold of his arm around her neck, steadied herself, and received the full amount of his weight—except for what was distributed on his good leg.

"Now, think you can take a step forward?" she asked, taking it slow, until he got used to walking this way.

"I guess I don't have much choice."

"Don't think about the pain… just focus on getting past those trees," she instructed, knowing that if he accidentally placed too much weight on the foot while running, he would be in excruciating pain.

Fluid anxiety rushed through his veins in anticipation of the pain, but bravely he gave her a nod that he was ready and braced himself mentally for what was coming.

"Alright, on the count of three. Ready?"

Again, he nodded—not taking his eyes off the trees ahead.

"One… two… three!" Together, they lurched forward!

CHAPTER TWENTY-TWO
The Hollow Within the Wall

S wiftly, the two sprinted towards the trees and ducked beneath their unhinged swinging branches! "Whew! We made it!" Amora cheered, coming to a halt on the other side of them in order to help Magnar steady himself—his arm still gripped her firmly across the shoulders.

Heaving his chest in-an-out, he took in a few gulps of air, then confidently said, "I knew we would… didn't have a doubt."

"Yeah. I'm sure," Amora replied, smiling as a small laugh left her throat.

"Now, we just need to get through… *there*," he said, gesturing at the hole within the shrubs comprising the wall in front of them.

"Hold on. You can't possibly think we're going through there?" Amora asked, pointing at the dark mysterious gap. "No!

We can't! Those bushes are covered with thorns! We need to find another way," she fussed, shaking her head and refusing to take another step.

"I don't like it any more than you do, but unless you see another way inside... we have to."

"Maybe if I walk the length of the wall, I'll find another way in."

"No. I'm not leaving you alone. Whatever we do... we do together," Magnar insisted, giving the wall a good thorough look for any other ways inside, but there was only the one hole. "Right here is our best chance, but we can't stand around any longer talking about it. Looks like the sun is already starting to set... that means the white werewolves will be coming out to hunt soon, and I don't want to be caught between them and those trees... if you know what I mean."

Agreeably, Amora shook her head, *yes*, as Magnar carefully leaned his head into the hole and inspected it. "From what I can see—which isn't much—looks like something mid-sized forced its way through the wall right here, all the way clear over to the other side. I think there'll be enough room for both of us to squeeze through... one behind the other, but we'll have to take it slow."

"What do you think it was? What could have gotten through there?" Amora asked, trying to look over his shoulder into the mysterious hollow.

"I don't know, but I'd guess it was one of the white werewolves probably trying to escape the trees... same as us."

"Magnar... I'm scared. What if it's still in there?"

The pupils in Amora's eyes widened with fear as she calculated the numerous ways they could die if they foolishly entered inside the wall—neither knew what was waiting for them beyond the narrow passage, but their options to do otherwise were limited. With the dense canopy of foliage blocking out the sun's light overhead, the forest was quickly dimming, and nighttime was approaching earlier than its normal due within Kembrull Forest. If there was hope of finding another town, they would have to journey into the wall—stepping deeper into the deadly heart of the forest in order to find a way out.

"Alright," Amora grumbled. "Let's get this over with, but are you going to be okay on that ankle? I won't be able to help you."

"Don't worry. I'll manage. I can crawl just fine, so getting through the hole won't be much of a problem. I'll figure everything else out once we're on the other side of this thing," he answered. For a moment, he looked at the worried expression on her face and tried hard to think of something that might comfort her. "Hey, things will be alright... you'll see. Before you know it, we'll be in another town in our cozy beds with soft warm blankets nuzzled up to our necks. Then, after a long nap, we'll take steaming hot baths to scrub the grime away, and stuff our faces with plates piled high with stacks of hot griddle-cakes, maple sausages, creamy grits, fluffy eggs, and fried potatoes served with gallons of syrup and ketchup next to tall glasses of orange-fizzy-cream juice topped with mountains of sweet orange foam that has been drizzled with hot chocolate fudge, swirls of caramel, and cookie crumbles! You'll see… it won't be long now!"

As long as his friend, *Amora*, was right there with him, he was sure they would find a way out of Kembrull Forest… one way or another.

Briefly, Amora closed her eyes and thought about the happy images Magnar had described to her. They sounded absolutely delightful and she knew there was a possibility, no-matter how slim, of them coming true.

However, a heaviness took hold of Magnar's heart as he looked upon her dirt-streaked face. *This is all my fault,* he thought, not saying a word for her to hear. *I'll find a way out of here… I promise.*

"You ready?" she asked.

Quietly, Magnar nodded and crawled into the hole.

Inside the long passage, the two crawled slowly on their knees—wincing as the thorns scraped at their clothing and skin.

Carefully, both intruders placed their hands against the walls to feel their way through it as they ventured through the narrow tunnel—crouching their heads low along the way. The frigid air stung and reddened Amora's nose as her hands grew numb to the pain of the thorns due to the cold.

It was not long before howls rang out in the distance. Were they sorrowful songs from the white werewolf who had made the passage? Neither of them knew, but the odds were in favor of it.

"Magnar, you still there?" Amora whispered, unable to see him in the pitch-black.

"I'm here," he whispered. "Wait... I think I see something."

"What? Magnar—" she asked, but there was no answer. "Magnar, are you still there? Magnar!" but he had left her with only silence in the dark.

CHAPTER TWENTY-THREE
The Wall

*A*mora's nostrils ached at the sharpness of the frigid air as she squeezed through the narrow passage, following the last sounds of Magnar's voice within the darkness. Sharply, the tunnel twisted left and right, making it hard for her to keep track of where she was, but still deeper she crawled into the belly of the wall. Soon, the air became tinged with a foul pungent odor—a mixture of what she imagined death and despair must smell like. In the distance ahead, she swore something had just moved and there was a faint sound in the dark… there it was again, but this time, behind her. Her mind was spinning within what had become *a maze*—each step driving her closer to the edge of madness. Was something inside the passage with her? Was someone watching her from within the wall? And where was Magnar?

Suddenly, a sharp pain struck her head as a voice forcibly entered her mind—distinct and separate from her own—speaking a warning.

"You're going to die here. You'll never leave our forest. You'll die within the wall... inside our prison."

Struggling to hold onto her sanity, Amora pushed onwards, crawling through the narrowing tunnel, which seemed almost too tight to continue inching through. Thorns scratched at her hands and tore tiny holes in her clothes as they became snagged on the fabric, and several times her hair got caught on the edges of prickly twigs, but still she did not turn back.

Vines, slithering like snakes behind her in the tunnel, broke apart the remainder of the silence surrounding her, except for the crunching of twigs beneath her weight. That was, until the sound she had feared most... cried out. A long, high-pitched, wailing howl pierced the air from somewhere within the maze, but it was impossible to determine from which direction! Immediately, the pace of her heartbeat quickened, and her breathing respirations increased as the metallic taste of adrenaline began to coat her tongue and surge through her bloodstream.

She knew Magnar must have heard it—no matter where he was—but he was likely remaining quiet to prevent alerting the creature to his position within the wall, too. That was the most reasonable answer as to why he had not replied to her.

Bravely, Amora continued crawling onwards over the shrubs and entwined dead vines—making sure to keep her movements as soundless as possible. The last thing she wanted was to come face-to-face with a ghostly-looking white werewolf, but the odds did not seem to be in her favor, because another voice had joined the howling song... then another, and another. Within minutes, the wall was filled with a chorus of different tones serenading her! Each voice sent a bone-chilling shiver down her spine. She needed to find Magnar, quickly!

"Magnar. Can you hear me? Magnar—" she whispered, trying to keep her voice as low as possible.

"Amora! There you are!" a welcomed voice whispered back from somewhere within the darkness. "I can hear you, but we shouldn't speak unless we have to. I think one of the white werewolves is coming towards us."

"Maybe we should go back the way we came... backtrack our steps, till we reach the forest again. We need to get out of whatever this place is... before those *things* find us," she replied, hoping Magnar would listen and agree with her.

Although, she knew how head-strong he could be at times, and that it wasn't likely he would listen. Still, without knowing what *the wall* actually was, or where the tunnel was leading them, there was the slight possibility he would agree with her and turn back without a fuss. Maybe the outskirts were on the other side of the tunnel waiting for them, but maybe the only thing they would find was more forest, man-eating trees, and white werewolves waiting to claw their eyeballs out and rip the flesh from their bones to devour them beneath the canopy in the few rays left of light... probably moonlight. Since there were no guarantees of anything *good* happening if they continued forwards, there was definitely the chance that he would agree... for once.

"No! We need to keep following the tunnel."

"But—"

"Shh! I hear it. Keep your voice low and keep moving. We're sticking to the plan," he said, continuing forwards quite a way ahead of her in the tunnel.

"Ugh," Amora huffed, arguing in her mind against his decision... even though a small part of herself agreed that they needed to find out where the tunnel eventually led to.

Silently, they crawled through it without speaking another word—each listening to the chorus of howls within the massive structure, until eventually, they began to fade into silence. However, even with the howls gone, the warning from earlier still nagged in Amora's mind, *"You're going to die here."* Why had the voice bothered to warn her, unless the creature it belonged to was being cruel for mere sport.

Amora's hands and feet ached as the tunnel sharply turned left and right (over-and-over) connecting to more tunnels, which seemed to stretch on endlessly—distorting her senses of where she had come from and where she was going as they journeyed deeper into the core of the maze. Due to being in the dark for so long, she was not sure if her eyes were even open or not anymore in the pitch-black. Her eyelids had grown so heavy, that it was entirely possible she had closed them hours ago without realizing it, and soon, might be laying on the tunnel floor fast asleep.

"Amora—" Magnar's voice interrupted her thoughts.

"The walls are getting farther apart," he said, sliding his hands against them and feeling his arms lengthen as he moved forwards and began seeing a faint glow of light being emitted up ahead. "My arms are stretched out really far now, and I… I can stand! Amora, there's enough room to stand! I think I'm out… I'm out of the tunnel! We've made it!" he exclaimed, thrilled to no longer have his body crawling on hands and knees. "I can see a light. It's soft—" he whispered, his words trailing off as he stumbled out of the tunnel towards it; his injured ankle throbbed at the pressure.

"Magnar, wait! Magnar!" Amora said, hurrying her pace, but it was no use. Magnar had already exited the tunnel and disappeared into the soft glow ahead.

What is that? she thought to herself, but before she could think of an answer, the voice from earlier again spoke to her.

"Is it light that you see? Oh yes," the voice hissed. *"Of course, it is. I've seen it, too, but that was a long time ago. I know the light*

235

that flickers in the distance. Little lights... twinkles of starlight stones... is what you see within the glow. It happens when the moons are joined together at their apex, and they shine their combined lights through an opening at the top of high a wall down into... the <u>Room of Stars</u>. You have come far, but that is of no matter. You will join us soon enough. You and the one who travels with you. You will die within the wall... with us... with me. This is a tomb for those caught between life and death... not alive... nor dead. Home of the white werewolves you have found... part ghost... but alive enough to still hunger for flesh. Your flesh will do just fine. See, it is as I told you... you will never leave the wall... our maze... at least not alive," the voice explained, laughing maniacally. *"You will never leave... you have come to Kembrull Forest... deep into the dark woods... into the maze... to die."*

"No! Stop it! Leave me alone!" Amora shouted, banging her fists against the shrubs and jerking her body around wildly... seconds before Magnar ran up to her and pulled her free from the tunnel.

"Amora! Stop it! It's me!" he pleaded, shaking her from her confusion. "Are you okay? What happened? I heard you screaming."

Blinking in the soft light, Amora opened her eyes to see Magnar holding her—although half expecting someone else to be in the room. "I'm sorry. The dark must be playing tricks on me," she blurted, not wanting to explain the voice in her head. "Why did you leave me earlier? I was calling to you, but you didn't answer," she said, quickly changing the subject.

"Yeah... about that, I'm sorry. I wanted to come back sooner, but one of the werewolves got really close to me, so I had to stop moving and be quiet... I mean REALLY quiet. I laid down in the tunnel as flat as I could, and I felt its hot breath against my face. Amora, it was so close... I think it was over me, but it was too dark to see anything. I had to wait until it left and had moved far enough away that I could backtrack my steps to you without it hearing me. I'm sorry, but I didn't have much choice. Anyway, come on... you're not going to believe what I've found!" he said, pulling on her hand for her to follow him. "Through here, there's a room... the size of it is amazing! It's HUGE... like maybe a cave or something!" he exclaimed, but again Amora's mind was miles away and his words had become nothing more than mumbles underneath another voice.

"You both will die here, inside the wall, and our teeth will gnaw on your bones. There... is... no... escape!" the voice whispered.

CHAPTER TWENTY-FOUR

Stars

With an arm over Amora's shoulder, Magnar clumsily walked through the large doorway in front of them into an expansive room filled with millions of brightly twinkling lights lodged within dark rocky walls.

"I knew there was no way you'd believe this unless I showed you! It's amazing isn't it? The lights... they look like stars, don't they? There's got to be millions of them... maybe more!" he excitedly said, removing his arm from her shoulder and walking towards the center of the room to stand among the radiant lights. "Wow! Amora, come here! You've got to try this! It feels like I'm walking on stars! This must be what it feels like in space! I wonder if anyone has ever named this place? Maybe we're the first ones to discover it! If that's true, then we should be the ones to name it.

Hmm, what should we call it? Amora, are you listening to me? What should we name this place?"

Amora wanted to share in Magnar's excitement, but she couldn't... not with the sickness growing in her stomach about the information she was withholding from him. The room was real! That also meant the voice that had invaded her mind had been real too. "But how?" her voice trailed off, saying the words loud enough that Magnar overheard her.

"What did you say?" he asked.

"The lights," she softly replied. "They come from *starlight stones.*"

"Starlight stones. How do you know that?" he asked, stepping closer to her.

"That's not all I know about this place."

"Amora, what's wrong? You're starting to scare me a little," he said cautiously. "You're not acting like yourself."

"This place... this room inside the wall... it's called, the *Room of Stars.* I'm sure you're wondering how I know that... aren't you?" she asked, looking around the room to avoid staring in his direction.

"Yeah. A little," he answered, standing in front of her no more than a couple feet between them. The flickering lights of the *starlight stones* provided enough illumination to see her face clearly—a welcomed break from what had felt like endless dark inside the tunnel. Carefully, he took a moment to study her eyes and noticed the forlorn expression etched in the soft lines on her face… something was deeply bothering her.

"I heard a voice… it spoke inside my mind," she finally whispered, staring down at the twinkling lights near her feet. He was right… it did feel like what she imagined walking on stars might be like.

"Okay, whose voice was it?" he asked softly, taking both her hands into his, then giving her chin a gentle nudge upwards to encourage her to look at him instead of down at the lights. He could read her eyes and they were filled with fear, but at what— he hoped it was not at him or of what he might think of her for telling him about the voice. Maybe that fear was not directed at him at all, but rather at something else… something she was holding back, maybe to protect him from whatever had spooked her.

"Amora, you need to know everything is going to be okay, but I need you to tell me what's going on. Tell me what's happened so we can deal with it… together. Now, whose voice did you hear?"

Hesitantly, she nodded her head in agreement and looked around, expecting to see whoever had spoken inside her mind to be spying on them from some far corner within the room, however no one was there, except for her and Magnar—no faces were lurking in the dark, nor anyone waiting to jump out to attack. So, slowly she breathed in a deep cleansing breath and began explaining to him about the voice she had heard and everything it had said. She explained that it had told her about the starlight stones and the Room of Stars, and that it had kept saying they would die within the wall and would not make it out of Kembrull Forest alive, and that she did not know who had been forcing their way into her mind. She also explained that she had tried to keep this worrisome information to herself in hopes that the voice would stop contacting her and they would reach the outskirts, which would prove the intruder's words to be wrong. However, something in the voice's tone had changed the last time it had contacted her—something about it felt angry. Whoever the voice belonged to, the owner carried a hateful dark energy.

"You really have no idea who the voice belongs to?" Magnar asked, worried and pondering over different scenarios in his mind as he tried to figure out who could be the culprit and why.

"No, but it's angry, and if whoever it is, knows where we are… let's just agree we should get moving."

"Agreed, but I don't see a door leading out of this room anywhere. Do you?" he asked, searching the twinkling walls for any signs of hidden passageways concealed among them.

"I don't see anything either," she said, gliding her hands over the rough stones embedded within the rock—looking for lines that might indicate the wall could be shifted or moved somehow. "Do you have any ideas about what the wall in the middle of Kembrull Forest is for?" she asked, walking over to a section across from him to investigate it.

"Just one," he answered, concentrating hard to find any obscure patterns the twinkling stones might reveal—thinking he would notice something if he stared hard enough. However, the moons' lights were beginning to shift away from the large opening at the top of the ceiling and their rays were touching less of the stones, causing the lights to dwindle.

"I'm listening," she persisted, gliding her hands along another section of starlight stones. As she did so, a stone loosened from the rock at the touch of her fingers and tumbled down to her feet. Gently, she picked it up off the ground and slipped the rough, jagged-shaped, clear stone into her coat pocket and then continued her search.

"I think the wall is a cage of some kind and it was made with shadow magic," he answered. Although he did not want to tell her this, but a part of himself was worried the voice Amora had heard inside her head might be right. Maybe the wall—the maze—would become their tomb, especially if they could not find a way out of the Room of Stars before the last ray of moonlight faded, trapping them in the dark with no hope of escaping the white werewolves if they attacked. "I believe this place was constructed as a prison for the white werewolves… a way to keep them inside Kembrull Forest, but maybe over time some of them found a way to escape… those that did, were the ones we heard howling after we first entered the forest, but—"

"But there might be others who remained inside the cage, and now we're stuck inside with them," she said, finishing his sentence. Immediately, cold chills shuddered down her spine. "They could be watching us right now," she whispered, glancing around the room in every direction for hidden eyes peering behind invisible holes in the walls. "The voice inside my mind could have been… a white werewolf!"

"I thought that, too, as soon as you told me what it said, but I didn't want to alarm you if you hadn't already reasoned that for yourself. I could see how worried you already were, and I was hoping you wouldn't have to find that out… at least not until we were out of Kembrull Forest."

"That much I understand, but why didn't you tell me they could do that! That they could invade our minds!" she snapped.

"Honestly, I didn't know till you told me it had been done to you. I just started putting everything together and it all made sense. I figured the voice had to be coming from their alfa… the pack leader."

"Alright, as long as you weren't hiding it from me. Ugh! I can't find anything by these stones! They're too bright and… and

243

twinkly!" she fussed, frustrated that she had not yet found a way out of the room, which had already lost half its light.

"Shh... keep your voice down! They'll hear you," Magnar whispered. "I think I have an idea. I don't know if it'll work, but we might be able to use one of these stones to help us."

"If it'll get us out of here, I'm open to anything! Here," she said, handing him the stone she had tucked away in her coat pocket. "One of the starlight stones loosened from the rock, so I took it. Can you use it?"

"I'll try. Here goes nothing," Magnar said, placing the starlight stone firmly between his index finger and thumb, and walking towards the center of the room with it held high over his head to catch the last rays of moonlight that were cascading down from the large opening in the ceiling. Instantly, the stone caught the white moonbeams and shined them brightly all over the room, revealing hidden glyphs on the walls! "It worked! This must be what we need... what we've been looking for!" he exclaimed, turning around in circles to look at all the shimmering symbols highlighted on the walls.

"You did it!"

"No, *we* did it!" he said, quickly turning his attention to studying the glyphs nearest to him. "Now, all we have to do is figure out what they mean. Can you read any of them?"

244

"I don't know. The symbols look like they stand for words, but they're nothing like anything I've ever seen before. Give me the stone. I'll hold it for you... let you take a closer look."

Magnar handed her the stone and she quietly stood with it upheld to the moonlight, while he took a closer look at the glyphs—particularly at the brightest one. It had beautiful lines that curved, swirled, and intersected, and it looked extremely old.

"I can't tell what any of this means. I feel like the answer is right in front of me, but I can't figure it out. Any luck on your end?"

"Not yet, but I'm looking... same as you." With great patience, she continued looking around the room at all the sparkling glyphs and traced their lines and curves with her eyes. "Wait!"

"What? Did you find something?"

"I think I know what they are... they're words to make some kind of spell... a spell that must be the key to opening the next door!" she presumed. "Some of these marks look similar to ones I've seen in a spell book back in Bernard."

"A book? But we've never read anything that had symbols like this. When did you see them?"

"Sometimes, when I would wait for you to finish cleaning up the bookstore, I would flip through books that were lying around on the messy tables. I remember seeing some of these glyphs in one, but I didn't have enough time to read all of them. I didn't think much of it then, but these marks are identical to the ones I saw in the book! I remember thinking how strange and beautiful they looked."

"Well, go on… give the spell a try. See if you can read them."

"I think the first two words are—" she paused, concentrating on her memory of what she had seen in the book. "I think they are… *Proferre Ostium*." Instantly, a bright light at the bottom of a section of the wall in front of them began drawing itself upwards, until it reached the height of the ceiling, and then it moved across horizontally, then back down vertically until it intersected with the first marked-line and disappeared. "It's a door! Magnar, we found it!"

"Great! Keep going! See if you can read the words to open it!"

Carefully, Amora browsed the remaining glyphs to figure out if any of them resembled words she knew. "There!" she said, pointing to more glyphs with the other hand. "I think those might be close to something I've seen. *Aperiesque Ostium. Illuminet Transitus*!" Swiftly, the outlined section of rock began to shift and break loose from the wall! Bits of dirt and rock broke free from its edges and slowly the door swung itself open! Immediately, smaller starlight stones in the newly discovered corridor began flickering, illuminating the passageway as they caught the rays of moonlight shining off the other stones.

"We did it! It's open!" Amora shouted, shoving the starlight stone in her hand back into her coat pocket—brimming with pride at figuring out the symbols, but quickly, she noticed that something was wrong with Magnar. He didn't seem eager to celebrate their victory.

"Shh," he said, hushing her and standing frozen as he stared past her to the other doorway.

"Magnar, come on. The door is open. We can finally get out of here! Magnar! Are you listening? What's wrong with you?" Amora fussed, running over to the new door with eagerness to explore the next passage and to find a way to the outskirts. Why was he not moving?

"Stop talking before you get us *both* killed," he ordered, barely moving his lips as he spoke... continuing to stare past her while keeping perfectly still. "I think there's a white werewolf standing just beyond the opening of the other door. I heard it snarling right after that spell opened this one, but for some reason, it stopped moving."

Suddenly, an all too familiar, gut wrenching, sour feeling returned to the pit of her stomach, and slowly she turned around to face the same door as Magnar. Quietly, she stood within the second doorway, staring at a tall shadow that began moving towards them, until a large, towering, white, ghostly figure, which stood erect on hind legs, stepped into view! The werewolf heaved

247

its massive fur-covered chest up and down with heavy breaths as it stared back. Its skin was pale and its soulless eyes were white without pupils. It had a long oversized snout with two grisly nostrils at the end of its nose, and its mouth was crammed with crooked jagged teeth—dripping with long lines of thick drool as it unflinchingly stared at Amora.

Next, there was another pair of white eyes from a form creeping out from behind the standing werewolf. It was another one, but smaller and walking on all fours! Unexpectedly, another set emerged from the darkness and then another, until there was a gruesome pack of predators coldly staring from the doorway across the room! Amora and Magnar had accidentally intruded into their den!

Immediately, two of the werewolves assumed attack formation and took positions on each side of their pack leader— the largest amongst them—and snarled as they paced back-and-forth on all fours.

Bravely, Amora locked eyes with the beast and stared back into the whites of the alfa, and it became clear that *he* had been the one who had invaded her mind, however this time she was not going to let him back in. This time, she was going to keep firm control over her thoughts and prevent him from gaining access!

Slowly, Magnar side-stepped closer to Amora—being careful not to make any sudden movements that might cause them to attack. "Amora," he whispered, reaching out to grab her hand. "I think the big one is the alfa... the one whose voice you heard."

Without glancing away (even for a second) Amora took hold of Magnar's hand and whispered, "I know."

"Is he speaking to you right now?"

"He's trying, but I'm blocking him. I'm thinking of a memory he can't possibly push aside... one of my parents and me at Christmas time, opening presents by a warm fire in the chimney."

"On the count of three, I say we make a run for it through the door behind us... no stopping, till we're out of Kembrull Forest. You agree?

"Yes."

"Okay. One—" he counted, the alfa's eyes finally broke contact with Amora's and turned to look at Magnar.

"Two—" Magnar whispered. Abruptly, the alfa let out a long high-pitched howl, which was quickly joined-in by the others.

"Three!" Magnar shouted, and together the two sprinted with extreme haste into the new passageway!

CHAPTER TWENTY-FIVE
Battle

*D*own the long corridor they ran, huffing-out burning cold gulps of air as their breath fogged along the way. The starlight stones embedded in the rock walls provided only enough light within the passage to see the white werewolves closely chasing behind them as they navigated the twists and turns—blindly running without the slightest idea of where the next opening would be. Their hearts pounded fast in their chests with each rhythmic heartbeat drowning out the werewolves' howls from their ears. The noise of the white werewolves' paws pounding against the ground echoed off the rock walls, sending Amora and her companion into a frenzy of fear!

"Oooooooo!" the werewolves howled, excited by the chase (their white eyes seeing perfectly within the dim light). Thrilled by the hunt, they swiftly ran after them!

Eventually, the rock walls began changing back to the familiar vines and shrubs Magnar and Amora had become familiar with in the maze, and several times they stumbled over the thick vines slithering along the ground!

Magnar's ankle burned with searing pain as he ran, but still he tightly held onto Amora's hand, making sure not to leave her behind for any reason. "Come on! Faster!" he urged, quickening their pace even more.

Her heart was pounding so hard that it felt as if it might burst through her chest as she struggled to keep up and stay ahead of the white werewolf pack behind them! Pain filled every muscle in her body as she pushed them past their limits and kept running (mile-after-mile) through the winding passageway. "Magnar, I can't... I can't make it."

"Yes, you can! There's got to be a way out of here!" Frantically, he continued running, searching for an exit or a sign that they were nearing the end of the passageway—close to exiting the wall, or better yet, nearing the outskirts of Kembrull Forest! "Come on! Don't let go of my hand!" he urged.

Again, the tunnel shifted directions, throwing Amora off balance and causing her to trip over a vine.

"Get up! They're right behind us!" he said, pulling her off the ground and resuming their pace, but abruptly the passageway stopped!

251

"No!" Amora shouted, grabbing desperately at the branches, ripping them away in hopes of finding a way through the wall of shrubs. "No! It can't be a dead end!" Savagely, she grabbed the branches and tore them off the wall—not caring about the thorns lacerating her hands. "There's got to be a way through... maybe another hidden opening! Something! Anything!" she hollered. "Faster! They're almost here!" Hectically, she tugged at the bushes with Magnar, pulling sections of them away, casting leaves and twigs down onto the ground around them.

"Can you think of any spells?" Magnar asked, looking over his shoulder behind him in the direction of the maniacal howling—the white werewolves were closing in!

"No! I'm trying... but I can't think of anything!" she replied, panic filled her voice as she, too, glanced down the dim passageway, expecting to see that the white werewolves had already caught up to them.

Suddenly, the howling stopped, and the passageway fell silent. Immediately, Magnar ceased what he was doing and whispered "Amora, stop." Gently, he grabbed her hand, "Do you hear that?"

"Hear what?" she replied, looking at him.

"It's gone quiet."

For a moment, she listened to the silence. He was right. There was nothing. It was as if they had vanished, but why?

"They were behind us. Why would they leave? This doesn't make any sense. Where'd they go?" A new wave of fear slowly crept up Amora's spine after asking the unanswerable questions.

For a few minutes, both quietly returned to removing the vines and branches from the wall of shrubs, hoping to create a hole big enough to climb through to the outskirts, or at least to hide inside of, but before they could achieve either... Amora began to feel a strange dark energy growing behind them. Suddenly, the air grew colder, fogging with every breath, and there was a foul odor to it. The chill stung her skin, forcing her to hold her coat closed even more with one hand to trap in what little body heat she had, while she pulled at the branches with the other. Still, she could not ignore the energy intensifying behind her, and soon, she had an unnerving impulse to turn around, slowly.

As she turned, she saw the tall alfa werewolf standing on its hind legs, heaving its mighty chest with every breath as it stared coldly at them with its soulless eyes—joined by the entire pack of over a hundred others! Without delay, the alfa howled a long high-pitched howl through the air. Obediently, the voices of the others joined in!

Doomed, Amora and Magnar interlocked their hands and stepped backwards, until their backs were pressed firmly against the dead-end wall. This was it! There was nowhere left to run nor hide. The voice that had intruded earlier into Amora's mind had

been right all along; they were destined to die within the maze…
within Kembrull Forest.

"Amora, I'm sorry. I never meant to drag you into any of this! Everything that's happened has been my fault," Magnar confessed, watching the snarling pack step closer. "If I could take back showing you that book… I would."

"Stop! This isn't your fault and even if it was, I'd forgive you. I wanted to read the book," she reassured him, giving his hand a firm and comforting squeeze.

Boldly, the ghostly-looking werewolves took another step towards them—each ready to devour their flesh and claim victory for the alfa.

"Close your eyes, Amora… don't watch what's coming next," Magnar said, closing his own.

"See you in the next life my friend," Amora replied, doing the same… bracing for the imminent attack. Surrendering to her fate, she took in a deep breath and prepared herself for the pain of death, but suddenly a war horn loudly bellowed behind them from the other side of the wall!

"Get down!" shouted a deep voice.

Obediently, Amora and Magnar opened their eyes and ducked down low! Still holding hands, they quickly fell (belly first) onto the ground a split second before a group of large horse-looking people broke through the wall, chopping at the shrubs with swords and axes! Swiftly, they poured through the opening and leapt over their bodies with weapons held high... ready to attack the white werewolves!

Stunned by the commotion, Amora turned her head to get a look at what appeared to be a man on a horse, but the dirt being kicked around by the hooves obstructed her view. The man seemed to be directing the others—men dressed in soldier apparel—who were creating a barrier around her and Magnar to protect them from the attackers.

"Hold your ground men! This is what we came for! Attack!" the leader ordered, thrusting his sword forwards at the snarling predators. "Kill the alfa... and the others will scatter like whimpering dogs!"

Immediately, the alfa took a more aggressive posture down on all fours with the hairs on his back raised. He had understood the man's words! The alfa displayed its sharp teeth in a fearsome snarl and its razor-like claws as it pawed at the ground—staring unflinchingly at the man.

"Do not try me beast! I will cleave the flesh off your bones... *these two* are coming with me! You will NOT claim them!" the man shouted.

Again, the alfa clawed at the ground with empty eyes glaring at him and it let out another howl—this one sounding more sinister in nature than the others had. It was clear the alfa was feeling defiant and was filled with rage.

"Then you have made your choice. I, *Zantharius*, will be the one to end you!" the man declared, boldly pointing the tip of his sword at the alfa.

Without fear, the alfa charged at full speed and sprung high into the air! Quickly, the leader of the battalion positioned himself for the impact (expecting the werewolf to land on top of him) and at once, the two were in the throes of a vicious fight!

Amora and Magnar watched in horror as the horses' hooves stepped all around them! The sounds of steel, howls, and bone-crushing noises filled the passageway as the soldiers fought the pack of white werewolves alongside their leader. The horses kicked and rose up high on hind legs as the werewolves bit and gnawed on their extremities. Clumps of white fur fell to the ground as the soldiers chopped off ears, tails, and sliced bits of flesh off their assailants in an effort to push them back down the passage!

Refusing to back down, the alfa maneuvered to the side of the leader—who rode high upon his horse—and swiped at the animal's rear, giving it a bloody claw-mark on its hind quarter! At the same time, the man slammed down the hilt of his sword against the alfa's jaw, sending several bloody teeth flying out his mouth! The alfa stumbled onto his side and spat a glob of blood onto the ground. However, he did not waste time getting back up to ram his stocky body into the man's horse, which knocked them both several feet sideways into another soldier on horseback—who was bravely fending off half a dozen attackers!

Time ticked onwards in slow motion for Amora and Magnar as they watched the battle from their disadvantaged low view point—surrounded by a blinding cloud of dust—for what felt like hours, but try hard as either of them may, the day's toll had worn hard on them. A black abyss filled with dreams was swiftly approaching to claim them where they lay—very little could be done to fight the wave of exhaustion washing over them. All of a sudden, Amora's eyes began to feel heavy, as if someone was pulling her eyelids shut. She struggled to keep them open, to watch the battle ensuring in front of her, but all her strength had left. Quickly, her vision blurred, and she turned to look at Magnar, but he had already succumbed to the abyss. Next, she looked back up at the man on the horse, who was still fighting the alfa and at the other soldiers fighting the white werewolves around him. Abruptly, a loud howling scream pierced the air as she watched the white beast fall with a long steel blade in its belly... then, the black abyss claimed her.

CHAPTER TWENTY-SIX
Ocean of Dreams

Helplessly, Amora sank into the depths of the black abyss. She had lost all control of her body and was suddenly free-falling weightlessly into an endless ocean filled with dreams inspired by memories from long ago. However, her subconscious mind longed for those moments to return, regardless of how the timeline had progressed—some memories felt as if they were only seconds away from reality, and she could reach out and grab them. As she fell deeper into the void, she saw memories of happier times floating by. Some of the dreams drifted in front of her eyes like scenes playing on misty windows of cascading rain, and slowly they passed by as she sank deeper and deeper into the void. Without pause, each of those dreams continued along their way, but other memories drifted in front of her and stayed—like frozen moments in time.

In one memory, people from long ago sat in chairs around the dinner table laughing at jokes, while others sat on the sofas chatting in what appeared to be frozen conversations. In other memories, people with joyous expressions etched on their faces stood like statues around a campfire with metal rods in their hands stacked with marshmallows to be roasted over an open fire. These pleasant memories did not drift in the dream currents of the ocean as the others did. Rather, they were anchored in place, and it was *her* that continued drifting along the abyssal current.

Gradually, as she sank farther down, the dreams with her happiest memories began to visit—each of them colliding with her to create a new ripple within the spectrum of dreams. They felt real with smells, sounds, and vivid colors. She felt as if she were really there and the past few days had never happened at all. In the abyss—in the ocean of dreams—she had found tranquility and happiness—a place where dreams mixed with memories, where past and present merged as one within the dreamer's mind... sweeping one's self away according to their needs.

There it was... the dream-memory she had longed for was sailing on the horizon and drifting within a current towards her. She watched patiently as it bobbed up and down, coming closer. Her fondest memory was playing on a cascading window of rain and she wanted desperately to relive the memory as if it had never slipped away in the first place. Happily, Amora closed her eyes and waited for it to reach her. Soon, warm cascading rain softly touched her skin as the dream enveloped her into itself and instantly, she was there… she was home.

In the kitchen, sitting on the floor in the middle of the room was a young child. She was clinging onto the skirt of her mother's crème colored silk nightgown with one hand and sucking her pointer finger with the other as she gazed up at the woman's gentle face. Her brown eyes were large with adoration for her mom as she watched her preparing a late-night snack at the kitchen counter.

"Mama, what ya making," the young Amora said, tugging at her mother's nightgown for her attention.

"Sweet girl, I'm making your favorite chocolate cream cookies," the woman softly answered, trying to step away to gather some materials from the cupboard. As Amora's mother stepped away, the young child scooted herself along the floor to follow her, and watched her mother pull out a mixing bowl, a whisk, and several dry ingredients from various cabinets—her favorite being a large bag full of chocolate bits for the cookies. "Amora, please dear, if you keep tugging on me like that, I'll never get these things made," she said, taking a moment to bend down and sweetly stroke the top of her head before gathering everything into a pile inside the large bowl, and heading back over to the center counter.

Amora watched the dream-memory continue to play with her inside it, but she felt like nothing more than a speck of dust— separate from everything inside the dream. She could only watch the young girl, but she wanted to do more! She wanted to be her again! She wanted to hug her mama and tell her how much she loved her! She wanted to warn her about what had happened and about what was going to happen in Bernard—she didn't know where she was in the timeline, but she wanted her mother to stay safe! She wanted to warn her about the goblins and to tell her about the book she had read in the Bernard bookstore, but she couldn't do any of those things. She could only stand within the dream-memory as a spectator and watch the young child on the floor.

"It's late. What are you two doing up?" asked a tired man walking into the room who was wearing a long brown robe tied with a sash at the waist, a pair of comfy pants, and some slippers. It was her dad! He was in his pajamas and rubbing the sleep away from his eyes.

"We're making chocolate cookies daddy," the young Amora replied, raising her arms for her dad to pick her up. She always loved it when he picked her up and carried her! It always made her feel safer and even more loved.

"You're making chocolate cookies... at this time of night?" he asked, smiling his charming smile at her mother, who was standing at the counter putting ingredients into the bowl and was preparing to mix everything with her large wooden spoon.

"Our little girl woke up after having some bad dreams and she couldn't go back to sleep, so I thought I'd treat all of us to a little something special," she answered, sweeping her long dark brown hair over to one side of her neck, signaling him to give her a little kiss there, which he pleasantly did.

Amora could see the look in her dad's almond brown eyes and every time he looked at her mom, they twinkled a bit at her. It was obvious how in-love they were, and it made everything feel perfect in Amora's small world.

Tears began to pool in the corners of the grown-up Amora's eyes as she watched the younger version of herself with her family. She remembered how much love there was that night. How her dad started making joke-after-joke, which made mama choke with laughter. How he got some cream and a whisk and said some kind of spell he didn't really know-well that started whipping the cream into a thick, white froth, but it wouldn't stop when he told it to. A moment later, the cream exploded all over the room and mama bursts out laughing even harder, and Amora's hair was covered with it! Then, her mom took out another bottle of cream and said a different spell that worked better than his. Next, once mama was ready, her dad held the young Amora up to the counter, so she could pour in the chocolate bits and help her mother to mix the batter.

The dream-memory showed her that while the cookies had baked, her dad had built them a warm, cozy fire and late into the night they had all cozied-up around it.

She watched her mother wrap her up in a soft blanket and hand her a small plate with huge chocolate cookies on it.

"Mama, I thought these were gonna be *chocolate cream cookies?*" the little girl asked, her round brown eyes blinking at her.

"That's right. I forgot the cream," her mother replied.

"Don't get up. I'll get it," her dad quickly said, sprinting from his seat to the kitchen to grab the new batch of cold frothy cream. Amora remembered seeing white splotches of the old batch in his curly, black hair as he walked away and returned with a small bowl filled with delicious sweet froth. Carefully, he sat the ceramic bowl on a small table in front of the sofa by Amora's mother.

Amora watched as he took a huge chocolate cookie from his plate, dipped it into the froth, and shoved a huge bite of it into his mouth! Cream was all over his face! Quickly, he reached over and gave her mama a big messy kiss! Mama laughed and took one of her own cookies from her plate, dipped it into the bowl of froth and also took a huge bite of it, covering her own mouth with loads of froth. Then, she planted a huge kiss on unsuspecting Amora's little cheek and watched her daughter giggle with a huge happy grin on her face!

As she watched the dream-memory of her family sharing cookies and laughs well into the late night by the fire, a happy, but sad expression crossed her face. She longed for those times again, but everything had changed. Gradually, she felt a dull pain enter her heart as she began to wonder if she'd find the place where the goblins had taken them, and if she'd ever see them again. Slowly, the aching in her heart grew and the cascading window of dream-memory removed itself from her and began drifting away with the current.

Helplessly, she watched the window playing the memory fade into the distance, and deeper she drifted down into the abyss. No more dreams followed after that one. The only thing left was silence.

"Mom. Dad. I'll find you…."

CHAPTER TWENTY-SEVEN
Grassland

"Amora," whispered a familiar voice, pulling her away from the deep slumber—out of the ocean of dreams within the black abyss. "Amora, wake up. Amora, you're gonna want to see this!"

Under the unfamiliar heat of a high noon sun, her eyes twitched open at the bright light and the uncomfortable feeling of hot, sticky sweat pooling against her skin beneath the overly warm coat. She felt her body gently sway from left to right, and through squinted eyes, she could see the backside of a tanned hide and a portion of a saddle fastened on it. The hardness of its leather ridge jabbed into her ribs as the horse she rode upon walked onwards, furthering her return to full consciousness.

"Zantharius, she's waking up," spoke an unfamiliar voice, but the brightness around her caused her vision to blur, and she couldn't quite make out the figure who had spoken—all she could see was a blurry outline of a man on a horse. "Sir, we'll be nearing the stream soon. Maybe we should stop there. Let them drink and rest awhile."

"Thank you Zanick, but I would prefer to put more distance between us and the outskirts. We can't be too careful when it comes to the white werewolves."

Again, Amora struggled to open her eyes against the sun's light to focus her vision on either of the men speaking, but it was hard, and the light hurt her eyes. They had become used to the darkness of Kembrull Forest and it would take time for them to adjust.

"Yes Sir, but white werewolves have never been known to travel past the outskirts of the forest, and the next source of fresh water isn't until we reach the city. We don't know the last time either of our guests had a drink. I fear if we don't make a stop soon at this stream... they could die, but we promised Sir Beaksmith we would find them and deliver them safely."

"Zanick, your point is well made, and you are my most trusted advisor... brother. We will stop as you have suggested, but we must do it quickly. Is that understood?"

"Yes, Zantharius. My respect for your trust. It is not ill placed, and I will ensure our stop will be brief. I will inform the others," she heard the man say, watching the blurry figure pound a fist against the leather armor on his chest in a respectful solute before

266

walking away. She tried to watch where he was going, but the sun still hurt her eyes too much, which forced her to shut them tight again for a few seconds.

"Amora, you awake yet?" she heard the familiar voice speak again.

Groggily, she turned her head towards the direction of the speaker and saw another blurry man on horseback trotting parallel alongside her carrying another rider, which she could make out enough to determine it was Magnar! Despite the light, she forced her eyes open wider to see him.

"Good! You're awake!" Magnar stated. "I was beginning to get worried. You were sleeping on his back like the dead for a while."

Her head ached as she lifted it off the saddle to get a better look at her friend, who was covered in clumps of dirt on his clothes and smelled badly... the same as she. "How long was I out for?" she asked, pushing the rest of herself up off her stomach and onto her rear to sit up.

"I don't know. Maybe a few hours I guess." Quickly, he noticed that as she sat up on the saddle, she was starting to lean too heavily towards one side of it. "Careful... you'd better take it easy... get your bearings straight. You don't wanna fall off the saddle," he said, gesturing at the long way down to the ground.

With a heavy head, she nodded and placed a hand up to her temple to massage it, "Where are we? Who were those men that fought the white werewolves for us?"

"As for where we are... I haven't a clue, but I think they're taking us to their city. No one wanted to do much talking until you woke up. Said they didn't want any noise waking you. I guess you had them worried, too, and they thought it would be best to let you sleep off whatever was going on with you. As for me, I woke up on the back of this one a couple hours ago. He hasn't said much either."

"What? A city? I don't understand," she mumbled, trying to fully wake up, but finding it difficult to break through the haze in her head due to the headache.

"I'll be the one to answer that," responded a deep voice near her. She'd heard the same voice earlier instructing the soldiers to attack in Kembrull Forest.

"Who are you?"

"My name is *Zantharius*. I hope you don't mind that I didn't wake you right-away after we left the forest. I thought it would be best to have one of my men scoop you off the ground and place you on my saddle... to rest. Your sleep appeared deeper than what I'm accustomed to, but it was necessary."

Again, she rubbed her eyes one last time and finally the blurry figure began to become clear. "Then, I am in your debt good sir.

You have my thanks, and I would like to thank our other rescuers as well, for surely neither my friend, nor I would be alive if it weren't for their bravery as well."

"Your words are kind, but not required. We were paid to find you both and rescue you if it be needed."

"Wait. I don't understand."

"I shall explain. I'm a ranger and am employed by Zeur's *Imperial Guard.* I track various things and use my unique talents to perform duties for them when hired to do so. A man who lives in our city, who has much favor with the leaders of the Imperial Guard, requested a group of the city's best soldiers to be formed for the purpose of finding you and your friend, and to bring you safely to our city. The Imperial Leaders approved his request and agreed to provide all necessary supplies for the endeavor if he was willing to supply appropriate payment to the men. He did exactly that without hesitation."

"That couldn't have been cheap. Who would pay such a price for us and why? What use could Magnar and I be to anyone in your city? Who are *we* to this man?" she asked, confused as to why anyone would have an interest in her or Magnar's well-being—much less pay what had to have been an exorbitant amount of currency to have soldiers search for them in the dark places of the world and risk their lives to save them.

"I don't know. Those questions will have to wait until you are with someone better equipped to answer them, but I can tell you who paid for our services."

"Alright, who?"

"The money was paid by a man named *Sir Beaksmith*."

At the sound of the man's name Amora and Magnar gasped in disbelief. It was the same name as the one they'd come across in the tattered book found in the forbidden section in the bookstore!

Right away, Zantharius noticed the surprised expressions on their faces, but chose not to pursue any questions into the matter at the present time. Instead, he continued to perform his duties admirably and allow whatever they were hiding to stay their own business... for now.

"You will meet with him once we've returned to my city. There is nothing more I can share with you, but I'm sure he'll answer the remainder of your questions, of which I can see there are many."

"Our thanks may not be required, yet you still have them," Amora insisted, overcoming the last bit of blurred vision.

Just then, one of the soldiers approached and interrupted the conversation among them with news for Zantharius, and Amora's eyes grew large as she looked at the entirety of one of her rescuers clearly for the first time since she'd awoken.

"Sir, I have news from Zanick. We have reached the stream and I am to escort the young lady and her companion to it."

"That is good. Help her down off my saddle. They can walk with you to the water," Zantharius instructed. "I'm sure they'd enjoy stretching their own legs for a while."

"Yes Sir. Right away," the soldier complied, stretching his hands out to help the young woman get down, but unexpectedly Amora jerked herself away.

"Amora, why did you do that? He's only trying to help," Magnar asked, stunned by her unreasonable reaction.

"What... what are you?" she whispered, her voice trembling with fear and eyes wide with curiosity.

"He is the same as me young lady. We are centaurs," Zantharius answered for the soldier, craning his neck around to look at her sternly as he awaited her next reaction.

Quickly, her eyes darted over to him and instantly she realized that what she had thought was the back of a horse she'd been riding upon, was actually Zantharius *himself* who was bound to the body of an animal! Without hesitating, Amora screamed and tried desperately to slide her way down off his saddle, but on cue from Zantharius, the soldier took hold of her waist to prevent her from falling or injuring herself. Without much thought into the matter, she feared they'd been kidnapped by new enemies sent by the Dark One to claim their heads! Instantly, Amora began wildly

271

kicking her legs at the soldier and flailing her arms—striking Zantharius' back several times as she struggled to free herself from the soldier's grip!

"Stop it! Amora! You need to calm down!" Magnar insisted, trying to reason with her. "I promise they're not trying to hurt us! They saved our lives and took care of your injured hand while you slept. If they had wanted us dead, they would have taken care of that detail when we were passed out and at their mercy hours ago! Amora! I mean it… stop fighting! You've got to get a hold of yourself! Are you listening to any of the words I'm saying? Amora! You've got to stop!" he yelled, but still she continued flailing her limbs as if she hadn't heard a single word.

Hot adrenaline was coursing through her veins and heightening her primitive survival instincts! Immediately, she bent down and aggressively gave the soldier a firm bite on his arm, causing him to release her and grip the injured flesh. It was bruised and turning a bluish-purple in color—due to the blood pooling underneath the skin—and a small amount of it was oozing out from a tooth mark where she had torn his flesh.

Now free from the soldier's clutches, Amora escaped into the tall grasses of the prairie surrounding them, but stopped to look up at Magnar, who was still sitting on his carrier's saddle.

"Are you coming or not?"

For a brief moment, Magnar weighed his options—to go with a woman filled with madness or stay within the safety provided by the centaurs. A tough decision at the moment, but the wild expression in her eyes suggested he wouldn't remain safe for long if he chose to stay with them. He felt a duty to be loyal to her and for that reason alone he wanted to go, but there was more to it. He knew in his gut that these people were trying to help and intended them no harm. He felt that he could trust Zantharius. Something about the man was more than just a ranger for hire, and although he knew nothing about rangers, he could tell this man was honorable and knew more than he was saying. Very calmly, he spoke careful and deliberate words that he thought would be most helpful in reasoning with her.

"Amora, these Centaurs are good people and Sir Beaksmith is the one who sent them. I know it doesn't seem possible that it could be the same man we read about in the book, but... what if it is? We owe it to ourselves to find that out, and the only way we're going to do that is to trust them and follow them back to their city."

Her eyes were wide with fear (and rightfully so) after witnessing the destruction of Bernard by goblin-fire, being attacked by flesh eating trees, and hunted by white werewolves, but despite her anxiety that they had stumbled upon yet another foe, he could see she was listening to him, so he continued.

"While you slept, Zantharius had one of his men lift you off his back and lay you against a large rock in the grass. I watched him tend to your injured hand myself. Look at it Amora."

Hesitantly, she lifted her injured hand and looked at both sides of it. It didn't hurt anymore! Since being injured by the enzyme, her hand had been burning and itching as if a dozen bees had stung it, but now the pain had completely disappeared.

"How?" she asked, looking down at her hand.

"Zantharius brought medicines, balms, and strips of cloth in case we had been injured in any way. After you were laid down, he took a vile filled with medicines out of his leather pouch that he keeps by his saddle, and he poured the liquid in it over the burns on your hand. He cleaned the areas affected by the enzyme and then rubbed a healing balm all over it. After that, he bandaged your hand with the strips of cloth. Then another centaur, I think I heard them say the name Zanick," he said, looking for confirmation from Zantharius that he was correct, who promptly nodded his head that he was. "Yes, Zanick was the one who scooped you up and placed you back onto Zantharius' saddle, so gently that you didn't wake, and he's been carrying you ever since. He also tended to my busted ankle and gave me medicines to help with the pain," he told her, lifting up his pant leg to reveal his ankle wrapped up tightly in clean strips of cloth.

Amora's breathing calmed as she listened and looked around at the faces of several other centaurs who had quietly joined the small group to hear the progressing discussion. She noticed that there was no hint of malice in any of their expressions. Instead, they looked tired and worn from their battle with the white werewolves. Some of them had bandages wrapped around their own wounds on arms and legs or had bloody jaws from injuries sustained during the fight. They stood as tall men attached to their horse counterparts at the waist, which were solid colors of either brown, black or white, and a few had patches of different colors mixed in. Each had an athletic build and was dressed in brown leather armor studded with bronze metal balls in a simple design upon their chest and lengths of their arms, with a sheathed sword by their side attached to a thick belt around the waist.

Amora looked at each of her rescuers carefully as they approached, forming a tight circle around her in support of their leader, Zantharius. The man carrying Magnar had short, curly, red hair and a beard to match, but the man standing next to him had loose, shoulder-length, black hair. Others had long light-brown, sandy-blonde, or dark-brown ponytails that were beautifully braided down their length of their backs—likely the work of the women back home who had diligently braided it for them before the men headed out on their dangerous mission to find and rescue herself and Magnar. The men were clean shaven and their brown, blue, and green eyes sparkled in the light of the sun.

Next, she turned to look at Zantharius, who was someone entirely different to behold. He stood erect with authority and his tanned chest was puffed with confidence as he watched her. She was somewhat intimidated to look at him in his large, round, dark-brown eyes, but still she did exactly that and could feel his intensity as he stared back at her. His athletic build was more muscular than the others, he was taller, and he seemed a bit lesser in years than them. He wore his black hair in a long braid down the length of his back, and it hung nicely over his armor, which was adorned with silver balls instead of bronze ones. The belt at his waist was thicker and sturdier, supporting a longer sheath and sword than the other centaurs, and he was the only one among them carrying a medicinal satchel, which she attributed to him being the only ranger amongst them.

"Magnar, do you honestly feel that we can trust them?" she asked, returning her eyes to rest upon her friend sitting upright on the saddle of the red-headed centaur.

"Yes, I do."

"Then I will follow them with you to the city," she agreed.

"A wise decision," Zantharius commented. "Although, be warned that we have wasted much time discussing this, and the white werewolves may be patrolling the outskirts of the forest—preparing another attack."

"Zantharius, I've spoken with the soldiers and none have heard of these creatures leaving the confinement of the forest. This is a worry we do not need to shelter any longer," Zanick assured.

"I hear your words brother, but circumstances have changed. We broke into the impenetrable wall and created a pathway for them leading out of Kembrull Forest—a thing they previously did not have. That action may provide the beasts with options that may alter their behavior. No one can be so bold as to anticipate the actions of these enemies moving forward... to know what they will choose to do with this new variable we've created. Either way, we must stay true to our purpose and valuable time has been lost. Get our guests to the water quickly... for our rest in this grassland will be brief. We must make haste to continue the journey and find a place far from Kembrull Forest to make shelter by the time the twin moons rise. At that hour I'd prefer to be far from here... far enough NOT to hear the howls that might fill this grassland for the first time," he ordered, looking back the way they'd come... towards the outskirts of Kembrull Forest.

"Understood Sir," Zanick acknowledged, respecting the decision of his superior. "You two," he motioned a hand at Amora and Magnar. "This way. Follow me."

Obediently, Magnar climbed down from the red-haired soldier's saddle and joined Amora at Zanick's side to walk with him to the stream.

"Amora," Zantharius said, stopping her as she began to walk away with them.

Silently, she paused and turned to face him.

"I give you my word that you will not regret your decision to remain in the company of the centaurs. There is much to be discussed once we reach the city… there's much you do not know. On my honor, I will do everything I can to keep you and your friend safe."

Without speaking a word, Amora acknowledged his words with a simple nod.

"If you're hungry, my brother has brought food for you and Magnar to eat that should be to your liking, and you should try to drink as much of the water as you can. The journey ahead will not be easy, and the canteens will go quickly. It may be quite some time before we find a place to camp for the night and are able to refill them with fresh water. You are not accustomed to heat such as this where you're from… your body will require more for this reason."

"Why is the sun warm here? I thought all places were cold— filled with clouds that blocked the sun's heat," she asked.

"Everything isn't what you've been led to believe, but beyond that, I can say no more. All your questions will be answered once we're safely inside my city, but *here* we must be careful with our words... not to share too many. Spies are hidden everywhere... even within a grassland such as this," he said, looking around and listening to the unfamiliar noises he was detecting with his sensitive ears—the grass was full of oddities that must be deciphered if he was going to spot any spies. "Remember, go and drink your fill. We leave this place at the half hour," he instructed, parting her company to join two soldiers waiting for him inside a temporary tent to plan the next portion of their journey back to Zeur.

The stream was a pleasant sight for the weary travelers. It cut through the grassland as far as Amora could see from north to south, and it glistened at the touch of the sun's golden rays. She couldn't remember the last time she'd had a drink of fresh water, and at the sight of it, her mouth ached to salivate, but it didn't have a drop of moisture to spare. A sharp pain pierced her lips as she raised a finger to touch them. They were cracked with dryness and her tongue felt rough as sandpaper. A sudden urge to grip Magnar's hand so they could run together and jump into the cool water almost overtook her upon seeing the stream, but there were centaurs there enjoying their rest, so she refrained from disturbing them.

The red-headed centaur was kneeling at the water's edge, dipping a canteen into the water and then gulping down mouthfuls of the cool refreshing liquid. His beard was drenched and dripping water onto his chest armor, but he didn't seem to mind. As they passed by him, he dipped his mug again into the stream and poured the liquid over his face, shaking his wet hair with exhilaration— enjoying a moment of relief from sweat and the heat of the sun.

As they continued walking with Zanick to their own spot at the stream, they passed by centaurs napping in the tall blades of grass, others eating small loaves of bread, and some engaging in spirited conversations as they guzzled down their full canteens— however, each became silent as Amora and Magnar passed by.

"I have canteens in my satchel for each of you," Zanick informed, twisting his torso slightly to reach for a large, brown, leather bag fastened with two straps across the front with silver buckles. It hung on the side of his saddle and from it he removed a canteen for each of them and one for himself. "Are you hungry? I brought the bread and blueberry cookies my wife baked for you."

Eagerly, both nodded and Magnar held out his hands first to receive the goodies wrapped in the delicate cloth the man's wife had secured them in. At once, he untied the top of the first package and stuffed one of the blueberry cookies into his mouth! "This is good," he mumbled in between chews. "I can taste the blueberries!" Crumbs fell from the corners of his lips as he

280

relished the feeling of food sliding down into the empty pit of his stomach.

"I'll let her know you liked them. I'm sure she'd be happy to bake another batch once we've reached the city… and I get back home to her and the little ones," Zanick replied, handing the other wrapped batch of cookies to Amora along with a small loaf of bread.

Greedily, Magnar swallowed down the rest of his cookies and received a round loaf of bread for himself. Without waiting, he ripped off a section and shoved it into his mouth—barely chewing before gulping it down into his gullet! "This taste great! What kind of bread is this?" he mumbled, stuffing another morsel into his mouth after barely finishing the first one.

"I believe my wife said it's rye bread with a sprinkle of parmesan cheese," Zanick proudly answered. His wife really was quite the cook!

"Well, tell her my compliments to the chef!"

Zanick nodded he would and took hold of his canteen, "Let's get our water… Zantharius will be moving the soldiers soon."

Quickly, Amora grabbed a few of the blueberry cookies from her package and stuffed them into her coat pocket. Then, she re-wrapped the rest in the cloth, along with her bread, and sat the package on the ground near the water's edge. "I'll follow you," she replied, taking hold of her canteen as she watched Magnar cram another bite of bread into his mouth, before putting down the rest of his package and grabbing his canteen to join them.

"You won't be needing that," Zanick said, kneeling his front legs down to fill his canteen with water.

"What do you mean?"

"Where we're going... you're not gonna need that coat anymore. My home, Zeur, it's a warm city. One of the seamstresses there sewed some new clothes for you and your companion... Sir Beaksmith requested it be done. I had one of the soldiers pack them in a bag for you and bring them along. Eat the cookies in your pocket and then find your new clothes waiting for you in that second tent by the tree over there. Get changed as soon as you're ready," he said, pointing to a skinny tree where the soldiers were putting up another tent for Amora's and Magnar's use—surrounded by tall blades of green grass that almost hid the shelter. "I'll make sure neither of you are interrupted and are given your privacy."

After her experience with the trees in Kembrull Forest, and then spotting the one next to the tent, Amora didn't feel good about the idea of being left alone next to one, but it looked harmless enough—it was normal and not likely to be interested in eating her. "Alright, but what about the water?"

"Don't worry. Magnar and I will handle that. We'll fill your canteen, and you can drink your fill after you've changed. The

282

soldiers didn't bring much... just the basic necessities, but if you require anything else, I'm sure you'll be able to find what you need at the shops in my city."

"Thank you, but we don't have any money and even if we did, it might not be the kind that's of any use to your people. The currency might be... well, different," she replied, handing her canteen to Magnar.

"That isn't a worry miss... arrangements have already been made for you and Magnar, compliments of Sir Beaksmith. He has made deals with all the shop-keeps in Zeur! It is my understanding that he has carefully taken care of every detail to make your stay in Zeur as comfortable as possible. The shops will supply you with whatever you require and lodging at the best inn has already been arranged."

Upon hearing this news, Magnar's curiosity peaked at finding out who this man was and why he had gone to such great lengths for them! "This... *Sir Beaksmith*, who is he?" Magnar interrupted, his face brimming with curiosity and excitement—thinking the answer he might receive would prove this man to be the same person he'd read about in the forbidden book back in Bernard, and that the man mentioned therein was still alive after countless years.

"I'm sorry, but I've said all I can. Any further questions will have to be answered by a more appropriate person once we've reached Zeur," Zanick answered.

"We understand. Isn't that right, Magnar?" Amora replied, nudging Magnar in the ribs with the side of her elbow—eyeing him hard that he shouldn't pursue his line of questioning any further at the present time. She could see it was making Zanick uncomfortable and she didn't want to get him into any trouble after all he'd done to help. Plus, he wasn't the one they needed answers from—that much was obvious. They needed to speak directly to the man behind all of the mystery... and that was *Sir Beaksmith!*

"I think I'll get that water now," Magnar said, relinquishing his question and rubbing the side of his aching stomach where her elbow had made contact.

Relieved that he had decided to leave it alone, Amora promptly returned her attention to Zanick, while Magnar began dipping their canteens into the water to fill them—lowly mumbling his displeasure at not having his question answered as he did so.

"Well, I think I'd better go change. Thank you Zanick for everything... really. I don't know what we would've done to fend off those white werewolves without you and the others."

"We were only performing our duty miss, but your *thanks* are warmly accepted."

"Well, I suppose Zantharius will be leaving within the hour. I'd better get going," she said, digging around in her coat pocket for the cookies, then feeling the smooth surface of the star stone. Along with one of the cookies, she pulled out the smooth stone and looked at it in her hand.

"If you don't mind me asking, what's that you've got there?" Zanick asked, curiously looking down at the smooth stone in her hand.

"Nothing, just one of the star stones I picked up."

"Ah, I see."

"Is your city far?" she asked.

"That depends on which way we take to reach my home."

Amora could hear the longing in his voice to return there.

"It was a few days journey by the dangerous roads we chose to take in order to quickly reach you in Kembrull Forest, but something in the air here is foul. We may have to take yet another way home... a longer way, because something doesn't feel right about this grassland, and I can see that my brother, Zantharius, feels this, too. That is why he chose to speak with the soldiers privately in one of the tents and left you in my care, instead of accompanying you himself to this stream."

285

Alarmed, Amora looked around at the wide-open prairie of tall grass. At once, her eyes became fixed upon a single spot where the blades rustled *against the breeze*, instead of swaying with it like all the others.

"You sense it too, don't you?" Zanick asked, fixing his eyes upon the same spot.

"What do you mean?" she asked, pretending not to sense it, even though she could.

"I believe someone has been following you. It remained hidden in the shadows while it tracked you through Kembrull Forest, and now it hides itself somewhere among the stalks of grass. Rest assured, my brother is the best ranger in Zeur, and he knows much about these lands and the creatures in them. Whatever has followed you here, to this place, is a foreign creature to this land, and although it is difficult to flush out, Zantharius will not allow it to follow you any further. For this reason, Zantharius will choose to take another way home that will prove to be much harder for the creature to stay hidden in."

Amora's heart beat faster as she stared at the grass on the other side of the stream. She could feel a dark energy hidden there, and she knew whatever or whomever it was coming from... it was staring back at her. However, she had no desire to confront it. Her focus needed to remain on finding Sir Beaksmith to get the answers she desperately required.

"Whatever the creature is... I'm sure Zantharius will handle it," she said, taking a bite of the cookie. "These really are very good," she mumbled, quickly following that bite with another, until nothing was left in her hand but crumbs. "Magnar, my canteen if you don't mind."

"Here. I filled it up to the top for you," he replied, handing her the wet canteen. Quickly, Amora took a few gulps of the refreshing water to wash down the globs of cookie in her throat. The cool liquid was a welcomed sensation on her tongue as it slid down. "Now, back to the matter of getting myself out of this coat. I'll be in the tent if anyone needs me." "Hurry up won't you... I can't stand being in this heavy oversized thing any longer than I have to," Magnar complained, itching to get changed, too.

"Alright, alright... I'm going!" Amora huffed, slipping her arms out of the coat and folding it over one arm. "I'll join the two of you in a few minutes." Quietly, Amora set her eyes upon the second tent near the skinny tree and headed over to it. Suddenly, she paused and looked down at the star stone in her hand.

"Guess I won't be needing this anymore," she whispered to herself, pausing to look at the smooth stone once more (it really was beautiful). "I wouldn't want those werewolves coming after me to find *you*." After a long moment of thinking about the Room of Stars and all that had happened in Kembrull Forest, Amora let out a deep sigh. "Goodbye," she said, skipping the stone across the water and watching it sink beneath its glassy surface before heading into the tent.

CHAPTER TWENTY-EIGHT
Onwards

"Up on your feet. Time to get moving," commanded Zantharius, walking towards the soldiers sitting in the grass by the stream's edge. "It'll be nightfall in a few hours, and no one wants to be near the outskirts when the twin moons rise."

"Come on. You heard the ranger... up on your feet!" insisted one of the soldiers, getting himself up and urging the others to do the same (a soldier much too eager to move up in rank by any means necessary). "Don't none of us want them howling beasts close enough to pick up our scent! You there! Wake up!" he ordered, giving a napping centaur a painful kick against one of his legs.

Right away, the centaur was jolted awake as the shouting man's hoof made contact against his leg. Immediately he hollered, "What was that for?" without expecting a reasonable answer.

Trying to decide in his sleepy state if he should be ready for a fight, he realized who it was that had struck him—the suck-up who unfortunately out-ranked him—and with a grumble, he decided against the action.

"No lip from you would do just fine and if you can't manage that, I'll shut 'em up for ya!" the soldier snapped.

Furious, the centaur hurriedly got up on his feet and brazenly puffed out his chest, pressing it up against the rude soldier's. "I'd like to see you try," he said, staring coldly into his eyes.

"That's enough you two! Break it off, or I'll leave you both here to take on any white werewolves who try to track us... if you insist on fighting, rather than performing the duty you've been paid for," Zantharius warned, his own chest puffed to see if either man would dare challenge his authority. However, obediently both soldiers backed down.

"Zantharius..."

"Yes," he responded, turning to look at Zanick buckling his satchel and walking over towards him.

"Everyone is ready to leave at your command, however, there's the matter of the hidden spy. We should take care of this problem before reaching Zeur," he informed, glancing in the suspected direction of the spy's location.

"It still hasn't shown itself?"

290

"No Sir. It has made no sounds or obvious movements towards Amora or Magnar. The only indication we have of its presence is the rustling of the grass when there is no wind blowing across the grassland. Each time this movement has been seen by one of the soldiers, it was in a different area than before."

"Yes, we must make haste to cut off its eyes from watching their journey. This spy in the shadows most certainly watches for its master... which every fiber of my body tells me is the Dark One. We cannot allow this watcher to learn of our city's location, because our people would become exposed and no longer be safe," he replied, glancing over at Amora and Magnar, who were standing with the soldiers and awaiting Zantharius to give word of their departure from the grassland.

"This makes little sense. Why would the Dark One be interested in those two, or go to such lengths as to send a spy to observe them?" Zanick asked, confused about why Amora and Magnar were worth so much effort from not only the Dark One, but also from Sir Beaksmith. "They can be of no threat to the DARK ONE."

"I have no answer for that, but it is clear that if the Dark One has an interest in them, then we must do everything we can to find out why. We must also do everything we can to keep them safe. After-all, Sir Beaksmith paid an enormous purse for us to do exactly that and we will perform our duties as requested."

"Even at the risk of jeopardizing the safety of our own city... our own people?" Zanick asked, worried that if the Dark One was to realize they were helping them, wrath might be brought against Zeur, and its citizens would be the ones to pay the price!

Zantharius faced his brother and placed a hand upon his shoulder as he looked him in the eyes, "Yes, my brother. I have been told in confidence, by Sir Beaksmith himself, that our highest priority is to protect these two and to get them safely to Zeur... at any and ALL cost. He stood with me then, as I now stand with you, and spoke those words to me from a heavy and worn heart. If you had seen the look in his eyes as I had, then you would know Sir Beaksmith does not ask this of us lightly. He understands the risks and for reasons not yet known... he would risk every life in Zeur to save Amora and Magnar... it's as if the world itself depends on our task being done," he affirmed. "Sir Beaksmith loves our people as much as we do, and he is a trustworthy, honorable man. If he says this is of the utmost importance, our highest priority, then we should without doubt in our hearts understand this to be true."

"I understand," Zanick relented and agreed.

"Now, let us leave this place and see if the spy continues to follow. If it does, then I will form a plan to roust it from the shadows myself," Zantharius instructed.

"Are we returning by the route we came?" Zanick asked.

For a moment, Zantharius paused and turned away from his brother to stare across the grass, which was rustling and swaying back-and-forth at the touch of a cool breeze passing over the prairie, but when he again spoke there was something chillingly different in his tone. "No. There are white werewolves at our backs and a spy hidden in the shadows. We have only one choice left to us now. We must take a different way to Zeur."

"I know that tone brother and it suggests an ill-advised plan has crossed your mind. By what route are you thinking of? Surely, it is any place other than... the dead city."

"Brother, you know my mind... that is exactly where my thoughts have settled," Zantharius answered. "We must travel through the place which has known much darkness if we are to have any chance at emerging victorious at the task charged to us by Sir Beaksmith."

"The deaths that happened in Zareck left the city desolate and barren. Nothing good survives there now and none dare travel through it, nor seek shelter within its walls anymore. It is a place of death and the dead still claim it. Their souls cannot find rest and are unendingly tormented by this—seeking revenge for their untimely deaths. Zantharius, you must reconsider! There are stories of mournful wailings being heard from the city's walls at night from those passing by. Zareck has become a place for foul creatures to lurk and hunt. They dwell in the abandoned buildings, but even their screams have been heard from those outside the city. The only thing any of us will find there is death waiting with open arms to give us its cold embrace. Please brother, there must be another way," Zanick pleaded, but Zantharius' mind was set firm to travel through the dead city and there was little that could change it.

"This is the way we must take, brother."

"You MUST reconsider,"

"No! We will speak of this no more. Do the job you were paid to do… follow the path your ranger has determined, and you will see Zeur again," Zantharius ordered, shifting his demeanor from a brother who would hear Zanick's opinions, into a ranger of high rank who was paid to do a job—to safely bring Amora and Magnar to Zeur. Although he loved his brother, he was not going to explain his reasons for traveling through the dead city any further.

"Yes sir," Zanick respectfully replied, promptly forming a fist with his right hand and pounding it over his heart with a hard *thud* against his chest armor in a respectful salute, which Zantharius equally returned before walking away to address the other soldiers.

"Alright, break-time is over. Everyone, let's get moving," the ranger commanded. With an extended hand, Zantharius approached Amora and reached for her, "My lady, you may ride on my saddle if you'd like? You need not walk, for the way is long."

Hesitant, Amora turned to look at Magnar, "What about him?" she asked, gesturing over her shoulder at her friend.

"He may ride on my brother's saddle," he replied, watching Zanick approach Magnar, extending his hand in the same manner to assist him.

"Or would you rather walk to Zeur?" Zantharius asked, smiling down at her to evoke a feeling of calmness to ease her fears—making his offer about riding on a centaur's saddle more pleasant. "It really is a long way, I assure you it's farther than you can imagine. I will carry you as far as I can, but even so, you may find use of your legs along the way if my strength wains even a little."

For a second or two, Amora contemplated walking—balking at the idea of riding on the centaur—but her body still felt weak and tired, and Magnar had already hoisted himself up onto Zanick's saddle and was waiting for her to do the same on Zantharius'.

"I suppose I'll ride… not much sense in walking if it's as far as you say" she answered, not happy about it. Firmly, she took hold of the ranger's hand and with his help, he pulled her up to sit on his saddle.

295

"A wise decision," the ranger commented, walking with his brother towards the head of the awaiting group to lead the way.

Amora took a moment to use her vantage point at the height of Zantharius' back to look out over the tall grass to the place where she'd felt the dark energy. Again, the blades of grass rustled without the help of the wind. She knew the spy was there watching her... staring at her as they departed the grassland.

CHAPTER TWENTY-NINE
The Dark Gate

S hortly after departing the grassland, the pinkish-purple hues of dusk settled in the evening sky and the twin moons began their nightly waltz above the travelers. Steadily, they journeyed across various terrains of wet marshes, steep hills, and edged along rocky cliffs as they walked onwards to the dead city, Zareck. Tick... tock... tick... tock. The minutes turned into hours, and the hours into days, as they traveled over high and low hills and through vast, barren valleys that had long ago been filled with grapevines as far as one could see—once owned by prideful farmers who boasted that the best wines came from their vineyards. However, much time had passed since those days, and what used to be fertile soil, had changed into grey hardened clay that gave life to only crippled trees with empty branches. Long ago, fresh apples, plump pears, and juicy oranges had once covered those branches, and wicker baskets overflowed with the produce picked by customers from the grand city at harvest time, but as shadow took over the lands, everything changed.

In Zareck, the passage of time had not been merciful. The plentiful rains had abandoned the sky and unyielding droughts took their places, forcing the trees to dwindle in number, until only a few dotted the dying landscape leading to the city's walls. No longer were magnificent fruits to be found, but instead, rotten mushy globs hung from brittle branches and dropped beneath them to the ground, forming rotten heaps covered with black corpse-flies and fat squiggling maggot-grubs that gnawed on the moldy fruit. As the insects ate, they covered the mounds with their waste deposits, which released an awful stench into the air—a dreadful mix of decay and death—forcing the travelers to hold a cloth over their noses as they passed by, but still much of the odor got through and caused everyone to choke and cough as they continued onwards to the dead city.

The closer the travelers got to Zareck, the colder the air became, bringing back the familiar chill Amora and Magnar knew too well, and it wasn't long before they yearned for the coats they'd left behind. Shivering in the cold, Amora clutched her arms around herself—the thin fabric of her long-sleeved shirt barely kept her warm enough not to shiver. Desperately, she hoped Zantharius would stop soon and make shelter for the night—where she could warm herself by a fire. However, that didn't seem likely to happen, because the shadow that lay claim to these lands had sinister intentions in mind, and it wasn't long before dark-grey ominous storm clouds began rolling in. Soon, most of the twin moons' light was gone and the wind was beginning to pick up. Next, loud *booms* of thunder began to rumble overhead in the night sky and suddenly there was a bright *clap* of lightning that jumped across the clouds!

While riding on Zantharius' saddle, Amora removed her hand from her nose and looked up at the storm clouds. One... two... three. The first few drops of cold rain splattered against her cheeks as she held her face up to the sky seconds before it opened up to dump a shower of rain onto them. Grumbling about getting wet, everyone shivered and quickened their pace towards the city— although not eager to seek shelter inside its high walls.

"How much farther?" one of the centaurs from the rear of the group asked, shielding his face with a hand cupped over his forehead as the rain whipped at him sideways by a powerful gust of wind.

Zantharius turned to see who'd asked the question, but the blinding rain blowing into his own eyes blurred his vision. The best he could figure was the question was coming from the soldier with the curly red hair and long beard, but he wasn't sure if it was him or the man next to him.

"It's not much further... over there. Those are the city's walls," Zantharius announced, shouting his words over the loudness of the storm and pointing ahead to a large stone archway in the distance, which was slightly hidden by a rising white fog creeping up the grey stones on the muddied ground. "The gate is within our sights."

Begrudgingly, everyone was silent and trudged onwards through the downpour and the thickening sludge toward the gate looming ahead, and within minutes they were standing in front of it. Amora's eyes lifted upwards to look at the towering arches as Zantharius approached the entrance, pausing to marvel at its impressive size and structure—surely, in its day it had been something quite impressive. It was the first time he had traveled to the city and had laid his own eyes upon the place he'd heard folktales about as a child, and Amora understood what it meant to him to be able to take this moment in and look upon the gate himself.

While he did so, she looked at the large stones along the wall and noticed burn marks on them. Many of the iron-hinges, which had been connected to the gate doors, were partially melted, twisted, and were lying on the ground at the bottom of them. Large splinters of wood were dangerously jutting out of the busted doors, and it was clear something terrible had happened here.

Immediately, Amora's mind began racing with thoughts centered around what she had read in the tattered book in the bookstore back in Bernard. *Wait… is this the place spoken about in the book,* she wondered? *Maybe, the ranger knows more than he's saying about this city and what it once was. Maybe he knows about the book too! Is the book the reason why Sir Beaksmith paid these people to find us,* she asked herself. *If I could just get him to tell me something… anything!*

Hesitantly, she leaned over to question the ranger, "Zantharius, what happened here? What is this place?"

For a moment, he craned his neck to the side to look at her. "Where I'm from, people used to tell stories about this city to young children, so they would know about the past, understand the present, and be able to prepare for the future," he answered, returning his neck to face forward and stare off at nothing particular. "However, many of my people have come to believe those stories are nothing more than myths created by wild imaginations, and this place is nothing more than an abandoned city, which was destroyed by greed and the destructive consequences of the passage of time."

"Something about you—maybe the look in your eyes — tells me you think those stories are more than myths though. Zantharius, what do *you* think this place is?" she asked softly.

"I'm not the one who should be speaking to you concerning this. That task belongs to Sir Beaksmith, but what I can tell you is this… Zareck has become a city of shadow and it is deeply scarred by evil. Whatever this place once was, it is no more, and there are things lurking in the dark here that will kill you if they can—if you give them the smallest chance—so keep your wits sharp and eyes open. Take nothing here for granted… for even a shadow in this place has the ability to kill any one of us."

"If this place is as dangerous as you claim it is, then why have you brought us here?"

"A spy hidden in the shadows has been following and watching you," he answered, peering through the open gate at several high roofs of buildings on the other side, which had been marred by tragic violence long ago. "Even now, I feel its dark presence staring at you from somewhere inside this city… out of my reach, but still close." Zantharius' eyes darted left and right, searching the roofs, but soon he continued, "I believe its master hides it from my vision, but I feel its energy coming from one of those intact roofs up ahead. This spy is the reason I have brought you here, instead of taking you directly to Zeur."

"I don't understand. If there are things here in the shadows that are going to try to kill us, then it seems to me the best course of action would be for us and your soldiers to turn away from this place and take a different path. After-all, you did profess your mission was to find and save us from whatever perilous situation you found us in and to deliver us safely to Zeur so that we may have a meeting with Sir Beaksmith," she argued, but then a realization crossed her mind. "Wait a second, there's not even a way through the dead city to reach yours... is there? What harm do you think will happen if we leave now and journey to Zeur?

"Shh," he ordered, silencing her. "I heard something! Up there on that roof!" Quickly, his eyes darted up to the rooftop of a nearby building and spotted dirt falling off one of the ledges. Carefully, he scanned the roof for the spy, but still the creature remained hidden. "I won't speak of this anymore. I MUST draw it out and prevent it from following you to Zeur. It mustn't be allowed to learn the location of my city, or else my people's blood will run like a river through the streets, and I cannot allow that to happen if there's the smallest chance of it being prevented. Before we enter Zareck, I will answer your question though. No. There isn't a way through the dead city. We're here for one purpose only... to rid you of your spy. This is the reason we must camp within the walls of Zareck tonight and risk the wrath of the dead that dwell here... of those unable to move on... trapped in limbo."

Amora sighed and nodded that she understood as the rest of the group approached the gate to join them. Quickly, she flashed a nervous glance at Magnar, who was no longer sitting on

303

Zanick's saddle, but had transitioned onto the saddle atop the curly red-haired centaur.

"Is everything okay? You and the ranger seemed to be having an intense talk a moment ago," Magnar asked, feeling a tense energy in the air between her and the centaur.

Amora gave a quick glance at Zantharius, "We're good. He was explaining what we'll face once we're inside the dead city. It wasn't something I wanted to hear, or anything I'm looking forward to, but I'm sure we'll manage well enough on the inside."

"Right. Well then, we should probably be getting on with it… I'm freezing in this rain," he relented, knowing it was futile to pursue the matter further, but something more than what she was sharing had obviously been said between the two and it had shaken her nerves.

"Soldiers, you have met our journey with unyielding bravery and have trusted me… your ranger… your guide… to lead this mission to victory. I know your hearts long for home, as does mine, but our duty is not yet over. I must ask you to again draw upon that same courage and follow me into the dead city, Zareck. We've all heard the same stories about souls that do not rest presiding here in this place overflowing with sorrow, but still our courage must lead us onwards. Even now, as we stand by Zareck's high-walls, the souls of the fallen have begun their wailings to us—mournful songs welcoming us to join them in death. Yet, let no one succumb to this cursed place, and let no person among us walk alone within the city. Soldiers, stay together and keep your senses sharp. There may be more than tortured souls dwelling behind these walls," Zantharius cautioned.

"What is our purpose here?" one of the centaurs called out to the ranger.

"A spy who hides in the shadows watches the two we protect, and it stays hidden from my sight. It cannot be allowed to learn the way to Zeur. If it does, I fear its master will bring terror to those we love, and rivers of blood will stain our streets," Zantharius answered.

"Then let us find and strike the spy down!" a soldier shouted. Instantly, the other soldiers erupted with loud cheers and pumped their fists into the air!

"Yes! We'll tear out its eyes and casts them down onto the rocks… see if it can watch them then!" another commented.

"What are we waiting for? Let's get in there and find it!" the curly red-haired centaur shouted—the group again erupted with shouts and cheers in support of the idea.

"First," Zantharius interrupted, "We must find shelter from this rain… a place to camp for the night, which may not be easy. We have to find a structure that hasn't become too rotten. Then, we'll get these two out of the rain and warmed by a fire," he said, gesturing at Amora and Magnar who were soaking wet and shivering in the cold. "After that, I'll take a group of men with me to search for the spy, while the others remain with these two for their protection. Everyone understand the plan?"

"Yes Sir!" the soldiers unanimously shouted.

Then, Zantharius turned his head to look at Amora before he stepped through the gate, "Ready?"

Briefly, she paused to think if there was anything she could possibly say to convince him NOT to enter Zareck, but no words came to her, because deep down she agreed this had to be done. Instead of arguing, she nodded and replied, "I'm as ready as I'll ever be," and together they stepped through the gate into *Zareck*.

CHAPTER THIRTY

Zareck

*C*arefully, everyone stepped through the gate and was met with the disgusting odor of mildew and decay in the stagnant air. The streets were unnaturally quiet for a city of its size and a thick blanket of fog crept along them—moving with a mind of its own down one street, and then another. Large banners on rusty hooks hung on doors and window ledges—some slumped down, but others were flapping and swaying *without* the slightest breeze. Chills ran down Amora's spine as she walked past one of them—searching for the cause of its movement in the absence of reason.

Quietly, everyone walked deeper into the city, looking at the ruined buildings and debris littering the streets from citizens who had lived there long ago. Everyone's eyes lifted upwards as they passed underneath a large, torn banner hanging across one lamp-pole to another, and although it had sustained heavy damage,

307

Amora could make out some of the faded letters... *W—lc—me Z—di—k's!*

The last few letters seemed familiar—she had seen them somewhere before. *What was that word,* she asked herself, thinking back to the old book she had read with Magnar at the bookstore in Bernard. She shut her eyes tight and tried hard to remember it—imagining herself sitting at the table with him, flipping through the book's pages. *What was that word,* she wondered again, but she couldn't remember. Frustrated, she opened her eyes and continued looking around at the ruined buildings as she rode on Zantharius' saddle, while he continued searching for a place suitable enough to make camp for the night.

Every now and again, low, mournful wailings and sobs could be heard—some seeming to come from behind windows of timeworn homes, while others with unknown origins echoed off random buildings. Cautiously, everyone searched for the owners of the sounds, but only puffs of dissipating smoke were ever seen. Several times, Amora and Magnar flashed each other uneasy looks—the hairs along their arms stood up as they traveled deeper into the city and passed by several more blobs of floating smoke.

Eventually, the mysterious Z-word from the banner began coming together (one letter at a time) in Amora's mind, but before all the letters could correctly be assembled, her concentration was broken by an odd noise coming from somewhere in the distance—

a moan from behind a partial wall up ahead within a crumbled building. Just then, her eyes caught a glimpse of something running across the far end of the street, but before she could make out what it was, it had dashed between two columns haphazardly supporting a crumbling section of wall, which connected the building to the tavern next door. She watched as the shadow clumsily knocked into one of its columns—sending debris and bits of broken stone to the ground. The noise alerted the soldiers to its position! There it was again—another long moan rang out from the location of where she had just seen the creature dart to!

"This way men!" Zantharius ordered, drawing his sword from his sheath to charge towards the direction the sounds were coming from. "Have your swords ready! We will end whatever foul creature makes those moans on this night!"

Obediently, the centaurs took hold of their swords and marched together behind the ranger towards the area they had heard the stones fall from, but before they reached the tavern, another gruff moan filled the air. This time, Amora listened intently to the pitch and tone of the moan. She remembered Zantharius' words warning her about the things living in Zareck and how they would surely want to kill everyone, but something about this creature's moan didn't feel menacing to her. Rather, the moan pulled at her heart for an unknown reason and it sounded like a plea for help—the creature hidden in the shadows was in pain and hiding from them in fear... but it wasn't evil. How she knew this, she didn't have the slightest idea, but the fact remained that she did, and she needed to trust her instincts. However, she was certain there would be no point in trying to convince Zantharius to trust her about this... about a feeling that couldn't be explained. He was much to stern and unyielding in his judgements to do such a thing.

For a moment, she thought about the next thing she should do. She needed to get to the creature before the centaurs did, but how? Amora leaned forward and whispered into the ranger's ear, "Zantharius, do you know what's making that sound or why? Maybe you shouldn't kill it."

"What *it* is... that's of little importance. Nothing good lives in this city anymore," he flatly replied. "Whatever it is... it will receive NO mercy." A forlorn expression crossed his face as he spoke—he went somewhere in his thoughts to a time when things were better in Zareck, much different from the desolate place it had become. "No, whatever calls out in this darkness cannot be trusted... no matter what it would have us believe. The soldiers and I will kill it. Rest assured you and your friend will remain safe... even within a deadly place like this."

Quietly, Amora nodded her fake agreement and wiped away the rain—turning into a drizzle—and the stray wet hairs off her face. Now, without the rain whipping into her eyes, she could see the city better, but there were only more crumbled buildings to observe and shattered window panes. Moss grew along the northern sides of those lining the streets, and there were broken columns, doors hanging off hinges, and shards of glass everywhere. Torn banners were slumped over doorways, balconies, and ledges, but the thing she wanted to see most—the creature—was nowhere to be seen.

Quietly, Zantharius and the others stepped inside the tavern with their swords held firmly. "This is where you last saw it?" Zantharius asked one of the soldiers, who nodded that it was.

Glass crunched beneath the centaurs' hooves as they walked around the room, searching for the creature. Amora watched the soldiers look for it behind the long, wooden bar and underneath tables, which they flipped over, but they found nothing. Two of the soldiers opened the large, dusty, pantry closets and searched the shelves, but the only things in there were expired goods, which were of no use. Others searched the cobweb covered bathrooms, but the creature wasn't in there either. Nothing was found in the tavern except for broken dishes, dirty silverware, and mugs filled with cobwebs and hatching spider eggs. After flipping one of the mugs over, a soldier was surprised by a grey, long-legged spider scurrying out of it onto his hand. Immediately, the burly soldier jumped and squealed, and the room erupted in laughter by the others, but the noise was short-lived. Soon, everyone was again silent.

Then, it happened! A long wail filled the air, and Amora's heart felt a pinch of pain at the sound. *That noise can't be coming from something dangerous,* she thought. *It sounds hurt!* She wondered how she was going to convince Zantharius not to kill it, but she knew any effort towards that would certainly be futile.

"There!" a soldier shouted, racing out of the tavern like a crazed man toward the string of buildings connected to each other across the street—holding his sword high and waving it wildly as he ran.

"I saw it too! A shadow going that way!" another exclaimed, pointing out the center of a window, trying hard not to get cut on the broken glass around the pane as he motioned a finger at something moving across the far side of the street—in the same direction the soldier had dashed off to.

"I think it went into one of those buildings over there!" another claimed; adrenaline rich blood rushed through his veins and his voice was hyper with excitement at the thrill of the hunt!

Immediately, Zantharius looked at Amora. "Hold on tight!" he commanded, sprinting out the tavern door towards the suspected location of the shadow.

As he galloped toward the creature—following behind one of the soldiers—Amora's heartbeat gained speed. Panic was setting in for the creature's well-being! She couldn't let the ranger, or the soldiers hurt it... no matter what! Within seconds, she saw a flash of white in the darkness, but oddly it wasn't in the direction Zantharius was running toward. The flash of white was across the street ahead of them. Then, again she saw the flash! This time farther away!

What was that, she wondered? *It's the creature's eyes! I know where it is! It's hiding inside another building, behind a half-crumbled column... peeking out from the side of it! Good! It's hiding, and if it stays quiet this time, then Zantharius and the others won't be able to find it,* she reasoned, but as soon as she completed her thought, the sound of someone stumbling over rubble up ahead was in her ears and the ranger's, too. Her eyes darted to where she had last seen the flash of white just in time to see the shadow for herself, and it was swiftly moving away from the column, dashing toward the back of the next building!

Suddenly, Zantharius stopped running to listen for it. As he waited for another sound, Amora caught sight of the white eyes and saw the shadow moving from the rear of a clothing shop, across to an adjacent back-alley! Then, it ran across several more alleys and disappeared into the night!

She was glad the creature was putting some distance between itself and the hunting centaurs, but she wasn't sure if that was going to be enough to deter the ranger from pursuing the hunt!

Very quickly and without thinking, Amora jumped off the ranger's saddle—surprising him—and took off running as fast as she could towards the building where she'd last seen the shadow!

"Amora! What are you doing? Get back here! Amora, wait!" Zantharius shouted, but she wasn't listening. Faster, the young woman ran, disappearing into the night to find the creature without any regard to what else could be lurking in the city—thinking only of desperately wanting to reach the creature before any of the others did!

Hearing the commotion and watching Amora run off through a tavern window, Magnar urged the red-haired centaur carrying him to run and see what was going on. Swiftly, the soldier ran, but he couldn't catch up to Zantharius, who had already sprinted off to find the young woman.

"Did you see what happened?" the soldier asked, coming to halt in the middle of the street. He was unsure of which direction Zantharius had taken off to, after seeing him dash away in an alley.

"Not much. Amora hopped off his saddle and took off running... over there I think," he answered, pointing to a different alley. "Zantharius was yelling and took off after her, but she didn't stop. Whatever happened... it can't be good."

"I'd say not. I've no idea what got into her head... running off in a dangerous place like this. This is not a good city... shouldn't no one be alone here... not even the ranger."

"I have to go find her. I can't let her be alone," Magnar insisted, hopping down from the saddle.

"I don't advise that. No, better to just let the ranger find her," the red-haired soldier replied, stroking his long curly beard and looking around at all the alleys she could have run through that led to... he didn't know where.

"I don't have a choice... she's my best friend. Can you help me?"

"No... I don't think it be wise. The ranger wouldn't want no one deviating from his plan. I'd better stay here," the soldier answered, shaking his head.

"Fine, I'll look for her myself," Magnar replied, picking an alley at random to head off to.

"Alright. Don't suppose there's any way I could convince ya not to, but just do your best to meet back up with one of the soldiers as soon as you can. Don't stay out here too long by yourself, or you'll be in the same predicament as your friend. I'll regroup with the others and tell them what happened. We'll set up a shelter somewhere and then come find you soon as we can. Remember lad, keep ya wits sharp in this place. Things worse than that wailing creature be lurking in this place."

Without hesitation, Magnar agreed with a quick nod and a fist salute, which the soldier returned, and then took off running after Amora! For a moment, he paused to look back at the soldier,

315

hoping he was going to change his mind and help him, but he was already returning to where the other men had gathered down the street. However, just as he was about to turn back around to go after Amora, he spotted something unusual. At the corner of a building there was a transparent blob of smoke hovering in the air a couple feet above the ground, but quickly it vanished into thin air. Not a trace of it was left, but something odder than seeing the smoke gripped the pit of his stomach… the smoke felt as if it had been *watching* him. Magnar had felt something was terribly wrong about this place… ever since he'd stepped through the front gate.

"Don't worry Amora. I'll find you," he said to himself, then rushed off to do exactly that!

CHAPTER THIRTY-ONE
Alone

Quietly, Magnar walked up and down the long narrow alleys tucked tightly between the buildings in search of Amora and Zantharius, but there were no signs of either of them anywhere. The night had become eerily still with no more rain or wind. It was silent, except for the sounds of his feet stumbling over chunks of rubble, which littered the streets and alleys from a tragic event that had happened long ago. The deeper he walked into the city, the deeper the white fog along the streets became—reaching his knees and making the steps over the rubble more difficult, because he couldn't see beneath the white blanket.

The night air was chilly, and a soft hazy mist was beginning to settle throughout the city as the hours ticked on. Carefully, he continued his search for signs of where either of them might've gone, but he was becoming more worried after spotting nothing for quite some time.

Amora, where are you? he asked himself, searching for bits of torn cloth snagged on fragmented stones along the walls or on corners of buildings, figuring that a piece of her clothing might have gotten ripped off if she had been running away from something—searching for any signs of a struggle. Maybe he would find a bloody handprint somewhere on one of the walls, or strands of her dark hair, which had been pulled out lying somewhere, yet there was nothing; he was feeling extremely relieved he hadn't found any of those things.

Maybe something happened to her after she ran away from Zantharius, he thought. *He's not protecting her anymore, and the centaur warned me about being alone in this place.* His mind created new horrible scenarios, one-after-another, with each passing second that he wondered through the streets searching for her.

Maybe one of the blobs of smoke found a way to kidnap her, he wondered?

It could've stolen her and sucked her into a place filled with them... the smoke-blobs could be the spirits of people that died in this city and they are still wondering around here, seeking revenge! That could be why I can't find her, he thought, out of his mind with worry.

No! Magnar, get a grip! That kind of thinking is crazy, he fussed, shaking his head.

Amora is still somewhere in the city, but I haven't looked in the right place yet... that's all. Wherever she is... she's alive and that's all that matters. If anything's got her... it'll have to fight me to keep her! Right now, all I need to do is to keep searching, he encouraged himself, filled with determination to find her somewhere within Zareck.

For a minute, he closed his eyes and inhaled a deep, mind-cleansing breath, but when he opened them, something strange had appeared, and it was hovering above the fog only a few feet in front of him. It was a dense, grayish-white blob of smoke with a long, oval shape, and there was a smaller one floating above it! Magnar nervously stared at the two—afraid to move—but neither smoky blob made an attempt to come nearer to him. Still, something about the situation felt sinister in intention. He was definitely in the middle of something he didn't want and was an unwilling participant! His instincts were telling him to run, but his mind was racing with thoughts about how the forms might react if he suddenly did so. They could become violent and rush over to him if his moves were not slow, deliberate, and careful, but that would mean the masses of smoke were more than a collection of random gases.

Could they somehow be alive? Are they spirits, he asked himself, studying the forms for visible signs of self-awareness.

319

Ever-so-slowly, he positioned his back against the farthest brick wall in the alley and moved away from the smoke. Perhaps, these were only two of the many spirits drifting around the city, which he had been forewarned about—those seeking revenge for their untimely deaths! With little thought required, Magnar quickly realized that if anything were to happen at this moment—alone without the aid of the soldiers—he wasn't equipped to battle enemies such as this with the little magic he knew. It had become more important than ever that he find Amora and Zantharius… with haste!

Slowly, he slid his body against the cold wet stones of the wall by stepping his feet to the side (inch-by-inch) away from the blobs of smoke. His back was pressed firm against the hard bricks, and several times their rough edges snagged against the soggy fabric of his long-sleeved shirt as his body moved along them, but still he kept his eyes focused on the blobs—their positions unmoved. As he stared at them, he could see the various hues of color swirling within them, and their smell of rot made his nose twitch. Bravely, he stared, but a chill was rising up his spine as he did—causing goosebumps to erupt all over his skin. Even the hairs along his arms were reacting to the entities near him by rising in alarm to the phenomenon. Then, suddenly the temperature in the alley dropped around him, causing his breath to fog! Something was about to happen, and he didn't want to stick around to find out what!

Quickly, he took in a deep breath, but this time when he blew it out, he felt like someone was standing close behind him... too close! That was impossible... right? Except for the smoke, he had been alone in the alley. The long wall of the building behind him was at his back and another stood across on the other side, so there couldn't be anyone behind him. Still, he felt someone was close— almost close enough to reach out and touch him.

Slowly, Magnar stepped one foot next to the other and resumed scooting his body along the wall away from the formless blobs of smoke. One, two, three, four, five feet away... six, seven, eight, nine, ten more feet of distance he placed between himself and them. Within a couple minutes, he had reached the end of the alley and turned to see if the smoky blobs were where he had left them.

Good! They haven't moved, he reassured himself with great relief, but just before he was about to turn away from them to continue his search down a different street, he saw out of the corner of an eye that the blobs were moving towards him.

They're moving! I knew it! They're not smoke... they're spirits, he said to himself, not sure if he was happy that he had been right all along, or more terrified now-than-ever as he realized the danger he was in.

321

Immediately, his mind spun with thoughts about Amora. Had she encountered one of the vengeful spirits too? Was she lost in the city and hurt? Where was Zantharius? Had he found her and kept her safe? Question-after-question popped into his mind as he stared at the spirits.

Suddenly, the spirts turned and floated away in the opposite direction and took off out of the alley, but why? Confused about what he had just seen, Magnar realized he'd been holding his breath, so he let out a huge sigh of relief. Then, his eyes caught sight of something else... something larger was phasing through the wall from where he'd felt like someone had been standing behind him!

From nothingness, a much larger blob of smoke was coming through the wall and it began to form a shape... a person! The hairs on his arms and back stood erect, and he could feel that this spirit was different than the first two he'd encountered. The energy emanating from it felt... hateful. Magnar knew that if he didn't get moving right away, then he might join the dead sooner than he thought!

Despite the cold air, sweat ran down Magnar's forehead as the entity began drifting closer toward him with arms held out. He could feel it glaring at him—making the energy in the air feel dense. The organ pumping blood inside Magnar's chest began working harder and faster as fear froze his body in place—

becoming nothing more than a statue staring at an ominous fate. He could feel the tension rising steadily in the alley between himself and the smoky form, and more goosebumps were popping up everywhere along his skin beneath the wet clingy clothing.

All of a sudden, Magnar found his strength to break free of his fear and without thinking... he ran! With hurried steps, he took off sprinting down street after street, crossing one alley, and then another! Swiftly, he dashed around corners and ran through alleys without losing a bit of speed—putting as much distance as possible between himself and the spirit! Huffing with lungs burning, Magnar ran down one more street and an alley for good measure—finally stopping to catch his breath and looked around to see if the spirit was anywhere to be seen, but the street was empty. In the middle of it, he stood alone, and everything was again quiet, except for random sounds of rubble falling off decayed buildings.

Where is everyone, he wondered, thinking that he should have run into Amora, Zantharius, or any of the soldiers by now. *Where did the spirits vanish to?* However, he could live without finding out the answer to that last question!

Quietly, Magnar began walking up a street—trying to decide the next way to go to search for Amora. Everything looked the same: crumbled buildings, moss growing on the northern sides of them, shattered windows, broken doors with bent hinges, caved-in roofs, columns leaning against walls, and filthy banners drooping on rusty hooks in the windless night.

What horrible thing happened here?

For a moment, he thought about the bookstore and he remembered the images he had seen in the forbidden book's tattered pages. *Could these be the same buildings,* he contemplated? Magnar paused in the middle of the street and carefully studied the details of the surrounding buildings before continuing on. He looked at their architecture and thought about what the structures might have looked like before they became damaged ruins.

Next, he compared his mental reconstructions to the drawings he remembered in the book, but so much had happened since then, that his memory had become vague at best. *I don't know… maybe it's the same place. Everything looks like it could be, but it's too dark to see enough. There has to be something around here that'll help,* he thought.

As he searched for clues to the mystery, he spotted a large torn cloth hanging from a hook on a high window ledge of what appeared to be a building that had once served as an inn. The dirty, rain-soaked cloth looked like it might have been a bed sheet that someone had written on, but the letters had long since faded, and part of the sheet had folded-in on itself—probably during a windy thunderstorm, but he could still make out the letters not hidden within the fold. Quickly, Magnar walked closer to it, until he was almost standing directly beneath it. Cold drops of water dripped down the cloth and splashed onto his forehead while he tried to read the sign.

"WELCOME ZODIARKS! WE LOVE YOU!"

"Zodiarks! This is the place! This is the city in the book... where it all happened!" Magnar exclaimed, barely blinking as he stared up at the sign in amazement that he had found the area spoken about in the book. Even after the horrible things that had happened since reading the daft thing, he'd been wondering if the stories were anything other than made up tales. After all, it did require quite an imagination to think that the DARK ONE had been real, or that there had been people with extraordinary magical abilities that kept the world in balance, and that was only the beginning of what he'd had time to read.

That means the Zodiarks were real and this is the city where the parade was held. This is where they were going to announce the newest Zodiark, he reasoned, connecting one logical conclusion to the next. Deep in thought, he turned away from the banner and continued walking along the street, barely paying attention to anything else. He looked down at the knee-deep fog as he walked the dark streets, one after another, aimlessly making lefts or rights as he thought about the things he had read in the book. Street-after-street, he turned one corner after another without paying the slightest bit of attention to where he was going, while he focused on the flood of thoughts passing through his mind.

If this IS real, then that means there was the **DARK ONE**... *there was the* **DARK ONE**... *there was the* **DARK ONE**, the thought echoed in his mind. *What if that also means there still is,* he questioned, fearing the answer. Suddenly, the energy around him began feeling heavy and thick.

This city is where the DARK ONE killed them... the Zodiarks... the citizens... everyone. They all died... here... on these streets and inside these buildings, he thought, glancing around at the small shops, taverns, and inns that lined the streets as he walked.

That must be why their souls are trapped here, because this is the city where they were all... murdered. Magnar's hazel eyes began to well-up with salty tears that stung the corners, but then from nowhere, screams suddenly filled his mind—thousands of voices were in pain!

"Stop it! Please!" he begged, dropping instantly to his knees with his hands gripping the sides of his head at the temples. He shut his eyes tight at the sharp stabs of pain the voices were causing to pierce his brain, but still they grew louder.

"Stop! I beg you! Stop screaming!" he shouted to the air, but again the volume increased and drowned out his own thoughts, till every part of his mind was consumed with the pain and sorrow of those screaming.

"Stop! It's too much! I know you died here, but what can *I* do? Please, stop the screaming and I'll try to help you!" he pleaded, beating his hands against the sides of his head as he fell to his knees in the fog and hunched himself over in pain.

Abruptly, all the voices quieted down into whispers, but then a loud voice among them spoke—worsening the pain in Magnar's head.

"**YOU!** YOU CANNOT HELP US!" the voice angrily bellowed.

Without warning, Magnar's body stiffened and his spine was forced to straighten while he knelt in the fog. He wanted to stand and run, but as he tried to lift himself from the street, he felt as if an immense amount of weight was being pushed down against his back, and his legs were being forcibly held to the ground. The droplets of mist drifting through the air started to harden into tiny pellets of ice as the temperature around him began to rapidly plunge to zero. For the second time that night, he could see the exhalations of his breath appear as a frosty white fog in front of himself, and his body was beginning to shake and shiver. Quickly, he gripped his hands around his arms and began rubbing them vigorously up and down in an effort to warm his frozen skin. However, it did little to help. Still, his body shivered with chills as the temperature dropped lower with every passing second.

Magnar closed his eyes and tried to focus his thoughts on warm memories—sitting by a roaring fire, sipping hot apple cider beneath a cozy blanket—but the bone-chilling cold was too strong to ignore. A violent chill shot up his spine and shook his limbs mercilessly, forcing his eyes to re-open as it did so, but when they did, he saw something even more disturbing than the blobs of smoke he had witnessed floating earlier. The thick fog that had been creeping along the city's muddied streets had begun to slowly move in swirls around him! Right away, his mind raced to the worst idea about what the phenomenon could be as he watched the fog swirl and break apart into multiple sections—thousands of various sized smoky blobs were forming around him at an alarming rate!

"Anything but spirits… anything but spirits… anything but spirits!" he whispered aloud to himself, shutting his eyes again and crossing his fingers with empty hope.

"You!" a voice hissed behind him. "You have come to the wrong place!"

Slowly, Magnar opened his eyes. There, two feet in front of him, he saw a large blob of greyish smoke drifting closer to face him—sizably larger than those he had seen in the alley—and it was taking on a human form! The energy in the air was static and palpable with intense anger! Quickly, the other smoky blobs surrounding him began taking on human forms, too and were making a tight circle around him.

"Intruder! You die here. FILTHY! Filthy scum... the living... they invade... trying to lay claim to it! *This* place be claimed by the dead. You... have... NO... place here!" a man, who appeared to be the leader, shouted. Suddenly, the others gathered closer around Magnar, tightening the circle around him!

Magnar could feel the intentions of the angry mob... they wanted his head on the chopping block... they wanted his blood!

"Why did you kill me?" a young boy's voice rang out.

Magnar turned his head to see a small smoky form of a boy drifting nearer towards the front of the mob—the others respectfully moving out of his way as he came close to Magnar's face and lifted his tiny hand to touch Magnar's cheek.

"Why did you attack my city? Why did you kill me and my mother?" the young boy softly asked, his voice gentle and his eyes filled with tears. Instantly, Magnar felt sorry for the boy, but why did he think *he* was the one who had killed him and his mother?

"You heard the boy. Answer him!" an angry woman's voice yelled from somewhere within the mob of spirits—inching together tighter around him. "Why did you kill my innocent child? Why did you kill any of us?"

"What? But… I didn't. I'm not the one who murdered him… you… or any of you! You've got it all wrong!" he pleaded, but the spirits weren't listening.

"He wanted the Zodiarks dead! That's why he did it! He wanted to stop the parade, so he murdered us!" a man shouted. "He's a MURDERER! MURDERER! MURDERER!"

Suddenly, the entire mob began shouting in rhythmic unison the same word over and over, **"MURDERER! MURDERER! MURDERER! MURDERER!"**

"He must die for his crimes against the city!" another man's voice shouted from within the mob.

Quickly, Magnar turned toward the direction of the yeller just in time to see a large blob of smoke vanish from the air and re-appear no more than an inch in front of his face. Up close the smoke smelled of rotten flesh and the odor made Magnar's skin crawl.

Viscously, the spirit encouraged the mob. "The intruder must die! Bash his head upon a rock! Break his skull and spill his blood upon the same streets as our own blood spilled!"

Immediately, the mob erupted with sinister cheers and began chanting, "DIE! DIE! DIE! DIE! DIE!" They wanted him executed as payment for crimes Magnar had not committed! They were ravenous for the shedding of his blood to fulfill their need for revenge, and they were blinded to all else!

Something was strange about the mob—it was as if they could see him, but at the same time, they were oblivious to reality. He had not killed these people, but no matter how hard he tried to convince them of that fact, they still thought he had. Something else was going on! Suddenly, Magnar realized that everyone who had died in the city by the deeds of the DARK ONE, was still trapped in an alternate reality that kept them bound to Zareck! They couldn't believe him, because they were under an evil spell—trapped as spirits who were being withheld from moving on.

"Wait! Please, it wasn't me that wronged you... any of you! You're trapped by some sort of spell! I want to help, but first you've got to believe me! I'm not the one who did this to you!" Magnar tried to explain, but he was barely able to hear his own words over their ranting for his death.

"Lies! He lies to us! Venomous words he speaks to shake our minds from the truth!" a little girl's voice shouted from the midst of the mob—her scull bashed and bleeding from an injury sustained long ago. "Don't listen to him, mom!" she said, gripping her mother's hand. "Make him pay for killing me! Make him pay for killing all of us and our Zodiarks!"

Again, the mob cried, "KILL HIM! KILL HIM! KILL HIM!"

"Rain bricks and stones down upon him! Stone him till his veins empty of their red!" the mother's voice shouted, agreeing

331

with her daughter—a large gaping hole was at her center where something had speared her, which had caused her death.

"We could scorch him with fire! Make his flesh crackle and peel!" another yelled, grinning wildly with crazed bulging eyes glaring at Magnar.

"No! Please! I beg you... hear me! Listen to what I'm telling you! I'm not the one that killed you, or the Zodiarks! It wasn't me! I'm not the one you're after," Magnar begged, struggling to free himself from the road to get up and run, but he was being forced to keep his kneeling position on the street no matter how he jerked his body to free himself. "Let me go! I didn't do anything to you... to any of you! I can help, if you'd just listen to me!"

"LIES! LIES! He speaks filthy lies!" the apparitions angrily shouted, tightening the circle around him.

"We saw you do it!"

"We saw you kill the Zodiarks!"

"You killed us!"

"There is no escape."

"It is decided."

"The intruder will die for his crimes!" the leader declared.

Frantically, Magnar searched for a way out, but the spirits had not left even the smallest gap between them as they closed in tighter to make the kill. Slowly, they began circling him—a swarm moving as one to form an impenetrable wall of thick smoke.

"Stop! It wasn't me! I swear it! I'm not the one who killed any of you!" Magnar insisted, but the spirits refused to listen and steadily increased their speed, until forming a gigantic soul-storm swarming around him! Its high winds drowned his voice from the air, and it kicked up dirt and debris that stung his eyes, rendering him partially blind as he knelt helplessly in the center of the massive storm. It appeared to be expanding as the spirits whirled by him!

Again, he tried shouting his pleas to the spirits, but the debris flying through the air invaded his mouth and coated his tongue with textures of sticky clay and coarse sand, causing him to cough and choke. Beyond desperation for the spirits to listen to reason, he spat out a thick wad of the clumped dirt from his mouth and held his hands against his face. Once more, he shouted his pleas to the swarming soul-storm, but through squinted eyes he could see something else horrible was beginning to happen. The spirits were conjuring a colossal form—yet to take a shape other than a funneling mass of smoke that towered him!

At the sight of it, a nauseating rush of panic overtook his senses, and Magnar began to violently jerk his body left and right in another attempt to free himself from the muddied road beneath him, knowing that if he didn't successfully do so within the next few seconds, then he never would! Suddenly, a simplistic childhood spell crossed his mind. It was something he had learned in, Bernard, and he had only used it a few times while working at the bookstore. It had helped him to lift heavy stacks of books off the tables when preparing to put them away on their shelves at the end of his shift every night. Maybe that same spell would be enough to free him. It was definitely worth a try!

Quickly, Magnar looked down at his legs, which had gone numb from being in the forced position for so long, and calmly he waved his hands over his lower half. Then, he said the spell, *"Pondus de Pluma, Levate, Supergreditur."* Abruptly, the ground beneath him began to rumble and shake, but still his body stayed pinned to the street.

Louder this time, Magnar yelled the words, *"Pondus de Pluma, Levate, Supergreditur,"* and he began to feel a small bit of space push itself between him and the street beneath his legs, but it was only a little—not nearly enough for him to unfold them from their kneeling position to take off running.

Once more he repeated the spell, declaring in his mind that it was going to work this time! *"Pondus… de… Pluma,… Levate,… Supergreditur,"* making sure each word was clearly pronounced as he shouted them with all his might as loudly as he could in order to carry the spell over the roar of the soul-storm's powerful winds. At the finish of his words, dark swollen clouds rolled through the night sky and the souls erupted with angry moans. Several bright flashes of light streaked across the clouds with claps of thunder following them, and suddenly Magnar's body lifted free from the spirits' bonds that had held him! The spell had worked! Immediately, Magnar took off running, forcing his way through the swarm of spirits without stopping!

Engorged with rage, but unable to stop him, the souls continued converging into the frightening form. The tornado of swirling smoke was shifting and twisting as the spirits collided together to conjure a formidable foe to carry out Magnar's execution. Groans and growls filled the air as the form shifted into an enormous smoke-giant with two thick legs, and six arms—three on each side of the monstrosity—and it stretched forth its massive hands at the sky just as another streak of lightening jumped across the clouds above its head. Loudly, the giant growled at the sky, but quickly its focus was drawn down at Magnar!

The giant took several steps towards the running miniature—scurrying along the ground far beneath the giant—and the vibrations of his feet caused the street to tremble and the buildings to shake. Stones in decomposing walls were shaken loose and columns crumbled to the ground as the giant stomped towards him.

Filled with fear, Magnar looked over his shoulder to see the giant stomping behind him. Smoke swirled within its faux skin from those that had become a part of the creature in order to summon it! Its eyes appeared as dark pits without emotion, but soon enough, fires from deep within the creation became lit! The fires in its eyes glowed crimson, and the giant stopped to heave its mighty chest up and down, oxygenating the flames to make them burn hotter. An evil grin crossed the giant's lip as it stared at Magnar.

Knowing he couldn't defeat the giant alone, Magnar thought about the centaur soldiers! He needed to quickly find them if he was going to have any chance of defeating the monstrosity the souls had conjured. However, there was a crucial problem. He didn't have the slightest idea about where they could be! Hours had passed since he'd left their protection to search for Amora. Where should he run to look for them? Instantly, his brain flipped through images of the streets and alleys he'd traveled, but he still couldn't figure out which direction to go!

"DIE!" the giant bellowed, swiping its lowest two hands down at Magnar a split second before he chose a direction. Luckily, he dodged the first swipe, but immediately a second came from one of the giant's middle hands that he didn't see! Right-away, Magnar felt it strike his back hard with great force as he became airborne and was flung across the street—hitting the side of a building with a hard *thud!* Pain filled his body and the breath in his lungs was emptied upon contact with the wall. Magnar heard the clinking of glass shards and rubble falling down around him as he shook his head and coughed, trying to force the air back into his lungs. He gripped his chest at the painful rush of the cold air flooding back inside and his body ached. Then, he reached for his temples and felt something wet oozing down the side of his forehead onto his cheek. Carefully, he touched the substance to investigate it—moving strands of hair away from his face, but they were wet too. Gently, he touched his forehead and withdrew the finger to look at the coated tip through blurry vision and he realized it was blood. His head had hit the wall! Again, he touched his forehead—searching for the gash—and it stung the moment he found it, but with some stitching it might prove manageable.

How I am going to find the centaurs if I can barely see, he asked himself, placing the palm of his hand against the gash on his forehead. "Ouch!" he whimpered, flinching at the pain as he made contact with the bloodied skin at his hairline.

First, he needed to push aside the rubble lying around him on the ground and get back onto his feet. Then, he'd have to muster all his strength to take off running again in any direction that led away from the giant—hoping that choice would lead him to the soldiers. Slowly, he did the first thing and pushed aside several chunks of broken stones. Next, he got onto his feet, but as he straightened his body upright, a wave of pain flooded him and sent severe throbs pounding through his head. Still, he staggered to his feet, up-righted himself and got prepared to run like the wind—

337

fully aware that he would have to sprint as fast as he could, because the giant would be chasing close behind him.

Then, it happened! The giant began stomping faster towards him with all six hands wide open!

"YOU... DIE... NOW!" it bellowed, stomping its flat feet against the ground, shattering the stones beneath them.

Quickly, Magnar ducked around the corner of what was left of the building in order to hide from the smoke-giant's sight. Then, he made a decisive decision about which direction he needed to run towards, but just as he was about to take off, he felt searing hot heat and the force of something huge knocking into the building at his backside! The smoke-giant had rammed it—knocking down the building's walls and columns! Immediately, Magnar was flung once again into the air and he crashed onto the ground with huge sections of stones falling around him!

In a daze, Magnar tried to get back up, but pain ripped through him from his injuries as he tried lifting himself with his arms. Instantly, they buckled underneath him, and he collapsed back down onto his stomach. All he could do was to lift his head to look up at the smoke-giant standing over him in the midst of the debris. The heat from the smoke-giant's eyes was intense, and Magnar looked up to see the blazing furnaces staring down at him without the slightest hint of emotion. It was obvious that the smoke-giant was not going to waver from its purpose... to kill him for the spirits. It was at this moment that he was beginning to think the smoke-giant was enjoying itself.

Not sure of what to do next, Magnar closed his eyes and took in a painful deep breath into his sore lungs. The energy in the air had become more static and seemed to beckon his impending doom. The air tingled with bitterness and hatred; Magnar knew the spirits were anxious for their evil creation to carry out the deed! In his mind, he knew what the spirits were thinking: *We have him*, or, *Do it! He's ours!* Maybe they were right. He could see no way out of his predicament. It felt as if death itself were reaching for him, and soon he would be within its smoky grasps.

"Get up! Get up now Magnar!" a new voice called to him, but the throbbing pain in his head quieted the voice. Magnar tried to lift his head to see if anyone was actually there, calling to him, but quickly the pain forced him back down onto the rubble.

"Magnar! Get up! Get up if you want to live!"

Again, he heard the voice calling him.

With great pain, Magnar forced his head up this time to look through blurred vision for the owner of the voice… though, still plausible it was imagined. Quickly, his thoughts returned to Amora. *Did she meet the same fate? Did she and Zantharius find each other? Was the ranger able to keep her safe from the spirits? Why did she run off in the first place?* With no answers, he hoped for the best, and knew he needed to find a way to stand up so he could find her. If Zantharius was half the ranger the soldiers had claimed, then surely, he had found her, and was keeping her safe somewhere in the city. Maybe the soldiers had already found and rescued both of them, and they were now safely outside the city's walls.

"Magnar! Get up! Do it NOW!" the voice forcefully shouted.

Through blurred vision, Magnar saw a centaur running up the street toward him with several soldiers close behind!

"We'll distract the giant, but for goodness sake, get up and RUN!" the soldier shouted, motioning with his hands and directing the others.

They found me! The soldiers found me! They're here... I'm not alone anymore! Right-away, Magnar was rejuvenated with hope! Despite the whooshing noise in his ears from the pain in his head, he could hear the soldiers' hooves pounding fast and hard against the street as they charged towards the smoke-giant! They had come to rescue Magnar from his nightmare!

Quickly, he looked up at the smoke-giant. It was losing interest in him, but it was now angrily stomping toward the approaching soldiers—shaking the ground with every step as it neared them. The smoke-giant bellowed a horrendous growl, but the soldiers did not flee!

"YOU... STOP... NOW!" the smoke-giant demanded. "HE BELONG TO ME!"

"He is under the protection of Zeur's army. He is not yours to have!" the leading centaur boldly replied, coming to a halt with the soldiers behind him in an attack formation.

"Your claim means nothing! The man flesh is mine!" the smoke-giant declared, snarling at the soldiers. "Horse-men die if they try to take him," it threatened, eyeballing two large sections of a broken wall laying on the ground. "LEAVE... CITY... NOW!"

"He is ours to take! Stand down! Crawl back into the shadows from whence you came, or the end shall be yours alone," the centaur barked back at the giant, who was evilly glaring at him.

"No!" the smoke-giant shouted, shaking the walls of nearby buildings with the vibrations of its voice.

"Men, stand your ground!" the leader shouted, ordering them to hold the line in perfect unity with their swords drawn from their sheaths. Their faces were stern and unyielding with great intensity in their eyes as they tightened their grips around the hilts of their steel blades—each prepared to sacrifice his own life for the greater good.

Furious that its warning had fallen on deaf ears, the smoke-giant reached down with its many hands and scooped up the two hefty sections of the broken stone wall and hurled them at the soldiers! "HE... BE... MINE!" the smoke-giant yelled, watching the stones fly through the air.

Magnar's eyes widened with horror and his heart lurched into his throat as he watched the stones lift into the sky and whirl past him towards the soldiers. "Look out!" he screamed, pointing at the massive chunks.

Suddenly, a thunderous voice yelled, "*Claudicatis Petras!*" and abruptly the stones ceased their movements in mid-air halfway between the giant and the soldiers!

Magnar's eyes darted to see who had cast the spell as he ran past the suspended stones to join the soldiers. It was the curly red-haired soldier! He held his sword high and had it pointed at the stones.

"Magnar, good to have you back! Now, what do ya say... let's kill this smoke-giant and get out of here!" he said, welcoming him back without looking away from the stones. Spells were difficult for him, so it was important he keep his concentration on this one to prevent the stones from becoming loose to crush them as the smoke-giant had intended.

"How are you doing that? The spell I mean," Magnar asked, watching in awe at such magic. He had never seen a spell suspend large objects before, and he wondered what other spells the soldier knew.

"What? Ya never lain ya eyes on a proper spell before?" he asked, keeping his focus on the flat slabs, which were beginning to shake in the air as they itched to break free. Slowly, he lowered

342

his sword and placed it back into its sheath by his side without taking his eyes off the slabs.

"I've seen spells, but nothing like this," Magnar answered, looking around at the tired faces of the other soldiers. They were weary from their travels, soaked, cold, hungry and homesick for their wives and children. However, their bravery showed as well, because every man was ready to take on the giant and die, if it meant the world where their children grew up would be safer.

"Can't imagine what kinds of spells they taught you... if proper ones not be counted among ya lessons," he remarked.

"The world I was taught... let's just say it was different than this and spells were for chores. There, no one knew magic beyond that."

"That's a shame," he commented, shaking his head. "Then, I suppose all this is a shock to ya... centaurs, a city full of dead that can still kill ya, not to mention the goblins. Bet they didn't teach ya about them nasty things either did they?"

Magnar shook his head no.

"Guess you're gonna have to be trained up once we get ya to my city, and *THAT* you can be sure they're gonna do."

"You mean Zeur?"

"Yep, that's my home and a fine one at that. Zeur is one of the only places left in this world untouched by the evils that hide in the shadows. One thing's for sure, you'll know the world for what it really is once my people are done with ya. That is, if ya haven't figured it out already with what you and that friend of yours have been through. A nasty place that Kembrull Forest is, and ya both survived it. Ya already been up against goblins, and most people without strong magic don't live to talk about them after comin' face-to-face with *those* nasties. The truth is, most who live in this world are asleep to the truth, but they'll awake soon enough. Somethin' be changin' in the shadows... strengthening, but I can't say anymore. It's not my place. Some people in Zeur are waitin' to speak with you and ya friend about that," he said, his voice trailing off as he realized he had said too much. Briefly, he took his eyes off the stone slabs and glanced at Magnar, "Where did you say you're from lad?"

"I didn't, but it was a place called, Bernard. It's gone now. It was destroyed by goblin-fire when they were looking for me and Amora," he glumly replied.

"Were... lookin'?" the centaur asked puzzled, shocked at Magnar's naive assumption about goblins. "What makes ya think they've stopped?"

"What do you mean? Do you know something?" Magnar asked, his heart beating faster with anxiety as he paused for the answer. His gut was telling him that he wasn't going to like what the red-haired soldier was going to say.

"It's just that goblins aren't known for givin' up targets easily. Once they've become fixated on somethin', they hunt it down until either they've gotten what they wanted, it's dead, or they're dead.

"Oh. I see," Magnar replied, with a new rush of fear forming inside himself.

"No worries lad. Our job is to protect ya and as long as ya are in the company of the centaurs, protected is what you'll be."

With a respectful closed-fisted solute to his chest, the red-haired soldier continued, "Now, let's end this smoke-giant so I can get back home to me wife and wee little ones. What ya say... ya with me?"

Quickly, Magnar nodded his agreement, "Let's end this." He was ready to fight the smoke-giant with the help of the soldiers and the red-haired centaur, who was becoming a friend.

CHAPTER THIRTY-TWO
Giants Must Fall

*T*here, everyone stood at the far end of the street face-to-face with the smoke-giant. Each person was staring it down as it glared back. The furnaces of its eyes blazed with flames as it slowly heaved its chest in and out, preparing for their strike against it. At the same time, it was plotting the ways it wanted to kill the soldiers in return. Everyone's breath fogged white in the air as each person stood together as a united group and waited in anticipation for who would make the first move.

Magnar couldn't feel the cold against his skin anymore as the adrenaline boiled inside his blood. *Who would strike first to end this stalemate,* he wondered? *Was the curly red-haired soldier really as good at spells as he would need to be in order to protect his life from the smoke-giant? If all the soldiers were with him, then was Amora alone somewhere inside the city? Had the ranger,*

Zantharius, found her? Would he be able to protect her without the help of the soldiers? These were the questions that would have to be answered at another time.

For now, he stood there among the brave centaurs who held their swords firmly, waiting for the one word they needed to hear, from the person who had become their leader in Zantharius' absence. Out of the corner of his eye, Magnar noticed an approving nod from Zantharius' brother, Zanick, at the curly red-haired man who was keeping the line steady—making sure he didn't use presumptuous force if the smoke-giant agreed to back down.

Frankly, it made Magnar a bit annoyed that he was acknowledging this tactic, because he wanted the men to charge at the smoke-giant and render its head from its neck before it had enough time to end his own life. However, despite his eagerness to engage the battle, he understood that the soldiers knew better than him. Silently, he held his ground with them and waited for the word.

Then, something began to happen... the smoke-giant took a step forward and then another. It wasn't going to back down! It was conjured by spirits who wanted Magnar dead, and it wasn't going to stop until that goal had been achieved. Suddenly, he heard the word everyone had been waiting for, and it was shouted into the air by the red-haired soldier.

"ATTACK!" The battle for Magnar's life had begun!

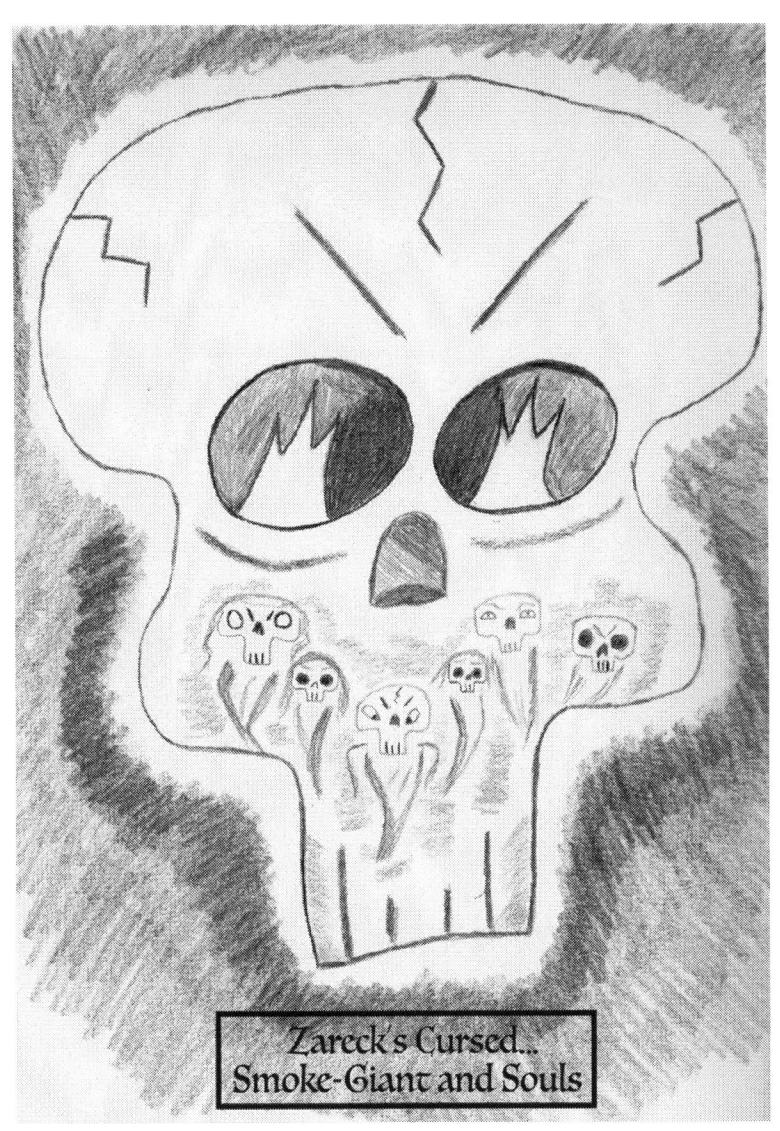

Zareck's Cursed...
Smoke-Giant and Souls

Brazenly, the centaurs stomped and excitedly pawed their feet against the ground and charged at the smoke-giant with swords pointed! War cries and galloping hooves striking the street's stones filled the air.

Right-away, the words, "*Reditum Petra!*" were shouted by the red-haired man next to Magnar, unsheathing his sword and pointing it once again at the suspended stones in the air. With a swift motion of his blade, the stones flipped their direction and flew back towards the smoke-giant!

Being unable to move away fast enough, Magnar watched in awe as the two massive stones slammed hard against the side of the smoke-giant's face and chest, knocking it backwards several steps, causing it to lose balance and fall to the ground! Without hesitation, the centaurs hastened their approach at this precise moment, and plunged their swords into its legs and feet. However, the smoke-giant did not holler as expected. Instead, the furnaces of its eyes blazed brighter—the scorching heat was felt against each centaur's skin—and the energy in the area became electric!

At that moment, Magnar looked up at the smoke-giant's eyes. There was something different about them... more sinister. It felt as if the spirits that had conjured it were no longer in control. Something *evil* had taken hold of the creation. Whoever was controlling it now... was malevolent and much stronger than the spirits had been.

Who is the new puppet master, Magnar wondered? However, before his mind could find a plausible answer... the dark master made its puppet speak.

It glared past the centaurs and looked down at him and declared, "Your parents are as good as dead. Your eyes look sad," the smoke-giant wickedly laughed. "Are they watering for your parents? Then, do not worry. You will join them in death soon enough... and your companion will join hers, too," the smoke-giant said, grinning.

Without thinking, Magnar flinched at the comment and the smoke-giant took notice of his emotional reaction.

"Yes! Amora is the one I speak of. What? Did you think I didn't know about her? That I would spare her life and only kill YOU! Now, why would anyone do that?" the smoke-giant sneered.

Magnar was shocked the smoke-giant knew of her, but it didn't make any sense *how* it knew about her. Was it the work of the spirits? No. It couldn't have been. They would've attacked her outright as they had him. Plus, whoever was talking through the giant seemed to have insider knowledge about their parents being kidnapped, and the spirits wouldn't have had any information about that. One thing was clear, whoever the new puppet master was, this person was evil and enjoying the taunts.

"Leave her out of this! It's my life you're here to claim, not hers!" Magnar shouted back, trying his hardest to keep a brave face as if nothing had shaken him, but he feared the puppet master controlling the smoke-giant had already figured out that the expression on his face was fake. Undeniably, he was shaken to his core with worry about Amora and their parents' safety.

"Do you really think these half-horses will be able to keep either of you safe? They're mindless animals!" Abruptly, the furnaces in its eyes blazed hotter as it swooped all its hands down and grabbed several of the soldiers! The centaurs screamed as the smoke-giant lifted them up and squeezed them mercilessly! "They make better food, than they do as soldiers!"

Magnar's eyes widened in horror as he watched blood burst from their flesh and drip down the smoke-giant's fingers! Bone-chilling cracks filled his ears as their bones broke and shattered beneath its grips! His body cringed as the centaurs screamed, until no more sounds came forth from their lifeless corpses.

Mischievously, the giant grinned at him as it held one of the bodies up by the hind legs and dangled it over its wide-open mouth, dropping the centaur down into its stomach! One-by-one, it dropped the other dead bodies in there too.

"Stop! You'll claim no more of my brethren ye foul blaspheme from the shadows!" the red-haired soldier yelled, outraged about their deaths. "Ya should've left this city while ya could. I won't let ya touch a single hair on Magnar's head, or his pretty friend's either! I'll have to be cold an' in the grave first!"

Then he then turned to Magnar, "Don't ya worry lad. We're not done and outta this fight yet! There still be a smoke-giant to kill... and kill him we will! We won't let him get nowhere near Amora. The sky will help us bring this thing down!" Immediately, the red-haired soldier sheathed his sword and looked up at the cloudy sky, stretching both his open hands at it. *"Tonitrui et Fulmen. Fulminibus Percutio!"* he shouted. Instantly, the tips of his fingers began to spark with electricity!

"I feel an electrifyin' comin' on!" he cheekily said, confident that he was going to end this fight once and for all. Next, he flung his hands towards the smoke-giant! Huge bolts of lightning shot out of his fingertips and struck the smoke-giant—sizzling and zapping along its smoky skin! Instantly, he flung bolt-after-bolt with great excitement, and each bolt reached its mark! Twice, the smoke-giant was knocked to the ground, but got back up— shattering the stones on the street and splattering mud high into the air each time it fell. Until finally, it fell once more—its body twitching as the lightning coursed through it.

Altogether, the remaining soldiers became silent as they watched and waited for the smoke-giant to get back up—for the fight to continue—but there was nothing.

Quietly, Magnar thought, *Was that really it? Had the centaurs won? Had the puppet master really been defeated? Was it that easy?* Silently, he stood with the others and waited for any movements that would signal the fight wasn't over, but it wasn't long before the centaurs had started cheering their victory!

Hoorah's were joyously shouted by the soldiers, and hooves pounded the street as they gave one another celebratory fist-to-chest salutes. However, what came next was something no one had expected....

CHAPTER THIRTY-THREE
Midnight

"Amora, stop! It's not safe to be alone in this city," Zantharius shouted, galloping after her as she ran from one dark alley to another, chasing after the wailing creature in the foggy mist that had settled in after the night's rainstorm.

"Zantharius, I'm not gonna let you or the soldiers hurt it! It's not dangerous!" she yelled, picking up speed as she caught a glimpse of its white eyes looking back at her as it darted around another corner into a narrow alley between two buildings pressed tightly together.

Right-away, Amora ran past that same corner and squeezed her body through the narrow alley with her face turned to the side and chest pressed against the stones as she side-stepped to fit through. Unable to expand her chest even a little, she held her breath as she squeezed past the wet stones threatening to crush her! Carefully, she stepped one foot next to the other, trying to keep as quiet as possible. Her eyes strained hard to see down the alley in the dim light as she inched through, but suddenly she heard something knocking around some rubble. She was getting close to the creature and her heart instantly jolted to a quickened pace!

There, she thought, spotting the white eyes and its shadow sprinting off to another alley.

"Amora, get back here! That's an order!" Zantharius demanded, coming to a full stop at the entrance to the narrow alley—unable to fit himself through. Quickly, he looked left and right, trying to find another way to reach the young woman, but without knowing the layout of the city, Zantharius ran towards the wrong direction.

Quietly, Amora followed the sounds of the creature from one alley to another as she trailed behind it; until finally ending up on a dead-end street surrounded by buildings on all sides, except for the way she'd entered. It was darker than the others, but if the creature was there, then there would be no way for it to escape.

I've got you, she thought, walking slowly down the passage as she looked around through squinted eyes in the dark. The only sound was her heartbeat whooshing in her ears from her nerves as she stepped deeper into the darkness… everything was perfectly still and quiet. Then, a flash of white at the far end of the alley grabbed her attention. Something was huddled against the stone-wall that sealed off the alley! Little-by-little, she approached the figure huddled against it, and her ears homed-in to the sounds of nails scraping against the stones as she got closer.

"I'm not going to hurt you," she softly said, stretching out a hand towards it. "I want to help."

Again, the scraping sounds were heard, but this time they sounded faster and more frantic. Whatever she was moving closer towards, it was becoming more frightened—realizing that it was trapped with nowhere left to hide. The situation had grown more dangerous because of this, but still Amora wanted to help.

"I promise... no one is going to hurt you. Will you let me help?" she asked. Her voice was gentle and filled with genuine concern as she rid them both of the last bit of distance between them.

Finally, she was close enough to see the scared creature huddled against the wall and a soft wail emerged from its throat as it, too, stepped towards her. As it neared, a ray of moonlight pierced the storm clouds to shine down upon the creature. In the beautiful bright beam, stood a baby dragon the color of night! Its eyes were sad and filled with tears, and it fearfully looked up at her and softly wailed... it was a cry in the night for help.

"Amora! Stop! Not another step!" Zantharius ordered, charging into the alley with his sword drawn at the baby dragon.

"Zantharius, NO! I know you think it's dangerous, but it's not! It's only a baby and it's not going to hurt me," she pleaded, throwing herself between the ranger's blade and the terrified baby dragon who clutched onto her leg to hide behind her. "I'm NOT going to let you hurt it! You'll have to kill ME first!"

"Amora, don't be deceived... even small things in a place like this can be deadly," Zantharius replied, looking around as if he was expecting something else to emerge out of the darkness. "Step aside and let me end it while we have the chance. Then, we'll find the others and your friend. We must leave this city before worse things lurking in the shadows find us," the ranger insisted, pointing the tip of his broad sword at Amora to urge her to hand over the baby dragon.

"I mean it Zantharius! Not another step, or I won't come with you to Zeur to meet Sir Beaksmith! If you hurt this dragon, I'll find Magnar and we'll go somewhere that you'll never be able to find! Sir Beaksmith will blame YOU for not bringing us to Zeur, and whatever he wants from us, he'll never get, simply because you wouldn't spare the life of one baby dragon. When you return to your home, what kind of life and reputation will you have as a ranger if Sir Beaksmith and your people no longer trust you? I don't think you want to risk any of that happening, but I promise I'll not go with you, if you harm this dragon!" she warned, with her eyes fiercely staring into the ranger's as she held her position to shield the baby, who was gripping one of her legs with its tiny claws while peeking out from the side of it at the big, bad centaur.

For a moment, Zantharius stood silently looking at her and the baby dragon. "If the life of this dragon means that much to you, then I will make no more claims against it. You have my word. No harm shall come to it from me unless your life be in danger from the beast. That is the best I can offer," he replied, sheathing his sword. "Do you accept my word?"

"Yes," she answered, stooping down onto her knees to embrace the frightened baby, who was lowering its head in submission with gratitude. Then, she noticed it was favoring one of its front feet, refusing to place weight on it.

"What's wrong little one?" she asked, holding out her hand in hopes that the baby dragon would trust her and place its paw there. "Is something wrong with your foot? I'll look at it if you'll let me."

"Amora, must you touch it? The animal could bite," Zantharius interrupted, frustrated at the young woman for not heeding any of his warnings—realizing this was probably going to become a pattern of behavior that he'd have to get used to.

"I don't care if it bites me… its foot needs to be tended to."

"How? We have no medical supplies for treating baby dragons, and I doubt you know of any spells that'll do much good."

Defiantly, Amora ignored Zantharius' skepticism and kept her focus on the baby dragon, who was tenderly licking one of its unfurled wings with its long, grape-colored tongue. The wing was torn, as if something had been shot through it, and the tear was large enough to disable the dragon from being capable of flight.

"That's why you're stuck down here isn't it?" she asked, gesturing at the baby's wing.

For a moment, the baby dragon stopped licking and followed her eyes to its wing.

"You understand me, don't you?"

Again, the baby dragon briefly paused its licking.

"Yes! You do understand! Well, what happened to you?" she asked, not expecting an answer, but wondering where the little one's mother was. "Did you get separated from your mother?"

Immediately, the baby dragon stopped licking and looked at her. Water filled its large eyes and spilled over their edges down onto its charcoal cheeks.

"That's exactly what happened isn't it. You must have been learning to fly with your mother when something attacked you, and your wing became injured, causing you to fall from the sky into Zareck. You're as afraid of being here as us!" Amora realized, putting together the clues to figure out the dragon's story.

Slowly, the baby dragon lifted its paw and placed it in Amora's hand for her to examine. There was a piece of broken wood sticking out of it—likely from the same weapon that had been used to shoot at its wings.

"I'll have to remove this from your foot if it's going to heal properly. Understand?" she asked, looking at the baby dragon. It didn't pull its foot away from her, so she knew that it did. It wanted the wood gone from its foot. "Zantharius, do you know any spells that could help with the pain?"

"No. I know of nothing that will help this creature," he answered, his voice kinder this time as he looked down at it.

Amora nodded and then kindly looked into the dragon's eyes. "I'm going to remove this from your foot. It's going to hurt, maybe even a lot, but that's no reason to bite me!" she said, smiling and hoping it really did understand at least that part. "I can't leave it in there. If I did, your foot would get infected and it might hurt worse over time. I need you to trust me."

Without flinching, the baby dragon allowed its paw to remain in her hand, and it turned its face to look away as she prepared to pull out the wood. Amora took in a deep breath and gave the wood a hard tug. Immediately, the baby dragon cried out from the pain as she pulled the wood free from its foot!

"There! All done!" she said, ripping off one of the long sleeves from her shirt to wrap around the baby's foot to stop the bleeding. "You did so good! Now, let's take a look at what was sticking in that foot," she said, taking a closer look at the

361

splintered wood. "There's something on the tip of it," she said, bringing it closer to her face to get a better look, but still she was confused about the object and its origin.

"Zantharius, come take a look at this," she said, noticing an odd, small, pointed stone on the tip of the wood. "Have you ever seen anything like this before?"

Carefully, the ranger picked up the small piece of wood with the tiny stone and studied it. He lifted it to his nostrils and took in a whiff of its foul scent and pulled it away with great alarm! "We've got to get this dragon moving, find the others, and get ourselves out of here! Time is against us!"

"Why? Zantharius, what's wrong?" she asked, hearing the panic in his voice. She hadn't seen him like this before—not even in Kembrull Forest when he was fighting the white werewolves. Whatever had him alarmed was something horrible!

"This is a broken piece of a goblin's arrow. I recognize the stench that still lingers on it. Goblins must've attacked the baby and its mother, trying to shoot them down to feed a horde of their own."

"If that's true… then,"

"Yes! They're somewhere close… too many for me to slay alone. Goblins don't leave prey behind, and if they know the baby has fallen, then they'll come here to claim their prize. They could already be within the city's walls searching for it! Amora, if they find *you*, they'll stop at nothing to claim your life," he informed, pausing before continuing on. "I'll do what I can to protect you... even if that means my death, but I am only one man. I cannot stop a horde of goblins without the help of the soldiers we came here with. We need to find everyone and leave for Zeur. Do what you can for the dragon. If you can get it flying again, then it might have a chance at finding its way home. I've heard dragons have great memories."

"How can I do that? I don't know any spells that'll help its wing to heal."

"Search your heart for the spell. All you need to do is to feel what you want inside yourself, and then let the words come to you... like water flowing over a waterfall. Focus. Place your hands over the dragon's wing and close your eyes. Think about healing it," he urged.

Hesitantly, Amora closed her eyes and placed her hands over the baby's wing. She tried to think about healing it, but the words weren't coming to her and nothing was happening. "I can't do it!" she sighed.

"Concentrate. Calm yourself and think of nothing else... only healing it. Let the spell flow from inside you... from your heart to the dragon's heart," Zantharius encouraged, looking around for goblins after hearing some rubble tumble down the side of a nearby building within the darkness.

Again, Amora closed her eyes, but this time she shut off her mind and allowed her feelings for the baby dragon to take over. She had already grown fond of it and wanted it to be without pain... she wanted both its wounds to be healed. At that moment, she felt a warm sensation flood out of heart all over her body, and the energy radiated outwards. Next, her lips began to move with unfamiliar words. At first, they were soft, barely audible, but the whispers grew as she spoke the spell, *"Draco Amor, Cor, et Sanitatum Virtus. Existo ut Sanetur!"* She spoke the spell several more times, *"Draco Amor, Cor, et Sanitatum Virtus. Existo ut Sanetur,"* and with each repetition, her hands became warmer as healing energy flowed into the dragon!

Gradually, she opened her eyes and watched in awe as the wing became healed—the skin closing itself. Quickly, she unwrapped the dragon's wounded paw and it had healed too! Amora had found the first spark of magic hidden inside herself, and deep down she knew this was only the beginning.

"I did it!" she exclaimed, giving the baby dragon a tight hug. "You can fly back home to your family!" she happily said, watching it step away hesitantly.

"I knew you could, but now we really must go and find the others. It's not safe here!" Zantharius stated, hearing the rubble once again. Something was watching them from the shadows... maybe the spy, or possibly a goblin. Either way, it was time to go!

"First, I have to give you a name. I'll call you, *Midnight*. Yes, that name suits you, but now you've got to go. Go on! Now! You're healed," Amora insisted, giving the baby dragon a shove. "You can't stay here. If the goblins find you, they'll kill and eat you! Go! Now!" she yelled.

Hesitant to leave her, but willing to obey, the baby dragon stretched out its injured wing and tested its strength by flapping it up and down a few times. Then, it stretched out the other one and took to the sky, flying up above the stormy clouds... out of her sight.

CHAPTER THIRTY-FOUR
A Cry in the Distance

Without another word, Amora stared up into the night sky for the baby dragon, but it had vanished as she had hoped it would high above the clouds. A pang of sorrow struck her heart at the thought of it being gone, but she had done the right thing. Silently, she climbed onto Zantharius' saddle, and he led the way through the alleys to search for Magnar and the soldiers, but the streets were quiet, still, and empty. Only the sounds of his hooves stepping on stones made noises throughout the streets as they journeyed deeper into Zareck's heart.

"Amora, did you hear that?" Zantharius asked, pausing his steps in the middle of an alley.

"Hear what?" she asked.

"Listen." For a moment, he stood still and they both kept quiet, listening for the slightest sound in the desolate alley. "There it is again!" he whispered.

"What was it? I didn't hear anything."

"Voices... yelling from somewhere, but they're faint."

"Are they from the soldiers... do you hear Magnar's?"

Zantharius closed his eyes and focused on the voices crying out in the distance, until they became clearer. "Yes, it's them, and Magnar's is among them. They're in danger! They need our help! We must hurry!" he answered, turning his face to the side to look at hers without realizing how much worry filled his eyes.

Right-away, Amora realized something was horribly wrong by the expression written on the centaur's face. "Zantharius, what aren't you saying? What's happened!" Her heart sank with dread as she thought about Magnar. This was the first time she had stopped to think about him since running off to chase after the baby dragon. She thought about what he had probably done in her absence: running after her, getting separated from the soldiers in pursuit of her, finding himself in some sort of trouble somewhere in the city... all because she had left without any explanation. Her foolish decision to run off may have put everyone's lives at risk! Maybe he had run into the goblins that had attacked the baby dragon... or something worse. She had to find him and do whatever it would take to make things right! *Magnar, I'll find you... I'm coming,* she thought.

"Amora, wrap your arms around me and hold on tight," Zantharius said, preparing to gallop towards the voices.

"Zantharius, for what it's worth... I'm sorry if I've caused any of this. I only wanted to help the baby dragon, but I didn't mean for anyone to get hurt."

"Whatever has happened, you were not the cause of it. This place is shrouded in shadow. The only thing you are guilty of is bringing light into it by your deeds of helping the innocent. Speak of your guilt no more. It needn't be a burden you carry," he comforted.

Amora knew his words were true, and for that, a fraction of a smile crossed her lips, but still, the guilt weighed heavily on her heart. She needed to find Magnar, and she desperately wanted to know if he was alright. Only then would her emotions be eased.

"Ready?" Zantharius asked, positioning himself to race towards the sounds.

"Let's go!" she replied, tightening her grip around the ranger and feeling the power within his body as he lunged forwards and began galloping across the dead city. The heat of anger boiled inside her blood as her adrenaline increased and coated her tongue with a metallic taste.

"I'm coming Magnar... and I'll kill whatever has you!"

CHAPTER THIRTY-FIVE
Not What It Seems

*L*oudly, the soldiers cheered victory over the defeated smoke-giant as it lay motionless on the ground not far away from the celebrators—none having a single care in regard to the twitching of its limbs from the random flickers of electricity surging throughout it. Triumphantly, the red-haired soldier pumped his fists into the air with the other soldiers who had gathered around to celebrate him for saving Magnar's life!

The battle was over, and it had been won, but something pulled Magnar away from the urge to celebrate. It caused an ill sensation in the pit of his stomach. Something felt odd about the ease at which the smoke-giant had fallen. Quietly, he stood apart from the others and refrained from joining their victory cheers, while he stared coldly at the smoky form lying on the ground only a few footsteps away. He searched his mind for a reason to explain the strong feeling, but all he knew was that he was expecting something more from his foe and its puppet master.

"If your face looked any sourer, I'd think you hadn't wanted your life to be saved," one of the soldiers walking by remarked, giving Magnar a curious look with a hard pat on the back. "Best put a smile on that face, for soon we will be in *my* city where a great celebration will be held in our honor… filled with adoring pretty women, food that stretches across tables for miles, and more mugs of frothy ale than a man can drink!" he boasted, loud enough for the others to hear as he pumped one of his fist a couple times high in the air with a rowdy cheer—others quickly joining their voices to it.

"I for one can't wait to return home. Zareck wreaks of death and I'm sickened by its repugnant smell," another soldier commented, wiping his runny nose against his arm.

"Anywhere is better than here," stated another.

"I don't be needin' to go home. There's nothin' special waitin' for me there, but still it'd be better than here. In this place, death be lurkin' around every corner waitin' to jump out and claim ya," remarked one more.

"When we return home, we'll tell heroic stories of our deeds and travels. The people will talk of our bravery and the number of foes we've slain! We will be heroes!" one of the centaurs encouraged, beginning a slow intermittent pump of his right fist

370

against his armor over his heart, increasing the beating rhythm of it steadily as he began a joyous battle song the others soon joined:

STEADY BEATS HEARTS OF WARRIORS
(BOOM...BOOM...BOOM...BOOM)

GIVE OUR LIFE FOR HONOR
(BOOM...BOOM...BOOM...BOOM)

MIGHTY MEN OF VALOR
(BOOM...BOOM...BOOM...BOOM)

AXE AND SWORD OUR POWER
(BOOM...BOOM...BOOM...BOOM)

CUT THEM DOWN, CUT THEM DOWN
(BOOM...BOOM...BOOM...BOOM)

STEEL AND SWORD, AXE AND STONE
(BOOM...BOOM...BOOM...BOOM)

TRUE HEART, OF A WARRIOR
(BOOM...BOOM...BOOM...BOOM)

However, Magnar's face was still long without passion for the victory as he listened to the deep harmonies belting from the soldiers' mouths to the synchronized beats of their fists pounding against their armor with every *boom* as they repeated the song twice more, which grabbed the attention of the red-haired soldier who had saved his life.

Quietly, the soldier slipped away from the group chanting the battle song, to find Magnar brooding by himself a little-ways away. "What's the glum look for? I'd have thought ya be the happiest amongst all the men since it be your life the smoke-giant was wantin'. What's the matter? Ya wish I could return the smoke-giant back to life so it could be back tryin' to squeeze ya innards into out'ards to make good on its need of killin' ya?" the red-haired centaur sarcastically asked, trying to investigate the reason for his sour expression. "Aren't ya glad it's dead?"

"Yes, I am. I thank everyone who had a hand in saving my life. It's just that—" Magnar began to say.

"It's just what!" the soldier snapped, cutting off his response before he could finish. "Ya don't like livin' or ya don't know how to be properly celebratin' after winnin'… cause that's what we've done here—we won the fight all nice and fair, and you be showin' no gratitude."

"Listen to good ole Bartholomaus!" a soldier passing by suggested, overhearing their conversation. "He knows what he's talking about. Magnar, relax and join in on the songs! We've killed the smoke-giant. Now, this be our time for celebratin'!" the soldier said, pumping his fists high into the air with loud cheers, that several others joyously joined, before he walked away.

Magnar smiled to imply that he understood, but still he couldn't shake the sour filling in the pit of his stomach that something wasn't right. "No, it's not that. I'm grateful, but—" he paused, looking over at the smoke-giant.

"There ya go again... always lookin' at that blasted thing! Well, spit it out. What's botherin' ya and why do ya keep lookin' at it? Ya expectin' it to get up or somethin'?" Bartholomaus asked, laughing at the thought, but suddenly after hearing himself say the idea out loud, it sunk in deeper that maybe *that* was exactly what was upsetting Magnar—sobering him up from his own elation. The possibility of the giant not being quite as deceased as he had thought would mean that the soldiers, Magnar, and himself were still in serious danger. Everyone had moved closer to what they had thought was a corpse and were now within the smoke-giant's reach if it somehow suddenly woke up and attacked. In contemplation of the absurd idea, Bartholomaus squinted one eye and raised an eyebrow at Magnar as he waited for his answer.

Hesitantly, Magnar gave one more long look at the twitching smoke-giant whose arms, fingers, and legs were randomly jerking as streaks of electricity zapped up and down its limbs. Then, he turned to answer the question with one of his own, "Don't *you* think all this was too easy?"

At the proposed question, a contemplative look crossed Bartholomaus' face. Finally, he understood why the young man had been unable to celebrate. Without further delay, Bartholomaus shouted, "Run! Everyone get outta here and stop that daft singin'! The smoke-giant isn't dead! Stop standin' around! What are ya deaf or somethin'? I said RUN!" he urged.

Abruptly, the soldiers stopped everything and turned to look at the smoke-giant with confused expressions—each wondering why Bartholomaus had become frenzied with concern. However, it didn't take long for them to understand why. Seconds after Magnar had asked the question, the smoke-giant opened its black eyes and the furnaces inside them became lit with fury! Slowly, it turned to look at its enemies as it shook its head from left to right. Then, the smoke-giant pressed all six of its hands against the ground and pushed itself back up onto its feet!

Immediately, the centaurs scrambled for their swords, pulling them free from their sheaths to attack the smoke-giant! They began violently plunging the sharp silver blades into its smoky flesh, but the wounds were healing instantly, and their weapons were doing little to no damage at all!

"Magnar! Come wit' me! I need to hide ya somewhere safe till we deal wit' this thing for good," Bartholomaus ordered, but it

374

was already too late. Bartholomaus' eyes widened as he watched the young man standing helplessly in front of him be lifted off the street within the smoke-giant's grip!

Briefly, Magnar and Bartholomaus locked terrified eyes! Without thinking, the soldier leaped up and took hold of Magnar's feet with a powerful grip. Immediately, he could feel the strength of the smoke-giant pulling him upwards higher and higher, but the centaur pulled against the abomination with all his might in the unfair tug-of-war over Magnar; the soldiers took hold of Bartholomaus to prevent him from being carried off as well. The tug on his limbs made Magnar's legs feel as if they were going to rip free from the rest of his body, and within seconds he heard one of the joints in his hip pop, which sent searing pain shooting through his lower half! At that moment, Magnar wasn't sure if he wanted Bartholomaus to continue trying to save him. Feeling as if his body were splitting in two, Magnar closed his eyes at the pain ripping through him as the centaur shouted and pulled against the smoke-giant's unmatchable strength. He could feel himself lifting higher, and the red-haired soldier's grip loosening, until there was no grip on his feet at all.

"HE… IS… MINE!" the smoke-giant bellowed, with freshly burning fires lit in its eyes. **"I… CLAIM… HIM!"**

Magnar tried to free himself from the fingers by wiggling, pushing, and pulling against them, but no matter how he squirmed, they weren't loosening the slightest bit. Instead, the grip was becoming tighter and it was choking the precious breath from his lungs. He felt pressure building against his rib-cage and his breaths were becoming shallow, causing him to gasp for air. Several times he choked and coughed on his own saliva as the mucus built up in his mouth from being unable to slide down his throat. The last whiffs of life-giving oxygen were being forced out of his wind-pipe as the smoke-giant's burning eyes watched his life fade. Magnar's head grew heavy and his consciousness was beginning to leave him—falling away from his grasp as he began to blackout from the pain. Desperately, he tried to cling to the here-and-now to think of spells, but he was drifting away too quickly—unable to hold onto the centaurs' voices he heard shouting to him from the street below.

"Let go of him ya monster!" shouted Bartholomaus, who was raising both his hands to ready himself to perform another spell. "I'll teach ya a lesson or two!" Quickly, the centaur shouted, "*Electricae! Fulgur Percutiens ut Obes autem Ignis!*" with the palms of his hands facing the sky. Instantly, bolts of lightning shot down from the storm clouds and combined with the energy pulsing within his hands to ignite them on fire! Without delay, Bartholomaus flung orbs of fire at the smoke-giant—hurling them furiously one after another! Instantly, the fiery orbs struck the smoke-giant and ignited the smoke all over its body—

transforming the towering form into a fearsome sight of blazing flames!

Violently, the burning smoke-giant shook its head and swiped its free hands at the burning orbs coming towards it, but instead of knocking them away, the orbs struck and lit the other five hands on fire. **"HE... IS... MINE! YOU DIE!"** the giant bellowed, maintaining its grip on Magnar with the unlit hand, while balling up its fiery fists to attack Bartholomaus! With a loud growl, the smoke-giant swooped the burning hands at the centaur, but nimbly the soldier managed to duck and dodge them. Unfortunately, one of the other soldiers wasn't as lucky; he was consumed by flames when one of the hands made contact against his side, flinging him across the street against a building.

"I won't be askin' again... put him down nice n' easy and return to where ya came from!" Bartholomaus demanded, hurling more fiery orbs at it.

Defiantly, the smoke-giant held its ground and stared at the soldier through the fires in its hollow eyes and yelled, **"NOOO!"** as it squeezed Magnar tighter.

Thinking of what to do next, Bartholomaus placed his hands together and began creating an enormous orb of blue energy between them. Quickly, the orb of concentrated energy grew into a gigantic sphere three-times bigger than any of the other orbs, and then the soldier whispered, *"Ignis,"* to light the orb on fire!

Finally, (with a powerful throw) he hurled the flaming orb at the smoke-giant's face! Swiftly, it soared through the air and struck its target, knocking the smoke-giant backwards onto its back down onto the road.

Right-away, Bartholomaus cheered as he watched the smoke-giant fall and lay motionless—thinking that surely the impact of the orb had killed it. Confidently, he turned his back to it and closed his eyes to savor this victorious moment. He thought of his wife and kids, and about the grand stories that would be told of him defeating the foe, but then a strange tone began to emanate behind him. Slowly, Bartholomaus opened his eyes and turned around. The sound was the roar of the furnaces relighting in the smoke-giant's opening eyes. Instantly, the soldier could feel the smoke-giant's evil hatred for him through its stare, and being so close to it, he felt its scorching heat against his skin.

"Bartholomaus! Run!" the soldiers shouted, keeping a safe distance away from him and the smoke-giant as they watched the tragedy unfold—unable to help. However, it was already too late. There was nowhere to run, and even if there was, he wouldn't be able to reach it in time.

Balancing on the edge of reality and unconsciousness, Magnar heard all the chaotic shouting, and he squinted his eyes open to see what was happening through his blurred vision. "No!" he screamed, but the word was barely audible through emptied lungs and a raspy voice. Helplessly, he watched the smoke-giant grab Bartholomaus with a fiery hand as it stood up, and immediately the centaur was engulfed in brightly burning flames! Screams were gurgled with the blood in his throat as the smoke-giant evilly squeezed the centaur tighter—crushing and snapping his bones like twigs along with his organs within the strength of its grip.

Magnar tried to force his eyes to stay open as the blazing smoke-giant opened its mouth wide and bit into his friend, tearing his torso free from his bottom half, but the black curtain of unconscious draped over him as he heard the giant victoriously declare, "HE... belongs... to ME!" and then someone else shouting the name, *"Amora!"*

CHAPTER THIRTY-SIX
Only the Brave

"*A*mora, wait! It's not safe!" shouted a soldier, galloping towards the approaching ranger with the woman riding on his back. Quickly, the exhausted soldier ran up to them with his sword heavy in his hand—tired from the fighting—and gave them a nod of respect as he sheathed his weapon and began explaining the situation.

"Zantharius, you must turn back. It's not safe for her to be here," he pleaded. "Retreat back to the entrance of the city and leave this fight to the rest of what's left of us soldiers. We've suffered heavy casualties and cannot guarantee her safety if she stays."

"Soldier, you're talking about me as if I'm not right here. I have no need for the ranger to make that choice for me... I can make the decision for myself!" Amora fussed, upset that he wasn't acknowledging her. She could decide for herself if she was going to leave or not, and that depended on what condition Magnar was in.

"Sorry, it's just that…"

"No need for apologies, sir. I know what you meant," she interrupted, giving the ranger a stern look that she meant what she said, regardless if Zantharius agreed with the soldier or not, and knowing that it was pointless to argue with her, the ranger held his words. "Is Magnar with the other soldiers? I'm not leaving without him."

"I fear Magnar's fate is out of our hands now. There's nothing left that any of us can do to save him… he is to join our fallen brothers. That is why you must leave, or the smoke-giant will come after you, too, and so far, nothing we've done has stopped it. The blight on this city is unlike anything I've ever seen!" the soldier responded. "Zantharius, please talk to her… she will listen to you. Get her to leave this city, for I fear this battle has already been lost. At least we can get one of them back to Zeur… alive. The soldiers and I will hold the smoke-giant off while you take her back to the front gate!"

"No! I will NOT leave Magnar to meet his death! The smoke-giant will have us both or neither of us!" she refused, hopping down from Zantharius' saddle and looking past the soldier at the flaming figure up ahead—holding Magnar within its last remaining smoky hand.

"Amora, there's nothing for you here. You must accept this truth. Dying with Magnar will do nothing, but living to fight another day will make his death an honorable one that he would be proud of. Think about what *he* would want."

"No! You want me to think about what *you* want... what *you* think is best!" she argued, turning her face away from the soldier in order to speak with the ranger. "Zantharius, I know the soldiers have been ordered to protect me, but you must let me do this. You didn't think I could handle myself with the baby dragon, but everything worked out fine. I knew what I was doing. I don't know how I knew... just that I did. I'm asking you to trust me and to let me do whatever I can to fight for the life of my friend."

For a moment, the soldier stood silently waiting for Zantharius to side with him and refuse her request. It was logical and a good strategy to remove her from the smoke-giant's wrath before things got any worse, and the soldier knew Zantharius—a highly intelligent and well-fought ranger—would most definitely echo that same decision.

Silently, the ranger stared down at Amora's face, reading the depth of her heartfelt emotions through her eyes. Then, he looked at the exhausted soldier. Lastly, his eyes turned to the smoke-giant in the distance who was squeezing the last bits of life out of Magnar with one hand, while the other five swooped left and right at the attacking soldiers who were hopelessly fighting a foe that wouldn't be taken down by any conventional means. The only thing that would be strong enough to take it down would be a dangerously powerful magic spell. Finally, he made his decision.

"She will remain here and fight alongside the soldiers. She has every right to do so," Zantharius commanded, siding with Amora.

At once, Amora felt energized with hope, but was filled with rage towards the smoke-giant. She was ready to fight! *Magnar, I'm coming to kill it! Just hold on… and stay alive,* she whispered to him through her mind—hoping that in some way he could hear her, even if it was impossible.

"But Sir…"

"That is my order. Now carry it out. Your men are to protect her at all cost. Is that understood?" Zantharius commanded.

"Yes Sir," the dismayed soldier obediently replied without another word.

What was… that name… Amora, Magnar thought in between waves of consciousness and unconsciousness lapping themselves over him—black curtains of sanity opening and closing to momentarily let him peak through at their whims. Slowly, he opened his eyes to blurred shapes and distorted figures of grey hues. *Magnar, I'm coming to kill it! Just hold on… and stay alive,* he heard whispered inside his mind. "Is she here? She can't be… it's not safe… I… must warn her," he mumbled, just as another curtain closed itself once more. Unable to fight it, he drifted away with another black wave of unconsciousness into the abyss.

"Move! Everyone! Get outta here!" a soldier screamed, as if the lives of everyone around him depended on it. "We've got to move! Hurry!"

"What are you hollering about? Shut your mouth, grip your sword, and fight! We've no time for the ramblings of a mad man!" another yelled, not waiting for an answer as he ducked beneath one of the fiery hands swiping at him. "What! Why are they bringing Amora over here? Keep a vigilant eye men... we've got to keep it busy! Make it focus on us and not Amora!"

Without hesitating, the centaur held his sword high in the air and let out a profound battle cry! Then, he and the others made several more attempts to injure the smoke-giant with their blades, but nothing appeared to wound it, or cease the fires engulfing the abomination. Repeatedly, the smoke-giant's hands swooped down low to grab himself and the other soldiers, but quickly the centaur ducked and dodged two of them, but was unfortunately blindsided by the third. The fiery hand struck him across the side of his body with great force and sent him flying through the air, until he landed with a hard *thud* on the rough street! Instantly, the soldier cried out in pain and gripped what he could reach of one of his hind legs. The thigh bone had cracked on impact and had been thrust through the badly burned skin! His leg had become a bloody, tangled mess of hair, flesh, and bone! At the sight of it, the soldier screamed and fell silent as he passed out due to the pain.

"Zantharius, watch out!" another soldier at the heart of the battle cried, leaping towards the ranger to use his own body as a shield for him and Amora a second before stinking hot flames blew forth from the giant's mouth at them! Immediately, hot orange and red hues lit the air with blistering heat, and sent several soldiers running and screaming with flames dancing across their armor—melting the precious metals that studded it into their injured flesh! Without delay, each of the men dropped their sword and clumsily began stumbling around, frantically trying to extinguish the fires with fervent slaps against their armor and skin!

The soldier—who had used himself as a human-shield—flung his body down onto the ground and rolled himself back-and-forth, until he was covered with filth, mud, and grime, which extinguished the flames. Quickly, he sat up and searched himself for injuries, but luckily his burns were minor compared to what they could be. Still, they would need to be treated with healing balms and medicine the moment he returned back to Zeur, but at least he would recover.

However, the other men weren't as lucky. They hadn't thought to drop and roll. Instead, they took off running and their high speeds created oxygen-rich winds that fed the flames, and swiftly the fires were spread along the lengths of their entire bodies! Instantly, their armor became engulfed—turning each man into a blazing trophy of defeat for the giant to look upon—and screams filled the air, until numbing silence was upon the street.

"Zantharius, is there anything we can do?" Amora asked, rushing to kneel beside the injured man who had saved them. The soldier was alive, but his skin was badly burned and blistered, and spasms of pain were uncontrollably shaking his body. He would need to be carried out of the city by the soldiers who'd escaped the flames. Amora could already see signs of infection beginning to set in around the edges of the gooey red burns where the skin had peeled away, exposing muscle tissue.

Gently, Amora took hold of one of the soldier's hands and squeezed it, "We're going to get you out of here and get you the help you need. You'll be fine, and we'll get you back home to your family in one piece," she comforted, giving the soldier a kind smile, and despite his pain, he returned one as well. Again, she gently squeezed his hand, then left his side to rejoin the ranger standing nearby.

"Zantharius, you need to get all the wounded out of here. Tell the soldiers to bind as many wounds as they can with whatever they have and help everyone get back to the front gate."

"What about you?" he asked.

"*I'm* going to rescue Magnar. Then, we'll meet you at the gate."

"I'm sure trying to stop you would make little difference," he said, pausing to see if that was a certainty, which she quickly nodded that he was correct. "Then, be brave, be well, and be swift. I'll instruct the soldiers to take the injured to the front gate and we'll wait for you there," he finished, turning to walk away, but suddenly stopping as something important crossed his mind. Slowly, he crooked his neck to the side to look at her and continued, "However, should your fate be ill met, know that we will wait only a reasonable amount of time for your return. After that, we'll depart this city with our injured... with, or without you," he warned. "Is that understood?" he asked, needing her to acknowledge that she would be on her own if she chose not to depart with him, but rather to stay and fight.

"Zantharius, the next time we meet *I will* have Magnar at my side," Amora replied, with fire in her eyes as she turned away to run towards the flaming smoke-giant... alone.

CHAPTER THIRTY-SEVEN
A Matter of Words

With fire raging wildly in her heart, Amora ran to face the smoke-giant. This was it! She had no idea what she was going to do, but if she didn't figure it out quickly, Magnar was going to die! She had to find the right words for a spell powerful enough to defeat the smoke-giant and break the dark curse over the city. How was she going to do it? Up until now, the only spells she knew were simple ones, but that sparked a genius thought! Maybe those same spells were the ones she'd need to stick with—basic levitating, throwing, and the like. Still, she would need to be clever about how to use them to her advantage.

As she constructed a plan in her mind, she soon found herself standing in front of the towering smoke-giant, who was evilly staring down at her, while holding Magnar firmly in one of its six hands, forcing out the last remnants of precious oxygen from his lungs. His limp body was slumped over and at the sight of this, Amora's heart suddenly became filled with a surge of powerful energy and the words she needed flooded her mind. *"Leva Petram, Magnis et Gravibus, Navigare caelo, Percutio Gigas!"* she shouted with hands raised at the sky, the words flowing out effortlessly from deep within. Instantly, the walls of the nearby buildings violently shook, broke apart, and lifted high into the sky! Then, the stones plunged down and struck the smoke-giant with great force!

Immediately, Amora repeated the spell, *"Leva Petram, Magnis et Gravibus, Navigare Caelo, Percutio Gigas!"* causing several more time-worn buildings to shake, break apart, and their stones to lift into the air, and then crash themselves mercilessly against the smoke-giant—each shattering into thousands of jagged pieces that extinguished the flames all over its body as they struck the fearsome form! Relentlessly, she repeated the spell again and again until there were no more buildings left standing on the street, and in their place was rubble and rot.

"Let him go!" she yelled, demanding Magnar be released from the smoke-giant's grip, but despite the gaping holes torn through the smoky form by the stones, still it refused.

"HE... IS... MINE! But *I*... know... *you*," it said, sneering. "After I kill *him*... I'll rip the flesh off your bones... cast your meat to the ground!" the giant bellowed, becoming angrier. As it

389

did, Amora noticed something peculiar. Smoke was escaping out one of its open wounds!

Suddenly, she realized the smoke was a spirit! She watched the smoky human form reach its long arms through an open wound in the smoke-giant's chest and pull itself out with claw-like hands. Once out, the spirit's face craned backwards to look at Amora! Its monstrous appearance shocked her with disgust—appearing barely human—and she cringed to think that it was once a person. The limbs were grotesquely long, as if they'd been cruelly stretched, and the skull was badly deformed with sunken-in creepy eyes filled with hate. The spirit climbed up onto the smoke-giant's shoulder and contorted itself to get a better look at Magnar— thinking about jumping onto the smoke-giant's hand in order to strangle the last bit of life from his body. However, the spirit refrained from committing the violent act and vanished into thin air!

Then, Amora realized something. *There's something else wrong with these spirits—not just the way they look. Something more is going on inside the city, Zareck,* she thought, looking around at the crumbled buildings. *That soul looked tormented... a person who was removed from the physical life too soon and unfairly,* she reasoned, diving deeper into the scenario playing in her mind as she thought back to the images she'd seen in the tattered book she had left behind in her hometown, Bernard. *What if the person spoken about in that book—the DARK ONE—had placed a curse over this city after killing those people in the parade? What if that curse has never been broken and it's still affecting the citizens here, till even this day! That would explain why the soul appeared as a deformed mutation... but what if—* the voice in her head paused, her brain linking one idea after another as she carefully put together the pieces of a reasonable explanation, until all the puzzle pieces in her mind cohesively fit together and made sense.

What if I could find a way to break the curse and release all the spirits in this city from their torment... from the DARK ONE's hold over them. Maybe I can find a spell or a way to free them, and that's how I can destroy the smoke-giant! Yes! That must be the way to destroy it! The souls must have conjured the smoke-giant because they think Magnar is responsible for what happened to them. So, I must make the souls realize that Magnar isn't their enemy... the DARK ONE is! I must make them realize who trapped them here, and that there's no need to be angry at the innocent who pass through their city—at Magnar! They don't understand anything that's going on anymore! I'll find a way to free them! I have to!

However, before she could think of a decent spell that might do the trick, the smoke-giant was already poised to attack her! Straightaway, it slammed five fists down onto the ground around

391

her, trying to squish her, but by reacting quickly she was able to dodge them and roll out of the way!

"I... WILL... CRUSH... YOU!" the giant bellowed.

Frantically, she ran left, right, left, right, and then back again, constantly changing her direction as she dodged the repetitive pounding fists that quaked the ground around her, but she knew she couldn't keep the pace up forever with the smoke-giant chasing behind her. Something had to be done quickly! With the smoke-giant close behind, Amora's skin grew hot from the heat being emitted from its smoldering eyes and suddenly she felt the vibrations of more fists hammering down around her on the street! Then, the unthinkable happened... Amora looked up to see a massive-sized fist coming straight down on top of her! Without having a moment to think, she instinctively shielded herself with both hands above her head, shouting the word, *"Clypeum!"* Instantly, the smoke-giant's fist was halted only a few inches above her!

"How? How... can... you ...be... this strong?" it asked, confused and fuming with rage.

Immediately, the smoke-giant smashed down another fist over her! Again, she shouted the spell, *"Clypeum!"* but also added the word, *"Levo!"* Instantly, both fists were sent flying upwards and they smacked the smoke-giant's own face!

Stunned by the impact of its own hands, the giant growled and shook its face roughly from side-to-side. Amora knew this was her chance! Instantly, she unleashed an eruption of spells!

"Quinque Manibus,
Sui Impetum,
Levo Indu Aerem,
Gravitatis Deorsum Trahere ad Terram,"

At once, five of the smoke-giant's hands slammed hard against itself and the gravity beneath it became suspended. Unexpectedly, the smoke-giant began levitating high in the air, but abruptly the gravity became reestablished, and pulled it down onto the ground with a hard *boom* that shook the ground below! Still, it didn't lose its grip on Magnar as it laid on the ground moaning with frustration with eyes closed. However, when it reopened them the flames in its eyes were blazing brighter and hotter than before! Slowly, the smoke-giant turned its face to look at Amora and it stared cruelly at the young woman, who was standing not too far away at an unsafe distance—coldly she returned the same intensity with a stare of her own!

Amora could feel the searing, hot, sticky heat coming from its eyes and several times the furnaces roared to brighten the flames and stretch them higher.

"HE... IS... MINE!" the smoke-giant again bellowed, opening its mouth to unleash the full fury of the fires inside itself. Without warning, a river of flames spewed forth from the smoke-giant's mouth and began twisting in the air, forming a rotating funnel of fire that lunged at her!

Amora's brown eyes widened as she watched the rotating tornado of flames come towards her—transforming the air into a hot dry vacuum that sucked away the surrounding oxygen and stung her lungs, causing her to cough uncontrollably!

"Waters from the sky... help me!" she shouted, stretching her hands up toward the grey clouds above as she spoke the spell, *"Aqua! Adiuva Mihi!"* For a moment, she wondered how she knew the spell—it had popped in her mind from nowhere. However, there wasn't any time to think about that! Right-away, the element came to her rescue! Rain drops poured down from the clouds above her to form an impenetrable shield of water around her—creating a barrier between her and the tornado of fire coming from the smoke-giant.

Without losing a second, Amora continued her verbal assault against the smoke-giant—thinking about how she could break the dark curse over the city and free the souls trapped in Zareck! Immediately, the words filled her mind and poured from her lips to form the next incantation:

"City of Zareck with Curse of Old
Break Apart the Darkness with Light,
Free the Tormented Souls
Between Two Worlds No More,
Released from the Trap
Rejoice! Spirits Awaken from Your Undue Long Nap!"

"Civitas de Zareck, ad Olim Maledictio
Conteram Seorsum ac Tenebras ad Lucem,
Liberum et Spirituum Excrucior
Inter Duos Mundos Nullo Amplius,
Dimissi inde Captionem
Exsultate! Spirituum Evigilare Faciatis inde vestra indebite
Conquiescamus Longus"

As the last word gracefully left her lips and drifted into the air, rapidly the burning tornado ceased, and the smoke-giant began convulsing violently on the ground—its limbs twitching uncontrollably! Instantly, all the winds throughout the city picked-up speed—kicking up dust into the air and loosening the last remnants of Amora's messy black ponytail as her hair tossed wildly in the strong gusts.

Quickly, she ran for some shelter far away from the convulsing smoke-giant and found a half-intact partial wall with a torn awning. It looked as if the rest of it might fall down at any second, but still she crouched down low and hoped it would last as long as she needed it to! Her heart pounded swiftly in her chest as she knelt down a split second before a bolt of lightning struck the other side of the wall… as if someone had been aiming for her! The words, *the DARK ONE,* popped into her mind as the culprit! Seconds later, a barrage of electric bolts struck that same wall, while others randomly struck buildings all over the city—hot white streaks of fury rained down front the angry clouds above!

Crouched against the partial wall, Amora fearfully watched the electric storm, and saw the spy that had been following her get struck by a hot bolt as it hid within a pile of rubble not too far away. A screech left its throat a second later, but that was the only sound its charred remains made.

Soon, the lightning began striking the smoke-giant— pounding the smoky form with one bolt after another for several long minutes without slowing down! The *booms* and *claps* shook the wall at her side and the vibrations quaking along the ground were felt against her feet, but silently she kept still and watched as the smoke-giant rolled back and forth, hollering in pain. Eventually, the thunderous booms of the storm—along with the smoke-giant's hollers—dwindled into cold silence just as the smoke-giant became limp, opened the hand containing Magnar, and dropped his body onto the ground.

"Magnar!" Amora shouted, leaving the safety of the building's wall as she sprinted towards him. Quickly, she dropped onto her knees and scooped his weak body up into her arms, holding him gently as she spoke, "Magnar, it's over now. Come back to me... please. I can't lose you too. I've lost everything already—not you, too." Water welled-up in her eyes and tears dripped down her cheeks as she held her friend. Carefully, she placed an ear against his chest, trying to listen for a heartbeat and his breathing, but everything inside him was sadly still.

"You! You did this!" she angrily shouted at the smoke-giant, turning to look at it, but it was gone. The smoke-giant had vanished! Amora frantically looked everywhere, but there were no signs of it.

Then, a feminine voice softly whispered in her ear, "You did it."

"What? Who's there?" Amora asked, searching for the unseen owner of the words.

"You did it!" it kindly repeated.

"You saved us," whispered someone else.

"Yes! All of us," another spoke.

Suddenly, a bright white light broke apart the storm clouds and shone down onto the street below, and within the beam stood the form of an old man who began walking out of the light towards her.

"We've been waiting a long time for someone brave enough to save us," he said, smiling at her.

"Yes! Someone with magic strong enough to end the evil curse the DARK ONE placed on our city," another voice added, coming from an old woman who appeared with several young children by her side.

"We've waited a very long time for someone to help us, but then YOU came! You're brave and strong!" one of the little boys said, reaching up to hold the old woman's hand.

As Amora watched the two interact and saw the love in the old woman's eyes for the child, she realized the old woman was the child's grandmother. They must've died together in the city during the DARK ONE'S attack. Pain struck Amora's heart at the realization of this, but she was glad they had found each other after death.

"Who are all of you?" Amora asked, watching dozens of more spirits appear all around her—none of them having grotesque forms anymore, but rather pleasant looking human ones.

"We are the citizens of Zareck. We happily lived here once, and this city was a grand jewel to all those who visited," another spirit answered.

"Thank you for saving us!" a little girl joyously blurted out, her spirit quickly becoming visible and running up to Amora to get a better look at who'd saved her and her family.

"Thank you! Thank you for not giving up on us," spoke an older child.

"Yes! Thank you for not leaving us in that dreadful state. Most people fled at the mere sight of us. We couldn't contain our anger and didn't understand what was going on, but we needed help more than any could've imagined. Yet, no one stayed long enough to figure out what was happening here. Thank you for sticking around and helping," said another.

"You're welcome." Amora softly said, holding Magnar in her arms as she watched thousands of apparitions appear to offer their gratitude, until she was fully surrounded by a crowd of beautiful glowing lights. "But I don't understand... what had happened to all of you?"

At that moment, the old man who'd appeared as the first kind spirit drifted to the front of the crowd and kneeled down next to Amora to explain. "Amora, I am one of the fallen Zodiarks. After my brothers were killed, the DARK ONE attacked the rest of this city, killing any who dwelled here, and a most foul curse was placed over every corpse whose blood had touched the ground in Zareck. Everyone, including the children, were slain for their loyalty to the Zodiarks... for they refused to place any allegiances to the DARK ONE that sought to rule in our absence. Those that had died that day had no choice but to succumb to that curse... forgetting who they were and who had murdered them. The truth became twisted inside us like old vines that endlessly sought for the light both day and night, but never was able to be satisfied with either. It twisted our souls and turned us into abominations that were a plague upon the very place we had all once loved, Zareck. Only a person with exceptional magical strength and courage could save us. That person would be the only one strong enough to break our curse and release this city from the shadow magic suffocating it. Amora, there is strong magic inside you unlike anything I've ever known."

"No, not me... I didn't know what I was doing," Amora replied, doubting herself and the validity of her magic as nothing more than dumb luck.

"Evidence proves otherwise," an old woman insisted, suggesting that the mere defeat of the smoke-giant proved her strength and courage.

"No. I'm just someone who got lucky with a few good spells. Don't get me wrong... I'm glad I could help, but I'm just *me*... just plain me. I barely know how to do magic."

"My dear, you broke the DARK ONE's curse. You freed us! We can finally move on to the next part of our journey, so to *us*, you are a hero! But... there's something important we must warn you about before we go."

"What?" Amora asked, with eye-brows scrunched down to relay concern as she listened carefully for the next words to depart from the spirit.

"You must be careful and more vigilant than ever!"

"Why? What's wrong?" she questioned.

Next, a male spirit glided forwards from the center of the crowd to answer, "*You* freed us… that puts you in grave danger. The DARK ONE will know the curse has been broken and *you* will be hunted for breaking it! Know that ALL you love is in danger of being destroyed! You're NOT safe here! You must go! Get out of the city! Get out of Zareck before the DARK ONE finds you!"

"Must leave! Must go! Must leave! Must go! Must leave! Must go!" all the spirits chanted in unison.

"All must move on now," the spirit insisted, and Amora could feel his energy was overflowing with purpose—he was ready to do for himself what he was suggesting for her as well.

"Amora, he tells you the truth. It is time to go," a gentle voice called to her from the center of the crowd, but there were so many spirits surrounding her, that she couldn't decipher from whom the words had come from.

"Yes, the light is calling to us now," a mother's voice softly spoke, reaching down to hold the hand of a child.

401

"Thank you Amora... we can go home now! I'm not afraid anymore," a little girl's voice spoke as she grasped her mother's hand in hers.

"No, wait! Please, I want to leave, but I can't. My friend is badly injured, and I can't leave without him. Help me! Let us both be able to leave this place... together!" Amora pleaded, sadly looking down at his limp body.

With great compassion in his voice, the fallen Zodiark spoke, "We can help him. It is *our* fault he is injured. At the very least... we owe you this kindness. We were misguided in our darkness, but now we see the beauty of light." Then, he pointed to the sky and the last bits of the grey clouds dissipated to show the early morning's sun-rays beginning to beam down with their brilliant colors of pink, orange, and gold—colors Amora had never seen before, which were opposite to the cold gloomy grays she'd known in Bernard.

Quietly, the Zodiark placed his hands over Magnar's heart and from them a soft, warm, rosy glow emanated into the stiff organ and then quickly spread throughout the entirety of his body. Amora and the spirits remained silent as everyone watched the Zodiark work. Finally, Amora heard the sound she'd been longing to hear as Magnar slowly opened his eyes, stirred a moment, and whispered her name, "*Amora*." Immediately, she placed her head against his chest to hear the beating of his restored heart! *Thump!* *Thump! Thump!* It was a beautiful sound!

"Magnar! You're okay!"

"W–what happened?" he stuttered, trying to sit up.

"Slow down… don't get up too fast. I'll explain everything later," she advised, giving him a tight hug, and then quickly turning to thank the Zodiark spirit for his help, but he was already gone. Everyone was gone, except for Magnar and herself.

"Come on, let's get outta here," she said, helping Magnar to his feet.

"Wait," he paused.

"What is it?"

"My cuts and bruises… they're—" he said, nervous to finish his sentence for fear that she wasn't going to believe him, because he was having a hard time believing it himself.

"You're hurting… I know. We'll get you looked at as soon as we reach the next city, but first we gotta hurry and catch up with Zantharius and the others."

"That's just it… they're all gone," he said, looking for any of the bruises or cuts, but there wasn't a mark anywhere.

"They're gone? All of them?" she asked, curiously looking at him.

"Yeah, all of them… but how?"

"I'll explain that too, but first we've got to get moving," she answered, leading him back to the front gate to meet-up with Zantharius and the others.

As they walked, a large smile crossed Amora's face. She knew what the Zodiark spirit had done—that more than Magnar's heart had been healed. Also, she was happy that everyone in the city had finally gotten the peace they so greatly deserved.

While they walked, Amora explained everything that had happened, and after realizing that she had risked everything to save him—including her own life—Magnar took her hand into his to walk the remainder of the way in the cool morning breeze, until reaching a very worried Zantharius, who was more than anxious to depart the city.

Quickly, the ranger greeted the two of them and gathered up the soldiers! He looked forward to hearing Amora's tales of how Magnar had been saved and how the spy had been killed during the lightning storm, but only after they were well on their way to continue their journey to the centaur's home, Zeur.

Thanks to Amora, Zareck was no longer the city of the dead.

CHAPTER THIRTY-EIGHT
Peace with Blood

"**M**aster, th–th–th–there is newssss," Legion stuttered, cowering beneath his dark hooded cloak in the far side of the cold, stone tower.

"Out with-it goblin!" the DARK ONE yelled, blankly staring into the slow, swirling, silver liquid held by the gold basin within the marble pedestal in the center of the room. Only light from a couple half melted pillar candles placed on skinny, wrought-iron stands broke apart the consuming darkness that filled the drafty tower. The sour odor of the melting candles dominated the air as they dripped wax down their sides onto large puddles beneath them (collecting in mounds) on the stone floor.

Th–th–the vulturks have returned to the castle, Master. Our spiesssss bring you newsssss," Legion hissed. "They spotted the girl and the one she travelssss with."

"What of them?"

"They escaped Bernard, but we have their parentssss. They have been taken from the load-puller's cart and tossed into the dungeonssss—hear their screams we do," Legion informed, tilting its hairy pointed ears towards the sounds coming up through the floor vent.

"The girl, where is she now?"

"I peered into the memoriesss of the Vulturks. They showed them fleeing into Kembrull Forest."

"Was it there that she and that prying boy met their deaths?" the DARK ONE asked, still gazing into the swirling liquid—not parting from the deep concentration at hand.

"No, master. They lived to make it past Kembrull Forest," Legion whispered, sinking further into the dark shadows inside the room in fear of its master's temper.

"WHAT! How is that possible!" the DARK ONE yelled, slamming a fist down against the pedestal—breaking concentration. Immediately, the silver liquid stopped swirling and returned to a smooth mirrored-glass of silver.

"The centaurs are helping them. Rescued them they did from Kembrull Forest and killed many white werewolves they did," Legion hissed, flashing its eyes up at the DARK ONE before pulling its hood further over its face to hide.

"The centaurs! They're a meddlesome people that I should've dealt with long ago... like disobedient children. I shall teach them there is a cost to working against me. They interfere in things they shouldn't. They've grown too bold and have no loyalty to me. Now, they must be taught the price that must be paid by traitors!"

"There isssss more," Legion announced.

Slowly, the DARK ONE turned away from the pedestal and glared down at the trembling goblin. "SPEAK!"

"The city of the dead, Zareck... Master, the girl hassss broken your curse, freed all the soulssss, and killed one of your Vulturk spiesss," Legion hissed, fearing the DARK ONE's reaction to the unpleasant news.

"NO! She couldn't have! I placed that curse on the city and it's unbreakable! UNBREAKABLE!" the DARK ONE shouted. "Those people were supposed to suffer an eternity for glorifying the Zodiarks! *Amora* will die by my hands... just like the Zodiarks did. Assemble the Generals and the goblin soldiers! Blood of the disobedient will soon spill, and with that blood, my peace shall be restored."

"Yesssss, Master! Right away, Master!" Legion obeyed, and with a puff of smoke the goblin disappeared from the stone tower to gather up the Generals and their troops.

MEET THE AUTHOR

TK Fretresé grew up in the upstate region of South Carolina. As a teenager, she wrote songs, poems, and short stories. A love of fantasy and magical realms led her to write her first full length novel, Magic Unleashed.

She is a devoted mother and wife, and her favorite pastime is cooking! She loves getting into the kitchen to cook and believes sharing delicious food is a great way to bring people together.

A few other things about her are that she adores country living, beautiful gardens, and learning about cultures from around the world, while embracing everyone's differences along with their similarities. She also enjoys learning new languages, styles of dress, music, and recipes from across the world!

Being a budding author is both thrilling and challenging; she's filled with upcoming fictional stories and is eager to write and share them!

Interact with her via social media and find out about new or upcoming books!

Goodreads: www.goodreads.com/tkfretrese

Instagram: www.instagram.com/tk_fretrese/

Amazon/ Author Page: www.amazon.com/author/tkfretrese

Facebook: www.facebook.com/authorTKFretrese

AUTHOR'S NOTE

A sincere thank you for reading <u>Journey of the Zodiarks, Magic Unleashed.</u> This is my first fantasy fiction novel, and I hope you've enjoyed it. I spent several years writing this story, and the process has been thrilling, humbling, and educational. It has truly been a labor of love.

Every day I learn more about writing, editing, and publishing. Thank you for your patience as I continue to grow as a writer. I encourage you to provide a book review. Your review is important and beneficial. I am deeply grateful to anyone who takes the time to write a review—regardless of it being positive or negative.

Continue this exciting journey with me! What new obstacles and challenges await Amora and Magnar?

Find out in book two of the series!

!!Coming Soon!!

<u>JOURNEY of the ZODIARKS</u>

Darkness Reigns

ACKNOWLEDGMENTS

I have to start by thanking God. My faith is paramount and core to my beliefs and values.

Secondly, I want to thank my husband, for everything. Specifically, thank you for always encouraging me to keep writing during the times when self-doubt caused me to wonder if my labor of love was indeed a worthy cause. Furthermore, for reading my first, second, and third drafts. Only real love could encourage a person to do such a thing! (I'm laughing because those drafts were painful to read due to my inexperience as a young, budding author learning the craft.) Dear husband, you have my everlasting gratitude. You are my best friend and I love you.

Thank you to my brilliant children for supplying me with ample time to write while I indulged my imagination and worked on my art. Furthermore, thank you for taking the time to patiently listen to me try-out new parts of the story with you, testing story plots and characters, and for your loving encouragement, compassion, and continued belief in me as a storyteller, as your mom, and as a writer. I love you unconditionally... always, no matter what!

I am grateful to have two wonderful, big-hearted, loving parents. I am thankful to my mother for her encouragement, positive reinforcement, never-ending support, and love. I am thankful to my dad for encouraging the development of my imagination when I was a child and for always reading stories to me. Thank you for the fun trips to the toy stores when I was a kid! They will never be forgotten (I had so much fun), nor the excitement I enjoyed while playing with my toys! It was during that special time in my life that my imagination began to create grand adventures! Thank you both... I love you.

Thank you to my father-in-law and to Sonya. Your encouragement and belief in my abilities as a storyteller have been priceless. You are wonderful people that I am blessed to know.

A special thanks to all the *readers* who have given the Zodiarks an opportunity to show you their world! Thank you for being a part of their journey as they learn about themselves, magic, evil, and love. I am thankful for each and every one of you! Thank you for giving me (a simple storyteller) an opportunity to entertain you.

It is not my intention to leave out anyone who deserves acknowledgment (there are many people that have my gratitude). Thank you to everyone who has had an integral part in my adventure of bringing, *Journey of the Zodiarks*, book series... to life!

JOURNEY
OF THE
ZODIARKS

DARKNESS

REIGNS

BOOK 2 IN THE JOURNEY OF THE ZODIARKS SERIES!

Join Amora and Magnar as they continue their epic journey! As shadow strengthens, discover new lands, creatures, magic spells, and battles. Will Amora learn to control her magic and wield powerful new spells? Will Zantharius be the leader Amora needs, or will his heart begin to darken and turn against her? Does the bond between Amora and Magnar lead them closer to love or despair? Will the mysterious Sir Beaksmith be found? If so, will he be alive… or dead?

Continue the journey in book 2!

!!Coming Soon!!

Printed in Great Britain
by Amazon

32904887R00251